PRENTICE ASH

RAGE OF LIONS BOOK ONE

MATT BARRON

D1479230

BLADE OF TRUTH PUBLISHING

Copyright © 2022 by Matt Barron

All rights reserved.

Published in the United States by Blade of Truth Publishing Company

Cover art: J Caleb Design

Map art copyright © 2022 Blade of Truth Publishing

This is a work of fiction. All characters, places, and events portrayed in these stories are either products of the author's imagination or are used fictitiously. Any resemblance to actual persons, living or dead, events, or locales is coincidental.

No part of this publication may be reproduced, distributed, or transmitted in any form or by any means, including photocopying, recording, or other electronic or mechanical methods, without prior written permission of the publisher, except in the case of brief quotations embodied in critical reviews and certain noncommercial uses permitted by copyright law.

Contact the publisher via email at:

chadd@bladeoftruthpublishing.com

To Rachel,
The duchess of my heart.

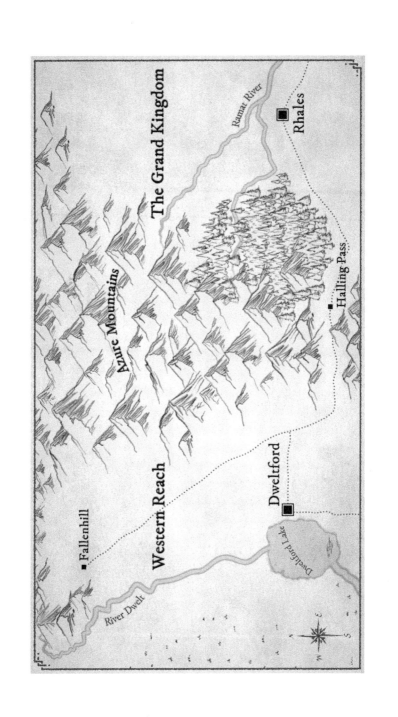

CHAPTER I

"No, it's not broken, but it's definitely twisted," Prentice said with a sympathetic smile. "You won't be standing easy on it for a while."

The young man lying in the dust looked up at him, grimacing in pain. He looked back down at his injured knee in the other man's hand. "Can't you do nothing? Like what you done for Turley?"

Prentice winced, and then forced a smile; the legend of the miracle of Turley's ankle was still spreading.

"Turley is tough as a plow horse," Prentice said. "It was his strength that made him heal, not any blessing in my hands, lad."

"I can be strong. Just help me, please."

Prentice sighed and nodded. "We can splint your knee."

The youth lay back in relief, as if the mere promise of help was a balm.

"What's your name?" Prentice asked.

"Bellam," the young man answered.

"And where are you from?"

"South, on Murr River, near the Vec. Our village didn't have a name."

"Well, Bellam of Murr River, we'll see about getting your leg straight, and you can show us how strong you are."

Prentice stood and turned to face his friend Turley. Prentice was tall, over six feet, but Turley was a bear of a man, taller by a clear margin and heavier built, even despite the leanness convict life inflicted on men. Together they were an intimidating pair, with their shaggy hair, uncut beards, and ragged clothes. Since Prentice had bound his ankle three years previously, Turley had been a loyal friend.

His only friend, most days.

"We need to find wood to make a splint. Up at the edge of the quarry, some of the fallen branches should suit," Prentice said.

Turley looked up the quarry wall to where the trees grew. In between were a dozen convicts, all in leg irons, hammering away at the rock face. At the end of the line of men was an overseer, a bored yeoman absently switching flies from his face with the coil of his whip.

Turley spat on the ground and turned back to Prentice. "Could be one of us could get up to the trees," he said. "But odds are good he'd be seen and flogged for trying to escape. Why not just grab a board from the side of one of the carts? Be easy enough to break off and split for two pieces."

"It's a fair idea," Prentice replied. "But that's theft, and Druce'll have us all before the magistrate. Young Bellam here can't afford that."

The two men looked down at the injured boy. His left hand was already missing its two lowest fingers, marking him as a twice-convicted thief. A third guilty charge would mean the loss of the whole hand.

"Your hand or your leg?" Turley whispered. "Sure, and there's a puzzle for the ages!"

"We'll just try to move before we're seen," Prentice said, but the harsh sound of a whip crack told him that it was too late.

Druce, the village headman, came clomping up, sweat trickling down the dust on his piggish face. "What's this, then, a late morning garden party? Just thought we'd stop for tea and cake, did we?" He glared down at Bellam lying on the ground, then up at Turley and Prentice. Around them the *tink-tink* sound of iron on quarry rock paused, all the convicts drawn by the echo of Druce's voice.

Druce cracked his whip again. "Back to work, curs," he shouted at the quarry, glaring around. The sound of rock work began again. "And what about you three?"

"Bellam's hurt his knee," Prentice reported. He had torn away the leg of Bellam's trousers, revealing a knee that was swollen and purple.

"Has he now?" The headman looked down at Bellam in contempt, clearly not impressed. "Doesn't look that bad." He planted a savage kick into Bellam's thigh, just above the injury.

Bellam screamed, a short high-pitched cry, which he did his best to choke off. He clenched his teeth, trying to keep from looking weak in front of the other convicts, but tears streamed down his dirty face all the same.

"That was a mongrel's act!" Prentice glared down at the shorter Druce, his fist clenched at his side. Druce glared back, as if daring the convict to hit him.

Turley quickly stepped between the two men, heading off any confrontation. "We were just thinking to get a couple of branches from near the quarry mouth," he said to Druce. "Make a splint for the lad."

"A splint?" asked Druce, dragging his eyes away from Prentice's scowl.

"Aye, a splint's the thing. And maybe a crutch, so's he can stand."

"He needs to rest his leg," said Prentice.

"He needs to work!" Druce spat back. "He works or he don't eat."

"Oh, he'll work," Turley readily agreed. "He's a good strong lad. Just needs a splint and a crutch is all. Isn't that right, lad?"

Bellam nodded eagerly and tried to push himself up a little, wiping away his tears. Anything to avoid the headman's cruelty.

"Stay there, lad. We'll get you seen to," Turley said, then turned to the headman. "We'll just have to find a few of branches of the right sizes. Shouldn't take more than an hour or two." To finish, he tugged his forelock in a show of deference to Druce, whose rank did not in fact entitle him to the honorific.

"An hour?" Druce repeated, plainly struggling to keep up with Turley's reasoning.

"I know, sir, it's a terrible waste of time. I suggested that we might take a board off the side of one of the carts, but Prentice here rightly chided me that such a taking without permission would be an act of theft, and it was that kind of behavior that landed us men here as convicts in the first place. So, we'll just be up there, scouting for some right branches."

Turley made to head off, and Prentice turned as well, happily following his lead. The pair had not gone four paces when the headman cracked his whip again, and they stopped and turned.

"We've lost enough time to this little garden party," Druce said archly. "I'm not letting you gallivant off for another hour. Take boards off the cart and be quick about it." He pointed down at Bellam. "And if he isn't working in a quarter of the candle, then he doesn't eat tonight, and you don't eat tonight!"

Druce stalked off to a patch of shade on the other side of the quarry. Prentice and Turley made their way to one of the half-laden carts, stepping around another convict emptying his basket of pale sandstone into the back. Once they had space, the two men took rocks and set about banging loose one of the side boards. Soon enough the plank came free.

"This'll make a much straighter and surer splint than a branch," Prentice said as they carried the board back to the waiting Bellam. "And you, Master Turley, are a truly cunning bastard."

"I'll take that as a compliment from a gent," Turley replied. "And not as a slur upon my good mother."

Prentice chuckled as the pair laid the board down beside Bellam and began splitting it into pieces that could be used for a splint and a crutch. They used a rusty iron stoneman's pick, which was ill-suited to the task, but they lacked any better tools. The board split easily enough and made for rough but serviceable work. As they bound it round Bellam's leg, the young man winced and hissed at the pain, but he did not cry anymore.

"Best wrap this job up soon," Turley advised as they levered Bellam upright. He cast an eye over his shoulder to where Druce sat in the shade. "Lest our lord timekeeper over there should be back."

"The man's a fool," said Prentice. "Half a candle? Who's burning a candle out here?"

He cast his eyes about the quarry. The midday sun poured down into the deep cut in the rock, making the pale sandstone almost blinding white and hot to the touch. The men sweated, and soon enough it would be too hot to work. The headman was due to call a rest, though Prentice suspected he would be deliberately late to the call, as payback for his and Turley's confrontation over Bellam.

"Whatever it is, we need to get back to work before he takes the excuse to get truly nasty," Turley said.

Prentice nodded and turned to the young man. "So, Bellam of Murr River, can you stand?"

Bellam tested his leg, leaning on the crutch. He nodded and gave a forced smile. "I'll do my best."

"Good man. Tonight when we get back to the village, we'll try and scare up some te tree bark for you. We'll wrap that round your knee, and that will help the swelling and the healing."

"Thank you."

"I'll get you a long spike to work with," Prentice finished off. "You can spend most of the day leaning on it so it'll look like you're working from a distance. Turley and I can do enough to make it look like the work of three. All you need to do is keep an eye out for the overseers. If one comes past, wipe your brow and start hammering the spike head into the rock face. That should pass inspection."

Prentice fetched a long spike. Turley took Bellam by the shoulder and helped him turn toward the rock face where the three would work.

"He's a good man," Bellam said when he thought Prentice was beyond hearing.

"That he is," Turley replied.

"You both are."

"I wouldn't go that far."

"Is he really a patrician?" Bellam asked.

"What?"

"You said he was a gent when the two of you were talking before; I heard you. Is that true?"

"Once, mayhap," Turley said with a nod. "He used to be a gentleman of sorts. Not of the blood, mind you, but refined all the same."

"What happened?"

"I don't know. And you won't go asking him."

"Why not?" Bellam asked.

"Because a twisted knee is one thing, but I'm not picking up the pieces of the fool who dug around in that wound!"

Bellam looked bewildered at Turley for a moment, but before he could ask another question, Prentice returned and handed him the spike. He gave Turley a silent, appreciative nod and the three men turned to the rock wall. They began to strike off chunks of sandstone, throwing them into the basket behind them.

CHAPTER 2

When Druce the headman finally called the afternoon rest, all the convicts slumped with thankful groans. They stacked their tools with the carts and waited while an overseer threaded a chain through the loops on their leg irons. Then, as one gang, they marched up out of the quarry to sit under the trees and wait for the midday heat to pass. A water cart with a huge barrel was filled in the village and four convicts were chained to it, marching it the quarter league or so back to the quarry.

The overseers drank first and tipped cups full of water over their heads and down their shirts. Then they went and sat in the shade to let the convicts slake their thirst. Each man took his share, and Prentice made sure Bellam got a good drink too. The barrel was three quarters empty by the time everyone had had enough, and the men sat their weary bones down in the shade. Some napped, others talked, and all just tried to endure the heat and prayed for any kind of breeze.

"I wonder if that widow is as lonely as she looks," Turley said, staring back toward the village.

Prentice was lying on the ground under a eucalyptus tree. The smell of the leaves was pleasantly heavy in the air. He propped himself on one elbow and followed Turley's eye. The road ran nearly straight and flat between the quarry and the village, with only a few stands of trees here and there to block the view. Prentice could just make out a tiny figure behind one of the village houses that could be a woman doing her laundry.

"What makes you think she looks lonely?" he asked.

"Well," said Turley, "she never seems to smile."

"Maybe she just never smiles at you."

"You could be right, you could be right."

The two men smiled at each other, and Bellam chuckled beside them. Prentice laid his head back down and covered his eyes with his arm.

"Oh, for a breath of wind," said Turley.

"That'd be grand," agreed Bellam, and then groaned as he shifted his weight around his injured knee.

A cry broke through the heavy, afternoon air. "Riders," came the call. "Riders coming in."

A few men stirred themselves to see, but most ignored the news. Not all high law applied in the Western Reach, so a horse didn't automatically mean a highborn horseman. Their disinterest was soon overturned as the riders came closer into view however.

"Knights! Knights and a lady, I think."

"Knights?" demanded Druce, forcing himself up from the ground. "What knights?" He stomped toward the road, and no sooner had he reached the edge of the trees than he swore under his breath. "Up, you buggers!" he commanded, unfurling his whip and cracking it over the convicts' heads. "Up and in your line!"

The convicts rose awkwardly, each man having to stand without pulling on or twisting in the chain that linked him to the others. Prentice and Turley supported Bellam until he got his makeshift crutch under his shoulder. The convicts were all mostly upright when the riders reached them. They came in at a canter, and their horses looked to be barely enduring the heat.

There were four men on horseback, each one a knight in armor. They wore dress armor rather than heavier plate and mail, and they had pennants and ribbons on their weapons and tack. Their finery looked dusty and bedraggled, and two of the men had dark sprays of blood across them. A fifth rider was a woman—a lady, by the fineness of her clothes, though she, too, was dusty and disheveled. Her once finely styled, dark golden hair was now coming apart with pins and curls hanging loose.

A sixth horse had no rider but carried the body of an armored man slung across the saddle. His arms hung down the horse's side, and a thin trail of blood ran down from his chest plate, along his arm, then dripped from his fingers to the ground. The mount's coat was smeared red with it as well.

"You there," called the leading knight, a tall man with gold-chased armor and red and blue livery.

Druce stepped forward and tugged his forelock. "Yes, my lord?"

"Do you know this village?"

Druce's expression showed he didn't really understand the point of the question. "I should do, my lord. I am the headman."

"Indeed," the knight observed dryly. "Do you know who I am?"

"No."

"Of course not. How is your village situated for defense?"

"Defense?" Druce asked.

"Yes, defense! Is your village defensible?"

"Defensible?"

The lead knight sighed in exasperation. From behind him, another said, "He has the wits of a dog, Sir Liam. You waste your time with questions."

Druce's expression soured. "Who are you lot? And who is she?"

"You forget yourself, churl!" said the leader.

The knight who had compared Druce with a dog trotted up and cuffed him across the back of the head. Druce rubbed the spot and then flicked his whip open, readying it to strike the knight back. The knight's hand went to the hilt of his longsword.

Before either could act further, Prentice called out, "She's the duchess, isn't she?"

All eyes turned to him, but Prentice fixed his gaze on the lead knight, Sir Liam.

Sir Liam returned his gaze, his eyes slitted like a serpent's. "It is true," he admitted at last. "This is Her Grace, the Duchess Amelia of Dweltford and the Western Reach, widow of Duke Marne. And your liege."

He spoke the last three words with vehement emphasis, but even before he finished speaking, Prentice lowered himself on one knee and bowed his head. Next to him, Turley helped Bellam to lower himself awkwardly, the ankle chain clanking loudly. The rest of the convict gang knelt as well, their ignorance of how to behave in the presence of nobility making them almost as awkward as Bellam. Even the overseers went to one knee.

With everyone around him on their knees, Druce looked lost. He was village headman and used to having no other authority above him from day to day. His nearest superior was usually the ducal magistrate from Longholm, who only showed up in frontier villages like Druce's once or twice a year. The sudden appearance of these knights, and with them the duchess of the entire province, plainly left him bewildered.

The knight with his hand on his sword rode around behind Druce and used his mount to knock him over. "On your knees, churl."

Sir Liam walked his horse along the line of kneeling men and stood near Prentice, Turley, and Bellam.

"You, stand!" he ordered. Prentice rose to his feet but kept his eyes downcast. "You seem to have wits enough. You will answer my questions. The village, how defensible—"

"Indefensible, sir, in the whole," Prentice cut the knight's question short. "There was a perimeter wall, but a wildfire three years hence burned the main to the ground, along with several of the houses and other buildings."

"That's true, my lord," added Druce, half rising and then sinking back again at the sight of the knight still mounted behind him. "That's why we've got these mongrels here in the first place. They're convicts sent from Dweltford to help with the rebuilding."

"Twenty men and the wall still not built in three years?" asked one of the knights. "Lazy dogs, all."

"Actually, we've only had them since early summer," Druce said. "At first we never asked 'cause we had no way to feed them. Then last summer we had a good harvest, but what with the duke dying and everything..."

"And that's all?" Sir Liam pressed. "No watch tower? A stockade, perhaps?"

"Nothing like that at all."

"God help us."

"The church might be held," Prentice said.

"The church?"

"Stone foundations and plastered walls a foot thick," Prentice continued. "The door's hard wood and cross barred. It could serve, depending on what was being defended against."

"That's true," Druce said. "The church's the stoutest place we got! It'll sure hold against... well, um... what is it you're running from?"

Sir Liam ignored the question, instead watching his men, who all cast grim looks at each other. Prentice took the chance to look up and gauge the knights and, most particularly, their commander. Sir Liam was tall and broad shouldered, with black hair and dark eyes. His face was blunt and cold but had no scars to speak of. Like all his men, he was clean-shaven, a fashion of nobility. Prentice involuntarily rubbed his hand across his own full beard. Convicts had neither money nor time to bother with facial grooming, not to mention not often being trusted to keep razors or similar blades.

Sir Liam gave his men orders. "You two, take the duchess and Trosus' body. Secure the church and bar the door. Sir Dav and I will parade this rabble and head off any pursuit."

The knights nodded, and one of them took hold of the reins of the dead man's mount—the deceased Sir Trosus. The other reached for the reins of the duchess' horse, but before his hand touched the leather, she took hold of them for herself. The knight nodded solemnly and allowed the duchess to guide her own mount as the two escorted her off to the village at a canter.

Sir Liam and Sir Dav, the knight who had cuffed Druce, wheeled their horses and stood together facing back to the south, the way they had come.

"Stand!" Sir Liam ordered. The convicts stood, and he turned to Druce. "Does your village have an armory? Bills? Something of that sort?"

Druce blinked in confusion. "No, sir, nothing like that."

"Then what do you do for defense? What do you use in case of violence?"

"I dunno, exactly." Druce shrugged. "We got tools."

"Then have these men issued their tools and parade them. Form the line here."

Druce nodded and sent the other two overseers to fetch the tool cart from down in the quarry.

While they were away, Bellam leaned in close to Prentice. "What's he mean by 'parade us'?" he whispered.

"It's army talk," Turley whispered. "They plan to use us in a fight of some sort."

"Looks that way," Prentice agreed. "But against whom?"

"But we're convicts, not soldiers," Bellam said.

"Same thing to the throne," said Prentice.

The overseers returned and began handing out picks, shovels, and pry bars to the convicts.

Sir Liam stood in his stirrups and addressed them all. "There is no higher service in life than to give one's life for God and the Kingdom," he began loudly, his raised voice echoing around the small stand of trees. A small stir of breeze seemed to accompany his voice, and a crow called from a branch above. "It is this service to which every knight devotes himself. It is a life of sacrifice and honor, which we welcome with humble hearts. You are not knights..."

Sir Dav gave a derisive snort at this. He and Sir Liam shared a knowing smile together.

"Nonetheless," Sir Liam continued, "in spite of your worthless estate, you are being given a rare opportunity today." He turned his eyes from the men to the distance again, looking past them. "Down at the river is the duchess' barge. We were escorting her upriver to Dweltford. Not an hour hence, a group of bandits ambushed us as we lay to shore. With treacherous cunning, these whoreson bastards caught us unaware, and we were forced to escort the duchess here temporarily to protect her life. Now we shall return and bring the king's justice upon these cowards.

"Today you are armed, and the call has come. You have sinned; you have fallen as low as any man might. Your crimes have been judged and you have been convicted to exile. But this day God has blessed you. If you fall in battle, your sins will be forgiven, and God will welcome you into paradise. You have lived like dogs, but today you will fight beside knights, and if called, you will die like knights!"

Sir Liam lifted his hand into the air and paused as if he expected his speech to receive a rousing cheer, but the convicts all stared at him in silence. He sat himself back in his saddle and then sighed heavily, as though their silence wearied him. He looked to Sir Dav, and they both rolled their eyes.

"Line them up and prepare to march," he ordered Druce and his overseers.

"Hey," said the headman, "we're yeomen—free settlers, not no convicts! We aren't marching into any battle with bandits."

Sir Liam dismissed his protest. "Your village is bound by king's law to field a militia. Today that is you!"

"With what? Whips?"

"Arm yourselves as you see fit."

The two knights arranged themselves on the road and waited for the convicts and overseers to form up behind them.

"I'm not going!" yelled one of the overseers. "You can't force me!"

Even as the man was shouting, Sir Dav wheeled his horse on the spot and spurred it into a springing leap. The war-trained mount seemed to explode with speed and power, and it barreled into the protesting overseer. He was thrown several yards by the impact, and he rolled over, groaning in pain. He was lying face down and trying to rise when Sir Dav drew his longsword and thrust it through the man's back. He collapsed back to the earth and died in the dust.

"Any man who thinks to refuse the king's call will receive this fate!" Sir Dav shouted. "You have heard the call, and you will fight. Try to flee, refuse to obey, or anything else, and I will cut you down like wheat."

Druce and his other overseer looked stricken, but the convicts simply lowered their heads as the knight walked his horse back to position, his blade dripping gore. Once beside Sir Liam, he drew forth a cloth and wiped the blood from the polished edge. "And for God's sake, get them unchained!" he ordered over his shoulder. "They can't fight bound together like that."

"You can't unchain 'em out here," Druce protested. "They'll try and run, I swear!"

"They won't get far," said Sir Dav, sheathing his sword but not deigning to look back over his shoulder.

CHAPTER 3

The two knights led the loose column of convicts, their horses prancing in parade step. Their riders sat proud, bolt upright. Behind them, the tired convicts walked on sore feet, tools over their shoulders. At the back came Druce and his fellow overseer; the two yeomen kept looking over their shoulders to the village, as if judging whether they could safely bolt.

"Can they really make us do this?" Bellam asked, stumbling along with his crutch and wincing with every step.

"Aye, lad, they can." Turley spat in the road dust, emphasizing his answer.

"It is the king's law," Prentice explained. "A liege can call upon any knight, serf, or convict to give military service. Only churchmen and some yeomen are exempt. In times of war, even free men can be compelled to serve in the militia."

"You grew up on the Murr," said Turley. "How do you not know this with all them wars?"

"Vec soldiers get paid, I thought." Sweat dripped down Bellam's red face, and he grunted from the pain of walking on his leg. His crutch twisted under him with every step, and already the trio was beginning to fall behind the rest of the convicts; Druce and his man were right on their heels. "We used to tell stories as kids, as how we'd run off and join a company of mercenaries or something, make our fortunes, and come home to live like princes."

"Well, that's daft," Turley said.

"It's true enough, though," said Prentice. "Vec princes raise professional companies to fight for them and pay them well. It's how they drove back King Falzen's crusade."

"King who?"

"King Falzen."

"Never heard of him!"

The three men's quiet conversation was interrupted by the sound of hoofbeats. Sir Dav had ridden to the back of the line and was looking down on them. They squinted back up at him, their eyes in the sun.

"You are falling behind," said Sir Dav. "Do not think to try my resolve. I will not hesitate to kill cowards."

"We seen that already," Turley whispered bitterly.

"What was that?"

"We have an injured man here," Prentice said. "He can barely walk."

Sir Dav eyed Bellam's leg, clearly assessing whether the injury was real or a ruse to escape by. "How did this happen?"

"Fell, sir," Bellam answered. "In the quarry this morning."

"That's true my lord," Druce added from behind them. "He's been needing rest since most the day."

"He cannot fight like this," said Prentice.

"Very well. Return to the village, boy," Sir Dav ordered. "But see that you are there when I return. If I have to search for you, I promise I will ride you down and geld you like a newborn foal. I'll feed your manhood to the dogs, I swear it."

"Yes, my... uh... lord!" Bellam looked as if he believed Sir Dav's every word, and he awkwardly tugged his forelock while gripping his crutch. Then he began the painful process of turning himself about to head back to the village.

"The rest of you will rejoin the company immediately."

"A guard should go with him," Druce protested, though half-heartedly. "He might try to escape."

"No, he won't," Sir Dav said, plainly confident that his threat had frightened Bellam into obedience. He cantered back to the front of the march with Sir Liam.

"Go as fast as you can," Prentice told Bellam, his hand on his shoulder. "And as soon as you get back, find a place to hide. This whole affair has a bad look to it."

Bellam nodded and hobbled off down the road slowly while the other four turned and jogged to catch up with the rest.

"This isn't right!" Druce huffed, even the short exertion causing him to lose his breath.

"'Tis no joy to live your life at another's beck and call, eh, headman?" said Turley.

"Watch your mouth."

"Or what, you'll have me flogged before a bandit can gut me? Could be that'd be a tough race to win!"

Prentice smirked grimly at Turley's gallows humor. Druce merely cursed under his breath. It was not long until the knights called a halt at the edge of the thin forest that grew by the riverside. The whole journey had taken no more than a handful of moments, and they were still barely half a league from the village, although it was now out of sight. The two knights discussed tactics while the convicts sweated in the sun.

"Should we attempt an assault?" Sir Liam asked. "Or would it be prudent to scout the trees first?"

"The dogs have not had time to set ambushes," Sir Dav averred. "They were far too concerned with looting her ladyship's barge, I'd say. Nevertheless, there is a risk of losing this rabble of ours in the trees before we even break through to the riverside."

Even as they were talking, there came the sound of movement from beneath the trees. There was the clink of leather and metal harness and the noises of armed men on the march.

"It seems they will bring the fight out here," Sir Dav said happily. "All the better for us! We shall engage them in the open, the way we like, eh, Raphael?" He drew forth his sword again and then rubbed his mount's neck, calming the eager beast. Sir Liam's mount was also becoming skittish at the sound of an approaching enemy, and he took a moment to retake control.

"Warhorses," Turley muttered, watching. "Powerful like a mountain falling on you, but higher strung than pigs in a slaughterhouse."

Prentice nodded. "We're in trouble here, Turley. Do not doubt it."

"Oh, that's for sure."

Sir Liam drew his sword. "Form your line."

No one else moved.

"You heard the order!" shouted Sir Dav. The convicts all stared at the two knights as if they were speaking a foreign language. Sir Dav looked like he was ready to kill another of them.

"On your right or your left?" Prentice called back.

Sir Dav looked to Sir Liam.

"On? On my left," Sir Liam said in an uncertain tone. Sir Dav nodded, and Sir Liam repeated his order with more confidence. "On my left."

"This way," Prentice said to Turley and the other convicts.

He positioned himself next to Sir Liam's horse, his shoulder all but brushing the knight's stirrup. Turley stood next to Prentice, and then the others formed a rough line. Druce and his man made the other end of the line. They made an unimpressive sight—bushy-bearded, dirty convicts dressed in little more than rags and carrying a mixed collection of rusty tools.

From within the little forest, the sound of advancing men grew louder, and shadowed shapes could be seen under the leaf canopy.

"How bloody many of them are there?" Turley wondered out loud.

"Sounds like twenty or thirty," Prentice guessed.

"What bandits move in that kind of company?"

"We're about to find out." Prentice hefted his pick as the first of the enemy emerged from trees. They were all armored in boiled leather, with chest plates, vambraces, and greaves. Mostly they carried spears and leather-covered round shields, each of which had a blazon of a snarling black wolf's head. It was not a heraldry that Prentice recognized.

Stranger than their equipment were the men themselves. Their skin was a burnished bronze color, and many of them looked dappled in odd shadows. When they came into direct sunlight however, it became clear that their skin was painted with blue patterns, as though they were covered all over with dark tattoos. They stalked forward, not in any apparent formation but with coordination to their movements so that each man seemed a part of a more dangerous whole.

"Skirmish order," Prentice said, recognizing the tactics. "These are no bandits!"

About ten men had emerged, shields and spears at the ready, when a second wave came behind them. Among this group, several carried their spears aloft and on the top of each spear was an impaled head, blood dripping from the severed necks and dead eyes staring forward.

They looked very fresh.

"Malbus!" Sir Dav cried. "Those bastards have cut off his head!" Sensing his anger, Sir Dav's horse, Raphael, began to shift and turn, losing control in response to its rider's own emotions.

"Wait!" Sir Liam tried to order his fellow, but had to struggle with his own warhorse, Sir Dav's disquiet infecting it also. "We should wait to see how they array before we attack."

"Bugger that!" shouted Sir Dav. "They just beheaded my squire!" Before anything more could be said, Sir Dav wrestled Raphael's nose around to face the enemy and, with a whoop, charged forward, his sword high.

At the sight of Sir Dav's approach, the blue-skinned skirmishers quickly fanned out, maximizing their chances of avoiding the thundering charger. Nonetheless, as he reached them, Raphael kicked himself into a leap and his forehooves landed on one man's shield, driving him down beneath the horse's weight. Sir Dav wheeled Raphael about on the spot, and the steel-shod hoofs smashed the man's body to tatters, while Sir Dav's sword swung with the momentum of the wheeling motion and cleaved another warrior's skull. The rest of the spearmen backed away from the dangerous knight, but they kept their shields and spears up, forming a loose circle about mount and rider.

Sir Dav charged Raphael again, trying to take down another enemy, but this time the man was ready for him. The warrior dodged out of the way, taking a sword blow that scored the leather of his shield. The spearmen behind moved in quickly, even as the charge began, so that as he wheeled again and struck heavily at his target, Sir Dav found himself still encircled. The man he had attacked could barely stand from the powerful blows; his left arm hung low, meaning likely a broken shoulder, and his shield was split almost clean through. But as the circle tightened, the wounded man slipped back out of Sir Dav's range.

Sir Dav attempted a third charge but aborted as he was forced to defend himself and his mount against spear thrusts from multiple sides. He checked an attack with his sword, and another scraped loudly across his breastplate before he forced his attackers back by rearing Raphael and bringing his hoofs down like twin war hammers on yet another spearman. It was clear that the attackers were trained to fight knights, but they were too few, and Sir Dav seemed confident that he could defeat them soon enough.

CHAPTER 4

Prentice watched Sir Dav's horse rear and its hoofs kick out, crushing a man's skull with the blow.

"We shall advance and rout this rabble," Sir Liam announced, appearing buoyed by Sir Dav's success. He began to move his horse forward, building it to a quick charge. As he did so, the convicts began to shuffle forward. The fight was stirring up a cloud of dust from the dry summer grass, and the second wave of painted spearmen was sweeping to the left of the melee to move around the cloud. The attackers were readying themselves to fight the convict line.

A sound like a huntsman's horn, though with an animalistic tone, sounded from the trees. The spearmen all shouted in reply, and their own voices sounded like the howls of wolves. Even the warriors ringing Sir Dav paused from their attacks to take up the ululation. From the shadows of the trees, a dark shape seemed to bound forth. In two strides it crossed the open ground to the fracas and leaped over the spearmen, to crash into Sir Dav, driving him from his saddle. He fell to the ground and tried to roll away, but the thing was upon him.

Whatever the creature was, it was covered in black fur and had a wolflike snout, but its limbs were built wrong for such a beast. Its strength was prodigious though, and it slashed wildly at Sir Dav's armor. Despite the fact that Dav wore no helmet, the monster did not strike for his head, seemingly too enraged to care where it placed its attacks. The hard-pressed knight managed to keep his grip on his sword as he fell, just as he'd been trained, and he swung it across the beast's snout, plainly thinking to sever its head. The blow was weak, though, and the strike glanced off the creature's skull without drawing much blood.

The wolf beast snarled at him angrily, spittle flying, and it pinned his sword arm to the ground with one claw. With his other hand, Sir Dav punched the damaged snout with his gauntlet. The creature roared at him with a voice that no wolf's throat ever possessed, and then it bit down savagely on his face and neck, tearing the flesh and killing the knight in a spray of blood.

Even as the wolf thing had leaped from the trees, the spearmen facing the convicts began to advance at a run, their eyes lit with bloodlust. The convict line broke immediately, several of the men fleeing even before any enemy reached them. Standing next to Sir Liam, Prentice hesitated, fearing that the knight might strike him down for trying to flee, but he knew that retreat was the only option. He looked up at Sir Liam, who had pulled short and now stared at Sir Dav's destruction, clearly unable to fathom the sight.

"We must go, now!" Prentice said to Turley as the first spearman reached the remains of the line. The two convicts turned, and as they ran, the line finally collapsed. All the convicts fled as best they could, but the slow were quickly taken by the spearmen who seemed eager not only to slay but to mutilate the bodies as well.

Prentice pushed himself to sprint, sweat stinging his eyes and his limbs aching. Neither he nor Turley risked throwing away their tools, though. To Prentice's surprise, Druce was keeping pace beside them, huffing with the exertion. His face was red, and his tiny eyes darted back and forth. The overseer was starting to slow when he made eye contact with Prentice. Druce reached out his hand like a drowning man.

"Help me!" he gasped.

"What does he bloody think we're going to do, carry him?" said Turley.

Prentice looked back the way they had come. Behind them, the painted men were slaughtering and advancing at a slow jog. He could see the figure of Sir Liam, still on his charger and galloping across the line of the spearmen's advance. As he reached the flank, Sir Liam turned his horse about and charged across their line, knocking enemies down with mount and sword.

Prentice turned toward the village, and through the heat haze he could make out the figure of Bellam, paused on his crutch and looking back toward the battle. He was probably trying to figure out what was going on.

Prentice made up his mind. "No," he said to Turley and pointed at Bellam. "We're going to carry *him*!"

He slapped Turley's shoulder, and the two men ran off toward their wounded compatriot. Druce cursed after them and even cracked his whip, as if to bring them to heel. The sound of the whip drew the attention of some of the spearmen, and they shouted fresh lupine war cries as they charged after him. Druce started running again, shuffling desperately, but he only made a few labored steps before they caught him and ended his life with savage spear thrusts.

Prentice and Turley sprinted to Bellam. They threw their weapons away at last and ignored the young man's confusion. Clasping their hands together under his legs, they lifted him up so that he sat between them, their arms like a seat. With grunts of exertion, they ran sideways toward the village, Bellam bouncing in agony with every step.

"Oh God, it hurts!" he cried.

"Better than the alternative," said Turley.

"Not far, lad," said Prentice. "Just endure. You will survive!"

"What happened back there?"

"We were given the chance to expunge our sins by dying in service to the throne," Prentice sneered.

"But we thought we'd look for a better offer," added Turley, and he flashed a forced smile.

Hoofbeats sounded behind them, and Sir Liam came cantering up. His horse was breathing heavy, its bit dripping foam and sweating with exhaustion. The labors of the past hours were hard on a beast bred for power and not endurance.

As Sir Liam approached, Prentice tried to hail the knight. "This man is injured," he called. "You can carry him to safety!"

Sir Liam ignored them and rode on toward the village.

"Bastard!" Turley cursed.

"Don't stop!"

The two continued to struggle forward. Prentice's arms burned with exhaustion, and only fear could drive his tired legs on. Soon, between the trees on one side of the road, they spotted the figure of the leading spearman, gleefully ranging ahead of his comrades. Prentice stopped, and he nodded to Turley.

Bellam slipped gingerly to the ground. "Don't leave me here!" he said in a panic.

"No one's leaving you." Prentice looked at Turley. "You have to carry him."

Turley glanced at the advancing spearman and then back. "You can't fight him! You have no weapon."

"Don't worry about me, just take him!"

Turley turned his back to Bellam and bent down. Prentice pushed the youth up onto the older man, who took hold of his legs. Bellam gave a short gasp of pain.

Looking over his shoulder, Prentice saw that the spearman had heard the noise and was now heading straight at them. "Go! Run for the church. Don't stop, though your heart bursts!"

Turley took off at the best trot he could manage with Bellam's weight on him. Bellam cried out, making no effort now to hide the tears of pain.

Prentice turned to face the onrushing attacker. Quickly, he ripped his shirt off over his head and wrapped it around his right hand. It wouldn't be much, but it was all he could think of. He did his best to calm his breathing, but the running and carrying had taken a lot from him.

He stood his ground and faced the onrushing spearman.

"All right, Lord God," he prayed tersely under his breath. "If you notice the fall of the least sparrow to the earth, then maybe you could take the time to notice me now."

Leading with the point of his weapon, the spearman ran headlong at Prentice. Just as the tip reached range, Prentice used his shirt-wrapped hand to knock the spear off its course. At the same time, he stepped into the man's body, deflecting his force and trying to take the spear from his grasp. The man stumbled past but kept hold of his spear, wrenching it back out of Prentice's grip. When he managed to regain his footing, he turned and charged once more.

Again, Prentice used his right hand to deflect the point, but this time ended up on the shield side. He tried to take the spear again, but his opponent slammed his shield into Prentice's side, twisting so that he was almost behind him. Prentice grunted in pain and pushed backward against the shield, keeping attention on the fight for the spear. Then, while his left hand gripped hard on the weapon's haft, he reversed his direction and whipped his right elbow backward. The strike at such close range hooked easily around the edge of the shield and crashed into the man's temple like a hammer blow. The spearman went limp and staggered, releasing his weapon. Prentice seized the haft as his enemy collapsed in the dust. A straight thrust of the purloined weapon took the man in the throat, killing him. Prentice paused a moment to look back to check for pursuit. Then he remembered his angry prayer and looked up at the sky.

There was no sign there.

Shaking his head and smiling ruefully, he turned and ran for the village.

CHAPTER 5

Prentice rushed to the village center, ducking between houses and animal pens. In the middle of the small settlement, he found chaos as nearly fifty people—farm wives, children, and the elderly, all dressed in dun-colored homespun—milled about, trying to make some sense of what was happening. They were gathered mostly in front of the church, whose doors were closed fast. Across the heads of the crowd, Prentice could make out Turley's tall figure standing on the church steps and hammering on the door.

Prentice made to push through the crowd, but as he started forward, several of the women turned to look at him and recoiled. He hadn't thought about how he might look to them, naked to the waist with a spear in hand, but he realized they were confronted by the scars on his torso and arms, and the spray of blood from the man he had killed. He had no time to waste for their sensibilities and kept pressing toward the church door.

He tapped Turley on the shoulder. "What's happening?"

"Our noble sir knights have ridden in and locked themselves in the church," Turley answered. "No warning to the village. No raising the alarm. Just straight in to hide, like a whipped mutt at the back of its kennel!"

Prentice lifted his captured spear and hammered the butt on the door. "Open up!" he shouted. "These people need sanctuary." He stepped back to see if the door would open, but nothing happened.

Bellam was seated on the steps, his back against the wall. The youth was drenched in sweat and looked barely conscious, almost delirious with the pain of his ride on Turley's back.

A stout village woman with an incongruously soft face stepped up onto the church steps with the convicts. "What is going on?" she demanded.

"Bandits have come, goodwife," said Turley.

At the mention of bandits, a whisper of fear passed through the crowd. Toward the back, one woman turned to her young boy and gave quick instructions. The child nodded and ran off across the village barefoot, disappearing down an alley between two homes. The running boy gave him a quick thought. If they stood here much longer trying to gain entry to the church, then this was where the tattooed spearmen would catch them. Then it would be a swift slaughter.

"Listen! Listen to me," he shouted. "You must flee, run to the fields! Hide! The village is under attack."

Some villagers moved off and, looking about fearfully, but most hesitated, not trusting orders given by a convict, especially one standing with a spear on the steps of the village church.

Before Prentice could say more to persuade them, there came a scream from the other side of the crowd. He could just make out a flash of black fur as the demonic beast burst into the crowd from another side of the village and began to tear flesh. A spray of blood and a scream cut short ended one woman's life. The crowd erupted and fled in all directions, and the wolf beast turned its head this way and that, seeking a new victim. It pounced on an elderly man and crushed him to the ground, then it chased others down the close alleys leading away from the center of the village.

"We have to go!" Prentice said, nodding down at Bellam at their feet. He and Turley reached down to pick him up, and as they did, he stirred.

"Time to go, son," said Turley.

"Aren't we going to church?" Bellam asked, his voice slurring. He grunted in pain as he was lifted.

"Church is closed today. They won't open the door to the likes of us."

"We should go to the vestry door," Bellam said, smiling like his wits were gone. "The sacrist always gives me a bit of extra bread each night from the vestry door, if I muck his sheep pen for him."

Prentice looked at Turley. "Is there a vestry door?"

"I don't know! I ain't been to any church in years."

"It's worth a try."

"It'll be locked for sure!" Turley protested.

"Maybe not," said Prentice. "Not the way these fool knights think. I wouldn't put it past them to have missed it."

Prentice put Bellam on Turley's back and then took up his spear, leading the way around the side of the church. Weeks in this village and Prentice had not once been on the other side of the settlement, keeping himself to the barn the convicts were housed in and the march back and forth from the quarry to the new wall.

All those weeks and not once to worship? he thought. *How far have I fallen?*

Following the wall of the church, the three men stalked as quietly as they could. All about them came panicked screams and the war cries of spearmen who must have reached the village outskirts. Sneaking around the corner footings of the building, they found a number of small trees, green-leaved, and bearing summer fruit. They crept between the wall and the trees and found the vestry door at the far corner.

"Good. Let's be quick," Prentice said.

As they hurried to the doorway, a noise came from beyond the trees. Peering under the branches, he could see a young woman crouching beside a hay pile, hiding. Her face and her torn blouse were bloodied. Prentice hissed and waved her over. When she heard him, she dashed from cover, moving awkwardly as if from an injury. She had not even reached the row of trees when the wolf beast leaped over the hay, scattering straw with its paws, and fell upon her. She did not scream, but they could see the despair in her eyes as it ripped her apart like a child's doll.

Abandoning any hope of stealth, Turley rushed to the vestry door and Prentice shadowed him, keeping the spear ready. The beast looked up at them, one of the dead woman's limbs still trapped in its jaws. As Turley reached the door, the beast closed its mouth with a snap, biting through bone and flesh.

Turley tried the door, and just as they hoped, it was not locked. However, he only managed to push it half open before it was blocked from the other side. The terrified face of the village sacrist appeared in the gap. He was a thin man with dark eyes and pale skin. His face was streaked with tears and wild with terror.

"No, no!" he said. "No more in!" The sacrist's bony fingers pushed on the edge of the door, but Turley jammed his foot in the gap and pressed. There was no way normally that the little man could have stopped Turley's push, but with Bellam on his back and the narrowness of the doorway, he could not get leverage. He wrestled at the door, making no progress.

Prentice kept his back to Turley and Bellam, his eyes on the beast. It stared back at him with hateful yellow eyes, lazily stalking its way forward. Prentice raised the spear so that the tip was directly between his and the beast's line of sight.

"What's going on, Turley?"

"This bastard priest won't let us in," Turley said with a grunt as he made another unsuccessful push.

Prentice risked a quick glance over his shoulder at the door. The beast seemed to follow his thought, looking past him for a moment at the two men behind him, as if it understood what was happening and found the situation amusing.

That's too much thought for a dumb beast, Prentice thought, following the creature's eyes. At any moment, he was sure the monster would spring, and they would have no chance.

"Turley! Bellam!" Prentice shouted. "Watch your heads!"

Turley took the order and ducked himself down, pressing his weight against the door. Without turning around, Prentice leaned back against his comrades and pushed with all his strength. The combined weight of all three was too much for the man on the other side, and they began to fall through the doorway. At the same time, the wolf beast surged forward, roaring and snarling.

"Keep going, damn you!" Prentice shouted, feet scrabbling on the dry ground as he pushed with all his might, desperate to get inside and close the door before the wolf beast caught him. Somewhere in the back of his mind, he doubted the wooden boards would even hold against the savage creature.

The four men—Prentice, Turley, Bellam, and the sacrist —collapsed over each other in the small vestry, scrabbling to get farther in. The beast leaped the last distance, and Prentice reflexively drew his legs up and just inside the doorway. One claw caught on the metal of his leg iron, which wrenched with a force that made him think his foot might be torn off. He shouted in pain, but the sound of the shout was swallowed in the beast's own shriek of agony and terror. The creature pulled its claw back as if burned, then tried to strike at Prentice once more. Again, it recoiled in pain. Its eyes blazed with rage as it gingerly pressed its paw forward a third time. Prentice watched in horrible fascination as the paw drew near to his foot then stopped, leaving a gap between them.

That gap was the threshold of the door.

"It cannot enter the house of God," the sacrist whispered. "Praise the Lord, it is a miracle!"

Prentice wasn't sure he agreed, but he wasn't going to argue. He gently pushed himself a little farther inside, eyes never leaving the beast. The creature's head swayed back and forth, snuffling the air, as if trying to find the invisible source of the pain that stopped it. Prentice pulled his legs slowly up to his chest, and he could hear the fearful breathing of the men behind him. The beast snapped and snarled suddenly, and all four of them jumped.

Once Prentice had drawn his legs in far enough, he slammed the door shut in the monster's face with a quick move locking the small iron bolt. Almost immediately, the creature began to howl and claw at the door, while Prentice threw himself against it with his full weight.

"Get the bloody table!" he shouted.

Turley and the sacrist wrestled the room's heavy wooden table to block the door. Bellam groaned and passed out on the floor as he was unceremoniously pushed out of the way. Prentice jumped away and helped to push the table right up against the door. Then they grabbed every object they could find, including the sacrist's little cot bed and even his chamber pot, and stacked it on and around the table.

Outside, the clawing continued, shaking the door, but the beast did not break through. The three of them stood watching, breath heaving, until at last the attacks on the door stopped and there was quiet. For another long moment they held themselves, then they sank to the floor with exhaustion and relief.

Prentice had just hung his head between his knees and closed his eyes when the inner door separating the vestry from the church sanctuary burst open. Sir Liam stood in the doorway, the other two surviving knights behind him. All three had their swords drawn. They looked bewildered by the sight of three convicts and the sacrist collapsed on the floor.

"Nice of you to join us," said Turley and he laid his head against the wall. "Better late than never."

CHAPTER 6

The church was dim and cool, even in the heat of the afternoon, with adobe walls over a foot thick rising from the sandstone foundations. The only light came from tiny slit windows high in the walls, just below the heavily thatched roof. The three knights marched Prentice and Turley into the sanctuary at sword point, the two men carrying Bellam between them.

"We need to get that te tree bark on his leg and soon," Turley said quietly.

"Odds are good it's too late. Likely he'll never walk freely again," said Prentice.

"Silence!" Sir Liam clubbed Turley on the back of the shoulder with the pommel of his sword. "On your knees, churls."

Turley sank slowly, lowering Bellam's legs gently to the floor. Prentice went down likewise, carefully lowering his burden to lie unconscious on the cool ground. The two convict men stared at each other.

Sir Liam walked between them and laid his sword on Prentice's shoulder. "You two cowards will now face the king's justice."

"What is going on here?"

From the shadows near the altar of the church, Duchess Amelia approached them. Her cream linen dress was still smeared with dust, and Prentice could see blood on the cuff of one sleeve. The duchess was an upright woman, long limbed and young, it seemed. Her face was strong and her eyes clear. She was not especially beautiful, but she was not unattractive either. "Pleasantly plain" was the phrase that came to Prentice's mind, and he couldn't help but smirk at the foolishness of thinking of a woman's beauty, or lack thereof, when facing his own execution.

"You think this is funny?" Sir Liam demanded. He drew his sword back for the strike, and Prentice closed his eyes.

"Sir Liam!" the duchess shouted. Liam froze in place, sword held high. "I asked you a question."

"These convict dogs are cowards who fled the battle. It is their fault we lost."

"That's a lie," said Prentice with a cold steel in his voice.

"You dare?" Sir Liam made to finish his swing.

"Sir Liam, lower your sword!" Again, the duchess held him with a command.

The knight obeyed, slowly lowering his blade to his side. "They are cowards and deserters, and the king's law condemns them to die for their crimes."

"Are you the duke, Sir Liam?"

Sir Liam looked up with a puzzled expression. "Your Grace?"

"Are you the Duke of the Western Reach, Sir Liam?" the duchess repeated.

"No, of course not."

"Well, since you are not the duke and since I am the Duchess of the Reach, I am the peer of rank in this assembly, would you not agree?"

"Of course, my lady."

"Then it falls to me to dispense the king's justice, is that not right, Sir Liam?"

Sir Liam lowered his eyes and nodded at the duchess. "Yes, Your Grace. Your servant, always."

"Very good." She looked down at Bellam's unconscious form. "Did this man fall while you retreated?"

"Yes, he did," answered Sir Liam, but Duchess Amelia gave him a sharp look that silenced any further answer.

She looked down at Prentice and Turley, waiting for one of them to answer her question.

"He was not in the retreat, Your Grace," Prentice said, not looking at the duchess directly but keeping his eyes ahead. "He could not be, since he was not in combat."

"What do you mean?"

"He was injured this morning working the quarry."

"Fell, he did, your ladyship," Turley added.

"Your knight Sir Liam sent Bellam back before the fight," Prentice said.

Amelia turned to Sir Liam. "Is that true?"

The knight nodded.

"If he was sent back, how did you two come to be with him?" she asked. "And have a care with your answer. If you are cowards, I will not hesitate to allow Sir Liam to fulfill his duty."

Prentice raised his eyes and looked straight at Amelia's face. "Your Grace, when the line broke and routed, every man present retreated. We were a handful of convict men with some stone working tools. We had no chance against that enemy. As we retreated, we caught up with Bellam still trying for the village with his injured knee. There was no way he could reach here before the enemy. We had already seen the savagery of these attackers and couldn't leave him to their mercy, so we carried him."

"You carried a wounded man to save him from an advancing enemy?"

"Yes, Your Grace."

"That sounds to me more like an act of heroism than cowardice," the duchess mused.

"Your Grace, do not allow this dog to sway you with a sweet story," Sir Liam protested.

"Did he lie?"

"That is not to the point!"

"Then what is the point?" the duchess asked. Her face was a study of reserve, but her eyes searched Sir Liam's.

"These men fled the field!"

"So did you!"

Sir Liam recoiled as if slapped. "It is not the same thing."

"How is it not?"

Sir Liam's eyes narrowed, and his lip twisted in a sneer. "I held my ground and fought until the position was untenable."

"By their account, so did these men. They fled when the line collapsed."

"That's right, your ladyship," Turley chimed in with a smile.

Sir Liam fixed him with a hateful glare, and Turley nodded his head down again. The knight softened his features with a visible effort and turned back to the duchess. "Your Grace, I feel that you have chanced upon something for which your birth has not prepared you. I would not normally raise the issue, but this is an extraordinary circumstance, and I feel I must explain and offer my guidance."

Duchess Amelia's composed face hardened at the mention of her birth; her eyes flashed fury, and she spoke through gritted teeth. "If you feel you must, Sir Liam, then let me not keep you from explaining how the meanness of my birth has caused my misunderstanding."

If Sir Liam recognized the anger in his liege lady's voice, it did not keep him from his point. "On a battlefield, it is the commander's role to determine the disposition of forces," he explained. "Only the knight commanding can determine strategy, and only he can order a retreat."

"Which you did."

"Only after they fled!"

"If they had stood their ground, would you have won?"

Sir Liam opened his mouth, but then he paused and looked away for a moment. Prentice imagined he was remembering the battle and the ferocious way Sir Dav had been torn apart by the wolf beast. Once that creature had attacked, defeat was inevitable.

"No, my lady," Sir Liam said at last.

"Then it seems these men only thought as you did and did as you did. I cannot condemn them and not condemn you too."

"You do not understand!"

"Perhaps not," the duchess shouted, her cool reserve finally cracking. "But I do understand that I am the peer of rank and you are my bondsman. You will do as I command. Now go and attend to our defense. These men have no case to answer."

Sir Liam stood straight and bowed, returning his sword to its scabbard. Then he turned and withdrew. His two companion knights went with him. They stood a way off and discussed how they might see what was happening outside without opening the doors.

Duchess Amelia bent down next to Bellam's body. "Did I hear you say that you could treat his injury?"

"Prentice here can, your ladyship," said Turley. "He's a man who knows some healing."

"A bark bandage will help. Te tree bark," Prentice explained. "Though I don't know if it will be enough. His injury has been left untreated for some time."

"Where will you find this bark?" the duchess asked.

"The sacrist'll have some," said Turley.

"What is your name?"

"Turley, your ladyship."

"And this is Prentice? Very well, Turley, go to the sacrist and see if he has some of this te tree bark and fetch it here."

He stood and turned to go.

"And Turley?" the duchess added. "You will address me as Your Grace or Duchess Amelia from now on, is that clear?"

"Yes, Your Grace."

"Very good."

Turley left. Prentice remained quietly on his knees, watching the duchess as she brushed her fingers over Bellam's dirty, sweaty brow. It seemed that she was seeing someone else, perhaps remembering the suffering of a loved one. She smiled gently for a moment.

"He wasn't wrong, Your Grace," Prentice whispered.

"What did you say?"

"Sir Liam wasn't wrong."

The duchess's demeanor changed, suddenly defensive and angry. "What do you mean by that?"

"It does fall to the knight commanding to order a retreat."

"Oh. Then why did you flee?"

"Sir Liam froze," Prentice said.

"Are you saying *he* was the coward?"

"No, Your Grace. He was unready for the fight, which is not the same thing."

"He wasn't the only one," Amelia said. She looked back down at Bellam.

"Your Grace?"

"I ordered a stop for my river barge this morning," she explained. "I was so cooped up on the boat, and we were starting to get close to Dweltford. I just wanted to pause for a moment, think about... about something other than my dead husband. I thought a simple picnic in the sun was the perfect solution. When we passed a little field between the trees, I told my servants to put in and lay out a luncheon for us. Oh God!"

The duchess slumped down completely on the floor, tears streaming down her face.

"It wasn't even hours ago. We were so happy. I was sitting with my lady-in-waiting. The knights had gone to get the horses so that they could have a run about. Those men, they... they just seemed to walk out of the trees so calmly, so relaxed. One of the servants went to ask what they wanted, and they just ran him through with a spear. They thrust it through his stomach until it came out his back. I saw him fall, and it... it seemed to take an age for him to fall. Then Dianda screamed and everyone was running. Those men, they were just killing and smiling, and they... they... why would they do that?"

The duchess looked straight into Prentice's eyes, then continued. "My father was leading a trade caravan ten years ago when they were ambushed by bandits. I wonder, is this how it felt for him? Was that how he died, running in terror while monstrous men like that hunted him down?"

"I do not think those men today were bandits, Your Grace," Prentice said. "I was exiled over the mountains to the Reach nearly eleven years ago, at the start of the last crusade against the Vec king Kolber's invasion. In all that time I have never seen nor heard of bandits like the men who attacked you today."

"Who are they?"

"I do not know. They moved like invaders, like a scouting force ahead of an army, but they were so intent on murder. And the beast that was with them?"

"Beast?"

"A black thing, like a wolf but more savage and with strange limbs. I've never seen an ape, but I've heard tales of such that were similar to this thing, so perhaps that is what this is—some kind of tamed ape."

Turley returned with the sacrist, who carried a small bundle of bark and twine.

"This is all we have," the man said with an apologetic tone. "It's a little old, but by God's grace it will help the young man's leg."

Prentice and the sacrist set about wrapping Bellam's knee in a bark bandage, the papery tree pieces pressed close to the skin. Bellam groaned but did not awaken.

When they were done, the sacrist sat back on his haunches and looked at Prentice. "Now, what about your ankle?"

"Fine for now," Prentice replied, and he showed the foot where the beast's claw had struck the iron. Though the skin was dirty and scratched from the retreat, there were no serious injuries.

"'Tis surely a miracle," the sacrist exclaimed. "I will fetch water, and you two men can wash your feet and hands. After all, this is God's house." He stood and left.

"What did he mean by a miracle?" the duchess asked.

Prentice shook his head, but Turley explained. "The beast attacked us at the rectory door, Your Grace. It reached a claw for Prentice's foot here, but it couldn't cross the threshold for fear of pain. Tried a number of times before giving up. The sacrist called it a miracle."

"Do you think it was?" the duchess asked.

Turley shrugged, and she looked at Prentice.

"It saved our lives," he said. "That's miracle enough, I suppose."

CHAPTER 7

The church had a simple vestibule, with a carved wooden screen dividing the entryway from the sanctuary proper. The knights had tied their mounts and the duchess's smaller horse to the posts of the screen, and every now and then a soft snort or whinny echoed from the vestibule. Otherwise, all was quiet until an hour or so before sundown.

As the afternoon waned, there came the sounds of terrified cries from the village square just outside the church door. The horses began to fret and push against the screen so that the knights had to calm them or else they would injure each other.

Prentice and Turley made their way to the door, listening. Behind them came Duchess Amelia and the sacrist.

"What's happening?" she whispered.

"I think they're bringing the villagers here," said Prentice.

"Why would they do that?"

"I don't know."

For some time, the miserable sounds from outside—the crying of children and the shouts of violent men—

continued. Few of the words the invaders spoke were comprehensible. Mostly they spoke in a foreign tongue.

"What language is that?" Duchess Amelia asked.

Prentice and Turley shook their heads. The knights, likewise, did not know. Even the sacrist could only shrug. After a while, they heard wood being cut, as well as hammering and other work.

"Sounds like they're demolishing the village," Turley said.

Prentice tapped him and pointed to a small round window directly over the door. "Give me a boost."

Turley bent down and interlaced his fingers. Prentice stepped up, one foot in Turley's hands and then onto his shoulders. Turley grabbed his ankles, and they moved close to the wall so that Prentice could look out.

In the open space in front of the church, the painted men were planting rows of stakes, cut from timbers of the village buildings. Already a number of the humble homes had been ripped apart, their roof and wall beams given points and thrust into the hard-packed earth. Most of the attackers did this labor, while a few kept watch on the villagers, who sat together in a crowd to one side. Beyond them the wolf creature prowled back and forth.

To Prentice's eye, it looked like the stakes were to keep the people in the church inside, similar to the fields of stakes used to fortify sieges and the like, but that seemed like a strange overreaction. Did they fear the knights sallying on their mounts, with only three on horseback? Maybe they did not know how many horses were inside.

"What are they doing?" asked Sir Liam, who had come to find out what was happening outside as well.

"I can't tell," Prentice answered. "It doesn't make sense."

Two of the men left a stake they had just planted and headed over to the prisoners. They grabbed a woman by the arms, pulling her up and toward the church door.

"If you do not understand, then let me see," Sir Liam demanded. "I will make sense of it."

The woman struggled, and the two men simply lifted her into the air and continued to carry her.

"Oh God," said Prentice.

The purpose of the stakes had become clear. The two men raised her high over the point of their spike and then dropped her onto it, impaling her through her belly in a gout of blood and gore. She screamed in agony, a scream that went on until it choked away into a gurgling moan. The two men, sprayed with the woman's blood, left her body and went back to the prisoners.

This time the villagers recoiled and cried out in horror. They tried to escape the grasping hands, but their guards beat at them with spear butts, and the wolf snarled and barked at them. The executioners grabbed a boy about ten years of age. He twisted in their grip, slipping free for a moment and bolting to escape. He ran to the side of the church. One of the executioners gave a barked command, and the beast leaped after the boy.

From around the church corner, there was a cry cut short. The executioners grabbed an elderly man who had a crutch in his hand. They threw away his crutch, and he seemed to crumple into their arms as they carried him to a spike.

Prentice bowed his head and could watch no more. He slid down off Turley's shoulders.

"Well?" Sir Liam demanded.

Prentice crouched down near the floor, his head in his hand.

"Answer me!"

"What is happening?" Amelia asked.

There was a short cry—the old man's.

Prentice closed his eyes. "They are killing them. They're impaling them on stakes just outside the door."

"What? We must do something!" The duchess rushed to the door, her hand on the heavy cross bar. As she stood there, a third scream rent the air from outside. Amelia turned on the knights. "Sir Liam, I order you to rescue those people!"

Sir Liam looked from the duchess down to Prentice, who returned his gaze with grim eyes. There was no need to say anything. The two men knew that, with their small numbers, there was nothing they could do.

"Sir Liam!"

"Your Grace, we cannot."

"You refuse?"

Sir Liam shook his head. "If we try to sally, we will certainly be killed. We all will." He looked about the vestibule at everyone present. "You as well, Your Grace. It serves no purpose."

Duchess Amelia moved until she stood over Prentice. "You!" she ordered. "You go."

Prentice stood and looked the duchess in the eye. "Sir Liam is right, Your Grace. It would only lead to more death."

"Cowards," Amelia whispered, and she placed her hand to her mouth as tears streamed down her face. From outside came another scream and what sounded like a desperate cry of prayer that trailed away. Amelia cringed away from the sound, watching the tiny round window above them as though it were a portal to hell. With a final look at the men around her, she fled into the sanctuary, weeping. The sacrist followed after her, stricken.

"Well," said Sir Liam as he watched the two recede into the late afternoon darkness. "It seems that a convict's heroism is a short-lived thing." He turned to Prentice with a look of withering contempt.

Prentice met his eye. "Innocent people are being tortured to death on the other side of this door," he said flatly. "Do you really imagine God is allowing such evil just so you can make a petty point about the social order?"

Before Sir Liam could answer the rebuke, Prentice stood and walked slump-shouldered to the nearest wall, where he sank down and closed his eyes.

CHAPTER 8

The killing continued into the evening until, a few hours after sundown, every villager had been impaled. The invaders hardly spoke, neither to each other nor to the prisoners, and the death cries of the slain devolved into low groans that had all faded by midnight.

Inside the church, everyone remained silent, though occasionally one of the knights could be heard whispering to a horse to calm it. The sacrist went back into the vestry and returned with a single candle, which he lit from a flash match. He placed the candle on the altar and sat next to the duchess in the first pew. He bowed his head in prayer, and shortly after, she roused herself from her misery to join him. Through the rest of the night, they looked to the simple wooden cross and prayed.

Prentice stirred a little around midnight.

"Why don't they come and get us?" Turley asked from next to him.

Prentice did not answer.

"I mean, they could if they wanted," Turley continued. "Surely they must know we're only a few. Even if we put up a fight, they'd take us fine. Or hell, they could just fire to the place for that matter. Why aren't they just throwing some torches up onto the roof? That'd burn us out in short order, I'd say. So why don't they?"

Prentice sighed. "Do you expect me to have an answer?"

"No, not really. These are just the questions that trouble a soul at times like these."

"They want to capture the duchess alive," said a voice from the other side. In the dark it was impossible to make out which of the knights spoke. "She will be valuable for ransom."

"I suppose," mused Turley. "But how are bandits like these supposed to ask for ransom? And who of? And if that's the case, why the bloody slaughter?"

The questions hung in the darkness, and all the men considered them in silence.

"I don't think they want us dead," Prentice said at last.

"What? Why not?"

"Because you're right; if they wanted to kill us, they could. Instead, they've spent the afternoon staging a brutal mass execution. And it doesn't even sound like they especially wanted to."

"What kind of fool's talk is that?" came the knight's voice again in the darkness. "Why would they do it if they didn't want to?"

"Do you hear any laughter?" Prentice asked, and the knight did not reply. "Any sounds of merriment or shouts that sound like bloodlust or fury run amok?"

There was quiet as every man seemed to listen to whatever he could hear from outside. A night bird cried in the distance, and there was still a soft moan from the dying every now and then, but otherwise there was nothing to hear.

"So why are they doing all this?" asked the knight.

"Again, I don't know."

The rest of the night passed quietly, and despite their exhaustion, no one slept.

The next morning, the unnatural quiet continued. A little after dawn, Prentice climbed up on Turley's shoulders again and looked out. Every one of the villagers was dead, their blood running down into the dirt to form an ugly red mud at the foot of the church steps. Of the invaders there was no sign. Prentice got back down and told the others what he could see.

"They've gone?" asked the duchess. It seemed incredible.

They waited in the church for another hour, listening for any clue about what was happening. At last Duchess Amelia ordered them to look outside.

"It is an ambush," Sir Liam averred.

"We cannot wait here until we starve," the duchess countered. "Do you think we will be rescued if we wait?"

Sir Liam shook his head.

The duchess looked to Prentice and Turley with a grim expression, and the two convicts lifted the bar as quietly as they could from the door. They lowered the heavy wooden beam and then turned back to the doorway, one on either side. Behind them, Sir Liam and his knights drew their longswords and held them ready.

Prentice and Turley slowly pushed the door and poked their heads outside. The morning stillness was almost beautiful, the sky fine and blue and clear. But the dead hung where they were impaled, their faces contorted in rictus, the blood of wounds sprayed about as if by a mad painter. The smell was metallic and so strong that Prentice could taste it in the back of his throat.

He stalked forward down the steps, and Turley followed. In the doorway, the two knights held the door, which creaked slightly. Looking over his shoulder, Prentice could see the two armored men ready to slam the doors shut again. He doubted they'd wait for him or Turley to make it back first. After calling him a coward last night, he wondered if the duchess would even protest.

They made a slow circuit of the dead and then another wider one around the village. They jumped once when some roofing from one of the half-destroyed cottages fell with a crash some distance from them, but ultimately there was nothing to fear. The attackers had gone. After a quarter hour of tension, Prentice finally shrugged and sighed. He looked at Turley and then waved at the knights still waiting in the church doorway. His gaze fell on a shovel sitting beside a tumbled wall, and he picked it up.

"Come on," he said to Turley.

Turley looked at the shovel for a moment and then rolled his eyes as he realized what Prentice meant.

Prentice cocked an eyebrow. "You know they're only going to tell us to do it in a moment anyway."

He headed back toward the impaled bodies, and Turley came with him, scrabbling about in the wreckage and finding another shovel on the way. When they reached the first impaled villager, they began to dig the first grave, there in the bloody earth.

They were already knee deep before the knights finally emerged from the church. Duchess Amelia and the sacrist came with them. They surveyed the wreckage and Amelia wept again, but softly and with control, as befitted mourning rites. When Turley and Prentice lifted the first body into its shallow grave, the sacrist came forward and began to offer prayers to the Lord for the dead woman.

"You can't do this here," Sir Liam declared. "This is the village square." The three men at the grave stopped and looked at him. "Take the bodies out of the village and bury them there."

"Sir Liam?" said the duchess.

"When the other villagers return, they will not want a mass of graves in their midst!"

"No one's ever coming back here," Prentice said.

The duchess and the knights looked at him, then at the bodies and the wreckage. Prentice was right and there could be no doubting it. With a sour expression, Sir Liam nodded his agreement. Then he waved for his men to go back to the church.

"Where are you going, sir?" asked the duchess.

"This task will take the day," he replied. "I will take the horses out so that they may be run. We will make a patrol to ensure that the enemy has truly withdrawn and to guarantee your safety, Your Grace."

"You will stay and assist in the burials."

"Your Grace, you cannot be serious." All three knights bridled at the suggestion they would do such base work.

"I am the Duchess of the Western Reach, charged with the defense of the province and the protection of its people. You are sworn to me in that service," she said. Sir Liam looked about to interrupt the duchess, but she did not let him. "I failed to protect these people, and you failed me in your service! We all failed them." She looked over the three knights and also Prentice and Turley as she spoke. "We will not fail them in this final moment."

"But, Your Grace..."

"Find shovels and picks, Sir Liam! Find them and commence to dig. We will not shirk this duty."

The duchess turned her back on the knights and climbed the stairs to the church. She then faced them once more, standing like a guardian caryatid, looking down on them. The three knights slowly brought themselves to the task, and the digging of graves continued throughout the morning. Except for the words of the sacrist's prayers, hardly anyone spoke, and the duchess kept her stern watch throughout.

CHAPTER 9

The graves were dug, and the prayers said by early afternoon. The knights had stripped their armor, and by the end they were as filthy as the convicts. The bloody mud smeared every man. Even the sacrist's homespun brown robe looked like it had changed color, wetted upward from the hem. Prentice and Turley lounged on the steps of the church, close to the wall in the little available shade. The knights stretched their tired limbs but steadfastly refused to sit, the ground or steps being beneath their station.

"We should go now," said the duchess. "Is it far to Dweltford?"

"Three days' ride, my lady," said the sacrist. "Two and a half if ridden hard."

One of the knights shook his head. "Our mounts will not bear hard riding."

"You might get a boat up the river."

"Yes, we'll do that."

The knights gathered the mounts, and soon they were all ready to go.

The sacrist begged off the duchess's invitation to go with them. "I shall remain and pray for them," he said, looking over the graves.

"Those men might return."

"Then as like I'll join my flock in one final service."

The duchess nodded. "I will send from my reeve when I return to Dweltford. You will have a stipend for life, to tend these graves as a memorial."

The sacrist bowed and returned to the church.

The duchess ordered that the three convicts should accompany her rather than stay in the dead village. She allowed Turley and Prentice to scrounge up a handcart, and the two men loaded Bellam on it. Thankfully, he was still unconscious as they passed the bloody stakes and fresh graves. The knights led the way, with the convicts pulling in the rear, and they all left the nameless village at the river bend behind.

Out on the road, passing through the farmed fields, they soon found out what had happened to the menfolk of the village. Here and there were bodies, some on the road, some amongst the crops. A small cluster lay around a lone tree, as if the men had tried to climb to escape, or else made a last stand. They found no one alive.

"So cruel," Amelia said.

"Yet strangely half-hearted," said Sir Liam. "They left us to live."

"They need someone to tell the tale," Prentice called from where he was pulling the cart.

Amelia let her horse drop back to walk beside him. "What do you mean?"

"The torture was thorough but not excited, like soldiers under orders," Prentice explained. "I think they are the advance of a larger army. They go ahead and commit these crimes, careful to leave a few survivors to spread the tale of their cruelty, and the terror of their reputation grows. The men they slew in the field and left them where they fell, but the women they made a show of slaughtering right in front of us, almost like a set stage. They wanted us to hear the screams and see the bodies."

Amelia considered Prentice's words for a time. "But what makes you think they are part of an army? Could they not be mere bandits, as Sir Liam thinks?"

"They could, but if that were all they were, they would not be enough to spread terror. Thirty brutal men would be frightening, but the king's law would soon be brought against them. The Reach is vast, but it is only open fields and low hills. Where would they hide?"

"You make a sound case," Amelia said.

"It is only conjecture," Prentice conceded. "And it still leaves important questions unanswered."

"Which are?"

"If they are an army, who commands them and where do they come from?"

Duchess Amelia thought again, weighing the question. "The south?" she ventured. "One of the Vec princes, perhaps? A new king?"

Prentice shook his head. "You were coming from the south. You should have seen them days before, if they were coming from the Vec."

"Unless they were cunning, using stealth."

"They didn't seem the type."

The duchess shuddered, undoubtedly recalling the painted men and their brazen approach. They did not respect or fear her knights enough to use stealth. "They were not from the mountains," she said, and Prentice nodded. "And if they came from the north, they would have been intercepted by city militias long before they reached here. So, if that is the case, then where can they have come from?"

Prentice nodded over his left shoulder as he hefted the cart poles in his hands. He looked to the unseen Dwelt River, just over a league away. "From beyond the river."

"The west?" asked Amelia, incredulous. "But there's nothing out there. Just grasslands, not even farmsteads. The odd hermit perhaps, but no more..."

She stopped, and Prentice could tell what she was thinking.

"But there are no nations out there," she protested, shaking her head. "Who is there to raise an army?"

"I do not know, Your Grace, but for many years the primarchs of the Church have urged successive crusades, telling us that God has called us to subjugate the evil of the west, the mountains, and beyond the mountains."

"The crusades are over. We have settled the Reach. The region is pacified. It is my duchy!"

"Men are still sent over the mountains," Prentice countered. "I was sent with the last crusade eleven years ago."

"Yes, but that was against a Vec invasion, seeking the metals from the Broken Baronies in the north. That wasn't a campaign against the pagans or monsters."

Prentice nodded again and made a gesture to tug his forelock, but he had to be quick to retake the cart pole before it dropped. The duchess looked thoughtful for a time, her eyes fixed on the distance, then she spurred her horse and joined the knights once more. When she was gone, Turley moved up from where he was walking behind the cart.

"You think that's right?" he asked. "They came from over the river?"

"It's the best guess I can make."

"Nothing but sun, monsters, and a few hermit farmers out there, far as any man knows."

Prentice nodded.

"God help us all."

Turley grabbed the cart pole, and the two men changed places to give Prentice a rest. Prentice looked back on Bellam, who was still not awake but now seemed to be less troubled in his rest. The bandage seemed to be working well. He grabbed a length of old sack and positioned it over Bellam's face to protect him from the hot sun, then fell into a march behind the cart. The little column marched all day and rested by the roadside, having a second night without food.

CHAPTER 10

The next morning, Bellam awoke just before dawn and nearly fell off the cart before he realized where he was. The motion disturbed Prentice and Turley, who were both sleeping by the wheels.

"Ho there," said Turley. "Look who's with us."

"How are you feeling?" Prentice asked.

"Hungry, I think. Aargh, and my knee hurts. Is it supposed to do that?"

"Fool," said Turley, but he smiled and thumped Bellam's shoulder affectionately.

Bellam looked around. "Where are we?"

As the sun crept above the horizon, they explained what had happened at the village. By the time they were done, it was full day, and the duchess and her knights were awake. When she saw that Bellam had woken, Duchess Amelia smiled and said she was glad. The knights all but ignored him, sparing no more than a glance in his direction. As soon as they were all fully awake, they began their journey again.

It was almost midday when they passed their first sign of life, a farmhouse some small distance from the roadside. Two women worked the field next to the little whitewashed cottage. Sir Liam suggested that they could get food from the farmers, but the duchess forbade it, instead ordering them on their way.

"Easy enough for her to go without," Turley muttered under his breath. "She's riding, not walking."

"A small farmstead like that won't have enough food to feed us," Prentice countered. "Not without the farmer and his family going hungry. She's thinking of her people."

"Aren't we her people?"

"You know what I mean."

After midday, the road crossed a creek, and they took time to rest and water the horses.

Prentice looked at Bellam's leg, removing the bandage and washing the skin with water. "I think the swelling's reduced. Try standing on it."

Bellam slid gingerly off the cart and tried putting his weight on his leg. He winced in pain but was able to stand, as long as he could lean on the cart.

"Looks like we're still pulling you around for a while," Prentice said.

"Lazy bastard," Turley muttered, but his grin showed he did not mean it.

Bellam smiled and then pushed himself back onto the cart.

Toward the end of the day, the number of farms increased, and the road turned westward toward the river. The riders had gotten some distance ahead of the handcart, and when the duchess called a halt, it took time for the convicts to catch up. At last, they reached the rest.

"It appears there is a small riverside trading stop ahead," she said, addressing the whole group. "Hopefully, they have a boat we can use to reach Dweltford. From there I will gather the duchy's men-at-arms. We will return and hunt those men down, and every last one will pay with his life. In the meantime, you must tell no one what we have witnessed, not a word. Not to the traders, not the boatmen, nobody."

"That includes after we leave," Sir Liam added, looking down on the convicts.

"How can we speak to someone here after we leave?" Turley asked, confusion written on his face.

"After *we* leave," Sir Liam corrected, glancing at the others on horseback. "You will remain here and continue to serve your terms. No doubt there is some local farmer or fisher in need of labor."

"They will be coming with us, Sir Liam," said the duchess.

"Your Grace?"

"They will be coming with us to Dweltford. Now ride ahead and secure a boat, some food, and feed for the horses."

Sir Liam scowled and then rode off ahead. Duchess Amelia straightened her back and gently walked her mount down the road, leading the other knights and her little gaggle of convicts. Prentice and Turley exchanged smiles.

"I don't think that fella likes us much," said Bellam, and the three of them chuckled until the duchess cast an imperious glance over her shoulder. They quieted like chastened school children.

The riverside trading post had several flat-bottomed craft moored at its little dock, and there was a barge easily large enough to take them and their horses. It took a short while to persuade the boatman that the handful of filthy men and the woman in the dirty dress were in fact the duchess and her honor guard. Ultimately the promise of silver swayed him. Soon after dark, the boatman and his two sons poled their barge out into the flow of the Dwelt. At the urging of their passengers, they pushed on through the night in shifts, one sleeping and the other two using long poles to drive the barge against the gentle current.

The horses were secured in the middle of the barge, and the knights took pains to care for them. They scrubbed them down, looked to their shoes and fetlocks, and fed them good oats obtained from the trade post. The duchess sat at the bow and ate a bowl of pease porridge. The convicts stayed at the back, splitting a loaf of rye between them and keeping out of the way.

The coolness of the air over the river and the night sounds were calming. The three exiled men soon dozed peacefully. After a while Prentice woke to find the elderly boatman nudging his shoulder. "You the one called Prentice?"

He nodded.

"Lady at the bow says to fetch you. She don't mind giving out orders, do she?" the boatman said.

Prentice stood up. "She is the duchess."

"A woman with airs and a rank. They's the worst kind."

The boatman sank down and pulled his hat over his eyes. Prentice left him to sleep and went to the front to see what the duchess wanted.

Amelia was still seated in the bow, looking up at the small crescent moon and the arc of the ribbon across the sky, the strange band of light bridging the eastern horizon with the west. There was a legend that said the rampart was different from all other celestial bodies, having been put in place by the knowledge of an ancient people. Scholars argued over why. Some called it a road that the builders of Babel would walk to their tower, which had offended God. Others claimed it a defense of some kind. They called it a rampart against the fire of heaven. And others still said God himself put it in the sky. The Church had no official doctrine but accepted that the ribbon dated from before the Second Flood, and otherwise discouraged further inquiry.

Prentice stood behind the duchess while she studied the sky, waiting to be acknowledged. When Amelia said nothing, he coughed quietly to get her attention.

"My first night in Dweltford was like this," she said, not taking her eyes from the heavens. "I stood on the balcony with my new husband. We spent hours just watching the stars, and the ribbon, and the moon. Then we..." She paused, then looked down at the water with a shy smile. "Then we went back inside and did more of what husbands and wives do on their wedding night."

Prentice could not think of anything to say. After a moment Amelia turned to look at him. Her face was barely visible in the moonlight and the little dancing flame of the barge's one lantern.

"Did you ever meet my husband?" she asked.

"No, Your Grace, though I stood on the battlefield with him a number of times during the crusade. Well, me and about five thousand others, but I saw him then, leading the charge."

"What did you think of him?"

"You know it is not my place to say, Your Grace," Prentice responded reflexively.

"Do not answer me that way," she insisted. "Be straight with me, as two people might speak without station to separate them."

Prentice stood quietly for a short while, not sure whether he could trust the duchess enough to be truthful with her. He had seen other nobles ask to be treated like ordinary men and women, only to take offense and respond with wrath and violence when it actually happened.

He decided to risk only a small truth. "He loved to fight, Your Grace."

Amelia nodded and smiled. "That was true. He loved many of the things of life, much more than I expected when we became betrothed. He did love me, though, and that came as a surprise."

"Why, if I may ask?"

"We did not marry for love, Prentice."

"But he loved you?"

"He did, but that was not what made our match. You have heard, no doubt, that I am not highborn?"

Prentice fumbled a moment for words. "Your Grace, I don't—"

"No, no," Amelia cut him off. "That's an unfair question; you have no way to answer without risking insult. It is true, my family are merchants from Denay on the east coast of the kingdom. We were wealthy, and my father worked so very hard. Before he was killed, he obtained a place for me as a lady-in-waiting to Baroness Jayne Switch. It was part of his plan for our family: I would learn to move in the circles of court, perhaps marry a landed knight, and my sons—his grandsons—would have his wealth and my husband's title. I don't think he ever dreamed his plan would be as successful as it was.

"My dear husband, the duke, was a lover of many things in life, but finance was not one of them. Ten years after the victories of the last crusade, he was deeply in debt to capital bankers and even trading houses in the Vec. Baroness Switch introduced us, and it seemed perfect to my mother. Father's money would buy no mere knighthood but a peer's rank—a duchy. But Mother was not quite the shrewd planner that Father was, and we did not know how much money a duke could owe."

Amelia looked at Prentice straight, as though it mattered to her to know that he understood what she was telling him.

"That is why I was in the south, you see? My family's fortune is now lying in the vaults of a Vec merchant house called the Golden Heron. The last coppers are gone, to pay a mountain of debt. While I was south, negotiating the final terms to discharge that debt, word came that my husband had died. And now, little more than a year into my marriage, I am a widow. Last of all, I return to my lands to discover that there is unrest and an armed band of the foulest men at large, who are either mad bandits or else, worse, the vanguard of an invading army. I am poor, bereft, and under attack."

She stopped speaking, and Prentice looked closely to see if she was crying. She was not. He did not think there was much sense of self-pity in the way the duchess recounted the story. Rather, she seemed to be quite calm in listing the challenges before her.

She sighed. "Why are you a convict, Prentice?"

"Your Grace?" Prentice responded, taken by surprise.

"Obviously, I know that you committed some crime and were transported across the mountains for it. What I suppose I mean is why are you *still* a convict? The term of transportation is seven years, is it not?"

"Seven years is usual."

"And you were sent across the mountains for the crusade eleven years ago? So, you should have been released by now, should you not?"

"It is not that simple," Prentice answered quietly. The duchess was cutting straight into difficult territory, and he could feel his anger stirring. He pressed it down and thanked God inwardly that she could not see his face clearly in the dark.

"Why is it not?" Amelia asked. "Seven years and more have passed. Why are you not released?"

"Release is at the discretion of the convict's liege. I think the late duke had more on his mind in recent years than my freedom."

"Such as our wedding?"

"Such as your wedding."

"And his debts?"

"If you say so, Your Grace," Prentice said through gritted teeth. Was she trying to get him to say something to condemn himself? He'd seen convicts flogged for direct speech like this.

"And I thought that all the men who fought in the crusade were released at its end. Wasn't that a part of the victory jubilee?"

"The Primarch did call for a jubilee amnesty, Your Grace. But again, it was at the discretion of individual liege lords. I do not know how many were actually freed."

"It seems to me that convicts suffer some injustices as they pay their debt of justice," Amelia mused.

Prentice clenched his jaw. Self-pity or no, this was not a conversation he wanted to have with the ruler of the Western Reach.

"Perhaps you will understand, then, what I must next do." She paused, but Prentice said nothing. There was nothing safe to say.

"I had thought to release you three upon our return to Dweltford," she continued. "The youth, Bellam, is too injured to be a good worker, and you and the man Turley both demonstrated admirable heroism in his rescue. I know I called you a coward that night, and I am sorry for that. I see now the wisdom of Sir Liam's decision."

"He is not a bad man, Sir Liam, merely ambitious. Sir Dav was my husband's knight captain, and he rated Sir Liam very competent; he was training him for a replacement. Now that Sir Dav is dead, I will have to make Sir Liam captain of my knights. He is well-liked among them. He will keep their loyalty for me, prevent them from abandoning the duchy now that my husband is dead and only a woman rules."

Suddenly Prentice could see where the conversation was going. It was unwelcome, but not as dangerous as he had feared.

"Because of all these things, I cannot release you," the duchess finished. "The conflict between the two of you is too sharp. If I pardon you now and commute your transportation, it will offend Sir Liam. He might quit my service, and I cannot have that—not at this time. I am vulnerable. You do understand, don't you?"

Prentice's face was entirely in shadow, the little lamplight coming from behind him.

The duchess pressed him for an answer. "Do you understand?"

"I am a convict, exiled across the mountains to the Reach," he said coldly, his voice like forged steel. "It does not matter what I understand."

"You must see that there is more to it than that!"

"No, I do not!" Prentice answered through gritted teeth. "You are making a decision that does not sit well with your conscience. Such is the nature of rulership. Sweet and gentle is for milk maids and seamstresses. Duchesses rule, and either they are iron or they break."

"You dare rebuke me?" Amelia said, but her voice was quiet rather than indignant.

"You do me an injustice and then ask me to forgive you while you remain unrepentant. And you know that you are unjust, which is why we are having this conversation. By your own actions, you rebuke yourself. Now with your leave, Your Grace, I am tired and need to rest."

Prentice did not wait to be dismissed but turned back toward the stern.

"I will make good on this," Amelia said. "I will make restitution."

He paused but did not face her. "You are the Duchess of the Reach. You will do what you must." Then he returned to the stern and tried to sleep.

CHAPTER 11

The town of Dweltford sat on the northeast shore of a glittering blue lake that opened in the bowl of a rolling green valley. The town had three distinct parts. The town proper sat on the shore behind the circle of a curtain wall that was five times the height of a man and thick enough for four to walk abreast on top. A tower gate stood toward the middle, and the circle of the wall curved back around near the shore and headed out into the water of the lake. A bridge linked this to the town's second part, the castle, which sat on an island in the lake with its own walls and towers.

The third part of the town was outside the walls, mostly out of sight for those on the barge. There, farmers and merchants set up tents and stalls, as well as pens for animals. In winter this section would dwindle to almost nothing, but at this time of summer heading toward harvest, it was only growing. As the barge traveled along the lake's bank toward the town, they could see heavy traffic on the road in the valley. The farms and fields all seemed prosperous, and some of the workers even waved to them.

"How does a man with all this end up in debt?" Prentice mused as he watched the farms roll past.

"What?" asked Turley.

"Just something the duchess said last night."

"Last night?" Turley cocked a curious eye at Prentice, but he did not say any more.

Just before midday the barge pulled up to a wharf, and Sir Liam led the way from the riverside into the town and up to the castle. One of the knights was left to bring the mounts later, as the duchess was in a hurry to be home at last.

"Make way!" Sir Liam called, using his sheathed sword like a baton to shove people aside. "Make way for the duchess Amelia."

For her part, Amelia seemed uncomfortable drawing so much attention, perhaps because of their filthy estate, but Sir Liam was effective in making their way and she did not try to stop him. Where people heard him coming, they turned and looked, then quickly stood back and either knelt or bowed according to their social station. When they passed through the market, called the Market Within Walls, Sir Liam's voice was swallowed at first by the noise of street hawkers and hagglers. His forceful driving soon spread calm ahead of them, though, until a hush fell across the entire square and everyone stopped to watch them pass.

They crossed the bridge to the castle and found the portcullis lowered.

Sir Liam called to the gatehouse, and a guard appeared. "Open the gate!" he commanded.

The guard looked down on them. "Gate is down while the duchess is not in residence," he said imperiously, clearly not recognizing them. "Order of the castellan, Sir Duggan. Any business comes through the council's herald in town."

"This is the duchess, fool!"

The man peered down at the bedraggled party. "Pull the other one, it's a beer tap!"

"Open this damn gate or I'll have you flogged 'til your blood pools at your feet!" Sir Liam stared up at him and the guard left the wall. Sir Liam kicked at one of the bridge's footings, the leather thudding loudly. "This is ridiculous."

"Has he simply left?" asked the duchess, her expression more bemused than offended.

"Ho there!" Sir Liam called, but no one answered. He walked up to the portcullis and looked through. "The inner gate is closed as well. What are they expecting, a siege?"

He made his way back out. Soon they heard the sound of people on the parapet above them.

"What is this bloody foolishness?" came the gruff voice of a middle-aged man.

"Sir Duggan," called Duchess Amelia. "It is I."

Sir Duggan's gray-haired head poked out over the top of the wall. He was a well-groomed man with dark eyes and a bushy mustache that drooped down the sides of his mouth. His brow furrowed as he stared at them.

"Come now, Sir Duggan," Sir Liam said. "We are filthy and tired, man! We all need hot baths and good meals."

"And strong ale," added one of the knights. Sir Liam nodded his agreement.

Prentice watched the interchange and tried to understand what was happening. It seemed odd for the duchess to be made to wait at her own gate, and just as odd that the gate was closed for no reason during the day.

At last, Sir Duggan spoke. "My lady," he said, dragging the words out. "I will... I will see to the gate immediately." He gave an order to the guard behind him, and in short order the portcullis was ratcheted up. The inner gate opened, and Sir Liam led the duchess finally to her home. Prentice, Turley, and Bellam followed quietly at a distance. Inside the gatehouse, Prentice noted the rows of murder holes in the ceiling. Dweltford Castle was no rich nobleman's folly; it was a ducal seat and a border fortress.

Inside the castle bailey they met Sir Duggan, coming down from the wall. The guards on the parapet were turned out in the cream livery of the duchy, but Sir Duggan's surcoat was purple and gray, the heraldic colors of his own family.

"This is an odd welcome home, Sir Duggan," the duchess said.

Sir Duggan approached her and went down on one knee. "Please, my lady, there have been strange reports coming from the south. It is an odd time."

"We know some of what you speak," she agreed. "And we bring grave news of our own."

"Truly, Duchess?"

"Sir Dav is dead," said Sir Liam. "We were ambushed and gravely assaulted. The duchess's survival has been a hard-won thing!"

Sir Duggan shook his head. "This is dread news. A great blow to the duchy. My report is not near so dire, but it is serious nonetheless."

Prentice watched the ease with which the two knights addressed each other, like old comrades. Whether they knew it or not, they were talking in the duchess's presence as if she were not there. Prentice was sure that she would notice.

"Well, doubtless we will have much to discuss," Sir Liam said. "I imagine Her Grace would welcome the chance to bathe and eat, perhaps to rest, while we confer and prepare a report for her. Would it suit you, Your Grace, to receive the report in your solar, or in the salon off the main hall?"

Prentice nearly scoffed to hear Sir Liam try to lead Duchess Amelia like that. He could see by Sir Duggan's expression that the castellan was shocked as well.

The duchess smiled sweetly and nodded. "Sir Duggan, you will escort me at once to the crypts."

"The crypts, Your Grace?" Sir Duggan and Sir Liam both were clearly taken aback by the instruction.

"I have not yet seen my husband's body," the duchess explained. "I will attend his memory there, as is fitting for a grieving widow. You will join me."

"Yes, Your Grace."

"Then I will receive yourself and Sir Liam in the great hall, where you will each inform me of your intelligences, and I will formulate any responses that are needed. In the meantime, Sir Liam..." She turned to him and pointed to the three convicts standing by. "You will see to it that these men are bestowed and fed; your knights as well. Then you will see to your own needs. When I am done praying for my husband's soul, I will send for you."

"Yes, Your Grace," Sir Liam said, his eyes narrowing momentarily.

Duchess Amelia walked away toward the entry to the castle's inner keep. Sir Duggan trailed behind her. On the threshold, she turned. "And, Sir Liam," she said loudly, "see that these three are handled gently, or I shall hear of it." Then she was gone and Sir Duggan with her.

Prentice had to admire the way she handled the situation. Without a single direct comment, she had put Sir Liam in his place and shown everyone present that she was fully capable of ruling her own household, widow or not. The young knight was seething in the wake of the encounter, but Prentice had no sympathy. The fool had humiliated himself, attempting so crass a manipulation in such a public setting. What did he think would happen?

"You see to yourselves," Sir Liam told the knights with him bluntly. "I must make sure Her Grace's new pets are properly in their kennels."

"Well, that sounds mighty fine of you, my lord," said Turley, tugging his forelock but smiling insolently.

Sir Liam whirled on him, but Prentice quickly inserted himself between the two. For a moment he and the knight stood face-to-face, Sir Liam's rough-shaven chin and filthy surcoat almost obliterating the social distinction between them. They could have been any two dirty, ill-groomed men.

"Have a care, my lord," Prentice said flatly as he met Sir Liam's furious gaze. "'Gently handled,' those were the duchess's words."

Sir Liam said nothing in response for a long time, only staring at Prentice's face. Prentice wondered how angry the young knight was. They were all tired and worn, in body and heart, from the past few days. The chances were good that Sir Liam's grip on himself would slip, and Prentice would find himself at the wrong end of a sword.

At last, Sir Liam blinked and then turned his back on them. "This way, dogs." He led them in the opposite direction across the bailey from the main keep.

CHAPTER 12

Amelia looked down on the plain stone of her husband's crypt. The cool air of the sepulcher smelled of earth, and somewhere she could hear the drip of water. In the back of her mind, she wondered how far they were from the lake itself and if it might burst in somehow and drown them. Despite her tears, she smiled at the foolishness of her own thoughts.

"Sir Duggan," she called, after dabbing the tears from her face with the dirty hem of her sleeve.

Sir Duggan stepped up beside her. "Yes, Your Grace?"

"Why is the casket so plain?"

"I don't understand."

"The stone of my husband's casket," Amelia said, stretching out her hand and laying it on the coverstone. "It has no engravement, not even his name. He died a duke of the realm; his deeds should be engraved about the crypt. His name should be in the arch above the alcove and his likeness carved into the coverstone. Why has none of this been attended to? My husband has been nearly seven weeks in his grave now. The work should at least have been begun!"

Although Amelia's tone was not strong, Sir Duggan nonetheless seemed taken aback by the question. He appeared to grope to form a reply. "You were not yet here, Your Grace," he said eventually. "A likeness couldn't be carved without your approval."

She was not convinced. "The name, at least, should be in place."

"He was Duke Marne," Sir Duggan countered. "Everyone knew him. He was the first duke invested of the Western Reach, when the prince incorporated the three Broken Baronies into a duchy. And he is the first duke to be buried here. There are no traditions yet to follow."

Amelia looked about the crypt and its numerous shelves and alcoves, all empty save for her husband's stone coffin and the statue of the Christ at one end. The savior was carved in marble, with his arms wide to welcome the souls into paradise.

One day, this place will be filled with my descendants, Amelia thought. *But not of the house of Marne.*

Her husband had been invested a duke and died without an heir. The duchy would be hers until she was ordered to marry again—something the prince would almost certainly soon command, or even the king directly if the prince did not. The Western Reach was a martial province, standing to protect the Grand Kingdom's western border. A woman was not likely to be trusted to hold such a strategic position. It belonged in the hands of a commander of men. She did not like the thought, but she knew no one in the Grand Kingdom would think otherwise.

"Regardless of the traditions that are or are not in place," Amelia instructed, "you will have masons brought and begin the work. It is fitting."

Sir Duggan bowed and stepped back. Amelia prayed alone a little while longer and then led her castellan out of the vault and back up to the great hall.

The great hall occupied almost the entire ground floor's length of the main keep of the castle, excluding the vestibule and a number of rooms on the western side, which overlooked the lake. The vaulted ceiling rose thirty feet into the air, with high windows allowing the afternoon sun to fall in shafts. Amelia stopped as she stepped into the hall, struck by how much the light in the hall resembled the light in the village church where they had sheltered. For a moment, her mind was assaulted by the cries of the tortured dead, and she felt she could even smell the vile stench of blood and earth and piss and filth mixed together.

"Are you well, Your Grace?" Sir Duggan asked.

"I am well, sir," she replied. "I was just reflecting on how good it is to be home."

Sir Duggan nodded.

"I will receive at the high table," she told him and began to walk the length of the hall.

The feast tables were all pushed to the walls, even up against the enormous main hearth, which would not be used again until winter. The fireplace was so vast that Amelia could stand upright in it if she wished.

At the far end she ascended the dais and moved around behind the carved high table, long enough to seat twenty knights and ladies along one side. The spine of the table was fitted with a long pane of glass, recessed into the wood. Under that glass was the banner of the Vec king Kolber, whom Duke Marne had defeated during the crusade that won him his title. Along with the dukedom, the castle, and the duty to the province, the king had awarded Duke Marne the enemy's banner. Six yards long and made of silk and linen, the banner had required two heralds to carry it on the battlefield. The duke had it placed into the table and had eaten his meals off it. The hall contained no separate throne; the duke had always taken audiences from behind his table, a reminder to all of his service to the kingdom and his prowess in battle.

As she made her way around the table, Amelia decided that she would continue her husband's practice and make it a tradition for her family. Audiences would be received at the table of the duke Marne's triumph. She sat down in the head chair in the table's center.

"Your Grace," said Sir Duggan, his voice sounding shocked. "That is the duke's chair."

"I know that."

Sir Duggan nodded and then took his own customary seat. He made himself comfortable as they awaited Sir Liam.

"What have you to tell me?" the duchess asked.

"You do not wish me to wait for Sir Liam?"

"I am sure he will attend presently. If he misses any important information, I will see that he is caught up."

A small scowl flashed over Sir Duggan's face, and then he began. "Just before he died, Duke Marne was receiving strange reports—of disturbances, of attacks on farms across the province, especially along the river. The very week of his passing, he sent a bird to the prince's court in Rhales requesting aid, more knights, and as many conscripts as the prince would transport. He offered a bounty of silver for the service."

"Of course he did," Amelia said, an edge of bitterness to her voice. She had only just bought the province back from the moneylenders, and her dead husband had sold it out from under them once again. She loved him, but he was a fool with a purse.

"Well, when he died, I sent word to the prince as well, Your Grace," Sir Duggan said.

"Why?"

"It was proper, for the defense of the Reach." There was something in the tone of Sir Duggan's answer that did not feel right to Amelia, but she couldn't tell for certain what it was.

"Very well," she said. "What was the prince's response?"

"He was... uh... sympathetic."

"Sympathetic?"

"Yes."

"Sir Duggan, I feel that there is something you want to tell me but are struggling to find the right way," Amelia said.

Sir Duggan seemed almost to be shifting in his seat. He was thrice her age, yet he was making her feel like an elderly wet nurse with a disobedient infant. It was most unbecoming of a knight of any rank, let alone a man of his maturity.

"Couch your lance, sir, and make the charge!"

"Yes, Your Grace." Sir Duggan eyes narrowed, and he swallowed. "He is coming here, Your Grace."

"Coming here? Who?" Amelia's thoughts caught up a moment later. "The prince? Prince Mercad is coming here to Dweltford?"

Amelia's annoyance bloomed to full anger. She stood up from her chair. "This should have been told to me as soon as I arrived," she said, her voice rising. "I should not have had to drag this information from you like a confession from a guilty child!"

She cast about as the full weight of the situation dawned upon her. A royal visit. That meant feasts and quarters for the myriad householders the prince would bring with him. Entertainments would have to be hired. Then there was the impact on the town.

"Is the prince sending the troops my husband asked for?"

"All those and more, Your Grace."

"Damned fool! How could you not tell me this immediately? The preparations that will have to be made —"

"Everything is already prepared," Sir Duggan said in a cold, reproachful voice. The menace of it sent a shiver through Amelia.

Before she could gather herself enough to ask what he meant, Sir Liam entered the hall, walking quickly. He had bathed since they returned. All the dirt of the trail was washed away, and he wore a fresh surcoat of blue and red checked squares, black linen trews, and soft boots. His hair was still wet from washing. In spite of herself, Amelia was struck by how handsome he was.

"Your Grace, news!" Sir Liam announced. He rushed to the dais and quickly knelt before Amelia, then rose.

"What news, sir?" she asked.

"A rider has just arrived at the castle, Your Grace. A herald."

"From Prince Mercad?"

"You have already heard?"

"No, Sir Liam, but I have just been informed that the prince is coming to visit us here very soon. At the head of an army, no less, raised to aid us in our troubles."

"Indeed?" Sir Liam looked excited. It made him seem boyish, in a charming fashion. Amelia was struck by how easily he cast off the miseries of the preceding days, like taking off a dirty cloak. It spoke to his resilience and strength, she supposed.

"The rider bore this message."

Sir Liam stepped forward and handed her a scroll on fine paper, not the rough parchment of common correspondence. The kingdom's highest communication was always with paper, which would not crack or fade so badly as it aged. As she broke the seal and unrolled the missive on the table, Amelia marveled at the smoothness of it and the beauty of the writing.

"The prince's hand," she said. The fine script flowed across the page, and at the top was the imprint of the prince's seal—the lesser royal eagle, wreathed in laurel leaves.

"It will have been written by a scribe," said Sir Duggan, somewhat churlishly.

Amelia ignored him and read the message. A gasp escaped her lips.

"Something troubles you, Your Grace?" Sir Liam asked.

"Fallenhill is attacked," she said as she continued to read.

"Attacked?"

"Prince Mercad has received word of an army besieging the town, for two weeks now."

"An army? But how?"

Fallenhill was the northernmost settlement of the Western Reach, the former seat of one of the Broken Barons. A fortress town nestled into the mountains, it guarded a series of rich mines and provided much of the province's wealth. Its location made it an odd choice for an army to attack. It was too far north for any of the rival princes from the Vec to invade, without first passing Dweltford, and it was on the west side of the mountains, putting it out of reach of the wild people of the northern jungles.

"Do you know of this, Sir Duggan?" Amelia asked.

"No, Your Grace."

"How could you not? Why would Baron Stopher inform the prince and not send to Dweltford for aid?"

"Perhaps his messages were intercepted," Sir Duggan replied tersely. "A pigeon might pass over an enemy, where a rider would be trapped."

"It is common enough in the confusion of war, Your Grace," Sir Liam agreed.

"It seems my husband's death is not the only advantage this enemy has enjoyed. Well, their advantages will soon be outweighed. Prince Mercad has summoned us to meet him upon the road to Fallenhill. He commands the contingent of our full strength, every knight and man-at-arms not indispensable to the peace of Dweltford."

Amelia sat down heavily. She had thought to return home to mourn her early widowhood. Then when her barge was attacked, she had just wanted to come home. Now the weight of a royal visit and, worse yet, confirmation of a foreign invader had fallen upon her. How could she be expected to deal with these events? How could she even have anticipated all this?

The duchess stood, firm resolve on her face. "Sir Liam, as of this moment you are brevetted Knight Captain of the Western Reach. There is no time for full honors now, but upon completion of this campaign, your rank shall be confirmed. Go now and raise every sworn knight of the Reach—by rider, by bird, or by knocking on their doors yourself if you must!"

"By your command, Your Grace." Sir Liam saluted her like a commander in the field.

"Sir Duggan?"

The castellan took a moment to respond to her voice. "Yes, Your Grace?"

"See to the provisioning of the column. Everything Sir Liam's knights need will be provided from this household. Also, gather every convicted man and send to the town council. Announce that the province is at war, and a free militia is to be recruited."

"Such a thing would take weeks!"

"You have two days."

"Two days? That's ridic—"

"This letter from the prince is four days old, sir," Amelia interrupted. "It was written while the prince was still in the Halling Pass. We have no more than two days to ride, or we will be late to his meeting on the road. Mark me, I will not be late!"

Amelia walked from the table toward one of the hall's lesser exits.

"All this will need many orders, Your Grace," Sir Duggan called after her. "Where shall we find you?"

"You shan't," she said. "I will find you before you have the need. Now go to, gentlemen, in the service of the Prince of Rhales and our Grand Kingdom."

Amelia exited and went to look for Prentice.

CHAPTER 13

Prentice, Turley, and Bellam found themselves in a vast stone barn. The structure had a shingle roof and dirt floor, which was dug deep into a slope so that the door they entered by had stairs down to the floor below. At the other end was a larger door that looked chained closed. Despite the heat outside, the inside was reasonably cool because of the height of the roof.

Bellam shambled unevenly down the stairs and then sank against one wall, sitting on the cool earth. His gaze settled on a solid iron ring embedded in the stone of the wall next to him. He looked around at dozens of similar rings around the walls of the building. "What is this place?"

"Don't you remember?" Turley responded with a laugh as he sat next to Bellam. Prentice sat on the other side.

"Remember what?"

"This is where they transport you to, silly twit. Every convict in the Reach comes through here. Every spring they get us here, straight after the passes thaw, then send us out wherever the duchy needs us. What, were you unconscious when they dragged you over the mountains too?"

"I didn't come over the mountains, you dumb ass! I lived on the Murr. They sent us up the Dwelt on a boat. I got as

far as that village when the headman came on board with a
letter and had us all turned out to build that useless fence."

"Well," said Turley, somewhat chastened, "you just watch
your manners with your elders, young man. And you're
right, that fence turned out to be bloody useless."

They both chuckled, but Prentice couldn't join them.
His thoughts were too grim. He hated the confrontation
with Sir Liam, and he doubly hated having to bite his
tongue.

"Your heart troubled there?" Turley asked him.

"I'm just thinking."

"Oh, well, that was your first mistake," Turley quipped
and Bellam laughed. "Oh, by God, I need a pot of stout."

"Just one?" asked Bellam.

"Until the second one arrives."

Prentice smiled. He knew the two men were trying to
cheer him and while he felt he didn't have the heart for it,
he was glad for their efforts. He closed his eyes and leaned
his head back against the wall.

Get your rest whenever and wherever you can, Prentice
thought. That was a reality all convicts quickly learned.
There was no point waiting for the mercy of overseers.

For a time, there was only the pleasant coolness of the
shadows and the sound of their breathing. Prentice let his
mind drift, careful to keep himself from remembering.
"The past was a country best never returned to" - it was a
saying he lived by. Instead, he listened and was mindful of
little pleasures, like the buzzing of insects, the smell of the
earth.

An unexpected sound caught at the edge of his hearing,
and he cocked his head. Outside, there were running
footsteps, followed by a banging at the barn door. Prentice
launched himself to his feet, pushing off from the wall and
looking back up the stairs to the doorway. He waved to the
puzzled Turley and Bellam to get to their feet.

The door burst open, and three young men rushed in. Each one wore sacks for shirts with holes cut for their arms, as if they were too poor to own a proper shirt, and they had mud smeared on their faces and arms. Prentice snorted in derision. They were trying to disguise themselves as peasants, but they looked exactly like what they were: rich boys playing at poor. They rushed down the stairs, and each one wielded a brass-bound cudgel, the kind of weapon an armored knight would use for training—unable to do much damage against steel plate or even mail, but able to break bone and crush unprotected flesh.

Turley pushed himself up.

"Get Bellam out of here!" Prentice hissed.

"What?"

"If one of them hits his leg, no healing short of a miracle of God will save it. Get him to safety."

"How?" Turley asked, but he held his hand out to Bellam, who used it to get up as quickly as he could.

"One of the windows down by the big doors."

Bellam and Turley looked down to the other end of the barn. The windows down there were cut closer to the floor. It might have been possible for Bellam to climb up there with help, assuming the windows' wooden shutters were not locked like the barn doors, which Prentice knew was unlikely.

The three intruders fanned out as they reached the bottom of the stairs, hefting their cudgels. They were each wearing breeches and riding boots of fine leather, which made Prentice think they were probably squires or grooms. He put himself between the three attackers and his two companions. He heard Turley grunt as he lifted Bellam's weight, and he hoped they were moving away like he'd told them. He kept his eyes on the newcomers.

"Sir Liam sends his compliments," the one in the middle said with a sneer.

"I'm sure he does," said Prentice, and he sneered as well, just to show his contempt.

"We're to make sure none of you ever walks proper again," said another.

The three of them stood confidently, limbs held loosely. They had come armed and undoubtedly expected to find lowborn convicts easily cowed by the prospect of a beating.

"Let's make this quick," said the first.

Prentice nodded, his sneer growing into a savage smile. "Yes. Let's."

He surged forward. The short rest and the prospect of fighting gave him a rush of blood. The three squires blinked in near disbelief as he charged straight at the center man of the three, moving with predatory speed. The two on either side froze and watched as Prentice intercepted their companion, one hand on the wrist of his weapon arm, the other seizing him by the throat and pushing him backward. Prentice didn't stop, but kept rushing forward, pushing his opponent off balance. The man stumbled and tried to get his feet under him, but Prentice kept pushing him while half lifting him, so that in a moment the man slammed backward into the stone wall, his head cracking loudly. Even as he staggered, Prentice slipped his hand from the young man's throat and slammed an elbow across his jaw. He fell as if poleaxed, and Prentice took the cudgel from his insensible grasp.

Prentice turned to the other two and brought the cudgel up in guard. "Well, gentlemen, was there anything else from Sir Liam?"

The man behind him groaned.

"You bastard!" said one of the other squires. "You just struck a freeman of rank, convict! You'll hang when we report this."

"Don't be a fool, boy," Prentice retorted. "You're never going to report anything. You're going to die right here, and we're going to throw your bodies in the river. No one will know who did it because you've kept this a secret like Sir Liam told you to, haven't you?"

The two men shared a worried glance. Prentice kept his gaze level and did his best to not give anything away in his expression. He needed to keep them off balance if he was to have any real chance. Surprise and their overconfidence had allowed him to take the first one quickly, but if these two ever got their nerve back, they would likely turn the tables. They were well enough trained, as well as rested and well fed.

Over their shoulders, he saw Turley holding Bellam by a wall, watching the confrontation. They weren't moving.

"Shouldn't we be trying to escape?" Prentice heard Bellam ask Turley as they watched the fight.

"Don't be daft," Turley replied quietly. "We'll never get out. Either he wins or we get a beating—that's all the options we have. Besides, if I know our man Prentice, this is something you're not going to want to miss seeing, lad."

The two squires shared a nod, and one of them struck high while the other came a fraction later, aiming for his legs.

Good tactic, Prentice thought. He used the cudgel to check the high strike, flicking it aside and twisting into a riposte thrust that did not quite land. He lifted his foot away from the low strike, cocking his leg and kicking back out, catching the attacker in the stomach. With an *oof* sound, the young man bent double and stumbled backward, getting back out of reach. Prentice let him retreat, concentrating on the other man. He drove forward with a quick series of strikes and thrusts, but none of them landed to any great effect.

The squire was clearly remembering his training and held his stance and guard well.

He'll make a strong knight one day, Prentice thought. The young man's strong defense didn't worry him too much. Prentice's intent had not been to land any good hits, only to put his opponent on the defensive and drive him back so that he was at a longer distance from his companion.

Prentice ended another series of passes and strikes, and before the squire could put himself onto the attack, he turned on his heel and rushed at the other man. This one had not fully recovered from the kick to his midsection, and it seemed the blow must have caught him in the groin as well. His guard was weak and badly held, and Prentice readied himself for a quick finishing strike.

"Prentice, what is going on?" Duchess Amelia's voice rang out through the barn.

Prentice turned to the doorway. The duchess stood there, still in her dirty traveling clothes. Reflexively, he went to one knee and laid his cudgel on the ground. He felt so vulnerable to the man he had just been about to strike down that he could feel his skin twitch on that side of his head. The man did not strike him, however, for he had gone down on his knee as well.

The other opponent came near his compatriot. "What are you doing?"

"It's her, you fool. The duchess!" said the squire on his knees.

"No, it isn't!"

"Yes, it bloody is! I saw her come in this morning with Sir Liam."

The standing young man blinked for a moment and then he, too, sank to his knees. Duchess Amelia made her way down the stairs as the three men kept their eyes down.

She walked until she stood in front of Prentice. "I asked you a question, Prentice."

"Yes, Your Grace," he replied, eyes still down. "These three young men had heard I was skilled in singlestick fighting, and they asked me to demonstrate for them." Out of the corner of his eye, he saw the two squires look at him. They then quickly turned their faces down once more.

"Two of them at once?" she asked.

"It is a sophisticated technique, Your Grace." Prentice risked a cheeky glance at Amelia. Her face betrayed no amusement.

"And what of this poor fellow?" The duchess looked at the squire stunned on the floor.

"He hit his head, Your Grace."

"You hit him," one of the squires muttered, but he did not look up.

"Is that true, Prentice?"

"Of course, Your Grace," Prentice said easily. "We were practicing. I did strike him, and he did hit his head on the wall. We all thought it best to let him rest after that."

Amelia turned her head, and Prentice glanced up. She let her eyes wander over the whole space, and she stopped when she saw Turley and Bellam some distance off, both on their knees with their heads bowed.

"So, this is merely weapons practice?"

"Yes, Your Grace."

"But I gave orders that you and your companions were to rest."

"The fault is entirely mine, Your Grace. I was overly enthusiastic."

Duchess Amelia smiled. "Very well," she said quietly. "I forgive you. And it is good to know that this is simply practice, if a little rough. I would hate to think that Sir Liam was remiss in his duty to see you safely bestowed. It would be a serious lapse for a knight that could mar his honor, not to mention the honor of men in his service."

The two kneeling squires shifted.

Prentice shook his head. "Sir Liam saw us here directly, Your Grace, neither remiss in diligence nor success."

"Excellent." Amelia paused for a moment. "I think you should take your friend to be attended to," she instructed the squires, and the two men eagerly stood and carried their unconscious comrade up the stairs. "I will see your practice sticks are sent to your quarters."

The men left, and Amelia stood over Prentice. He didn't move.

"Oh, for God's sake, stand up!" she said in exasperation. "I've had enough of plays and charades for one day."

CHAPTER 14

"Have you heard the news?" the duchess asked.

She led Prentice out of the barn, and he now stood behind her as she looked southwest, down the castle's island to its lakeshore. The rear of the castle was an open, grassed space, neatly trimmed and maintained like a park. The preceding summer, just after their wedding, the duke had held picnics here for his new wife. Knights had competed in games and told tales, and once, a company of players and minstrels had set up their stage and given performances throughout the afternoon and into the evening. The duchess smiled as she led him into the sunlight. It was the broadest smile he had ever seen on her face.

"News, Your Grace?"

"The Western Reach has been invaded."

Prentice said nothing, and Amelia turned to look at him. "How did you know?" she asked.

"I didn't, Your Grace," he replied. "I hadn't heard."

"But you did know," she insisted. "Those men who attacked the village. You said they were soldiers of an invading army."

"I said they might be. It was the assumption that made the most sense."

"How? How did it make sense? Sir Liam dismissed them as bandits, and I saw only monstrous figures of nightmares. How did you see it?"

"It was in the way they moved with each other, Your Grace," Prentice said solemnly. "Long practice and experience in war breed a kind of familiarity between men. They move in a particular way. Like the way a true warhorse knows its rider, and the two function as one on the battlefield. It is why knights never ride each other's mounts into battle. The bond between knight and destrier is particular. It is the same sometimes with men."

Amelia was silent for a space. "And bandits would never develop this bond, you say?"

"Some might, Your Grace, to a degree. But that would be between individuals. Two men, or perhaps three, who know they can trust each other because of their past together. For a company of men to have it, that takes discipline or something similar—loyalty, pride, something in that vein. I've not known many bandits, but none of them had those traits to any great degree. Soldiers can develop it."

"I've always heard that soldiers were little more than bandits on a tight leash. After all, why else does the Grand Kingdom use convicts for the main of their armies?"

Amelia led Prentice along the bank of the lake and found a pleasant spot under a willow. She sat down. Prentice thought that, from a distance, they might well look like two peasants skiving off from their work and courting in the sunlight.

Especially under all this dirt, he thought.

He went to the lakeside and scooped up some of the water, using it to scrub his face. The dirt came away like mud on his fingers, and he could feel it running down into his beard.

"You were not born a convict," Amelia said.

"No one is, Your Grace."

She sighed. "How do you know so much about war?"

"I have fought wars."

"So had my knights," she said sharply. "I was defended by a dozen knights by the river, and more than half of them died. Sir Dav and Sir Liam said it was surprise, that it was the cowardly tactic of ambush that caught them unready. When they found your convict gang, they were so sure that they could turn and crush our attackers. Yet Sir Dav is dead, and Sir Liam commanded a rout. Not one of them saw what you saw or survived the combat as you did, carrying a comrade from the field."

"Do not make too much of that act, Your Grace," Prentice said, and he turned to look back out over the water. Far across the lake, sheep and cattle fed in fields.

"You shy from praise, but you know what I say is true. How do you see what others do not?"

Prentice shrugged and turned to face her. "I can give you answers to your questions, Your Grace, but you may not be pleased by them."

"I am a young woman with no heir and a limited hold on a province that is under assault from a foreign invader that no one can even name. There is little about today that pleases me. Answer me and let me look to my pleasure."

"Very well, Your Grace. Sir Dav was an arrogant fool, and Sir Liam follows in his footsteps."

The duchess drew in a sharp breath. Prentice wasn't surprised his bluntness shocked her. He made a point of being almost uniformly polite, especially with nobles, if they deigned to speak with him, careful in points of speech and respectful of the social order. No matter how she professed to want his opinion, the truth of his thoughts would not please her, that much was obvious.

"These are knights in my service, and Sir Dav was loyal to the death! You speak very bold to call them fools!" She let out a long sigh. "I suppose you did warn me."

"Your pardon, Your Grace, but do not mistake me," Prentice answered. "Sir Dav and Sir Liam are—or were— brave knights and skilled warriors. That is not the point."

"No? Then what is?"

"They are knights. They fight in a fashion that has not greatly changed in hundreds of years. A knight in armor, on horseback, is an engine of destruction on a battlefield, no mistake. But warfare has been changing, and the Grand Kingdom's knights are being left behind. In the Vec, the armies have been learning. The Vec princes have been perfecting their techniques of war for a generation. They hire scholars to study new tactics and new weapons for them."

"You mean the exploding weapons called bombards?" Amelia said. "Cannons? Like the king's Red Dragons?"

"No, not completely. Cannon are powerful and useful, and the Red Dragons are..." Prentice paused, trying to think of the best way to convey his thoughts. "In the simplest terms, Your Grace, in fifty years no Kingdom army has defeated a Vec army in the field."

Amelia snorted derisively and rolled her eyes. "Do you think me a fool, Prentice?"

"I speak the truth."

"That cannot possibly be. You yourself, by your own admission, were a member of the last crusade, against Kolber's invasion. A successful crusade, fairly obviously!" She waved her hand at the castle and the town, as by their presence they proved her point.

"The crusade was a success, but only because Kolber's son tried to take his throne in his absence. Kolber withdrew from the Reach, and we hounded him the whole way south, but in his entire invasion, he never lost a single battle. It is possible to win every battle and lose a war, Your Grace."

Amelia looked at Prentice for a moment and then turned her eyes across the waters of the lake. After a while she shook her head. "This makes no sense to me."

"I doubt there are a hundred men or women in the Grand Kingdom who would accept it," Prentice agreed. "But in the Vec there are manuals and treatises published on all aspects of war and battle, from dueling to skirmish to the battle of armies. Some of it is mere speculation, but much of it is tested—in the campaigns the Vec princes wage against each other, against Masnia, and even, it is said, against the jungle peoples of the north and across the sea."

"Have you read some of these works?"

"Many, Your Grace."

"You were an educated man, before you were a convict?"

Prentice refused to answer, turning his eyes down to his feet and then looking away. Amelia nodded and then offered her hand to him. He took it and helped her to her feet.

"Could a woman read these manuals?" she asked.

Prentice nodded in surprise. "Of course, Your Grace. I mean, I can see no reason why not."

"Excellent. Then when we return, I will have ink and quill sent to you, and you will list some for me. I will have them obtained."

"Some may be hard to find, Your Grace, or command high prices."

"Nevertheless. War has come to my province, and I do not know enough of it. I must prepare in every way I can before my lack becomes a threat to us all."

The duchess turned and began to walk back toward the castle. She watched her steps, looking down at her feet, then gave a loud tut. She pointed her toes on one foot, and the seam of the slipper was split, allowing her stockings to poke through. The soft, cream-colored leather was filthy and marked with dark streaks of ash and mud.

"I loved these shoes," Amelia said, then she looked back down at herself, at the clothes she hadn't yet had a chance to change. "And this dress. It's ruined. It will have to be..." She ran her fingers over one particular stain and fell quiet. It was a spray of little dots that ran around the left side of her skirt. They were a rust-brown color now, but Prentice knew they had been bright red when they fell. He knew that in her mind the duchess was seeing again the spray of blood, the falling crimson, possibly even from her lady-in-waiting as she was slain by the riverside.

Amelia started to weep. "I can't do this," she cried, and she looked straight at him. "I can't do this! I'm just a girl, a merchant's daughter." She dropped to her knees in the grass.

Her tears fell freely, and Prentice was surprised at how much they touched him. He had thought he had nothing but contempt for the nobility, but this girl, reaching to do the best she could in a role for which she was never prepared, she touched a place in Prentice he did not know he had. He suddenly remembered long hours studying, training; working to carry the hopes of his family—the family that now disowned him.

"I've made a terrible mess," Amelia said. "I didn't know what to do when those men attacked, and my knights died saving me. They were loyal and brave, and Sir Liam..." She stopped once again and looked up at Prentice. "Sir Liam sent those men to beat you to death! They were going to kill you, and I said nothing. He defied me, defied my express orders, and I was going to let him." She hung her head again, using her sleeve to wipe her tears.

She was ashamed, and Prentice felt an ache in himself for her. She looked so much like a little girl, not much older than Bellam. He wanted to disdain her tears and keep his distance, but he could not do it. He crouched beside her.

"Like as not, they wouldn't have killed us, Your Grace," he said. "We probably wouldn't have walked right again, and Bellam was sure to be fully crippled, but murder wasn't on their minds."

"You talk about such violence so casually."

"I am a convict, Your Grace. My life is violence."

Amelia nodded, and Prentice was impressed to see firm resolve return to her face. He could tell that she was a strong woman, and she knew what was needed from her as duchess.

"Regardless of their intent," she said, wiping the tears away and standing once more, "Sir Liam defied me, and I must act. I will strip him of rank and have him banished from the Reach. I will have the three of you freed as I originally planned, and his goods will be given to you as restitution. His horse will fetch some money, I don't doubt."

The duchess had begun walking to the castle again as she spoke, but Prentice stayed where he was.

"You must not do this, Your Grace," he said after her.

She turned. "What?"

"You cannot free us, and you cannot dismiss Sir Liam."

"Do not forget yourself, Prentice! You are still a convict yet, and I am the duchess."

"Yes, Your Grace, and the reasons why you could not dismiss Sir Liam before have not changed—an army is invading, and your position seems weak. If you dismiss him now, especially over the issue of mere treatment of a couple of convicts, it will lead to dissension and potentially even to revolt."

"He defied me! This is not about mistreatment, it is about rebellion!"

"Forgive me, Your Grace, but your knights will not see it that way."

Amelia shook her head. "Are you counseling me to keep you in chains? Do you not want your freedom?"

"Freedom is just a word, Your Grace," Prentice said reflexively, as he had told himself most days since he was convicted and transported. Then he sighed. That wasn't the whole truth. "Yes, I want my freedom. But you are the Duchess of the Western Reach. The province and the kingdom need you to judge what is right for more than just me and my friends."

"You are a strangely complex man, Prentice."

"I will not argue with Your Grace on that point."

The duchess smiled and then led the way back into the castle walls by the postern gate.

CHAPTER 15

For a day, Prentice, Turley, and Bellam sat in the barn, coming out only to fetch water and food. No one troubled them, and they enjoyed the rest. True to her word, the duchess sent a steward with ink and paper about an hour after her conversation with Prentice. The man turned up his nose at Prentice's filthy condition and had almost left, unable to believe that the duchess would have sent him to such a man.

At first Prentice had found the man's discomfort amusing, but his hesitation soon grated. "Just give me the damn parchment," he said.

Half an hour later, the steward left with the list on the dirtied sheet.

"He's just a servant, isn't he?" Turley remarked. "I don't see how he's got cause to turn his nose up at us."

"There are hierarchies inside hierarchies. Inside everything," Prentice said. Then they went back to resting. With no call upon them, the three men mostly slept, though Bellam spent a little time moving about during the day at Prentice's urging. By midday on the next day, he was limping about on his sore leg without aid or having to lean much against the wall.

"Won't be long and I'll be fine, I reckon," he said.

Prentice shook his head. "You'll still be limping when summer's long gone, lad. You'll be able to walk, but the final healing will be quite a while."

"How do you know about healing?" Bellam asked. "Was you a churchman? Or some sort of scholar, like a chirurgeon?"

"That's a fancy word for a little lad like you," Turley mocked.

Bellam's eyes narrowed. "I know some learning! My family's yeoman stock. I'm not just some peasant."

"No, lad, you're a convict now, which means you must be all kinds of stupid. Dumb enough to commit a crime and even dumber to get caught!"

"Well, I'm still young! What's your excuse?"

Prentice chuckled, and Turley looked at him. Prentice shook his head at the big man. "He's got you there."

From outside there came the sound of servants running and fetching. Turley stood and hoisted himself up to a window, looking out into the lesser bailey. "Well, that's odd."

"What do you see?" Prentice asked.

"A bath."

"A what?"

"A whole bunch of servants have carried out a bath, and now they're running to fill it."

Prentice went along to another window and pulled up to look for himself. "I wonder what they're doing."

"We should go and look," Bellam suggested.

They were not strictly confined to the barn. The door was not locked—staying put was just safer. A convict anywhere without an overseer or clear task was too easily accused of theft or attempting to escape. To stand just outside the barn would likely be all right, though. The three slowly eased out the door and stood by the wall, watching the servants rush back and forth.

There was a small commotion in the entry to the keep, and several of the rushing servants stood aside and bowed as Duchess Amelia emerged. She led a trail of three new servants, one older woman and two male stewards. The stewards carried large wooden trays piled high with cloths, small jugs, and pots. Amelia herself was clean now, her honey-colored hair washed and pinned high on her head. Her cheeks were lightly rouged and her lips glossed bright red. She wore a chemise of undyed linen and over it a surcoat, ducal blue with a bleached white lion sewn rampant upon it.

Prentice thought the surcoat might have been one of her husband's, though it had been taken up and cinched about her waist with a belt. The lion did not sit quite right, too low upon her chest.

As she passed each servant, they paused and bowed, and she nodded to them in turn. It took Prentice a moment to realize that she was headed straight toward them. When she arrived, the three convicts each went to a knee and waited.

Duchess Amelia looked at the three men with a smile and then turned to the matron behind her. "These are them, good Bettina."

The matron turned up her nose. "They are worse than I expected, filthier than the worst pigs. Do they sleep in the midden heap?"

"Do not be rude, Bettina."

"They are convicts," said Bettina, as if it were impossible to be rude to them.

"Yes, and they labored to preserve my life with the knights who saved us."

"They clung to your skirts to save their own miserable lives, more like."

"You were not there!" The duchess's face grew hard. She had had enough talk from her chamber matron, it seemed. "They served me well, and I will have them rewarded. They will be given the chance to bathe and replace their clothes.

The grooms will cut their hair and their beards, and you will see that it is rightly done."

"I don't see why we can't just throw them in the lake for a spell."

"Enough, Bettina. You will see them groomed and their clothes replaced. It is little enough reward for their role in my escape, and it will see them better fitted for the service I will require of them."

The duchess turned and left them. The three convicts stayed on their knees. Once the duchess had left the bailey, Bettina took charge. "Right, you lot, on your feet and out of those rags. You heard Her Grace!"

They stood and began to undress in front of the gray-haired woman. Both the stewards stood behind her, like an honor guard at attention, with sour looks on their faces. Clearly, they felt as disgusted dealing with convicts as Bettina did. She turned to one of the waiting stewards and grabbed a lump of launderer's soap from his tray.

"This is soap," she said to the convicts. "You know how to use it, I trust?"

"I think I saw it done once," Prentice said archly.

"I can imagine," she said and threw it onto the ground at his feet. It landed on his discarded tunic, looking pale against the filth and bloodstains. "I will stand away over there, since I do not wish to see you more naked than this. When you are cleaned, you will dry yourselves and put on these fresh clothes. I will inspect you, and if I am satisfied, these men will cut your hair and beards. You will be polite and submissive throughout, or I will have you flogged. Do you understand?"

They tugged their forelocks, and Bettina left them to cross to the other side of the bailey. She stood facing away from the three of them, preserving her honor. Now that she was gone and the servants had withdrawn from the bailey yard, the three stripped off their loincloths and quickly made their way to the large wooden tub. Prentice handed the block of soap to Turley and then took a second block from one of the stewards' trays.

"Thank you, good man," he said. The steward sneered and stepped away from him.

The tub was not large enough for three, but they each ducked themselves and then hopped out to use the soap. The water was cold and the harsh launderer's soap stung their skin, but the feeling of becoming clean was intoxicating. Soon they were smiling and scrubbed pink. Beneath the suds, the water in the tub had turned the color of mud.

They took cloths from the trays and wiped off the water, then stepped into their fresh new clothes: small cloths, loose trews, and cotton tunics. Bellam struggled with his sore knee to get the trousers on, but otherwise the process was quick and pleasant. Prentice almost sighed as he sat on the edge of the tub in the sunshine.

"We await your inspection, your ladyship," he called.

One of the stewards hissed and glared at him. Bettina came over to the tub. She looked at the stewards angrily, and one of them nodded at Prentice. Her eyes narrowed, and she leaned into him so that her angry features were only inches from his face.

"Did you just address me directly?" she asked.

"Politely and submissively, as instructed," he said, smiling as he tugged his forelock. He knew he was being provocative, but he had been in two fights with armed men in the last few days, not to mention being sneered at by armed knights. He wasn't about to kowtow to a lady's maid. Bettina stared at him a moment more, as if hoping her displeasure would diminish his smile, but when it did not, she began to look him up and down, inspecting him. Then she moved on to Turley and Bellam.

When she decided she was satisfied, she nodded to the stewards, who came over and pushed them down on their knees. Using straight razors, the two men began by hacking away long chunks of their matted hair. It fell to the ground and Bettina made a choking noise, as though the sight of it made her sick.

"Rats' nests. It is a wonder you aren't infested with the vermin."

"Rats? No rats in my hair," said Turley, turning to look at Bellam. "Though that'd explain why *your* hair smells like it does!" The steward gripped Turley's head and roughly turned it so he could keep cutting.

"No rats in your hair. Maggots ate them all," Bellam quipped back.

"Silence, you worthless villains!" Bettina commanded. "How dare you behave like this? What is my lady thinking, bringing you into service?"

Turley's eyes widened. "I'm sorry, mistress? Taken into service? Can she do that for convicts?"

"Not so that you'd be free!" Bettina said, her eyes narrowing at him. "But she has pity on you and seems to think you will be learning yourselves a place in her household so that, in time, you might be pardoned and elevated. Perhaps in a decade or two. You might even be given permission to marry."

"I've already been married," Turley said. "Not taken with it."

"Enough," she shouted. "One more word and I'll have you at the post for twenty lashes, hear me? One more word!"

The three men chuckled some more, but they did not speak. Soon enough they were cut, cleaned, and shaved. They stood, brushing fallen hairs from their new clothes.

"Her Grace has generously afforded you each a pair of shoes," Bettina said grandly. "You will be sent to the cobbler later in the day to be fitted. For now, you are passable enough and will follow me." She headed to the keep, head high and back straight.

"Thank you," Prentice said to the two stewards, smiling but not entirely mocking.

"Something for your trouble, my good man," Turley said like a patrician, a man of means. He slapped at his trousers as if looking for something. "Tush! I seem to have left me purse in me other britches."

The steward gave him a withering glare. "Get gone, dog!"

Turley tugged his forelock and moved to catch up with Bellam, who was limping as quickly as he could behind Prentice and the lady's matron.

CHAPTER 16

Prentice, Turley, and Bellam followed the lady Bettina into a salon flooded with afternoon light. The windows were open, and the smell of flowers from planter boxes perfumed the room. Duchess Amelia sat upon a chaise, which had a large table pulled up to it. Across the table were spread a wide variety of parchments and scrolls, as well as a large map of the Western Reach. A small stack of books sat on one corner.

Bettina curtsied, and the three men went to their knees.

The duchess looked up and smiled. "You've done well, Bettina. They look quite presentable."

"I just hope it isn't a wasted effort, Your Grace."

"I'm sure we all do." She addressed the men on their knees. "I will be taking you into my household service. You may thank me."

"Thank you, Your Grace," Prentice said, though he was puzzled by the duchess's decision. The other two looked at him, and when he nodded, they added their own mumbled thanks.

"Bellam, I will send you to Cook. You will serve in the kitchens."

"Yes'm," Bellam replied.

Bettina's hand whipped out and clipped him across the back of the head. "You speak only with permission," she commanded.

Bellam bowed his head. Although he'd seen the duchess filthy on the road, he seemed to find the formal surrounding of the solar intimidating. "Yes'm. Sorry."

"And Turley," the duchess continued. Turley nodded his head. "You will go to my chief steward. You strike me as a strong fellow who doesn't mind a bit of fetch and carry." Turley nodded again and smiled. "You will each be given household quarters and be permitted to keep a purse so that you may save for your freedom. When the campaign against these invaders we face is completed, there will be amnesties for convicts. Should you conduct yourselves appropriately in the meantime, you will receive amnesty then and be given status as servants of the ducal house. This is my thanks to you for your assistance in our recent difficulties."

Bellam and Turley nodded again.

"Bettina, see these two to their respective places."

"As you say, Your Grace."

Bettina curtsied and ushered them from the room, sparing a suspicious glance for Prentice, who remained on one knee. When the three were gone, Amelia sat quietly for a moment, looking over the table and its various documents.

"Rise, Prentice," she said after a moment.

He smiled. She understood the power of her rank and the timing of command. For a girl not born to power, she had a better instinct for it than she realized.

"Come here and tell me what you see," she said.

Prentice stood beside the table. The map was obvious, with key features marked: Dweltford in the middle, and the river Dwelt twisting a course from near the top right corner toward the south, south, west exit the map at the bottom. The town of Fallenhill and the mountain passes were all marked, as well as the province's only other major settlement, the town of Griffith, just north of the Murr in the south. A large circle had been drawn around a crossroads in the east of the province, where the main road to Dweltford crossed the mountains and split, sending smaller roads to Fallenhill and Griffith.

About the table were various lists. Prentice recognized a roster of knights, listing their number of squires, pages, and horses. Another list seemed to be of foodstuffs—cattle, sheep, and sacks of grain were all mentioned. One sheet of paper caught his eye particularly, topped as it was with the seal of the royal house and the Prince of Rhales.

"Well, what do you see?" Amelia asked.

"I see preparations for war," Prentice said. "You will be marching to meet an army from the east, to rendezvous at the crossroads. I would guess that the Prince of Rhales himself is coming. Do you then plan to march to Fallenhill? Is that where the invaders are?"

Amelia blinked several times and shook her head. "My respect for your opinion grows every time we speak, Prentice."

"Thank you, Your Grace."

"Have you heard rumors of our preparations?"

Prentice shook his head. "We spend our days in that barn, Your Grace. We hear nothing but the buzz of insects and the howl of lonely dogs."

She looked at him, and he could tell she wasn't sure whether he was being deliberately poetic. He smiled to remove her doubt.

"So, you obtained your entire opinion from one glance of this table?"

"I knew there was war already, Your Grace. You told me that."

"I suppose. Tell me, are you curious what position I have chosen for you in my service?"

"Your Grace will inform me when you are ready."

"How are you so controlled?"

Prentice only shrugged.

Amelia reached over and took one of the books from the pile. "*Rossman's Precepts of War*," she said, showing him the title. It was one of the books from the list he gave her. "I found it in my husband's chamber. Rossman, the author, was a knight. He served King Lioll IV."

"Yes, Your Grace, I know."

"I thought you said knights were fools," the duchess said.

"Not all. Rossman was a genius, and he wrote over a hundred years ago."

"Yet you believe his writing relevant in this age, where you think warfare is changing too quickly for knights to keep up?"

"As I said, Your Grace, a genius."

Amelia flicked through some of the worn pages of the book. There were pages of neat script and occasionally a diagram or woodcut print. "I think I understand some of it, but not all." She looked up at him, and he got the sense that she was waiting for him to say something. Not knowing what to say, he stayed silent.

"You will not offer to explain it to me?" she asked.

"If Your Grace requires my assistance, you know you have but to command it."

"Any one of my knights would be eager to explain it to me. Sir Liam had only to see the book in my hands before launching into a diatribe, listing its virtues and faults at length. Have you no ambition?"

"Ambition is for men who seek advancement," Prentice replied. "My ankle chains slow my prospects for advancement."

"Sir Liam is quite ambitious," Amelia continued, ignoring Prentice's gibe.

"No doubt."

"He was willing to share all of his wisdom with me on the slightest pretext. You make me draw it from you like a chirurgeon pulling teeth. However, the one thing Sir Liam did not do is encourage me to read it. He was of the opinion that I should simply trust the advice of my knights in these matters—his advice being preeminent, of course." She put the book on the table. "What do you think?"

"I think that you should learn for yourself, as much as you can. Otherwise you'll be at the mercy of your advisors. You would never be able to know if their advice was sound or useless."

"I thought exactly the same thing. That is why I have decided to move you into my household. I will have you advise me and instruct me in matters of war, at least until I feel comfortable to make my own judgments."

"I am to be your tutor?" Prentice could not believe her suggestion. "You will not need your knights to render an opinion on that notion; your household staff will revolt." He looked out the door of the salon, thinking of Bettina's disgust at his mere presence in the keep. The notion of him having such a powerful place in household staff would be unthinkable to her.

"No, such an appointment would be even more impolitic than simply pardoning you," Amelia agreed. "But having read some of this excellent book, which Sir Liam reluctantly conceded was among the most important treatises of war ever written, I find that Lord Rossman himself recommends that all foot troops be given commanders from among their own number. Something about freeing the knights from the considerations of the lesser ranks in the field."

"He also saw the value of different troops being commanded by officers of experience with the strengths and limitations of those troops," Prentice added before he could stop himself.

"Quite so. Since we will be joining the prince's army in a few days, and he is bringing a large number of convicts on foot to bolster the duchy's ranks, I have decided to make you the captain of my convict foot company. Tell me, what do you think?"

Prentice blinked in surprise. His mind raced, and he hardly knew what to think. So many possibilities and dangers presented themselves. He grabbed the first one from the list forming in his mind.

"They will still sneer," he said. "Rossman's work is respected, but many of his ideas have long been dismissed as too radical in the Grand Kingdom. Even the Vec princes that have made concessions to their own republicanists find him nearly seditious sometimes."

"They may sneer," Amelia conceded. "Sir Liam was quite vocal in his dislike for my decision when I informed him this morning. However, I need advice from a man who can keep his ambition in check, and I choose you as that man. Lord Rossman's advice will give me sufficient excuse. They already think of me as a silly girl out of my depth, but this, at least, is not the action of a complete fool. If they sneer, they will not do it to my face."

"Yes, Your Grace." Prentice was still so surprised at his change of fortunes that he could not think of anything more to say.

"There are few enough convicts available at the moment across the province, but most have orders that they be sent to the crossroads in time to meet with the prince's army. We will march from here shortly. That is why I have paid for you to have shoes—make sure they are good ones. Lord Rossman recommends that every footman have the best shoes he can afford. Long marches on bad shoes can hobble an army, defeat them before they even reach the battlefield."

"As you say, Your Grace."

"The steward in the great hall has orders to find you quarters. You will make whatever preparations you think you need to and be ready to march when we leave. At the end of this campaign, I will free you with good cause, I trust."

Prentice knew he had been dismissed. He bowed and headed to the salon door, then turned back. "May I ask you something, Your Grace?"

"When we are alone, I give you leave to speak your mind," Amelia answered. "Providing, of course, that you do not forget yourself. You will make a poor advisor otherwise."

"Very well, Your Grace. Then I have to ask. You said you thought I had no ambition, but that you needed a man who kept his ambitions in check. Which do you really think it is?"

Amelia smiled at him—a surprisingly warm smile, almost affectionate. "Silly Prentice, you are an educated man. You may have fallen as far as any man can in our great land, but at one time you were a man with ambitions, enough to devote yourself to study and to survive in war. You may think you have no ambitions left inside you, but I think the opportunity to serve in the private household of a peer of the realm will bring some of those ambitions back to life. When they are resurrected and you begin to look to your own advancement, I want you to remember how completely you depend upon me for that."

Prentice returned her smile and found that he could not help but admire this cunning young woman. "If fate had made you any less than a duchess, Your Grace, then God's handiwork would have gone to waste. You were born to do this."

"Thank you," she said and then waved him away in dismissal.

CHAPTER 17

Prentice felt like an acrobat walking a tightrope and forever in fear of losing his balance. None of the firm facts of convict life that he had used to ground himself for so many years were present anymore. Amelia had been right about his ambitions. Whatever plans or desires he had in his youth, he had only survived his years in the Reach by burying them deep under a pattern of calculated obedience and watchful caution. The prospect of having a promising future stirred up feelings long buried deep. He felt like a villain in a minstrel's poem, suddenly confronted by the ghosts of his past.

To overcome his unsteadiness of heart, he forced himself to focus as diligently as he could on the business of his new role as a captain of convicts, starting with a new pair of shoes to march in. He tried to have the cobbler make him a pair of strong leather boots, with high laces and hobnail soles, but the ankle iron on his leg made it impossible to fit them. He was forced to settle for simpler shoes, little more than leather clogs. Because it was forbidden by law for him to conceal the ankle iron, he could not wear hose either, and he settled for socks of homespun wool instead.

"You know, it might be possible to make boots that fit beneath the iron," the cobbler had mused. Then he appeared to realize who he was talking to, and his gentle musing gave way to a stern face. "But it would take a lot of money and time, which I'm sure your mistress won't want wasted."

"You're probably right," Prentice said. The shoes were to take the rest of the day, and he deliberately sat down on the street outside the cobbler's shop, his convict presence scaring away business. It was petty revenge, but no pettier than the cobbler's own behavior.

As he watched the people of Dweltford walking past on the stone-lined street and ignored their looks of suspicion at his iron-shod ankles, he began to think of things he had not thought about in many years. He looked at the houses and the various shops on the street. Everything seemed in good repair, and the people looked healthy and strong. They mostly wore homespun, but he found that finer cotton, leather, and even linen were common as well. He saw rosy-cheeked women and plenty of children. The street was not a main thoroughfare, but traffic was regular, with numerous carts and wagons coming back and forth.

A dirty-faced charcoal burner in a leather hood led a donkey-drawn wagon up the street, selling his charcoal as he went. When the cart was in front of the candle maker's shop next to the cobbler, the donkey pissed loudly on the stones and dropped a pile of turds. The candle maker came out and shouted at the charcoal burner, who returned the abuse with equal vehemence.

Prentice was distracted by the two men's argument but then was struck by a thought: where in the world was a town so clean that a shop owner noticed an ass relieving itself in the street? He looked up and down and realized that there was virtually no refuse. All the major towns and cities that Prentice knew of struggled to overcome the problem of animal dung and sewage, which had to be collected every day. The job was loathsome and usually fell to convict labor. In the Vec, where convict labor was typically outlawed, they paid teams of men called gong farmers to do the work. It was highly paid because it was hard to recruit for the task, and there was always a shortage of workers.

In the Vec cities, if a man were not proud, he would never go hungry. Prentice knew that Dweltford wasn't using convicts for the job because neither he nor his fellows had ever done it, which meant they had to be paying gong farmers. And given the clean state of the street, they must be paying well.

"What's a gong farmer earn here?" he asked the cobbler when the man called him to fit the new shoes.

"You looking to step up in the world?" the cobbler asked back, then laughed at his own joke.

"I just thought they were doing a good job. That's the cleanest street I've ever sat on."

The cobbler looked at Prentice as though he was strange, then shook his head and checked the fit on his feet. "You may be a criminal dog," he muttered under his breath, "but I'll be damned if I'll let any man out of my shop with shoes that don't fit."

"They're comfortable," Prentice said.

"Good. So you can get out of my shop!"

Prentice walked out, but the cobbler called after him, "You make sure and tell your mistress or whomever that I did a good job and it's worth what I charge."

Prentice gave the man a cold look, and the cobbler suddenly seemed shamefaced, as if he remembered that he was dealing with a man, not just an animal called a convict. He ducked his head for a moment and then looked up. "It's the sewers," he said suddenly. "Gong farmers only have to take the dung to a drain hole and chuck it down. The sewers wash it out into the lake and then down the river. I just... that's why it's so clean." He trailed off, apparently caught between his shame at treating Prentice so poorly and the further shame of speaking to a convict on the street. He looked up and down the long laneway, then ducked furtively back into his shop.

Prentice couldn't help a wry smile. The cobbler had despised him and mistreated him, but that was nothing new in convict life. And the poor fool was as ashamed of himself as he was of talking to Prentice. He was trapped whichever way he went.

Maybe not so different, you and I, Prentice thought.

On the short journey back to the castle, he watched the town around him and found it very curious. The people were prosperous, and there was commerce all around him. It seemed that most, if not all, trade in the province must flow through Dweltford, and there must be a lot of it, between the settlers' farms and the silver and iron coming from Fallenhill. By the time he reached the castle—another sign of the wealth and prosperity of the Reach—he found himself fixed on one simple question: how had Duke Marne gotten into so much debt?

All nobility tended to spend money to their limit, and unforeseen problems like drought, famine, or war could break even a great noble house, but how did any man spend away this much wealth? Since the end of the crusade eleven years before, the Reach had been at peace. And the crusade itself had been swift, not the kind of protracted affair that racked up heavy expenses. Kolber had fled so swiftly to try to stop his son's rebellion that he'd been forced to leave a great booty behind. Many knights had made their fortunes out of the defeated Vec king's baggage train. So where had the money gone?

He was musing over this question as he crossed the bridge back to the castle. He was so lost in his thoughts that he did not see two armed men in the shadows of the gatehouse until he had almost reached them. They were rough-shaven and dressed in tunics dyed and bleached in the ducal colors. One had a savage scar over his right eye. The other chewed a stalk of straw. Both held bill polearms, with spear points and back hooks on one side.

The one with the scar stepped into Prentice's path before he knew they were there. Prentice summed them up in a glance: bored guards, which meant trouble. He hadn't seen them there. Prentice lowered his head deferentially, while inwardly he cursed his own inattention. One shopping trip to buy a pair of ordinary shoes and he had forgotten all of his self-protective disciplines, wandering around with his head in the clouds like an apprentice given the afternoon off for a high holy day.

"What have we here?" said Scarface. He had an odd accent that Prentice could not quite identify. Somewhere south, perhaps. "You a convict?"

Prentice nodded.

The straw chewer let out a low chuckle. "Those are pretty new shoes you have there, little girl."

"They are a gift. From the duchess," Prentice said, hoping the fool would take the hint.

He did not.

"From the duchess?" The man laughed, clearly not believing a word. "How la-de-da! I ain't never got no gifts from a duchess. Show 'em to me."

Prentice slipped off the shoes and stepped back out of them, leaving them on the bridge boards in front of him.

"They look like a good fit," said Scarface. "What do you think, is they a good fit, Trolf?"

"Too small, I think," the guard named Trolf said. "Might be they need a stretching.

"A good idea. Isn't it a good idea, convict?"

Prentice did not speak but lifted his head to meet the man's eyes.

"No? You don't agree with wise Trolf?"

"Maybe he's dumb!" said Trolf.

"Well, if he's dumb, then we need to help the poor dumb beast. There's a proper way to stretch new leather. You need to get it wet and then you wear it in. Isn't that right, Trolf?"

"It's what my da always taught me. Still, my da was a right bastard, so take it how you will."

"Well, he was right on this. Here, I'll get you started."

Scarface tucked his bill shaft into the crook of his arm and reached both hands under his tunic. Prentice sighed wearily as he realized what the man was going to do. There was a loud splashing sound as the guard urinated all over the new shoes so that it pooled inside. The stink of his urine filled the air.

"There you go," he said as he tucked himself away. "Now that they're good and ready, you put them on and walk around in them. They'll stretch right to your feet. Go on, put them on!"

Prentice looked at the wet leather and the urine pooling in them. He clenched his fists by his sides, hands trembling as he struggled to control his fury. He wanted to slaughter this fool right where he stood. He knew he could do it, a quick strike to the throat, catch him off guard, take his bill, and run him through. Even if Trolf was good and quick, Prentice favored himself to take them both. With all his will, he first lifted one foot and then the other, pushing them into his shoes and feeling the warm urine soak into his new socks.

"There you go," said Scarface, while Trolf guffawed. "Now walk about in them. You can't take them off 'til they dry. You got to walk them in."

Prentice forced himself to take a few steps.

"See, they'll be perfect in no time. Now, piss off!"

Scarface struck Prentice in the back with the butt of his polearm. Prentice grunted in pain and staggered a little, but he took the opportunity to hurry away, leaving the two guards laughing behind him.

He rushed across the main bailey and took the long way to the lesser bailey, rather than trying to walk through the castle buildings smelling like a privy pot. He did not want to be anywhere near those two men—or anyone, for that matter—while he dealt with what they had done.

In the lesser bailey, he stopped by the stables and stepped straight into a horse trough with water, standing up to his calves so that the hems of his trews got wet. Then he leaned against the wall of the stable.

"Fool!" he cursed himself. "Stupid fool."

He punched the wall. In spite of himself, he knew that he had, in fact, escaped lightly. A guard's bullying could be savage, but that knowledge was no consolation. Abusing convicts was virtually a pastime for stupid thugs and bullies across the Grand Kingdom. And the strike with the bill was unpleasant, but bruises were nothing new. What scalded Prentice's thoughts was how unguarded he had been. Eleven years he had been a convict. He had survived whippings, beatings, six battles, and endless skirmishes during the crusade. Through it all he knew to be watchful, keep his wits about him. Now the duchess had dangled clean clothes and new shoes in front of him, and that was all it took to forget everything and step back in time to the first days of the betrayal that sent him here.

Prentice gradually pushed the anger down once more. He stepped out of the water and sloshed about in the horse yard. He would have to walk in his shoes until they dried, or else they would shrink and not fit. Shaking his head, he made his way over to the barn where he had been placed with Turley and Bellam when they first arrived. It was a good place to hide and walk up and down until his shoes dried off and the rage he felt lost some of its edge.

CHAPTER 18

The morning was bright as Duchess Amelia led her household guard and knights out of the castle and through the streets of Dweltford. A herald went before them, crying out to clear the way. People stood aside and watched. Some cheered, to see the twenty or so mounted men and twice that number of uniformed house guard marching in column behind. It felt like such a tiny group to Amelia—the ambush by the riverside still fresh in her mind —but she knew that the majority of her knights were scattered over the province, fetching supplies that would be needed to feed the army on the march, as well as the convicts who would be made to fight and any farmers who might volunteer to serve.

They would all meet at the crossroads, and she would field a force of just over one hundred knights on horse, fifty militiamen and household guard, and an uncertain number of convicts and volunteers. She knew also that this small force would be added to the prince's much larger army and united they would march three days and liberate Fallenhill. At least that was what Sir Liam and Sir Duggan assured her would be the outcome.

It all seemed too easy to Amelia. War was a violent business, with killing and death, but her knights seemed to treat it like a festival. They were so confident of victory. She looked down to see Prentice marching at her stirrup, and she tried to get a sense of him. He was tall and broad shouldered like Sir Liam, except there was something more to him than her fresh knight captain. Prentice was older, but only by about five years. He did not have Sir Liam's careful grooming or refined features, but now that he was shaven and his sandy hair cut, he was not unhandsome.

Is it in the eyes? she wondered.

Sir Liam's dark eyes always seemed full of laughter and charm and boundless confidence; always, except on the day Sir Dav had died. Then, he had looked like a wounded boy who needed to be comforted, at least in flashes. Prentice's eyes were gray and cold, like storm clouds, and they were impenetrable to her. Whoever he was, he kept that information to himself. Nonetheless, he seemed surer of himself than Sir Liam, which left her confused. He was a convict, and he filled the role to perfection. His manners were impeccable, with only a few lapses, yet Amelia felt it was a role—something he played at. Dig deeply enough and the man inside was neither bowed nor broken, but still angry. And this angry, unbroken man thought that they were not ready for this campaign.

Whose judgment should she trust?

The little procession passed through the town gates, and Amelia noted armed men on the parapet. She waved at them, playing the duchess, but they did not acknowledge her. They held weapons and had buff coats and broadbrim steel helms, but they wore no colors.

"Sir Duggan, who are those men?" she asked of the knight riding next to her.

The leather of his armor harness creaked as he craned about to see where she was indicating. Looking up at the walls, he blinked and hesitated. "They are... I think... militia, Your Grace."

"You seem unsure, Sir Duggan."

"No, Your Grace, they are most definitely militia."

"Will they not march with us?" she asked. "We gave orders for the raising of militia, and you assured me that only fifty could be raised in time. Surely we will need every one of those men?"

"Of course, Your Grace," Sir Duggan stumbled.

He seemed embarrassed by her questions, though she couldn't think why. Sir Duggan had behaved strangely often since her return. Perhaps it was her husband's death that had unsettled him. Loyal men were often thrown off by the death of their liege, she had heard. If Sir Duggan's will was lost with the duke's death, then he was another problem she would have to look to.

While she was thinking, a heavyset man in a black frock coat and broadbrim felt hat ran along the line from the city gate behind them. He called out for Sir Duggan.

"With your permission, Your Grace," Sir Duggan said. Without waiting for her permission, he rode to speak with the man, who was already huffing with the exertion of the short chase.

Amelia kept riding while the two men conferred, and soon the column reached a flat space outside the walls, where teams of ostlers had arranged the baggage train ready for the march; pack mules in teams, oxen drawn wagons piled with sacks of grain, a small herd of cattle, and flocks of sheep. The campaign would take no more than a week or two, her knights assured her, yet Amelia felt they were taking half a season's harvest with them. Nonetheless, even her little reading of Lord Rossman's *Precepts* had assured her that an army needed much food if it was to be kept from pillaging the countryside just to feed itself.

Sir Duggan rode back to her side, and she glanced down to see Prentice having to fall back to keep from being sandwiched between the two horses.

"A word, Your Grace?" Sir Duggan said.

Amelia reined to a stop, and along the line the marching stopped with her. Sir Duggan looked back as if worried or further embarrassed to have caused the halt.

"Speak your mind, Sir Duggan."

"Your Grace, I have just been informed that there is a problem with the militia."

"A problem?"

"Yes, Your Grace. They refuse to march."

Her brow furrowed. "Refuse?"

"Some peasant grumbling about pay and loss of money from being away from their crafts, or some such nonsense."

"Surely this is a matter for the town's guild conclave?" Amelia said, puzzled by the strange timing of the issue. *Why wasn't it raised earlier?*

"Um, yes, as you say, Your Grace," Sir Duggan fumbled. "I do not think the conclave has had time to meet due to the swiftness of preparations."

Amelia sighed in frustration. "They are in a single town, and the province is at war. One would think they could find an hour in a tavern back room to discuss the defense of the realm and its implications for the town's patricians." She took up her reins and began to wheel her mount to head back into Dweltford. "Very well. We will meet with them."

"No, Your Grace," Sir Duggan said. "If it please you, let me. I'll handle this, I assure you. Do not delay the march for this foolishness. The prince awaits you."

Amelia thought about Duggan's suggestion. It was true that they had to march quickly if they were to reach their rendezvous without keeping Prince Mercad waiting. And negotiating with merchants and guildsmen could be a protracted process at the best of times. She wondered about Sir Duggan's strange behavior and thought she discerned its origin.

"Sir Duggan, did you anticipate this circumstance?" she asked. Sir Duggan's face paled, and he looked away quickly, as if seeking an escape. "Have you been worrying about this for some time?"

"Worrying, Your Grace?" Sir Duggan's voice was almost a quiet whisper.

"You should have brought these matters to my attention," said the duchess. "You are my castellan, my advisor, and my sworn sword, but you should not fear to be shamed in front of me because of other men's failings."

As she spoke, Sir Duggan's expression began to brighten, and his face showed relief.

"Go, meet with these men," she ordered. "Assure them that the duchy will not forget them or their needs, and then remind them that it is the Prince of Rhales himself who has ordered us to the march. It is him they are disobeying if they refuse."

"I am certain that will persuade them, Your Grace," Sir Duggan said, and he leaned forward bowing slightly in the saddle. Then he rode back into the town.

Amelia waved her hand and recommenced her journey.

Prentice trotted up and retook his position at her stirrup. "He's not your sworn sword, Your Grace," he said quietly.

"What?"

"He is a free blade. He has not yet sworn to you," Prentice explained. "He was the duke's sworn man. With Duke Marne dead, he must swear fealty to you; all your knights must, or else they remain free blades. Worth remembering."

"Thank you for that lesson in chivalric law," she said with a mocking tone. "I'm sure there will be opportunity for ceremonies soon, perhaps at the end of the day on the march. In the meantime, it is a pleasant sunny morning, and I would enjoy my ride in quiet."

"Very good, Your Grace."

CHAPTER 19

The march to the crossroads was a simple affair along dusty roads that at least had the virtue of being dry and firm underfoot. Each evening that camp was made—and even on the way—their numbers grew. By the second evening, the column included over fifty knights and their squires and pages. The first night, the encampment surrounded a village well, and the noise never seemed to settle as ostlers and squires moved back and forth throughout the night, working to make sure the horses were well groomed and all the livestock properly watered. The second night, they camped in a field bordered by a little stream, and the animals were simply led to the water.

Each night, Prentice kept close by the duchess's tent, keeping out of the way of the stewards who unloaded all the furnishings. He was impressed when, following his story of looting the baggage trains of King Kolber's invasion, Duchess Amelia had insisted on only the bare minimum of furnishings for her tent and camp. Her canteen had only practical pewter, rather than the silver of her dinner service in Dweltford. Even the plates were pewter. Not cheap, but much less of a loss should they be stolen or looted.

"I was bringing a number of expensive dresses and other items when my barge was ambushed," she told him. "Gifts from worthies in the Vec. Not things purchased with my own money, but a loss to my duchy's coffers nonetheless."

Staying close to the duchess was practicality on Prentice's part. She intended to entrust him with command of the rogues, the Kingdom's military term for the convict foot— and sometimes even for the free militia, if a nobleman was feeling particularly condescending. But even with that trust, he still wore the leg irons of a convict, and that was what most would see, just as the guards on the castle's bridge had. Prentice *did* have to wryly admit that after the piss and water, the leather of his shoes was soft and comfortable, and after two days' march, his socks just smelled of his own feet. He sat on a tuft of grass by the side of the duchess's tent and removed his shoes and socks, rubbing his sore feet, pleased to find only one or two small blisters. He would have to find some vinegar for them in the stores before he went to sleep.

From behind him he heard two men grunting as they carried something heavy toward the entrance of the tent. Looking over his shoulder, he saw Turley and another steward carry a walnut wood dresser.

The steward muttered and cursed as they moved around Prentice. "Look out there, dog," he said between huffing breaths.

Turley noticed Prentice and gave him a wink and a cheeky smile. "Not easy to fetch and carry after walking a day."

Prentice returned the smile. "You're settling in."

"Shut up, convicts," the steward said. "I want to get this in for her ladyship and go get myself some of that mutton before it's gone."

"Her Grace," Turley said primly as the two continued their carry into the tent.

"What?"

Turley's voice became muffled, but Prentice could imagine the rough man continuing to give his lesson on the proper etiquette for addressing a duchess. Less than a week ago, Turley would not have known a chambermaid from a chamber pot in a ducal household. The thought made Prentice smile. Inside the tent he heard the duchess's muffled voice addressing the two men, giving further instruction.

"Right away, Your Grace!" the steward answered loudly as he and Turley exited the tent. They came around the corner, and the man looked back to Turley, then pointed at Prentice. "That's your job!" he said and moved off, doubtless in search of his supper.

Turley sat on the grass next to Prentice and rubbed at the leather of his new shoes. They were the same simple design as Prentice's, but it seemed Turley had not thought to get himself socks to wear with them.

"Damned things are as much curse as blessing," he muttered. "How are yours?"

"Pretty comfortable, actually," Prentice said, pulling his socks back on. "But I had some help softening them in."

"Lucky you."

Prentice shrugged.

"Still, it's not a bad job, this stewarding. Bit boring though. Fetch, carry, walk, fetch, carry, sleep."

"You've had worse jobs."

"Ain't that the truth. And these pretty new threads make a man feel almost free again, wouldn't you say?" Turley brushed his hands down his tunic, which was already dusty and smeared with grease and dirt.

"Something like that," Prentice agreed. "Of course, we'll have to keep them clean now, especially in the duchess's own household."

Turley *tsk*ed at the thought and spat on the grass. "A sweet maid to charm in the laundry, that's what I need," he mused. "Someone who won't mind me lying naked on her bed while she helps me with me washing needs."

Prentice chuckled.

"Oh, you better get a rush on. The duchess was calling for you. That's what the steward wanted me to tell you."

Prentice stood up, his smile twisting into a scowl. He nearly tripped over trying to get his foot into his other shoe in the same motion. "You should have told me straight away! We're not simple convicts anymore, playing games to annoy some fool overseer, you bastard."

Turley only sat back on his hands and smiled up at Prentice with his mocking grin. He plucked a length of grass and put it in his teeth, chewing in his impression of a slack-jawed farmhand. Prentice rolled his eyes and rushed to the entrance of the duchess's tent.

Inside, Duchess Amelia was seated upon a chair and reading by the light of a candelabra stand beside her. There was a plate of half-eaten food on the dresser by her left hand, along with a jug of wine and a pewter goblet filigreed in brass.

"Is this how you respond to my instructions now?" she asked, without looking up from the page in front of her. "I heard you both talking out there for some time. You did not think my summons required urgency?"

Prentice dropped to one knee and bowed his head. "I apologize, Your Grace. The messenger saw fit to speak with me on other subjects before he passed on your command." He cast a hard glance at the side of the tent, beyond which he imagined Turley still lazing and smiling at the trouble he'd caused.

"Well, you are here now, so I will overlook your lateness."

"Thank you, Your Grace."

The duchess folded the book, marking her place with a length of white silk from which was hung a gold pendant. She picked a bit of bread from her plate and took a bite. Her every movement was elegant and self-possessed.

"Tomorrow we will reach the crossroads and the prince's encampment," she told him. "It is important that I be ready, and I already have so much to think about. Just this afternoon I had three different knights of mine offering to make introductions to important relatives in the prince's court." She shook her head. "It will only be days before the formal offers of courtship start to come."

"You are a young woman of position, and you are unmarried," Prentice said with a shrug.

"I am a widow mourning her husband and defending his duchy from invaders!" Amelia spat back, and her normal reserve slipped a moment to show a wounded but angry heart underneath. "I know what is said of us, that I married for the title and he only for the money, but we loved each other, I swear it."

"I would not presume to think otherwise, Your Grace."

"It ripped me apart like a wild animal when I heard the news of his death. I knew..." She paused, taking a sip from the wine goblet before continuing, using the moment to calm herself. "I thought I would have months, perhaps years, to mourn and consider my future. I know I will have to remarry, and for the good of the Grand Kingdom, not for my heart. I am not the silly girl they think me to be. But this war has accelerated everything."

"War has that power, Your Grace," Prentice concurred.

"I will prepare myself and be ready for it." She took a forkful of meat, chewing slowly before swallowing. "How go your preparations? Are you ready for tomorrow?"

"Tomorrow, Your Grace?"

"You are to take command of the convicts tomorrow, o captain of my rogues. We have been on the march two days. I expect you've used the time to make preparations?"

"What preparations do you think are needed?"

"The prince informs me that he has crossed the mountains with nearly five hundred convict foot. I assume preparations for a command that size take at least two days."

Prentice's mind ran wild for a moment. Five hundred? The prince must have emptied every prison in Rhales. He had never expected so many.

"Does the number surprise you, Prentice?" the duchess asked. "It is a larger number than I supposed. Is it too much for you?"

Prentice narrowed his eyes and watched the duchess impertinently for a moment. Was she mocking him? There was something in her eyes that said she might be, but she might just as easily be genuinely afraid that he wasn't up to the task. She could be about to take it away from him and be waiting for him to make it easier for her by agreeing that the task was too great.

"Authority, Your Grace," he said quickly and firmly. "I need your authority to appoint order and enforce it."

"You have it," she said lightly and turned to her plate once again.

"Forgive me, Your Grace, but that is not enough."

"Is it not?" Amelia lifted a cherry tomato in two fingers and popped it into her mouth.

"Here, in this tent with just we two, it is all. But when I move about in your army, the first and last thing that is seen are these." He pointed down at the ankle irons on his legs. "For me to be your captain, I need your authority."

Amelia nodded and brushed some crumbs from her fingers. Then she moved the plate on her dresser and drew a document from underneath it. She held it out for him, and he took it. Glancing over it, Prentice noticed first that it was marked with the ducal seal.

"My warrant," she said. "It authorizes you to command the rogues foot in this campaign and to raise their orders and equipment as you see fit. My reeve of the purse is commanded to accept your instructions for the outfitting of the rogues and compensate as required."

Prentice bowed. "Very good, Your Grace." He looked at the writing on the warrant, which covered all the issues she had just outlined. "You made me ask for something you already planned to give me?"

"Oh, no, I certainly would not have given it to you had you not asked," Amelia said. She sat back in her chair. "I am trusting you Prentice, but I will expect you to prove yourself at every step. If my judgment is wrong and you are not worthy of my trust, I will make sure you have every opportunity to reveal your weakness before the lives of others are at risk."

Prentice nodded. It made great sense to him.

"And that warrant is for my army, Prentice," the duchess continued. "If I find you have used it to get drunk or feast your convict friends on roast swan, or indeed in any way that will bring embarrassment to my house, I will have you flogged at a post until I can count your bones myself. Do you understand?"

"I would expect no less, Your Grace."

CHAPTER 20

Just after noon the next day, the duchess's column crested the last ridge and made its way down into the shallow vale where Mercad, Prince of Rhales, made his encampment. The crossroads themselves were marked by an inn and stables called the Merchant's Rest, just a little north of the main road. The inn had several corrals for mule trains, and two wells surrounded by pastureland. The summer grass of that pasture was now crushed by dozens upon dozens of tents and pavilions. While they were still half a league from the edge of the camp, outriders intercepted them, and upon learning that it was the duchess who approached, the scouts rode quickly to announce her arrival. By the time they reached the edge of the encampment, a herald and ten knights in parade armor met them and escorted Amelia directly to an audience with the prince.

Riding among the tents, Amelia marveled at the vibrant life of the camp. There were armed men, of course—knights, squires, and house guard—but that was only a fraction of the number. Washerwomen and seamstresses were everywhere, sitting in the lanes between the guy lines. Stewards cooked over innumerable fires and rushed about, carrying buckets of water. Carpenters, leatherworkers, and coopers plied their trades in tents that served as workshops. There was even a smithy, with a portable forge built ingeniously into a monstrous ironbound cart that looked like it would need a team of at least ten draft animals to pull. As she passed, Amelia saw the smith quenching a newly forged sword while a polisher was carefully putting an edge on another blade; the blade's owner, a dark-haired knight in sea green livery, stood by and watched.

At last Amelia and her honor guard arrived at the prince's pavilion, and she blinked, trying to understand its scope. No simple tent, it was a pavilion of many chambers, including a vestibule, an audience chamber with a central firepit large enough for a hundred men to stand in comfortably, a chapel (so she was told), and the prince's own apartments. It was made of silk dyed the rich burgundy of the royal house, and dotted all about it were heraldic eagles sewn with gold thread.

A page took her horse's reins as she dismounted, and the herald showed her into the tent. Sir Liam followed. She had ordered Prentice to wait for her with the rest of her column, and Sir Duggan had not yet caught up from his negotiations with the guild council, which annoyed her deeply. It was one thing for the guild to advocate for its members, but days of negotiation were keeping an important advisor from her, not to mention her militia. At dawn that morning, she had sent a rider to see if Sir Duggan was bringing militia along the road and how far they were.

In the pavilion's vestibule, Amelia waited and suddenly thought to fret about her appearance. She was fresh from the road, and while she bathed nightly on the short journey and kept her clothing fresh each day, she was about to be granted an audience with the Prince of Rhales, the second most powerful man in the Grand Kingdom. She had only met him once before, on the day of her wedding, and then he had not deigned to say more to her than "Congratulations."

The herald announced her, and she entered the audience chamber. The room was dim but warm, the midday sun beating down outside. There were a number of servants around the room holding enormous silk fans on long rods. They waved the fans up and down, circulating and cooling the air a little. Across from the entrance was a gilded throne set on a small wooden dais and seated on the throne was the prince.

Amelia's first impression was that he was older than she expected. She knew he was in his sixties, but his hair seemed lanker and his skin grayer than she remembered. She thought it must have been because of his rushed march. He stood, and as he did, his red and gold surcoat seemed to hang about him, as though he was too thin for it. Even his gold diadem did not seem to sit right.

While she was still walking toward the throne to present herself, Prince Mercad surprised her by stepping down from the dais and crossing the distance between them. She promptly curtsied at his approach, bowing her head. He laid one hand on her shoulder and stroked the side of her face with the other. Then he quickly raised her to her feet. She blinked in surprise, then complete confusion as the prince took her into his arms and embraced her.

"Dearest Duchess Amelia," he said, his voice surprisingly warm and deep. "The kingdom weeps with you for the loss of Duke Marne."

"Thank you, Highness," she managed to force out through her bewilderment.

"He was a hero to all of us in the west, and doubtless even to the capital." The prince waved his hand about as he spoke, and Amelia could not look past how thin and weak it looked. "The times we rode together into battle, the victories we won. He was very dear to me, almost even as my brother."

"You are kind to say so, Your Highness. I mourn his passing and the loss of the time I might have had with him. I loved him very much."

"We all did, my dear. We all did." The prince looked over his shoulder at Sir Liam, who stood just inside the entrance to the tent. "Is this your man?"

"The captain of my knights," Amelia answered, and for a moment the prince looked at her as if she had said something strange. She wondered what was wrong. Before she could puzzle it out, the prince held his hand out to Sir Liam.

Sir Liam took an eager half step and started to lower himself into a kneel, then snatched himself back. With a bow to the prince, he unbuckled his sword belt, handing it to the herald who also still waited in the entrance. The herald received the weapon with a nod of approval and Amelia also felt pleased. It was forbidden for anyone to wear a sword in the prince's presence without dispensation. She was glad Liam had remembered the etiquette.

Finally, her knight captain knelt before the prince. "Sir Liam, Your Highness," he said, keeping his head bowed. "Your servant and sworn man."

"Of course," said Prince Mercad with a wan smile. "Sir Liam, no doubt you are tired from your long journey."

"I am quite well, Highness. You are kind to ask."

"Nonetheless, you should seek your rest."

Sir Liam appeared as puzzled by the prince as Amelia had been, though this time, she understood his meaning well enough. She hissed, and Sir Liam looked up.

"Leave," she whispered. Even then he seemed to struggle to understand, so she had to explain. "You are dismissed, sir."

Finally, Liam realized what was happening. With another quick bow, he stood, retrieved his sword, and backed out of the audience chamber.

"Please forgive him, Your Highness," Amelia said, curtsying quickly. "I think he was overawed to meet you. It is the highest ambition of many young knights, I am sure."

The prince smiled benevolently. "We understand, of course."

The prince led Amelia back toward his throne, where he once more took his seat. He waved to a steward, and another chair was brought for her. She sat, keeping her smile but feeling increasingly wary. Something was not right in the prince's generous behavior. He was being too kind. Goblets were brought and watered wine poured, which Amelia drank gratefully, washing the road dust from her throat. The prince waited until she had finished her cup before he spoke again.

"Please know that the crown and I held your husband in the highest regard, and our care for you is limitless. However, as this newly sprung war shows, the needs of our Grand Kingdom are always first. None of us, not even the princes of the land, are spared from its duties. God is our father, but the Grand Kingdom is our mother, and when she is assaulted, we must put aside our own tears and rush to her defense."

Amelia felt herself shifting in her seat and had to force herself to be still. She was struggling to understand why the prince was making so much of her grief for her husband. Even if the late duke was every bit as dear to him as Mercad said, it felt strange for the crown prince of the realm to take such time to comfort a grieving widow. And what had any of that to do with divine fathers and assaulted mothers?

"I know you mourn the dear lost duke, and I'm sure you intend to observe the proper time for that, but I can assure you that I am well pleased to hear of Sir Duggan's suit and commend you on your readiness to make swift action for the good of the Reach."

"Sir Duggan's suit?" Amelia repeated, as if the words were a foreign language. Her mind struggled to make them make sense.

"Indeed," the prince said with a condescending smile. "You did not think he would begin to seek your hand without first obtaining my consent, did you?"

"No, of course—of course not." Amelia fumbled for the right words while her thoughts ran to catch up to the conversation. Sir Duggan had asked permission to court her for marriage? When did he think he might mention it to her?

"I know he is an old man like me, my dear, but he is of birth. His father was the former Earl of Calmain, did you know?"

"No, Your Highness."

"His older brother holds the title now." A look of pity entered the prince's eyes. He leaned in close, seeming to Amelia that his withered frame might even topple over, and placed a hand on her arm. "I know, of course, that he is no Marne. You were truly blessed in the person of the late duke for a husband, my dear. Duggan has little of the bearing and none of the heart that made Marne the man he was. It's why we gave the duchy to Marne in the first place. Duggan had the birth and had served well enough in the crusade, but Marne was a duke at heart. You could see it in his every gesture. And Duggan took it well enough, accepting the offer to be castellan in the ducal capital when he could well have thought to be duke. He impressed me with that, and now our Lord God has seen him rewarded."

Amelia was doing everything she could to school her face from revealing her shock. She knew that she would have to work to keep her title and her place in the kingdom, but she had not even dreamed that the duchy would have already been traded out from under her. And by Sir Duggan? As the prince's words wound on, she found herself losing control.

"Sir Duggan is not with me!" she blurted out, unable to help herself during a momentary lapse into silence. She wasn't exactly sure what she meant by those words, but the prince gave them his own meaning.

"Traveling separately?" he said, nodding knowingly. "Very sensible. Avoid all hints of impropriety, at the very least until we have sorted this violation of Fallenhill. He follows along, I take it?"

Amelia nodded.

"And he will command your force when he arrives?"

"Sir Liam is my knight captain," she answered woodenly.

The prince's brows knotted momentarily into a frown. "Perhaps a little too circumspect." Then his smile returned. "Will you return to Dweltford after this, or will you remain here? I understand the inn is surprisingly fine, for a roadside affair. Something to do with all the merchant traffic, I suppose. Wealthy nobodies accustomed to more than is good for them."

"I will travel with my husband's forces until the threat to his lands is passed," Amelia averred through gritted teeth. She did not know whether to smile or frown—or indeed what face to show. It felt as though her expression were frozen in place. She desperately wanted time alone to think, and in her heart she only prayed that this horrendous audience with this too-kind old man would end as soon as possible.

CHAPTER 21

Sir Liam left the prince's pavilion utterly out of sorts. He had been presented to Mercad, Prince of Rhales, the second highest man in the whole Grand Kingdom. It was the highest of opportunities for a Reach knight, and Sir Liam was thankful to God for this little war that made such a rare occurrence possible. Advancement was made or broken by such opportunities. But the prince had dismissed him almost immediately. He had barely waited to hear Liam's name. How could that yield him any advantage?

He tied his sword belt around his waist with a rough tug and pushed it into place on his hips. Then he looked about for a page to fetch his horse.

"That is the expression of a man ill at ease with his thoughts," said a voice to his left.

Sir Liam turned and his eyes lighted on a knight standing a handful of yards away. With pale skin and his fair hair worn long and untied, held in place only by a polished copper circlet with a graven cross in the middle of his forehead, he was a figure of youthful vigor. His armor was silvered and his surcoat was church green divided by two overlapping crosses—one in gold and the other in black.

Sir Liam's eyes narrowed. "My thoughts are my own."

"Of course they are, but if they are not too private, may I say that it might benefit you to share them."

Sir Liam looked about for a page or a steward or indeed anyone he could send to have his horse fetched. There were all manner of people moving back and forth and around, but none of them paid him the least mind.

"If you seek your mount, it has been returned to your liege's people," said the blond knight. "They have been sent to encamp near the willow grove, I understand."

Sir Liam sketched a stiff bow of thanks.

The knight nodded and smiled. "Come, sir, let me purchase you a stoup of ale, and maybe we can wash some of those black thoughts white."

"I do not even know your name, sir!"

"Of course, how rude of me. I am Brother Whilte." He bowed again.

"Brother?" Sir Liam asked. "You are not a knight?"

"I am a knight of the Church. Of the Order of the Hind."

Sir Liam bowed again, less stiffly than before. "Sir Liam, of the Reach."

"It is a true pleasure to meet you, Sir Liam. Come, let me buy you that stoup, and thence I will show you the way to your lady's encampment. I hate to drink alone, and I swear by my hair that you have the look of a man that needs a drink!"

Sir Liam did not really want any company, having no specific plan except to ride his horse and brood, but Brother Whilte was genuinely charming. And since his mount was already at the camp, he saw no good reason to refuse the invitation. He smiled and waved Brother Whilte on.

"Lead the way, Brother," he said, trying to match the churchman's charm. "But you must at least allow me to pay for the ale, for the service of hearing my sorry thoughts."

"If you insist, Sir Liam."

Brother Whilte led them in search of a brewer's merchant.

"Tapster, another!"

Sir Liam waved the empty stoneware jug at the heavy man in the leather apron. Bald with corded muscles, the man resembled a village blacksmith, but he was in charge of a large cart stacked high with barrels. From the rear he tapped two barrels at a time and served ale. The cart's sideboards were wide enough to act as long bars, and Liam and Whilte were leaning against one side as they began their third jar, drinking from simple wooden tankards. The large barrels behind them gave a little shade from the afternoon sun.

"So, you have struck the first blows in this war of ours?" Whilte observed in between pulls from his tankard.

Sir Liam found the refreshment had improved his mood considerably, and over the course of the previous two stoups, he had regaled Brother Whilte with the tale of the ambush and the subsequent defense of the church.

Liam nodded. "Some, but it was a grim encounter, and I am eager to receive my justice for the loss of Sir Dav."

"Your mentor, was he?"

"Of a sort. A fine knight and braver than a lion."

"Death claims all indiscriminately," Whilte intoned. He took one last swig, then refilled his tankard from the jug. "And what of the beast that slew him?"

"Some sort of trained wolf," Liam explained. "Though faster and more powerful than any creature I have ever laid eyes on. In one leap it tore him from the saddle."

Whilte clicked his tongue and shook his head. "At least, good Sir Liam, you were able to fulfill your sworn duty— your first duty—and rescue the good lady, your liege lord's wife!" Whilte lifted his tankard in a toast.

Sir Liam met it and the wood clunked together. "Indeed," he agreed, draining his mug. As he lowered it from his face, his expression soured once more. "Though that's an overshadowed achievement too!"

"Overshadowed? How so?"

"A damnable convict."

"One of those that you led to counterattack? I thought you said they were useless."

"They were," Sir Liam said, and he slammed his tankard down hard.

The brewer's merchant looked around the rear corner of the cart with a disapproving scowl at the mistreatment of his equipment. Brother Whilte waved him away.

Liam slouched against the sideboard with both elbows, drunkenly recalling the day of the battle. "The dumb bastards could not even line up straight! And they ran at the first sign of trouble. Not one order. They obeyed not one of my orders!"

Whilte clapped his shoulder. "You know what is said? You don't waste good iron to make a nail, and you don't waste a good man to make a soldier! Certainly not a convict rogue." He frowned. "But you said 'overshadowed.' I know it must grate to have your command flee from under you, but how are you overshadowed?"

"Because the cowardly bastards didn't just flee!" Sir Liam then began to outline the story of the church and the two convicts who managed to reach its safety while carrying their comrade.

Whilte listened sympathetically. "So, the duchess favors these men for their belated courage? Frustrating to be sure, but does it really overshadow you? You were the one who led the successful retreat, so credit for the duchess's rescue falls to you."

"I would that it was so simple, new friend. This one convict—a bastard named Prentice, curse him—has her charmed or something. She favors him and lets him advise her. Advise her! Can you imagine such a thing? A convict advising a duchess?" Liam looked earnestly at Brother Whilte, hoping to find a fellow who could share his indignation, but the fury he found caught him completely by surprise. The Church knight's features contorted in a scowl, and his eyes flashed with rage.

"A convict named Prentice?" Whilte demanded through clenched teeth.

"Yes. Have I said something that offended you? Do you know him?" It might have been the drink slowing his wits some, but Liam could not see a way that a knight of the Church would take the convict's side against him.

Brother Whilte seized Sir Liam by the arm. "A convict named Prentice? Describe him!"

"Tall, I suppose, and strong. He has a directness about him that isn't easily cowed, like a stubborn ox."

"Gray eyes like two pieces of smoky glass? Like the eyes of a snow wolf?"

"Perhaps. I have never looked closely."

"What about scars? Is he scarred?"

"All convicts are scarred. They've all been under the lash more than once." Sir Liam waved a hand in exasperation.

"A convict named Prentice transported to the Reach? It must be the same one," Brother Whilte muttered.

"Do you know him?"

"Know him, Sir Liam? I am the one who found him out! Were it not for me, he would be a cankerworm biting at the sweet root of the mother Church to this day!"

Sir Liam blinked. Far from defending Prentice, Brother Whilte had a hatred for him even deeper than Liam's. The young knight listened with a fascination that grew to near glee as Whilte outlined the tale of Prentice before he was a convict, and what caused him to be sentenced and transported.

CHAPTER 22

With the duchess's warrant in his hands, Prentice set about preparing his command of the rogues foot. He went first to the head of the household stewards and had Turley released to him to be his sergeant. Although skeptical at first, once the chief steward saw the warrant, he was only too pleased to see Turley go, calling him a lazy rodent. Turley had smiled at the comment.

"It's better than cat vomit," he said to Prentice as they walked through the camp. "That's what he called me yesterday."

Prentice then took Turley to an armorer and used the warrant to obtain two brown leather jacks for them both. The armorer had a few he had made in anticipation of demand from militiamen in the army, and though they were ill fitting, they were serviceable enough. Prentice would have preferred buff coats, which were longer and had protective sleeves, but marching in the heat made the sleeveless jacks more practical—and the extra expense of the coats might have drawn the duchess's ire.

Before they left the armorer, he paid the man extra to sew strips of dyed cloth in blue and cream, the duchy's colors, onto the left breast of each jack. It was no knight's livery, no chivalric standard. It was less even than a militiaman might wear, but it did something to mark them both as the duchess's men, and not merely runaway convicts trying to pass for soldiers.

After the armorer's, they stopped by the smith with the impossible moving forge and persuaded him to give them two cudgels: ironbound, similar to the ones the ambushers had used at Dweltford Castle when they had fought Prentice. The smith looked at their leg irons with suspicion, and when Prentice presented the warrant, the man waved for his apprentice to go fetch a scribe or someone who had their letters. The dark-haired lad raced away, and Prentice and Turley stood quietly as they waited for his return.

He came back with an elderly washerwoman, whose face was lined with deep creases and whose mouth was missing half its teeth. The smith demanded she read the warrant, and while it was hard to understand her phlegmy speech, she confirmed what the warrant said. The smith accepted her word and allowed Turley and Prentice to take their hardwood rods. Prentice also acquired a serviceable fighting dagger, a poniard with a narrow point designed to push between the gaps in armor.

Before they headed back to the willow grove and their part of the encampment, Prentice diverted them via the field where the convicts that the prince had brought were being held. They were a miserable-looking crowd, seated or lying on the ground in long rows of thirty men, each group linked by a single chain running through the rings on their leg irons. Only a handful of overseers were around them because of the chains. Aside from the ubiquitous whips and the lack of leg irons, there was little to choose between the convicts and their guards, the overseers being an almost equally filthy collection of humanity.

One of the overseers stopped them as they looked over the manacled crowd, and he pointed to their leg irons. It looked like he was about to accuse them of being escaped members of one of his chains, and when Turley hefted the cudgel, he called to the two nearest overseers for support. By the time they arrived, Prentice had brought out the warrant and was showing it to him.

The overseer looked it over and then back at Prentice and Turley. "You stole this."

The other two overseers arrived and stood behind him. One of them took the warrant from his hand and looked it over while the other assessed Prentice and Turley, clearly noting the condition of their clothes and shoes, their leather armor, and the fact that they were armed.

"I assure you, we did not," Prentice answered the first overseer's accusation in an even tone. "It is a warrant from the duchess's own hand."

"No," the fat man insisted. His filthy shirt bulged open to the waist as he planted his feet. "You stole it or found it, and you think we're stupid!"

"I don't know," said the one behind holding the warrant. "It looks real to me. It's got a seal right there."

"And they don't look like they've just come off the chain," said the other one. "They've got shoes and shirts and all. And they got those colors. Those are Reacher colors, seen them everywhere since we crossed the passes in the mountains."

The fat overseer clearly did not want to be persuaded by his comrades' logic, but he couldn't fault it.

"You could send for the duchess's man, if you like," Prentice offered. "He will confirm the warrant and who we are. We arrived today and have just marched three days with the ducal household."

The fat man took back the warrant and gave it one last look over. He clearly could not read it. At last he handed it back to Prentice and, with a sneer, turned away, likely looking for someone on a chain he could use to vent his ill temper. The other two went with him.

"I'm not sure a piece of writing is much of a mark of authority if no bugger can read the damn thing," Turley observed.

"Indeed. Where's a friendly washerwoman when you need one?" Prentice joked.

He and Turley looked over the convicts for a moment more.

"No more use than we were," said Turley, arriving at the same obvious conclusion Prentice had. These convicts would be no better in a battlefield than any other group of men chained up and forced to fight.

"We'll probably march for Fallenhill in a day or two, and that's a three-day journey, so we've got less than a week to get them into shape."

"Oh, that much time? Well then, I needn't have worried. After all, it only takes a lifetime of training to make a knight. Most of them get their first blade to learn with before their sixth birthday. But if we have a few days short of a week, well then, you should have no trouble making soldiers out of them."

Prentice scowled at his friend's sarcasm, but he knew that he was right. Trying to command these convicts would be like trying to herd a swarm of rats—and likely just as dangerous. As the two of them made their way back to the willow grove, Prentice sank into his thoughts, trying to figure out any ways that he knew or could devise to make the convict rogues something more than animals for slaughter.

It was early twilight by the time they returned to the duchess's tents, and Turley slumped down beside a fire where a brace of fat hares turned slowly on a spit. Prentice went to a barrel and fetched them both tin cups of watered wine.

Turley watched the turning game and rubbed his stomach. "They look good."

The maid turning the spit gave him a cold look but said nothing. Prentice sat down and handed the second cup to Turley.

The chief steward arrived and seeing Prentice kicked his leg. "Where have you been? The duchess is looking for you!" He looked over the roasting rabbits and sniffed at the meat. "Not enough rosemary. I told you!" he said, then stalked off into the night.

"What is his name?" Prentice asked.

"Graycen, don't you know," Turley answered with mock sweetness in his voice. "A right ray of sunshine he is, too." He nodded to the maid at the spit. "I think they smell delicious!"

The young woman smiled, for a moment then looked back to the fire, likely unsure how to take a compliment from a convict.

Prentice levered himself upright and drained his cup. "Better go and see what is required of me," he said, dropping the empty tin cup on the ground in front of his friend.

"What do you expect me to do with this?" Turley asked indignantly, but Prentice was already walking away.

Prentice entered the duchess's tent and stood just inside the flap. Within, the duchess was seated in her chair while Sir Liam stood nearby. They were conversing quietly, and the duchess did not seem happy with the conversation. When she saw Prentice, she fixed him with a cold stare. Sir Liam noticed and he straightened, beaming a triumphant smile. Whatever was going on, Prentice knew it was not going to be good for him. He approached with his head down, the model of an obedient servant, or convict.

"Finally, he deigns to grace us with his presence," Sir Liam said. "You can see what I say, surely."

Duchess Amelia did not answer Sir Liam but gestured for him to be quiet. He bowed his head with exaggerated graciousness.

"Where have you been, Prentice?" she asked, and the tone of her voice revealed a barely restrained anger.

"I have been about Your Grace's business," Prentice replied.

Sir Liam strode toward him, giving him an appraising look. He glanced at the color ribbons tied to the front of Prentice's leather jack, and he flipped them dismissively with his gauntleted hand. "Looks to me as though you have been wasting your liege lady's money on fripperies!"

"Her Grace has instructed me to captain the rogues on the field during the campaign. It is only fitting that I do so wearing her colors." Prentice did not meet Sir Liam's eyes, but the knight grabbed him by the chin and tilted his face upward.

"You are a convict, less than Her Grace's dogs! The only color you get to wear is crimson—when you receive the lash."

"Enough, Sir Liam! I will conduct my own interview."

Sir Liam bowed again, but as he did so, he sneered at Prentice. Then he returned to Duchess Amelia's side.

"I have received unpleasant news today, convict Prentice," the duchess said. "Perhaps you might assist me with it."

"I will do as you will, Your Grace, as always."

Prentice kept his voice steady, but in his mind he was desperately searching to figure what accusation Sir Liam was bringing against him. It was clear the knight thought he had some damning secret to reveal, but what? Prentice had spent the day doing exactly what the duchess had instructed him to. Even the minor confrontation with the overseers had not breached the bounds of propriety. Had Sir Liam lied to her, invented something?

"How were you made a convict?" she asked.

With that question, Prentice guessed what the duchess must know, and his heart sank. Somehow Sir Liam had learned his past, and now the duchess knew. In spite of himself, Prentice smiled—a tight, wry smile that flashed across his lips before he could control it. Faced with forces beyond his control, what else was there to do? He straightened his shoulders and lifted his head to look the duchess and Sir Liam directly in the eyes.

"I was found guilty of heresy against the Church and the faith, Your Grace."

Sir Liam looked as if he might dance for glee hearing Prentice's statement, but the duchess only stared at him, her face like an ivory mask.

"Is that all?"

"That is all I was convicted of, yes."

"How dare you dissemble," Sir Liam said, pointing at Prentice. "Tell her everything. The whole foul truth!"

Prentice wanted to kill him, but before he could lose his temper, the duchess lost hers.

"Leave us, Sir Liam!" she all but shouted.

The knight was so shocked by the command that he did not at first respond. His mouth moved, but no words emerged.

Duchess Amelia did not give him time to find his voice. "Get out, sir, or you will quit my service by midnight. You'll be a hedge knight by dawn."

"Your Grace?"

"Get out!" she nearly screamed, and Sir Liam finally moved, scowling as he passed Prentice. He did not pause or bow on the tent's threshold.

When he was gone, Prentice remained stock still, not moving and not speaking.

"Tell me everything, convict. All of it."

Prentice could see that Amelia was tightly gripping the side of her chair, working to keep her temper.

"I was charged with heresy, witchcraft, and perfidy within the Church, Your Grace," he began, outlining the facts of a story he had worked hard to forget. Even though he had not spoken of it for years, the details were clear and fresh in his mind. "I was a squire of holy orders, studying at the academy in Ashfield. I was accused, and an inquisitorial court was convened. I was cleared of the charge of witchcraft, but the charges of heresy and perfidy were considered proven."

"Considered proven," Amelia repeated rhetorically. "You are careful not to admit any guilt, I see. What heresy were you charged with?"

"Does it matter?"

"Answer my questions or—"

"Or I'll be more damned than I already am?" Prentice knew it was a mistake to vent his anger in front of the duchess, but the comment came out before he could stop it.

She looked taken aback by his disrespect, but she still managed to keep her calm. "What was your heresy?"

"I was found with a copy of *Memories of Far Jerusalem* by the heretic Argensius."

Amelia shook her head, showing that she did not recognize the name of either book or author.

"He was a monk who lived some centuries ago," Prentice explained. "His book argued that since the holy land of Christ existed after the flood of Noah, then there must have been a second flood that obliterated all the lands of the Bright Age."

"And for this he was cast out of the faith?" asked the duchess, clearly trying to grasp the import of Prentice's words.

"No, Your Grace. For that he would only have been considered controversial. But he also believed and taught that the sacrist priesthood were not wholly ordained by God, were not the sole inheritors of the apostles' authority and that they were not necessary to the salvation of mankind. According to Argensius, any mortal man or woman, could be led to the Lord without the intervention of any other man or woman, even the Primarch or the Grand Sacrists of the College. And he claimed that no one possessed the power to put another out of God's kingdom but our Lord in heaven."

"Do you agree with this teaching?"

"I did."

"But you no longer do? Have you changed your mind?"

Prentice's eyes narrowed as he thought she was mocking him. This was the most painful part of him, and he resented the thought that she would make sport of it.

"I believed what seemed right in my heart, Your Grace," he said through gritted teeth. "I made no attempt to spread the teaching or undermine any others. I only pursued the faith I thought was true. When I was convicted, I was cast out of the Church for my refusal to recant. In the words of the sacrists, my salvation is utterly forfeit and only hell remains for me now. If Argensius was right, if God disagrees with the judgment of the Church fathers, He has not seen fit to speak on the subject."

Amelia paused, and for the first time since Prentice had entered the tent, she looked away from his face. It seemed she was considering his answers. Even angry, she had self-control and thoughtfulness. Prentice hated how admirable he found her. After eleven years of living like a dog and trying to think of himself as one, she kept making him want to do better.

"How were you found out?" she asked him.

"I fought a duel, Your Grace."

"A duel? How?"

"I fought a duel with a young knight named Sir Khalte, a wealthy man from Waverly, eldest son of a count and due to inherit the title. I won, and he..." Prentice paused at the difficult memory. He was surprised at how much shame he still felt for the duel that had happened over a decade ago. "He was humiliated, Your Grace. He lost his sword hand from an injury in the duel, and he couldn't face life like that. He killed himself."

"What has this to do with heresy?"

"Sir Khalte's younger brother, Whilte, was another student at Ashfield. He blamed me for his brother's death, which was not unreasonable, and he watched and waited for a chance of revenge. When he found Argensius's book in my cell, he informed the college synod. Charges were brought. Every one of Whilte's friends testified that I had proselytized them, trying to convert them to heresy. Sworn testimony from a dozen squires, each one the son of a noble father."

"And they all lied?" she asked.

"Every last man."

"You never proselytized?"

"No."

"When Sir Liam learned this today, there was talk of scars. The man who informed him said to confirm your identity by specific scars. Sir Liam wanted me to have you stripped. I told him that if I asked you directly, you would not lie to me. You have the virtue of honesty, at least."

"Bereft of all else, virtue is all a man has left, Your Grace."

Amelia nodded. It seemed the anger was leaving her. Prentice wondered if his story had touched her in some way or if she was merely reaching a decision.

"What are the scars?" she asked.

Prentice's wry smile reappeared. She knew most of it now, so there was no point trying to hide the rest. "After I was expelled from Ashfield, before I was transported, I was handed over to a sacrist inquisitor. For three days I was interrogated concerning the book. Who had given it to me? Where were they? How many were they?"

"What did you tell them?"

"That there was no one else. I found the book tucked away on a dusty shelf at Ashfield. My heresy was my own."

"And did he believe you?"

"It is not an inquisitor's job to believe, Your Grace. He must be certain. He only asked the same questions over and over while the interrogation became more severe."

"The scars? Show me."

Prentice sighed and then began to loosen the side laces on his jack. He pulled the stiff leather over his head and dropped it to the ground. He lifted his tunic and turned side-on to show the scars under his left arm; they were not the only ones, but they were distinctive.

"Hot irons, mostly," he said as Amelia crept closer to see the scars. Her face was filled with horror as she no doubt imagined the tools and wounds that had left the scars. "There was dripped boiling water once, and he had my legs beaten with sticks frequently. Oh, and he flayed two of my toes personally."

"Dear God!" Her hand came to her mouth. "How did you survive?"

"The crusade, Your Grace. On the third day, the crusade west across the mountains was declared. The Primarch announced that every prisoner in the Grand Kingdom should be transported to help break the heathen invaders from the Vec and thereby redeem their own souls. As simply as if he were a sculptor and I a piece of carved stone his client no longer required, the inquisitor stopped his work and sent for a healer. My wounds were treated, even healed with prayer, and I was sent to prison, to be transported to the Reach and the crusade that raised your husband to his dukedom."

"That's why you're still a convict," Amelia said, stepping back. "You're a heretic; you can't easily be released without dispensation from the Church."

Prentice nodded and lowered his tunic. Amelia returned to her chair.

"I believe your story, Prentice," she said thoughtfully. "But the truth of it still puts me into unwanted risk. My position is precarious enough without angering the Church fathers. And they will find out. Your accuser, Whilte, is in the prince's camp. It was he who shared your past with Sir Liam."

Prentice cursed inwardly.

"I cannot leave you in command of the rogues," she went on. "It is too great a risk. I will have to give their command to Sir Liam. You will serve as a sergeant or corporal under his banner. But I will watch, and if you serve as I have asked you, then I will speak for you to the Church at the end of this campaign. You have my word."

"Thank you, Your Grace." Prentice believed that she meant what she said but did not think it mattered. If Whilte was on this march, and already friends with Sir Liam, then the odds were excellent that Prentice would not survive to the end of the campaign, regardless of what the enemy did.

CHAPTER 23

When the duchess dismissed him, Prentice stopped just outside her tent. He half expected to find Sir Liam waiting for him, looking to gloat, but there was no one. The sun had set, and the stars were beginning to appear in the sky. To his left he could hear Turley's voice and glancing around the edge of the tent he saw his friend lying on the ground by the fire, propped up on one elbow. He was chatting with the maid and picking at a plate of roast hare. Prentice almost went to them, then realized that he did not want to face them—or, indeed, anybody.

Instead, he stalked away in the other direction, seeking solitude in the shadows under the willows. Twisting the cudgel in his grip, he tried to get his thoughts and feelings under control, but like an unbroken animal, they kept bucking and clashing inside him, turning him back upon himself.

Whilte?

After all these years, the bastard was back and making more trouble for Prentice. Was he not low enough? How much further did he have to fall? Or was it that he had a chance to rise again? Was even the sniff of relief in his torment enough to bring enemies back to harass him? Did fate loathe him that much? Or was it God who tormented him?

Pressing through the hanging tresses of the willow branches, he came to a small pond hidden in the middle of the grove. On this side, two large willows drooped over the pond while the rest of the water's surface was edged around with wild cattail reeds, taller than he was. The pond was still and muddy, buzzing with midges. There was a quiet privacy about the little body of water, and though he could still hear the sounds of the encampment not too far away, Prentice suddenly felt very alone.

As if the unexpected peace was unbearable, rage erupted inside him. He began to thrash the cudgel in the air, striking at the cattails and willow fronds, which simply turned aside inconsequentially. His strikes became wilder and angrier, turning his whole body with their force, until he lost his footing and slipped on the mud. Landing half on his side, he continued his raging for two or three more strokes, hammering the cudgel into the mud until at last he stopped.

In the dark he couldn't see himself, but he imagined he looked quite ridiculous, splattered with mud. He sat up for a long moment, listening to the sounds of the night insects over the water. A sliver of moon began to poke above the top of the reeds, and he saw its reflection on the water. It was a calm moment, but the more he tried to appreciate it, the more he felt the rage rise again inside him.

"Was it so evil, what I did?" he demanded of the air, though in his heart he knew that he was praying. It was not the first time he had muttered a private prayer since being sent over the mountains, but almost every time he had, this was the theme. What did God want of him?

"They're nobles," he said, and the bitterness in his voice was like poison on his tongue. "They kill each other every other day for any cause they can dream up. Then you let them go to your church, and the sacrists bless them and grant them absolution, and on it goes. What was so wrong with someone else getting that chance? Is it birth? You gave me a mean birth, and I was supposed to be thankful, tug my forelock, and let them ride over me and my family. Is that what you wanted?"

He stopped, as he always did. He was certain that whatever God thought of his troubles, He would remain silent, as He always had. Prentice truly believed in the heresy for which he was convicted. It could not be right to put something eternal, like the salvation of a soul, into the hands of fallible men, even sacrists. Yet the Church remained, the sacrists still absolved the corrupt, and Prentice was still an exiled heretic.

"Isn't that enough? Send me over here to fight their pointless wars and kill and die and go to hell for my sins! Did you have to send Whilte after me? Hound me with a petulant little child, worse than his brother?"

Finally, Prentice lapsed into silence, slumping down upon the mud, his arms resting on his knees and his head hanging down.

"Just do what you want," he whispered. "You will anyway!"

For a long while, Prentice sat in the quiet, head down. Then when he thought that it was probably time to return before someone accused him of attempting to flee, he looked up. The moonlight was brighter than before. The thin moon still barely reached above the rushes, but the pond water was almost silver with the light, and every tree and bush was lit from its reflections. Even if it had been a full moon, with the light of the ribbon across the night as well, it should not have been this bright. The sound of the insects had gone; the buzz of the midges and the chirrups of the crickets had stopped. The stillness pressed down like a tangible cloud.

There was movement on the other side of the pond, a rustling in the rushes. Prentice pushed himself onto his feet, crouching still to watch as the long fronds parted, and a lion's head pressed toward the water. It was a magnificent creature, with fur pale as snow in the moonlight and a vast mane that waved and shook about its head like a halo. It dipped its head to the water, and Prentice heard the lapping sound as the big tongue drew up the silvery liquid. Then it stopped and its ears pricked up. Prentice held his breath, keeping himself deathly still. Slowly, the noble beast raised its head, and its golden eyes looked straight at him.

Prentice swallowed, gripping the cudgel tight, and the lion held his gaze. At any moment, he expected the beast to attack, and he was not sure what he would do.

"Three times you will challenge me," said a voice that seemed to echo from all about him. "Three times, and then I will defeat you and give you victory."

Prentice gasped, disbelief forcing his held breath free in shock. The lion's mouth did not move, and he somehow knew it was not the lion itself that spoke but that the creature was like a herald, bringing a message for him to hear.

He had no thought to understand the words he heard, because before he could overcome the shock of seeing the lion and hearing the voice, another creature emerged from the rushes: an enormous serpent. It slithered and coiled out of the reeds and swept its body out into the water. Its scales were vibrantly multicolored, but its belly was gray, as though the beast was diseased, and its eyes glittered with menace.

The lion growled at the serpent as it coiled within itself over the pond's surface. The serpent's head was lost in the coils of its body for a moment, then it emerged again, seeming to open like the hood of a cobra. But instead of one hood of flesh, six separate necks arose, all but one ending in the head of a different animal: an insect, with eyes like cut crystals; a mighty horned bull; an elk with horns broad and tangled like the branches of a tree; a dragon-like serpent's head; and finally a wolf, black in the silver light. This last one was exactly like the head of the beast Prentice and Turley had faced in the flight through the village.

The sixth neck was empty and looked as if whatever had grown there had been severed or torn away. The monster's heads all looked down upon the lion and uttered their cries —hissing, barking, wailing, and howling from five mouths as one terrible, mingled chorus. The lion roared a challenge in response, but it seemed so much smaller now that the five-headed monster reared above it.

Then the serpent struck, the wolf head first and then each of the others, and the lion fought with them. The serpent tried to coil its body about the lion, but it was thrown back as the lion pounced, driving it back into the water. As the two beasts thrashed the shallow pond to foam, Prentice bolted away through the willows, the animal cries of battle hounding him as he fled. He did not think they were after him specifically, but the conflict felt as if it was on his heels continually until he burst out of the grove and into the firelight of the encampment. As soon as he did, the sound ceased, and the suddenness of it made him stop dead. He turned and looked behind him, but the willows were silent as the grave and black as a starless sky. For a long while he gasped for breath and tried to figure for himself what had just happened. He was still standing there when Turley found him.

"There you are, boss," Turley said. "Been looking for you. Hare's all gone, but I saved you some."

"What?" Prentice asked like a man emerging from a trance.

"I saved you some roast."

"No, you called me boss. Don't do that. Sir Liam is in charge of the rogues foot now."

"Truly?" Turley's face was equal parts puzzlement and disgust at this turn of events. "Why?"

"Politics."

"Well, that's a bastard's dog's leavings and no mistake. I'll bet you're not happy!"

"I..." Prentice thought about it for a breath. "I don't know what I am."

He walked off and Turley followed him with a shrug, picking at the plate of meat he had saved for his friend.

CHAPTER 24

When the next day dawned, Prentice was tired and sore.

Uncomfortable sleep was nothing new to him, but the strange vision of the lion and the many-headed serpent had troubled his thoughts throughout the night so that he hardly slept. He wondered if perhaps something strange, perhaps an unknown vapor in the pond water or the trees, which might have caused him to see a false vision, such as opium might cause, but that did not seem true to the experience. The creatures had been truly there, he was sure of it, but that thought only led to new, frightening questions.

In the end he rose before dawn and sat with his back against a cart wheel, staring at the embers of the night's fire. Later, as the sun rose, he did not move, but let the business of the day turn about him.

Turley found him sitting there after breakfast. "Haloo," he said, still chewing on a piece of black bread. "You still here? You know we have the run of the camp?" He sat next to Prentice and held out a chunk of the bread he was gnawing on.

Prentice looked at it and then took it. It was fresher than he expected. He nodded his thanks as he chewed.

"Good, huh?" Turley observed. "There's a baker has a whole set of tin ovens he's half buried in the sand but can dig up and bring on the march. I swear this place is as daft as you can imagine. Who knew this was what a war was like?"

"This isn't a war," Prentice said through his mouthful of bread. "It's a bloody carnival! How well do you think these people will cope with one of those wolf things running through here?"

"Now there's a grim thought." Turley looked about, likely imagining the creature rampaging as it had through the village. "Still, we got a lot more than two knights with us this time."

"What if they have more than one beast?" Prentice remembered his vision, the five different beast heads falling upon the lion and the wild violence of the conflict, savage and merciless. "And even if that was the only one, don't forget that we still have those spearmen to face."

"Sure, the knights will do that at least, won't they?"

"Usual battlefield tactic is to march the rogues foot at the enemy, with militia on either side of us to keep us from trying to flee. And once we've got them bogged down, the knights charge the flank and hope to break the enemy before we're all chewed up."

"What? That's it?" Turley said.

"Mostly, though if the other side has knights of their own, they start trying to chase each other down. A captured knight can be ransomed back to his family."

"Ah, there's silver in it? Makes some sense. Still, if they just want to fight each other, why do they need us? Why the rogues at all? It must be a devil to control men on the field who don't even want to be there."

Prentice nodded. "Mostly it's to disrupt anything else the enemy might bring," he explained. "A charge of footmen can distract archers or crossbowmen if the enemy has them. Or ballistae and catapults."

"Ballis... what?"

"War engines. They fling stones and spears and other savage things. The big mass of rogues foot rushing forward at the center of the field tends to draw the shooters' attention. It keeps the knights safe."

"But again, if the knights are the point, why not save your arrows or stones or whatever? Why waste them on men so mean that no one cares if they live or die?"

"Because you can't ransom a dead knight. Look, Turley, don't try to have it make sense because it doesn't. It's war— war the way they were taught to fight it by their fathers, and their fathers' fathers, and their fathers' fathers' fathers. It hasn't changed in hundreds of years, and they won't change it to keep some worthless convicts alive. It's like a game to them."

Turley shook his head.

"In one battle during the crusade," Prentice went on, remembering a particular example, "the crossbow militia were forbidden from shooting at any mounted man."

"What?"

"It's true, I swear. A baronet from Ongatta had a company of crossbowmen. They were well equipped and hard drilled, so effective they could break a horse charge, even at less than fifty yards. But the other knights got so worried that possible ransoms were being lost that the baronet's men were ordered never to shoot any group of men with horsemen in it, for fear of killing a man who could be ransomed if captured."

"Bloody madness!"

"War."

They sat awhile more in the early morning sunshine until the sound of approaching hoof falls disturbed them and Sir Liam walked up to them on his horse. This mount was his riding horse, a less temperamental beast, more suitable for long marches. His warhorse would be kept somewhere to itself, only released for the day of battle.

Sir Liam's hair was combed, and his armor shone in the sunlight. He wore a clean surcoat in his own colors, sky blue and red. Every part of his equipment flashed clean and polished; a squire must have worked through the night to ready it all. Had he lost a squire or page when the duchess's barge was ambushed? If so, who took the role now? On the back of the horse's saddle were what looked like lengths of hempen rope rolled in neat bundles. Their mundane appearance seemed odd against all the finery.

"On your feet, convicts," Sir Liam ordered, and they stood slowly. "Follow me."

He geed his horse, and they were forced to jog behind him to keep up. He led them to the paddock where the other convicts were being kept.

When they reached the field, Prentice and Turley stopped, but Sir Liam rode his horse around the crowd of chained men, bringing it close and forcing the convicts to pull back or be trampled. Most jumped to their feet, causing the chains between them to ring and jangle. Some fell over others to get away, and the knight soon had the entire contingent unsettled and angry. With a satisfied look on his face, he brought his mare back around to stand in front of Prentice and Turley, confident every eye was on him.

"I am Sir Liam of Dweltford, Knight Captain of the Duchy of the Western Reach," he announced grandly, standing in the saddle. "I am your commander, which gives me power of life and death over every last one of you."

The convicts stared back at him with sullen eyes. They were dirty, clearly tired and filled with bitter resentment, but none of these things seemed to trouble Sir Liam. If anything, the sight of them seemed to cheer him further.

"You are scum!" he continued. "You are failures as men, and you deserve your lot. But merciful God and glorious

Prince Mercad have deigned to give you a magnificent opportunity. A glorious opportunity! A chance to redeem yourselves and your souls."

"I seem to remember this speech," Prentice muttered quietly.

Turley nodded surreptitiously. "A lot more 'glorious' in it than last time."

Sir Liam continued, sweeping his arm around to point at Prentice and Turley. "You will fight for the Grand Kingdom, and these two men have been chosen by Her Grace, the Duchess Amelia, to show you how to do it. Do not fear, for they are convicts like you. They understand your meanness and will give you the benefits of their wisdom. I have seen them in battle, and I assure you they are as fine as any convicts I have ever laid eyes upon. They will instruct you. My only purpose here today will be to see that they do their work properly."

"You bastard," Prentice whispered. He could see where Sir Liam was leading and could guess what would come next. He wanted to kill the man.

Sir Liam turned his horse about to face Prentice. "You will teach them to stand in ranks, just like you showed the other convicts on the day Sir Dav died." His mouth twisted into a mocking smile, and his voice suddenly lifted to a shout. "And if you fail, you will be punished!"

Turley looked askance at his friend, but Prentice's eyes were fixed on Sir Liam. After a long moment, Prentice hefted his cudgel and walked toward the convicts. Turley followed until they were both a few paces in front of the manacled men.

"You're going to form lines," Prentice bellowed. He waved his cudgel back and forth, indicating a line in front of them. "Three chains across, here, all standing next to each other. Behind them the next three and so on, until you form a rectangle. One solid mass."

The convicts only watched him dully, not moving. Their faces had no expression. Prentice looked about him for a moment, noticing the dozen overseers that stood by, watching. They were more curious than their disinterested charges, but there was no chance they would actually help him. Odds were that they had no more idea of how to lead convicts to battle than the convicts themselves.

He nodded to Turley, and the two of them approached the first chain of thirty men.

"Up," Prentice ordered. "Stand up and form that line."

The convicts were slow and resistant, but by threatening with their cudgels and applying the occasional light whack, they managed to get the first chain to stand in a rough line. Then they left them and went back for the next chain. This group was more intractable, slower to move and more willing to take a hit. Prentice could see they were being deliberately difficult, and he looked up at Sir Liam, who sat his horse and watched imperiously. Most of the group was finally standing when he saw out of the corner of his eye that a number of the men in the first line had sat down.

Before he could do anything about it, Sir Liam's voice rang out. "You have failed, Prentice!" he announced. "Punishment must ensue. Overseers!"

The overseers started at hearing themselves summoned, and it took them a moment to respond. Soon enough they presented themselves before Sir Liam's horse.

"These men have failed. Punish them!" Liam reached behind himself and grabbed the ropes from his saddle, tossing them to the overseers. They unwrapped the bundles to find them already tied into narrow nooses, of the sort used to restrain prisoners, especially during a flogging.

Prentice sighed and his shoulders sagged as the overseers rushed over and seized him. He let them disarm him and put his hands through the rope loops. Two of them grabbed Turley, who resisted at first, only to earn himself a punch in the belly. His new armor took the brunt, but he clearly got the message.

The two of them were dragged in front of Sir Liam. "You think you are good enough to wear the duchy's colors? If so, then you must accept the responsibility." To the overseers, he said, "Strip them of those ridiculous shirts and give them fifty lashes each."

The leather jacks and their tunics were stripped, and there was a hiss of collective breath from the overseers nearest Prentice. They'd seen his scars. But if Sir Liam heard, he did not respond. The ropes were used to hold Prentice and Turley in place, a man on each cord forcing their arms apart. The other overseers uncoiled their whips and took up position. Turley tried to struggle once more, but with his arms pulled taut, he risked dislocating his joints if he struggled much more.

The whips cracked and the fifty lashes fell. Neither man called out in pain, but both grimaced and winced and hissed. The whips were of leather and not finely made, more flat than woven. Nonetheless, every few strokes drew blood, and by the end of the fifty, a thin sheen of sweat and gore was running down their backs.

"Good," Sir Liam said. "I hope you have learned your lesson."

The overseers released the ropes, and Prentice bent to recover his tunic and armor.

"Uh-uh!" Sir Liam said. "You may have those tunics back, of course; they were a gift from Her Grace. But if you choose to pick up that armor again, then you will have to show yourselves worthy. You'll have to get these dogs into ranks."

Turley paused, but Prentice took the armor without hesitation. He pulled his tunic over his head easily enough, in spite of the pain, though his hands fumbled with the laces of his armor when he moved to tie it over the top. Eventually he was done and nodded to Turley, who had also managed to shrug himself painfully into the leather, though he did not bother to lace it up.

They moved back to the convicts and tried again to get them in lines. This time the prisoners did not even bother to cooperate a little but sat down and resisted from the start. When threatened with the cudgel, they only smirked, and if Prentice made to strike, they pulled back out of the way but did not obey. They were broken men with nothing to look forward to; the humiliation of two other convicts was as good a sport as any they might have. Even though they had no idea what the knight's complaint against Prentice and Turley was, the two of them were cleaner and better dressed than any other convicts, so the group probably thought they needed to be taken down a peg or two.

Soon enough Sir Liam called a stop once more. "You have failed again!" he announced.

This time the overseers did not need orders. They quickly grabbed hold of Prentice and Turley, roped their wrists, and stripped them to the waist again.

"Another fifty. Lay on," Sir Liam ordered, and the flogging began again.

This time Turley gasped with the pain, and toward the end he was whimpering with some tears running down his face. He fell on his knees when the overseers released him. Prentice clenched his teeth and tried to remain silent, but by the fifteenth stroke he was grunting with pain after every impact. The overseers released his wrists, and he stumbled as he tried to keep his balance. He just managed to stand. Above him Sir Liam smiled condescendingly.

Turley looked at Prentice. There was pain in his eyes, and Prentice knew the meaning of the look. He knew that his friend wanted to be loyal, but Prentice shook his head. Turley nodded and took up his linen tunic, leaving the leather jack and the cudgel behind on the ground. He cried out once as he pulled the tunic back on, and the cloth stained quickly with blood.

Prentice struggled into his own tunic and then reached down awkwardly to get his leather. Sir Liam watched him closely and then sat back in surprise.

"Have you not learned your lesson yet, cur? Unbelievable."

Prentice glared at him while he pushed his arms into the armor. He gingerly let the jack settle on his shoulders but left the side laces untied. He knelt to pick up the cudgel and slowly walked back to the convicts.

This time many stood to get out of his way, but they more stared with disbelief or disdain than amusement. Prentice waved the cudgel weakly, pointing where they should go, but he made no pretense of threatening them with it. The convicts shuffled around him, but only a few moved off, and the chain soon stopped them.

"Why are you doing this, fool?" one old man hissed at him. "Are you trying to kill yourself?"

Prentice turned to look at him. One of the overseers' strikes had flown high before, and the whip had struck around Prentice's head. The lash had missed his eye, but the skin on the side of his face was bruised and swelling. He fixed the old man with a cold glare.

"If he wanted me dead, he could draw that longsword and take my head any time he wanted. All he wants is the only thing he can't take: my submission. I won't let him."

"He'll kill you anyway!" said another convict.

"Maybe," Prentice admitted. "But he will not make me submit."

"We do not have time for you to try persuasion on them," Sir Liam called loudly. He was no longer smiling. "Another fifty!"

The overseers pushed their way among the convicts and marched Prentice out. When they stripped him this time, he fell to his knees, and though they lifted him again by the wrist ropes, it took a long time for him to get his feet back under him. The skin on his back was ripped raw and nearly flayed in places. Many of the convicts turned away, and a grumbling arose among them. The overseers looked at them, nervous expressions on their faces. The one with the whip looked back to Sir Liam.

"No mercy for dogs too dull-witted to learn," he shouted at them. "Lay on. Fifty!"

The whip lashed again, and Prentice fell to his knees after the first three. The ropes kept him from falling flat, but the overseers left him on his knees until the fifty were done. The blood flowed down his back, and the strike of the lash sprayed fine droplets on the overseers, on Sir Liam, and on Turley, who stood by where he had been released from the previous flogging.

When they were finished, one of the overseers released Prentice's wrists, while another threw his tunic at him. His eyes could barely focus, and there were more bruises on his face.

Sir Liam regarded him disdainfully and then stood once more in the stirrups. "I hope this lesson has been well learned!" he shouted. "You are less than dogs to me, and your only salvation will be purchased with your deaths. You will march, you will fight, and you—"

He was interrupted by a sound from the prisoners, who were watching Prentice. Sir Liam looked down. On his hands and knees, Prentice was making his way over to where the overseers had cast away his armor. Like a baby unsure of its movements, he crawled to the jack and began to drag it onto himself. Sir Liam's face twisted, and he walked his horse over so that he was beside Prentice.

Prentice's breath was low and ragged, and he grunted with every movement, but he gradually pushed one arm into the jack. He refused to give in.

"Stop!" Sir Liam ordered.

But Prentice ignored him. He kept pushing feebly at the leather.

"Stop!" Liam swung out of the saddle and kicked the armor out of Prentice's hands. "Stop, scum!" he shouted, leaning down until his face was mere inches from Prentice's. "Don't you see? You can't have it. You're not worthy! You're a mangy dog, and you're going to die. She won't save you again. Not this time!"

He stood back and drew his sword. As he did so, the crowd of convicts made an angry noise, like the snarl of a wild animal. The sound caught Sir Liam's attention, and the overseers stepped back nervously. The convicts were clearly on the verge of rebellion. The knight's sword hung loosely in his grip, and his face showed indecision and, for the first time that morning, genuine uncertainty.

Prentice half smiled in spite of the pain. He tried to lift his head, but his muscles refused to work. "Even a cur can turn and bite you," he slurred, but he knew that Sir Liam would not understand him. The knight looked down on him, and that was all he knew as the darkness closed in and he passed out.

CHAPTER 25

P rentice came to, lying face down somewhere dark and cool. He lifted his head to see where he was and immediately regretted it. Pain lit up his skull like a fire, and he coughed and retched momentarily.

"Uh-uh," came Turley's voice from behind him. "You aren't ready to move yet! Let the unction do its work."

Prentice tried to turn his head and realized he was lying on a sleeping mat somewhere. He could see the edge of a tent wall where it met grass. Outside it was still daylight. He blinked and realized the pain he felt was mostly in his head. His back felt strangely numb. He tried to flex his shoulders, but a hand gently pushed him down onto the mat.

"Lie still, will you?"

"Where am I?" he asked, but did not move his head anymore to look. "What happened?"

Turley moved up beside him, kneeling on the ground and leaning in toward his face. "What do you remember?"

"I remember Sir Liam," Prentice began, then he coughed again. Turley offered him a wooden cup, and he awkwardly took the lip in his mouth and sucked some of the liquid. It was cool but bitter, and he suspected it was some tea of sorts, made from herbs. "I remember Sir Liam trying to kill me."

"You did a fair job of that yourself. A hundred and fifty lashes, and still trying to resist. You're a bloody fool, you are, and no mistake!"

"You took a hundred, as I recall."

"Sure, I did, just for loyalty's sake! Besides, you usually have a smarter plan than walking into a flogging three times in a row."

"Four, if I hadn't passed out," Prentice said with a smile. He closed his eyes and lowered his head. "Where are we?"

"An apothecary's tent. I found one and had your wounded bones dragged here."

"I'm impressed you found one that would treat a convict." Prentice lay quietly for a moment before a further thought opened his eyes. "How are you paying an apothecary?"

"I'm not," Turley said, and Prentice could hear the smug tone in his voice. "The duchess is."

"The duchess?"

"Through the magic of the warrant!" Turley waved the rolled page in front of Prentice's face.

Prentice snorted a half laugh and then winced at the pain. "You were lucky to find one that could read."

"I'll have you know I could read very well before my tenth birthday," came a woman's voice from somewhere behind him. "And recite the line of kings going back to Rapton the First and the founding of the Kingdom!"

"My apologies, lady," Prentice muttered painfully into the mat. "Knowing my friend here, I would have expected him to find a mountebank selling magic mud from the watery grave of St Eustace."

"Here, that's enough of that talk," Turley protested. "I'd be insulted if it weren't for the fact that I already tried that. The huckster said he was out of magic mud, but he had six of the Lord's finger bones on a string. Said it would cure any intimate ailments, so I naturally bought his whole stock!"

Prentice laughed and coughed. Turley was a roguish, belligerent man for the most part, always ready to challenge authority or start a fight, but he was a loyal friend and could find a joke in almost any situation. Prentice felt something being peeled from his back and was struck again by how little pain he felt.

"Just changing your poultice," said the apothecary. Though he could not see her, Prentice got the impression by her voice that she was an older woman, and she seemed to have a caring nature.

"It's doing remarkable work," he told her. "I can hardly feel any pain at all."

"Oh, that's not the poultice, dearie. That's the opium."

Prentice sniffed and realized he could smell an acrid smoke in the air. Turning his head, he saw a small brass brazier with a little black lump smoldering next to him. He took a deep inhale.

"Enjoy it while it lasts," she said. "'Cause that's all you're getting. I don't want no poppy fiends filching my stock. You are getting better, though. The poultices are working well."

"Getting better," Turley said with a snort. "His back looks like a lump of raw meat."

"Which is still better than when you brought him, isn't it?"

"Well, that is true enough."

"Right, that poultice won't need changing again for some time. I'll leave you two together." Prentice heard her stand and gather what sounded like metal bowls. As she left, she paused on the threshold of the tent. "And Master Turley, if you need help with those intimate problems, I'm quite happy to take a look!"

"I'll be sure to ask your help," said Turley. Prentice could imagine the smile he gave her.

"Is there any woman you wouldn't bed?" he asked, but Turley did not answer.

Outside the tent he heard the sounds of the encampment. They hadn't marched yet, he guessed. He wondered how long the prince would encamp before he thought to get to the business of actually lifting the siege. How many people were fighting and dying in defense of Fallenhill while the knights waited here only three days' march away?

"What happened?" he asked Turley. "Why didn't Liam kill me?" He remembered how furious he'd felt at the knight's petty but savage game. It was like the fury he'd felt the previous night, before he'd seen the vision.

"They'd have torn him apart," Turley answered. Prentice twisted his head to look into his friend's somber face. "A man on a chain is pretty much bound in place, but five hundred of them's another story. I don't think Sir Liam really thought of that. The overseers looked like they might crap themselves."

"A convict riot's not a pretty thing," said Prentice. "There hasn't been a big one in our lifetime, but I'd bet the average overseer hears stories about them every other day of his life. So, he just left me?"

"Oh, he spat on you for good measure, but he hopped back on his horse and rode off. I don't think he feared for his life, but maybe he didn't want to be present if there really was a riot. Then it'd be on his head."

"Coward."

"Whatever way he was thinking, all that matters is he left. Then the overseers didn't want any riot either, so they just left us and stood off to the side. After that, no one knew exactly what to do."

"You didn't carry me here by yourself?"

"Course not! I could barely bloody stand. I fished that warrant of yours out of your belt and got two pages to bring a cart. They wheeled you here, and the apothecary's been doing her work on you since."

"What about you?"

"Well, she saw to us both at first," Turley admitted. "I come back a lot quicker on account of my superior constitution and strength of character."

"That and the fifty fewer lashes."

"Eh, like that extra fifty made any difference on your scarred flesh."

Prentice knew his friend was being sarcastic. He closed his eyes and let the opiate smoke ease his aches. "Thank you, friend," he said, and faded into sleep.

When he woke, the air was clearer and the tent dark. He could hear the crackle of campfires and the quiet movements of the encampment asleep. He lifted his head to look around and found that the pain had receded from his skull, but he could now feel the stiffness and soreness of his flesh, especially on his back. Gritting his teeth, he pushed himself up from the mat and delicately peeled the poultice from his back. The skin was tender as the now-dry cloth came away, but the savage agony of the lash strokes was gone.

Prentice dropped the poultice and felt his way out of the dark tent. Pushing through the flap, he found himself in the back of a stall, an awning fronted by a wooden table with crates and chests stacked about. A candle burned low on the table next to a brass scale and a set of small weights. He blinked; after the dark of the tent, even the night seemed surprisingly bright.

"How do you feel?" the apothecary asked, and he turned quickly to see her seated on a box and leaning back on a barrel. She had crinkly hair that was impossibly fair, not quite white but like sun-bleached straw. It was loose and flared around her face like a cloud, reminding him of the white lion's mane, though it was neither as thick nor as bright.

"I feel sore," he said, then realized it would be churlish to leave it at that. "But better than I have any right to feel. How long have I...?"

"Since this morning," she said. "About twelve or fourteen hours of the candle."

Prentice smiled, eyes wide. "I should not be so well so soon! Your medicines are a marvel."

"An expensive marvel. I hope your letter is worthy and not a lie."

"It's worthy. You could send to the duchess's household, have it confirmed."

"I'll go myself soon enough," she said. "In the morning. I didn't want to leave you in my tent." She spoke with an unemotional tone, and in the dark, Prentice could not read her eyes or her expression. He could not tell if she feared to leave him for his sake or because he might steal from her. He decided to opt for the first.

"You are kind to show me such care."

"Care is the cause of an apothecary." She sighed heavily and stood. "Come now, turn around and show me how things fare."

Prentice turned about, and she took the candle from the table, it close to his back. Her small fingers pressed at the skin carefully in a number of places.

"How much pain do you feel?"

"Much less," he said.

"Wait here."

Prentice did as she asked while she walked around some of the crates. He looked over his shoulder but could not see what she was doing until she came back carrying a small bucket. She pushed his head forward and used a rag to sponge off the remnants of the poultice's herbs. The cool water felt fresh, and her touch was careful and delicate.

"I can see by your scars that you've been through this kind of thing before. And you're not as dirty as most convicts I've ever seen," she said. "That should work in your favor."

"I had a good bath only a few days past."

"Lucky you. You'll do well to keep this skin protected and washed every day, even twice a day if you can."

"With an army on the march?" he asked, and his tone revealed what he thought of that advice.

"Do whatever you can," she said and finished her cleaning. She put the bucket down and fetched his tunic from where it lay on a nearby chest. She walked in front of him and handed it back. "That's yours."

Prentice took the shirt. It was hard to tell in the dark, but it seemed that the shirt had been washed. It felt clean in his hands. He thought about putting it on but decided to leave his skin open to the cool air as long as he could. He noticed the apothecary looking at him, like she was trying to see something in his face.

"That one who brought you. Turley, is it?" she asked.

"That's his name."

"He's a charming rogue, and quite the big man."

Prentice nodded. There was no point arguing with the obvious truth.

"You're a big man too. And strong."

"Thank you," he said, but he sensed from her tone that she was not giving him a compliment.

"He told me what happened, or at least he told me a story. It was hard to believe. Did you really do it?"

"Yes." Prentice nodded.

The apothecary lifted the candle between them, using its light to look him in the eye. "That strength of yours has led to pride. They don't want you to have that pride. They'll beat you every time they see it in you. If you want to survive as a convict, you'll give that folly up."

Prentice pushed the candle away, shadowing their faces once more. "I've been a convict eleven years now," he told her. "I've survived long enough. If I don't take back my pride for myself, then what is survival worth?"

"The sacrists teach that humility is the path to godliness."

"Mercy as well, but I see precious little of that, present company excepted."

The apothecary nodded, unable to refute his point. She looked down at the ground a moment and then stepped back past him to her seat on the crate. "I suppose I don't like the thought that all my good work might just go to waste tomorrow because you can't or won't bend your knee to shirk a beating."

"Good woman, I have bent my knee every day since they transported me. I am not afraid to bow, but just because they push my head down to eat the dirt doesn't mean I have to chew."

"Well, take this." The apothecary threw a small leather pouch at him. "Chew on those."

Inside the pouch were small lumps of something hard and dark.

"It's myrtle and willow leaf in plant gum," she explained. "It'll help with the pain."

He nodded and tugged his forelock to her. Then he slipped out of the candlelight and went looking for his way back to the willow grove and the duchess's household.

CHAPTER 26

The camp broke the next morning, just after dawn. Heralds rode through on ponies and announced the march, taking special time to read the list of the order of the march—which knights were to have the privilege of riding in the van, which knights in the prince's company, and so forth. The camp's level of activity increased so that like busy termites, endless streams of marshals, pages, squires, stewards, and maids rushed about preparing, packing and stowing the camp.

For the convicts, it was a simple time. They had no equipment to pack or stow and were not even responsible for feeding themselves, so that after they had each eaten a bowl of grains boiled in water, they were left to themselves to wait on the progress of the line, consigned as they were to march at the rear.

Prentice had managed some hours of uncomfortable sleep, and he was stiff with ache when he woke. He started chewing one of the apothecary's gum lumps and tracked down Turley, waking him. Turley still had their ironbound cudgels, but Sir Liam had apparently taken Prentice's armor jacket with him and had it burned.

"I would not want to wear it, anyway. Not feeling like this," Prentice said.

Turley agreed. He had used his jack as a pillow and did not put it on when he rose. Instead, he gave it to the maid who had cooked the hares and asked her to stow it for him. She rolled her eyes but took it for him anyway.

After they had found a small bit of breakfast, Prentice led the way back to the convicts' field.

"We not going to march with the duchess like before?" Turley asked.

"I want to stay out of that bastard Liam's line of sight!"

"Aye, I suppose, but down with them we're out of sight of the duchess's benevolent grace as well. Ain't nothing to protect us back there. Or have you forgotten yesterday?"

"No, I haven't forgotten," Prentice said bitterly, biting down and spitting out part of the gum lump he was chewing.

When they reached the convicts, the twelve overseers were ranging about, whips in their hands. One of them noticed Prentice and Turley, and the surprise on his face was obvious. Like as not, they hadn't expected him to live through the night, let alone to be walking about. The dozen men conferred among themselves in small groups, seeming unsure how to treat these two convicts who had pretensions that such a savage flogging could not crush. The short, fat overseer strode toward them, his greasy black hair and beard already damp with sweat, even at this early hour. Prentice had no idea how the man would survive several days' march.

"All right, duchess' men," he said, and he slapped his whip against his thigh as he spoke. "What happens now?"

"What happens?" Prentice asked. "I don't understand."

"Well, after yesterday..." It was clear the man was wary and uncertain how to treat these two special convicts.

"Sir Liam said we were to act as corporals over these men, didn't he?" Prentice said.

The overseer nodded.

"Did he take back the order?"

"No."

"So, there it is."

"But we gave you a beating."

"We can't be the first convicts you've ever flogged," Prentice said, as if they were two merchants discussing the business of the day.

"Well, no..."

"Then I think we should do as we've been told by our betters, don't you?"

"All right, but what's this 'corporals' mean? I ain't taking no orders from you, duchess's man or no!"

"Of course not," Prentice agreed solemnly. "You're a free man. Not even the duchess can give me the right to give you orders. That's King's Law."

"Right!" The overseer nodded vehemently, and Prentice had to work to keep himself from smiling. He doubted the man knew one word of the King's Law, but as long as it worked in the overseer's favor, Prentice expected the man would just agree.

"We will order the ranks for battle," Prentice continued, using a carefully neutral tone. "Your job is to keep the convicts from escaping on the march or in camp. There's no reason our two roles should ever conflict, goodman...?"

Prentice waited for the overseer to give his name.

"Tuke. Overseer Tuke!" The man nodded purposefully. "Good. That's good. Well then, get to it, whatever it is you come to do." He went back to his compatriots, and the rest of them listened while Tuke relayed the situation, no doubt taking a good deal of credit for the thinking. The others looked from their leader to Prentice and Turley a few times, and one or two appeared ready to maybe make an argument of it, but Tuke browbeat them into submission.

"That was cleverly done," Turley said.

"He's not that much different from Druce," Prentice said. "They just want peace and ease. If they were ambitious men, they'd have found another type of work."

Turley snorted and followed Prentice as he walked to the waiting convicts. From their faces it was clear they were as surprised to see Prentice and Turley again as the overseers were. They watched the two approaching men with sullen curiosity. Prentice planted his feet in front of them and let them all look at him while he scanned the group.

Some of them won't even survive the march, he thought. Those ones were easy to pick out—men who were thin and old, their skin already gray and sickly from the hard journey over the mountains. Then there was the coming battle. Prentice studied their faces and tried to imagine how he could tell who would survive and who would not. There was no way to know. Some would live and some would die.

"What now?" whispered Turley.

"A speech seems traditional," Prentice answered half-heartedly, though he hated the notion of trying to rouse the enthusiasm of these broken men. The idea just seemed cruel.

"Well, they've always worked so well in the past," Turley said, echoing the bitterness that Prentice felt. The image of Sir Liam standing in his stirrups and trying to inspire them with his blend of pointless glory and spiteful disdain sat sourly in Prentice's thoughts.

"Perhaps just something practical to start," Prentice muttered, head down, then he looked up and scanned the chained crowd once more. "Any moment now, we'll get the order to march!" he shouted. "No one's going to stop for our convenience, so unless you like it running down your leg while we're walking, I suggest you dig yourselves holes and get it all out of you now."

The convicts seemed a little confused.

"You're ordering us to take a piss?" one shouted back.

"And a crap, if you need it!"

They looked at each other. Some shuffled in place, but none moved. They seemed surprised by such a basic instruction.

Prentice stared at them for a long while and then made a show of shrugging. "Well, it's up to you." He turned away.

From somewhere in the crowd, another voice shouted at him. "So, what, they beat you senseless and now you're in charge? What, do they pick 'em for stupidity in the Reach?"

There was a chuckle among the convicts, and Turley glared at them. For a minute it looked as if the big man might wade into the crowd and try to find the raw wit who made the joke, but that was a fool's errand.

Prentice had a different approach.

"That's right," he said loudly. He leaned on his cudgel like a walking cane. "Any time one of you thinks he might like to move up in this world, you know what you have to do. The overseers are here. Just ask for your hundred and fifty lashes and you can have my job!"

Several of them laughed at that.

"I'm in charge because the Prince of Rhales gave you to the Duchess of the Western Reach, and she decided to put a cold-hearted bastard in command over you. You met him yesterday, the noble man on the horse with all the talk of glory. And finally, she asked me to help to keep you all alive. When you don't like the orders I give you, do feel free to take your complaints to him."

Prentice walked into the crowd, and several of the convicts stood to make way for him as he spoke.

"There's a whole army of people around you—most of them with swords and maces and picks and lances—who think you're nothing more than an ugly pile of horse dung, and as far as they are concerned, I'm just the crowning turd on the top of the pile. So laugh at me if you like. Make trouble. Turley and I have seen it all and done most of it ourselves."

Prentice glanced at Turley, who made a show of nodding his agreement. "But all that means is that Sir Liam has to make more visits here to look after us, and you know that he won't just stop with me next time."

Several of the older men in the crowd muttered at that comment. Yesterday's beatings had been diverting, but they knew a show like that could easily spill violence over all their heads. The crowd that had threatened to rebel against one knight and a handful of overseers would quickly crumble against twenty or thirty men on horseback.

"The duchess has had a touch of madness and developed a soft spot for her rogues foot, which is you and me. Her knights and her captains, just like the prince, are like little boys in the street; they're happy to throw turds like you and me at their enemies in the hope that something sticks. But the duchess is a girl at heart. She sees turds and wants to think of manure, of growing flowers, of happy, pretty things."

Prentice stopped and watched. He could see that he had their attention. That they were trying to understand his point. It was the most he could hope for. Even Turley was hanging on his every word.

"So you can make your choice now, because at the end of this march we are going to be thrown into a battle by little boys who won't care as we fall under their enemies' feet and get trampled to death. I'm here from the only person who gives a damn whether or not something different happens, and it's my job to see that something different does. Turley and I are going to do everything we can to give you a better chance of living through that battle. It's a piss-poor chance, but it's a whole hell of a lot more than the knights and princes want you to have. It's your choice!"

He declared the last words and let them hang in the air before he turned and walked back out of the crowd, stepping over the chains.

"And like I said," he finished off as he walked, "the order will be coming soon, so if you need it, now's the time to dig a hole and do whatever you have to."

He tried not to look, but out of the corner of his eye he could see some of the men in the crowd start to kick divots in the sand and drop their trousers if they had them. Turley followed him out, and soon they stood once more on the little sand rise where they had both been flogged bloody the day before. They watched five hundred men relieve themselves and kick dust over the leavings.

"What was all that about?" Turley muttered.

"What's one of the things a convict never gets?"

"What, a crap in the morning before work?"

"A choice."

Turley looked confused. "To piss or not to piss? It's not much of a choice."

"No, it's not," Prentice agreed. "But it's more than they've had since they were convicted. And it's all I've got to offer them for now."

"Why offer them anything?"

"Because if I have nothing to offer them, then they have no reason to follow me. We all know what waits at the end of this march, and you're right when you say we have no chance to train them at anything. By God's mercy, we'll be lucky if they even give us a weapon each before throwing us at the enemy. So if we're going to do any good at all, I need to give them reasons to trust what I say and do what I want. This morning the best I had to work with was to piss or not to piss!"

Turley nodded thoughtfully. He might have said more, but a marshal rode up on his horse and gave the order for the convicts to march. The overseers cracked their whips and began to drive the crowd of prisoners forward. Prentice walked beside them, looking at their bare, dirty feet, scratched and torn from weeks of marching, shuffling along in the dust. He had new shoes, but here he was again, still a convict and marching off to war.

CHAPTER 27

For the first morning, the march north to Fallenhill progressed much like any of the other war marches Prentice had been on. The prince's army set a reasonable pace, and even with their shackles and chains, the convicts of the rogues foot had little trouble keeping up. Only the rear-guard horsemen, made up mostly of squires with just a few minor hedge knights, were behind them. The horsemen ranged off the road in small numbers infrequently, making a casual pretense of patrolling the column's rear. For the most part, however, they practiced their lance work on low bushes and startled rodents for short spaces before returning to the road and walking their horses again.

"Like children at play," said Turley as he watched several squires making mock passes against each other in a field beside the road, easily keeping up with the shuffling convicts.

"I did say that," Prentice answered, and he was quietly pleased that the other convicts had the chance to see the playfulness. It reinforced his speech from the morning and hopefully made him seem wiser and more reliable in the rogues' eyes.

A halt was called at noon, and the army rested for over an hour. A marshal appeared on his horse and questioned the overseers about the convicts' behavior. With no escape attempts or discipline problems, he quickly rode away again, and the rear guard went with him.

"I guess we won't be ambushed during luncheon," Prentice said.

"It's a considerate enemy we seem to be facing," Turley added.

"Very considerate, I'd say."

When at last the rear guard returned, the convicts were whipped to their feet once more and the march recommenced. The summer sun beat on their sweaty faces and backs. By mid-afternoon, Prentice was in near agony himself with his wounded back, chewing hard on one of the little medicinal lumps. He was fully expecting to see his first convict fall from the heat, when the marshal returned and ordered another halt. The overseers shouted and cracked their whips, and the convict chains shuffled to a thankful halt, more than half of them quickly sinking to the ground or casting about for any bit of sparse shade they might find.

"My lord, marshal," Prentice called as the man wheeled his horse and was about to head back up the column. When the marshal looked at him, Prentice quickly tugged his forelock and made a show of politeness. "Why do we stop, my lord? Has something happened?"

"The prince has halted for the day," the herald answered, then he looked down at Prentice's leg irons. His expression hardened. "All you need to know is that you're commanded to halt, rogue. More than that is above your station."

Prentice bowed his head and let the man ride away with no more comment.

Turley glanced up at the sun. "Stopped already? There's hours of day yet. We'll be a week or more to Fallenhill at this rate!"

"Perhaps something has happened."

The overseers were similarly disdainful of the early stop, from what Prentice could see. They began to scout beyond the edges of the road, looking for places a convict might try to slip the chain and escape in the night. On either side was open pastureland with nowhere to hide. Tuke did a circuit on both sides of the dirt road and then made a big show of placing his men at equal points around the convicts. They stood with their whips in hand for an hour or so, while their weary charges mostly sat or napped. As the sun headed down, however, even the overseers sat, dropping all pretense of menace.

Eventually, a dozen or so servants brought down large leather-lined baskets filled with the same boiled grain porridge the convicts had eaten in the morning, along with a mule laden with skins of water that tasted stale and tepid. Nonetheless, the thirsty convicts drank greedily, and Tuke and his men had to lash a few to see that every man got some.

Prentice and Turley took wooden bowls of porridge and sat in the dust to eat it with their fingers, just like the rest of the convicts.

"I reckon I can scrounge up something a bit better than this once it gets fully dark," Turley offered.

Prentice shook his head. The gesture made him wince with the pain of his back. "We march with them and eat what they eat," he said, scowling.

"Seriously?"

"Yes!"

Turley looked disgusted, but before he could say any more, a young man slithered close to them from his gang, loudly dragging the chain through the iron rings of the men behind him. "What do you want?" Turley demanded.

"We were talking," the young man said. "Is it true what you say? Have you really met the Duchess of the Reach? Did she really give you orders herself?"

"We said so, didn't we?" Turley replied, but the convict did not look convinced.

"I don't believe it. No high and fancy duchess talks to convict scum like us!"

Prentice nodded. "You saw the beatings we got yesterday?"

The young man nodded back.

"Did you think to see me walking today?"

"I thought they'd probably leave you for the rats," the man answered with a smile. "You looked like a piece of meat and all!"

"That's right," Prentice agreed. "Yet here I am. It was the duchess who paid for my healing. And for Turley's here."

"Why'd she do that?"

"Because we helped to save her life."

"No!"

"It's true, lad, and don't you doubt it!" Turley averred. "Not more than two weeks ago."

The young convict rubbed his stubbled chin with his hand, showing missing fingers. With his youth and his punishments, Prentice was struck by how much this convict reminded him of Bellam, whom he hoped was safe and comfortable in the kitchens of Dweltford Castle.

"Why'd you save her?" the young man asked. "I'd have let the bitch die. Serve her right!"

"What's your name?" Prentice asked.

"Nulset."

"Well, Nulset, if we hadn't saved her then, there wouldn't have been anyone to pay for my healing, would there? I'd have been left for rat food, after all."

After a few moments, Nulset shrugged. "I suppose." He began to shuffle back to his chain gang.

"Also," Prentice called after him quietly, "if I ever hear you call Duchess Amelia a bitch again, I'll take to you with this cudgel so hard that you'll wish you'd been flogged and left for rats instead."

Nulset's shocked expression was obvious even in the dimness of twilight.

"That kind of talk will bring judgment down on all of us!" Prentice continued. "Think whatever you like but keep it to yourself. You will make your words and your actions sweetness every moment of this campaign, or you'll suffer for it."

Nulset moved away, head down and a frown on his face.

"I don't think he liked that idea," Turley said to Prentice.

"You know what happens if he doesn't learn to curb his tongue. How many idiots have you watched get beaten to death because they came over the mountains thinking they were the most brazen piece of brass the Reach had ever seen?"

"True enough."

A steward's servant carrying an iron lantern approached, led by one of the overseers who pointed to where Prentice and Turley were seated.

"The duchess summons you," the servant said, and he turned away, leaving Prentice to scramble quickly to catch up to his receding lamplight.

The servant led Prentice along the road through the middle of the army. So abruptly had the column stopped that most of the knights simply spilled into the near fields, their squires rushing to pitch tents and unload baggage. The farther up the road the servant led, the grander and more complex the encamping became. By the time they reached the duchess's tent, Prentice shook his head at the sight of the towering sheets of the prince's pavilion being raised by torchlight in a field beyond. If the army were to renew its full encampment at the end of every day's march, it would surely take Turley's week to reach Fallenhill, and then some. The siege could well be over, and not favorably for the people of the town.

The servant left him at the tent flap and he entered quickly, standing just inside. Duchess Amelia was seated in her chair as usual, her eyes focused on another book in the candlelight, another military manual he imagined. Her diligence impressed him. At the rate she was studying, she'd soon make an effective commander in her own right.

"You summoned me, Your Grace?"

"I did."

She did not look up from her book, but with one free hand reached under it to pull a single sheet of parchment from her lap. "What is this?"

Prentice took it from her and scanned it. The parchment listed the apothecary's charges for his and Turley's treatment. "It's a receipt."

Amelia looked up from her reading, and her eyes narrowed as she looked at him for the first time. "When I issued you my warrant, what did I warn you?"

"To not abuse it."

"And yet my reeve's man brings me this."

Prentice said nothing, schooling his face to neutrality.

"Do you think this reasonable?" she asked.

"I do."

Amelia stood, and even though she was considerably shorter, Prentice was impressed with the force of personality that she exuded. He was not sure why he didn't make more effort to appease her, but he felt he was just as angry as she was, and he couldn't vent it any other way. If she wanted him to explain the cost of his survival in her service, she could do some of the work and dig it out herself.

"Thirty-two royals?" she asked, her voice dangerously low. "You think spending thirty-two gold coins on yourself and your mate at an apothecary was how I wanted my little remaining wealth expended? I know you can read. You see that word there?" She stabbed her finger at the page. "Opium, it says. Opium! What did you two do, pitch up and spend a day smoking? And what of the rest? Some other exotic entertainments, perhaps? My reeve's man nearly lost control of himself trying not to laugh at me.

How could you humiliate me like this?" The duchess seemed on the verge of exploding.

"I did not think to humiliate you," Prentice said. "And Turley and I sought no entertainment from the apothecary. Truly, I doubt she would have sold to us for entertainment purposes. She takes her calling to physic and healing very seriously."

"Oh? Is that so? Well then, what *did* you spend my money on?"

Prentice grabbed the hem of his tunic and pulled it over his head. The apothecary's medicines had done exceptional work in healing him, and he had marched through most of the day with endurable pain, only having to chew on the one lump of gum. The act of pulling off his clothing was more painful than he expected, however, and he winced and hissed as he took the tunic over his head. When it was removed, he turned to let the duchess view his back.

She gasped at the sight of it. "Dear God! Again? What happened?"

Prentice heard her step forward, and he felt her hand hover just above his wounded skin. For a long moment neither of them spoke. For his part he could imagine her horror and disgust but couldn't think what to say. It was a brutally intimate moment and he just wanted it to end. He hoped she felt the same.

"A flogging," he said at last "A hundred and fifty lashes."

"One hundred and fifty? What did you do? How did this happen?"

"Sir Liam felt I was not fulfilling my duty."

"Liam?"

Prentice angled his head slightly and saw Amelia step backward, all but falling into her seat. She bowed her head and rubbed at her temples, as though the news of Prentice's most recent encounter with Sir Liam caused her actual pain.

"Tell me what happened, in detail. Omit nothing."

Prentice turned back around and quickly explained how Sir Liam had found him and Turley and taken them to the convict chains to enact his plan. Amelia listened quietly as he relayed every detail, including passing out from the pain and awakening in the apothecary's tent.

"She healed you both?" Amelia asked.

"Yes, Your Grace."

"And that is what my money paid for?"

Prentice nodded.

Amelia looked over the apothecary's list once more. She shook her head. "No matter what I do or what I command, he is determined to crush you. It seems I cannot stop him. What should I do?"

"Stop protecting me," Prentice replied without thinking.

"What? You cannot mean that."

"It will be the best in the long run," he explained. Inside himself, he seethed, but something he couldn't explain made him give the duchess the best advice he could. "I haven't seen him since he had me flogged. For all he knows, I'm still there, lying in the dust. Most likely he thinks I am dead—or hopes so. It will be bad enough when he learns I've been healed, but a thousand times worse if you let him know that you heard the story from my lips."

"You would not have me order him to leave you alone?" Amelia asked.

"You have already tried that, Your Grace. He disobeyed you twice; he will find a way to do it again."

"Why does he hate you so?"

"You listen to me, you value my opinion," Prentice answered. He felt Sir Liam's motivations were easy enough to explain. "He has been waiting years to be knight commander of your duchy, and now that it has come to him, none of the details are as he dreamed. Instead of being invested with the blessing of Sir Dav as he expected, his mentor is dead, slain in front of his eyes in a shameful rout. The duke he expected to serve is also dead, and now he must take the orders of his liege's young widow, who is not behaving at all like a little lump of grieving lace, but instead feels she has the wit and will to command him. And the crowning cream of his bitter cake is me, a convict dog who does not fear him and will not be chastened. Worst of all, I give you advice and you listen."

"It is good advice, typically."

"That doesn't matter to Sir Liam. Glory and honor are the method and the measure of a knight's career. Any honor you allow me, however small or humbly given, is an honor you have denied him, in his eyes."

Amelia nodded at his words. "You imagine that if I let him think I no longer favor you, he won't despise you anymore?"

"Oh, I think he will hate me until the day he dies, or the day I do. But his hate will have less fuel for its fire."

"I don't agree with you."

"Your prerogative, Your Grace."

Amelia thought quietly for some time, so long that Prentice became uncomfortable standing shirtless before her. He lifted his tunic to show he wanted to put it back on, and she nodded vigorously, lifting from her thoughts.

"Yes, of course," she said. "Does it still hurt?"

"Yes," he answered. "But the apothecary did good work and gave me some help for the pain. Besides, I've survived worse." He smiled wryly.

"God, yes, you have," she said. Prentice wondered if she was remembering the tale of his interrogation by the Church inquisitor. She fell silent once more and thought for a while longer.

"You should go," she said finally. "You've given me a lot to think about."

"Your Grace." He sketched a quick bow before heading for the entry.

"Why don't you hate him, Prentice?" she asked as he put his hand on the flap of the tent.

"What?" he replied, surprised enough by her question to break etiquette and speak to her with directness.

"He hates you," Amelia explained. "Enough to have you beaten to death, or near to it, but you never rage against him. You show almost no anger at all! He's given you cause enough; why don't you hate him back?"

"I do, Your Grace," Prentice answered, and seeing inside himself he knew he was telling her the truth. "I hate him with a fury!"

"Then how do you control yourself?"

Prentice thought about the question, and unexpectedly his mind was taken back to the vision in the willow grove, to the sight of the lion and the serpent monster fighting. The rage of that battle had terrified him, and in the shadow of that, his own hatred seemed somehow small, even petty.

He looked the duchess in the eyes. "I have seen true fury, Your Grace, righteous fury. It is a force that, when unleashed, cannot be resisted. I keep my own anger controlled, lest it turn and destroy me."

He left the tent.

CHAPTER 28

The next two days, Prentice marched with Turley and the rogues. The army was late to leave each morning and early to stop. Talk quickly spread that the Prince of Rhales was to blame. The nobility would not dare to openly question the crown prince, but whispers were common among the lower orders. For some, the story was that he was old and uncomfortable, unable to bear the march. For others who were more hateful or less polite, they imagined that the prince was growing cowardly in his dotage and was afraid to confront the enemy. Other tales circulated as well.

Watching the march, Prentice noticed that when the army stopped in the mid-afternoon, foraging parties quickly made haste into the surrounding lands and returned hours later with livestock and wagons loaded with produce. It took massive amounts of food to feed an army of this size. Prentice wondered if the prince was calling an early rest each day to allow the army this time to forage. In spite of the duchess's plan to supply them from her own herds and flocks, Prince Mercad's force seemed intent on stripping the near countryside of every possible resource. One group of squires even returned with a string of farmers, dressed in coarse shifts with jute belts, tied by their wrists, jogging behind the horses.

The bound men were handed to the overseers with the explanation that they were guilty of fleeing the King's Law. The half dozen men claimed they were only fleeing from the invaders in the north, but the squires countered that serfs had no right to leave their lord's lands, regardless of circumstance. Some tried to protest that such law did not apply in the Reach and that they were yeomen, but the squires only rode away, leaving the overseers to chain the miserable fellows to the ends of the gangs.

How many more refugees might they find from the north?

As the sun set, Prentice made his way to talk with the men. At first they were eager to speak with him, hopeful that he might be able to secure their release. But once they realized he was just a convict, most of them tried to shun him, maintaining the yeoman's disdain for rogues. The other convicts hissed in the twilight at the newcomers' pride, and some whispered mocking comments.

"You'll not last long on this march if you hold to this disdain," Prentice told them quietly.

"I don't intend to be long on this march," one of them snarled, and others nodded.

"Really? Well, that's excellent news," Prentice mocked. "I don't know what plan you have for escaping, but I wish you well for it. Every man here has dreamed of escape for years, and none of us has managed it."

"We don't need to escape," the man replied. In the dim light, his expression seemed disgusted, as if he were upset at being drawn into a conversation with a man he would much rather just disdain with silence. "We don't belong here!"

"Oh, well, of course. Your advocate is certainly presenting your case to the magistrate right now! Doubtless, your suit will be brought to the commanders of the army, the prince, and his captains within the hour, and you will be quickly found and freed from the chain."

From nearby shadows, the chuckles of other convicts could be heard. Prentice knew he was being cruel, but he also knew that the longer these men held to the vain hope of quick freedom, the greater danger they were in. He hoped they would soon understand that fact.

"What do you want? Are you just here to entertain the convicts and torment good men?" the angry farmer asked. More hissing came from around them.

"What have you seen?" Prentice asked, ignoring the hissing and the man's anger.

"Seen? Seen where? Seen when? What do you mean?"

"The enemy, the army that's besieging Fallenhill! What have you seen of them, of their forces?"

The farmer went quiet and said nothing. Neither did the others. Prentice waited. In the gathering dark, he heard one of them shift uncomfortably.

"I, uh... I seen something," a voice said. By his tone he was a young man.

"Shut up, fool!" said the angry man. "You ain't seen nothing."

"What? What did you see?" Prentice pressed.

"He didn't see anything. None of us did. We just ran away from war, that's all!"

Prentice stood and moved through the gloom to where he could just make out the owner of the young voice. "Tell me."

"Don't," warned another of the farmers, but Prentice ignored him and pressed for the young man's story. Slowly at first, the fellow unfolded the story of the attack that had driven him and his fellows from their homes.

"They weren't bandits; you could see that from the start. They had shields and spears like militia and the like, and boiled leather armor. But they weren't like any bandits."

"Like you've ever seen bandits to know what they look like," said the angry farmer.

"I know what they look like; leastwise how they should look!"

"They were painted, weren't they?" Prentice offered. "Painted skin?"

"That's right!"

"Blue?"

"No, green and red mostly. In all kinds of patterns, like unholy writing. And a couple had black or white. And I swear one was painted fully green, all over his face and limbs. His whole skin the color of new grass!"

Prentice hadn't expected this. The attackers at the river bend village had all been one unified group. News that there were diverse colors suggested that the invaders had multiple factions, like an army divided into separate noble houses or knightly orders. It suggested an even larger invasion than he expected.

"What were they like?" he asked.

"Wild beasts," the young man said vehemently. "They just attacked and killed, like they didn't want to steal anything, just slaughter!"

"Did they have anything with them, any animals?"

"They did. I seen them too!"

"Bollocks!" yelled the angry farmer. "You didn't see anything."

"I seen my wife ripped apart with me own eyes, you bastard, so just shut up about what I seen an' ain't seen!"

"Was it a wolf?" Prentice asked.

In the darkness, the young man's voice revealed his surprise. "A wolf? No, not really like that. They was more like hounds, big dogs, but they had beaks."

"Beaks?"

"Wicked savage beaks, like giant eagle heads."

"Giant eagle heads on dogs' bodies," scoffed the farmer. "Oh, aye, they were true gryphons, swooped down out of the sky to take folks away and eat them!"

"I never said they had wings, you potsherd!"

Prentice could see the similarities between the young farmer's story and his own experience—murderous soldiers accompanied by savage attack beasts—but the details were also quite different. What did that mean for the siege?

"Thank you for telling me," he said.

"That's not everything," protested the young man. "That's not the worst thing."

"Don't," said the angry farmer, and for the first time he sounded not furious but plaintive, almost pleading.

"We have to tell them! How will they know what's at Fallenhill if we don't?"

There was silence in the dark as none of the farmers spoke. They seemed to have no answer for their young comrade's question.

"What is it?" Prentice asked.

"They have a leader," the young man continued. "Taller than any man I ever seen, like a big bear on its hind legs. And he has... he has horns growing out of his head."

"Horns?"

"Antlers, like a big buck deer."

"Antlers?"

The young man nodded. "Aye! And he was powerful. He tossed men about like they were lambs, smashing them through walls of homes. Big men fell to him from single blows."

"Did he use a weapon?"

"No, sir, not that I saw. Just his big fists!"

None of the others argued with the young man's description, so Prentice guessed that they had all seen him. "Why don't they want you to tell me this?" he asked.

"We all know our catechism, no mistake! We don't want sacrists down on us spitting about heresy and blasphemy," the young man answered.

"Blasphemy?"

"We know what the sacrists say, that the Wild Hunt's just a folktale. But we seen him, the Huntsman! His big antlers and devil dogs. We seen him, and we know it's not just a folktale. He's real!"

Prentice chewed over their words as he left them and went looking for wherever Turley had found for them to bed down for the night, likely some grass on the side of a hillock. Prentice lay on his back and gazed up at the stars. It was a long while before he fell asleep.

CHAPTER 29

On the next day of the march, they came upon their first destroyed farms: a small cluster of burned houses sharing a single barn, not even enough to call a village. There was a natural spring in a field nearby and fences for animals, but no living thing to see, neither peasant nor beast. The sight of the destruction put an angry mood on the march as many saw it as a sign that the enemy was near, and more than a few talked of looking for revenge for these crimes. Prentice was not convinced.

"You don't think it's them like?" Turley asked him quietly as they marched.

Prentice shook his head. "Every night, those foragers ride in with swaths of food, like they've just ridden back from the most well-stocked market on God's earth. It must come from somewhere. It's as likely that this was the work of our army as the enemy."

"No sign of the murder and butchery either," Turley observed.

"Exactly," said Prentice. "No slaughter. Just burning and theft."

"Could be ordinary bandits, caught between the two armies."

"True."

"And the farther north we go, the closer we get to the lands of the Hills Riders."

Prentice gave his companion a disbelieving look. "Goblins and elves? Is everyone talking folktales now?"

"Now sure, not goblins, but true Fey Tribes folk. You know they exist!"

"The people who were called Fey Tribes are all gone," Prentice said. "They were killed in crusades or forced to intermarry. There haven't been odd folk in the Grand Kingdom for centuries."

"Not in the Kingdom proper, no," Turley reasoned. "But this is the Reach, isn't it? Here, things are different."

Prentice shook his head.

"Look," Turley continued, clearly not dissuaded, "we know that the jungles of the north have tribesmen, dark and mysterious, obviously bred from different stock than Kingdom men. And we know there used to be fey in the Grand Kingdom proper, till the Church and knights done 'em in! And now we have men with strange painted skin coming in an army to invade, so there's that."

"You think the invaders are fey?"

"Perhaps they are. Don't be too quick to dismiss what you don't know just because you don't know."

Prentice shook his head again and laughed. Then the two of them marched on in silence.

For the next two days, the army continued as it had, starting late and quitting early and in spite of the slow progress, the town of Fallenhill drew closer.

In the afternoon of the march's sixth day, Duchess Amelia summoned Prentice once more to her tent. He made his way through the camp, head down and eyes open for Sir Liam. He listened at the duchess's tent flap before entering, in case the knight captain was within. The recent days' marches had proved reasonably pleasant, with no sign of his tormentor and no other duties except to march and plan whatever tactics he might devise for the battle ahead. The overseers accepted his and Turley's presence and gave them no particular orders. His wounds were healing miraculously well and quick. Even the discipline of eating only the same gruel as the rest of the rogues was bearable, if bland. Running into Sir Liam would be certain to ruin that peace.

Inside her tent, Amelia was alone.

"You summoned me, Your Grace?" Prentice said.

Amelia stood toward the back of the tent, looking over an open chest of clothes. She was still wearing her riding dress, the dust of the day covering the dark material. She reached into the chest and tossed out a summer cloak so that it fell on the cot behind her.

"Prentice," she said, not looking at him. "How goes the rogues foot? Are they well?"

"Two men fell yesterday," he reported.

"They tripped?" she mused, hands buried in clothes, then she stopped and looked up. Her brow furrowed. "Oh, that is sad. The heat, was it?"

He shook his head. "They were old, Your Grace. Graybeards, both! They were never going to last long on a chain, no matter what task they were set to."

Amelia went back to searching through her clothes chest. "I would swear I did not pack so many garments back in Dweltford. It's as if they are breeding in here!" She threw a linen dress aside and kept searching.

"Forgive me, but isn't this a task for a lady's maid?"

"If only," she said, then sighed. She stopped searching again and looked at him. "I thought I was being terribly wise when we left Dweltford, insisting that my full staff not risk themselves on a march to war. I took just one maid and commanded that Bettina remain behind. But this maid— Teerah is her name—knows nothing of etiquette. She cleans and folds my clothes and fetches whatever I tell her to, but she cannot advise me what is best to wear or when. There are so many levels and layers in this army. Bettina always fusses, and I gave her so little thought as she did it, but now I see just how much I have relied on her advice in so many little ways. Hers and Dianda's..."

Amelia's voice trailed off at the mention of her slain maid, still not even dead a month. For a moment she looked as if she might be about to cry, but she sucked in a strong breath and steeled herself. "I wanted to protect them, appear so wise and frugal, and then I get to this damn army and look like a pauper! Every man jack of them casts money about like mana from heaven. If my father or one of his competitors had spent money like this, they'd be out of business and into a ditch."

Prentice smiled at Amelia resorting to a merchant's aphorism to express her frustration, her ignoble birth showing through for a moment.

"Nobility consider frugality a weakness, Your Grace," he said.

"So is spending yourself out of house and home," she retorted. Then she stopped and worked to recover her poise. "You are correct, of course, Prentice. Regardless of how I think about their behavior, these are the gentle born, and their way is the Grand Kingdom's way."

"Indeed, Your Grace."

"Which brings me neatly around to my reason for sending for you. Do you know what a Council of Forfeits is?"

Prentice nodded. "A Forfeits Council? Yes, Your Grace."

"The prince has called one this evening. I've searched through the books I was able to bring, your suggestions, and two gentry treatises on manners and courtly ways, yet none of them mention this council. What is it, and what will be expected of me?"

"It's an old tradition, Your Grace," Prentice explained, dredging his memory for facts he learned long years before. "On the eve of battle, a king—or, in this case, the prince—

calls all the ranking nobility before him and asks for advice on strategy. It is a war council."

"So why not call it that? Why a Forfeits Council?"

"The forfeits come from the knights themselves. They make claims of bravery and skill, then name some achievement they expect to make on the following day's battle. They then offer a forfeit to the crown, or the Church sometimes, if they fail."

"What kind of achievements?"

"'Tomorrow my mace will thunder with the trump of God's judgment, and I will lay at my liege's feet the shields of fifty of your enemy's sworn men,'" Prentice recited from memory, a line from one of the Grand Kingdom's earliest chivalric epics. "'If I do not do this for you, then all my lands and titles are forfeit to you, O King, and my sons to you will become the lowliest serfs, for my family and I will be shown unworthy.'"

"That's quite the forfeit," said Amelia, eyes wide.

"It is. It's called Garoman's Oath. At college it was written around the walls of the student commissary, a lesson to proud young noblemen that they are called by faith and throne to lives of sacrifice and service. Their pride has a price."

Amelia shook her head in wonder. "What do the knights gain from this? They boast and make promises, but what rewards are there?"

"Honor and glory," Prentice said simply.

"That's all?"

"For a knight, that is everything."

Amelia shook her head again. It was clear she could hardly believe the impracticality of the whole affair. Raised in a merchant house, she had learned to evaluate everything in terms of profit and loss, risk versus reward. This likely felt like all risk and no reward.

"You say that this council takes place on the eve of battle?" she asked.

"Traditionally."

"Then that means we are near to Fallenhill?"

"Finally," said Prentice. He did not manage to keep a tone of frustration from his voice.

"You see it too?" Amelia asked. "We move like a summer progress, not an army on the march."

"It is not for me to say," Prentice began to answer, but a sharp look from Amelia froze the polite words on his lips. "Yes, Your Grace, I think we are moving too slowly, and others have noted it."

Amelia nodded. "There have been whispers. Even among the knights, which I suppose should not be a surprise. They're eager to get to grips with the enemy, win glory, and plunder. But no matter who urges the prince, he refuses a faster pace. Every morning after breaking fast and every afternoon just after the heat of the day, he sends out his heralds. At first it was only a handful, but now it's every single one that came over the mountains with him. They go out twice a day into the countryside—scouting, I assume, though why he would give the task to heralds I cannot imagine. Surely they risk the capture of the prince's standard as they carry it about in such small numbers."

Listening to the duchess's words, Prentice suddenly realized what the prince's plan was and he wanted to despair. The army was being led by a fool.

"I think I understand Prince Mercad's intention, Your Grace."

"Tell me, Prentice."

"He is sending his heralds forth, looking for the enemy's heralds in turn."

"Why would the enemy be sending out heralds?"

"So that they might discuss the coming battle and settle on the time and place."

Amelia's eyes grew wider still, then she rubbed at her temple as if the things she was learning were so impossible they gave her a headache. "This is how wars are fought?"

"Not for nearly a century, Your Grace," Prentice said. His face was schooled to show no emotion, but his tone conveyed his misgivings.

It seemed the prince was leading the campaign according to ancient rules of war. Even the Forfeits Council was an old tradition. As far as Prentice knew, none had been called during the crusade against King Kolber, and Kolber had never let his heralds take his banner ahead of the army. The long pennant thus became one of the highest prizes of the campaign when it was captured during Kolber's retreat. If the prince thought he was fighting something like the ancient wars of the early Kingdom, when noble houses fought with high chivalric honor and courtly conduct, then it did not bode well.

"He cannot think this enemy to be like the knights of old, can he?" Amelia's thoughts seemed to follow Prentice's own.

"I do not know, Your Grace."

"But surely he's been told," she went on, pacing as she thought out loud. "The men who attacked us on the riverbank and the other reports. These are not noble knights, or even knights at all. They're savages! What can he be thinking?"

Prentice shook his head.

"I was not sure that I would be welcome at this Forfeits Council," she mused. "The invitation came to my knights, and I was almost ready to let them attend without me, but now I feel I need to be there."

"There would be no law against your presence, Your Grace. At least none I know of."

"If the prince thinks we face a genteel foe, then he must be persuaded of the truth."

"It is no easy task to persuade princes. Of anything."

"You could do it, I'm sure of it," she said.

Prentice was aghast. "Nothing forbids your attendance, especially not in your own lands, but the insult of a convict's presence would never be forgiven."

Amelia nodded. She knew he was right. "I will have to do it myself."

"Your lands, your responsibility," he said.

She gave him a cold look. "I value your counsel above your station, Prentice, but I do not need you to tell me my responsibilities."

Prentice met her gaze, and in her eyes he could see the strength of the woman inside, a strength that made her a duchess as much as any title could.

"That you do not, Your Grace," he said, and he bowed with genuine respect. "That you do not."

CHAPTER 30

Duchess Amelia paused on the threshold of the audience chamber and listened. Only a single heavy curtain separated the main chamber of the prince's pavilion from the canvas vestibule, yet to Amelia it felt like a fortress wall. Did she dare to enter the prince's council of war, to stand among highborn knights and skilled men-at-arms and represent her duchy's needs?

"No," she whispered to herself. It was not *her* duchy, not to these men. It was her beloved late husband's, and they would respect that.

She would make them.

Drawing in a deep breath, Amelia smoothed her dress's bodice and straightened her skirts. Just as she was about to draw the curtain aside, a steward slipped through from the other side, carrying a wooden tray with an empty silver pitcher. The man blinked when he saw Amelia standing there, and he froze, apparently torn between the duties of refilling the wine jug, parting the curtain for a lady of status, and deciding if he needed permission to admit a woman to the prince's council. After staring a moment, he opted to serve the needs of the noblewoman in front of him, stepping back and holding the curtain open for her. He opened his mouth to announce her, but before he could, Amelia raised her finger for silence.

"I am late," she said quietly. "I would not draw the prince's attention to the fact. It might be taken as disrespect."

The steward nodded and stood by as she entered, then he dropped the curtain and went off. Alone at the back of the crowd of men, two things struck Amelia immediately. One was the heat; the braziers in the center were lit and blazing to produce light, and torches were set all around. One accident, a shift in the crowd knocking things over, and the pavilion would be ablaze in moments.

Every man present was in full armor. Polished and primped plate and mail glittered in the firelight, and surcoats flashed colors of every hue, in patterns and designs of every conceivable shape. Nearest to Amelia stood the least knights, men with little more than a hereditary name or rank, barely wealthy enough to afford their weapons, armor, and mounts. Farther into the crowd, closer to the prince, the armor became more complex, chased in gold and silver, embossed with bold designs, mottos, and prayers. The helms they carried in the crooks of their arms had plumes of bright feathers or dyed horsehair, some so extravagant that, even held under their owner's arms, the plumes still reached above their heads.

The second thing Amelia noticed was the smell. So many bodies sweating in their armor could not help but stink and mixed with that was the rotten odor of dung. Most of these men must have come directly from the march and walked through rows of tied horses, hurrying to not be late and so while they stood clad in shining steel, their sabatons and riding boots were coated in filth. The combination of smells reminded Amelia of a stable where horses had been put away sweated without first being groomed.

Pretty colors and rank odors.

The men nearest to Amelia were mostly quiet, watching the proceedings from their less privileged viewpoint. She could hear talking from deeper in, and although she was less than fifteen paces from the prince's dais, over a hundred men stood between her and the crown prince. Looking at their steel-clad backs made her feel like a child standing among giants. She drew in a breath and hardened her expression, then she pressed at the elbow of the knight in front of her and cleared her throat.

The man turned, and for a moment his eyes were filled with contempt. Then he saw the ducal colors she was wearing and realized she was the duchess and not just a presumptuous maid. Amelia trembled inside as she met his gaze and prayed inwardly that her uncertainty did not show in her face.

The knight suddenly bowed his head—the model of courtesy—and stepped aside for her to pass. As he did so, he tapped the man in front of him, drawing his attention. This knight had the same disdainful expression as the first until he, too, noticed her colors. Then he also made way for her, and so she was passed courteously through a crowd of men who otherwise would sooner have thrashed a woman than allowed her presence in this martial gathering.

At last she came to the edge of the crowd, where a small space was opened in front of the dais for men to pay their respects and make their boasts. The prince was seated upon his throne, wearing heavy burgundy robes sewn with gold thread. In spite of the heat, he clutched the collar of his robe about him as if warding off a chill. On the dais at his feet were a helmet with an enormous feather plume and a sheathed longsword. Too old and weak to wear armor for pure ceremonial purposes, nonetheless these two items lent the prince's appearance a military aspect.

Standing at his right hand was a tall, gray-haired knight in full regalia. Amelia knew him as Sir Carron Ironworth, Mercad's knight commander and the highest-ranking man-at-arms in the Rhales court. He had served the prince for nearly twenty years, and although his face was lined and his beard fully gray, he still stood tall in his armor and looked as strong and competent as any man present. His eyes coldly surveyed crowd, as if they were as much his enemies as the army they prepared to face in the morning. Amelia swallowed at the sight of him.

Looking across the front rank of men, she tried to spy Sir Liam and eventually located him away to the right, standing with Brother Whilte. Both men were as resplendent as any other knight present and Amelia realized that since Sir Liam was her man, his appearance would add weight to her own presence in the council, if she could get him to stand with her. But Sir Liam and Brother Whilte were completely focused on the business in front of the dais and had not noticed her arrival.

She began to push across the edge of the crowd toward them when a huge guffaw caught her attention and she turned to see a huge bear of a man with black hair and a thick beard laughing at the petitioner on his knee before the throne.

"Twenty enemy spears?" the man almost bellowed, his booming voice quieting the crowd who all watched him as he stepped forward in front of the dais. "You could walk around the battlefield and claim them from the dead at the end of the day, like a camp follower! And what trophies are spears? Perhaps the prince's gardener might use them to build a fence around his vegetable patch to keep out small dogs." Many of the men around her chuckled, but Amelia noticed that the man on his knee clenched his fists.

"And what forfeit is ten bags of gold?" the bearded mocker continued. "Is the prince a merchant, that his honor might be purchased?"

The kneeling man surged to his feet and stood glowering at his tormentor, but as he did so the comparison between them only served to make him look smaller, more worthy of mockery. The bearded man was tall and heavyset, but his armor was well forged, gilded, and fluted. Even though he had a massive belly, his breastplate was shaped to accommodate it perfectly. His hair was oiled and his skin clean. In contrast, his victim was shorter and smaller of stature, with lank hair streaked with gray that hung untrimmed. His cloak was patched and threadbare, and his armor was serviceable but unpolished. He was the very picture of a hedge knight.

"Count Rothman," the prince said, his voice croaking but easily heard. "You interrupt the baronet before he has the chance to finish. It is not seemly for you to mock. Baronet Canton, please continue."

The baronet turned to face the prince, his head bowed once again, and although he had his back to Amelia, she felt there was something shamefaced about his manner, like a man beaten down to the very end of his pride.

"That is my forfeit, great prince," he said. "It is the whole of my wealth. I have nothing else except my title and my breath."

"That is exactly perfect!" the prince declared. "Your title it shall be. Return with your twenty spears and the captured men who wielded them, or else do not return! This forfeit we accept."

Baronet Canton made a small choking sound, and chuckles and sneers rippled through the men around Amelia. All she could think was that this man had committed as much as he sensibly could afford on a goal he could reasonably hope to achieve, but these others despised him for it. And the prince had responded by placing a crushing burden on his shoulders. Could any man, even a hero of old, capture twenty enemy soldiers alive in a single battle? The baronet slunk away like a whipped dog under the callous gaze of the snide Count Rothman. However, the prince was not yet done with the boastful and condescending count.

"And you, good Lord Rothman? What is your forfeit?"

The count bowed as low as his belly and breastplate would allow. "The tower on Reece Point has been in my family's possession for over two hundred years," he began, his voice loud but mellifluous. Amelia thought his words sounded like a well-rehearsed speech. "In spite of its longstanding attachment to my line, I will offer it forfeit, so confident am I of my success in tomorrow's battle. Twenty is the number, my prince, but not mere spears! Twenty of the enemy's sworn banner knights will fall beneath my blade tomorrow. No spears of peasants, but I will lay pennants and armor, knights' mounts, and all their panoply at your feet tomorrow evening, great prince. Or else give Reece Point to the Church so that they may make of it an abbey, a remote place of contemplation and prayer."

The count bowed again. From the left side of the dais, a small, bent-backed man in a scholar's coat appeared, carrying a quill and a heavy leather-bound ledger. He stepped up beside the throne and whispered gently in the prince's ear. Amelia assumed the man was a reeve, or a seneschal perhaps—some such person who handled the prince's affairs. She realized she had no idea who he was, and it occurred to her that she knew very few members of the prince's household by sight, or even by name. That was a genuine disadvantage for her, one she should work to correct.

As for Count Rothman, his offer sounded too easily given. To her it seemed he probably wasn't afraid to lose the tower at all and might even be glad to see it gone. In her mind, she imagined an ancient pile of uninhabited stones, only fit for bats and rodents. She looked over to Sir Liam, still unable to catch his eye, and then started her way toward him once more. She barely listened as the prince began to speak again.

"Given as an abbey, you say, dear count?"

"Yes, my prince."

"Could it be that you hope for a ready supply of pretty novices on your lands?"

Chuckles flowed through the crowd again, but the count joined them readily enough. "I had not thought of that possibility, Your Highness," he said. "Though I fear I am too old and fat now to go trying to charm neophytes out of their robes. They will outrun me."

Many of the knights laughed, while the prince smiled benignly at the count's joke.

From the crowd, an anonymous voice called out, "Have 'em brought to you! Any steward that can carry your food can handle the weight of a young girl!"

This brought further laughter, but this time the count turned to face the crowd, and for a moment his pleasant facade fell. Cold, angry eyes scoured the men present, looking for the jest maker.

The prince's voice called Rothman back to himself. "We are sure you offer your forfeit in earnest, Count."

Rothman bowed to the prince, and his face was again a mask of jovial courtesy.

"However, we are informed that the lands about the tower are unsuitable for an abbey," the prince continued. Although his face was turned to the dais so that Amelia could see only one side of the count's expression, it seemed to her that his smile was becoming quite brittle and difficult to hold. "Reece Point is rocky and windswept, is it not?"

"Somewhat, Your Highness."

"So, any nuns would be unable to grow enough food to feed themselves, isn't that so?"

"I suppose, Your Highness."

"What of the villages in the nearby valleys?"

"Villages? What villages?"

"We are informed that there are a number of villages in close proximity to the tower, and that these villages are healthy and productive."

"Yes, Highness," answered the count, and there was a tremulous undertone to his voice that was like the brokenness of Baronet Canton.

"Very well, then we accept the forfeit of the tower, along with the tithes and taxes from villages within four leagues of the tower's foot."

"Four leagues?"

Amelia smiled hearing the count's weakened voice, enjoying the thought that the bully was receiving his comeuppance and in so public a fashion. But she could not watch because she had reached an impasse. She was almost to Sir Liam, but a man armored in a coat of plates with a cloak of purple and red silk was standing firm in her way. The voluminous cloak was slung over one shoulder, and it was caught on the spike on the crest of the wearer's helmet in the crook of his arm. As such, the cloak blocked Amelia from the man's sight, and she could not easily get his attention.

She pressed gently at his elbow, but the man seemed not to notice, probably thinking it was just the jostling of the crowd. Being careful to seem as respectful as she could, she pressed more firmly. Now the man turned, but even as he did so, Amelia could see that her successful passage through the crowd had come to an end.

The man looked at her with the typical disdain, but his expression did not change as he took in her dress and its ducal colors. Looking into his face, Amelia saw what was coming the moment before the man opened his mouth to speak. She felt herself flinch and even shrunk back as the man let forth an angry parade-ground bellow.

"Cease pawing at me, woman! By what feminine presumption do you imagine yourself entitled to lay your least finger upon my person?"

CHAPTER 31

The entire pavilion fell silent, and all eyes turned toward Amelia and her confronter. In the quiet, she could hear muttered voices somewhere in the crowd speaking about the offensiveness of a woman's presence in the Forfeits Council. On his dais, the prince squinted his eyes as if he had difficulty seeing who had spoken. The seneschal at his elbow pointed him to where Amelia and the cloaked knight were standing. He whispered in the prince's ear.

"What troubles you, Lord Dunstan?" the prince asked loudly.

"This impertinent woman," Lord Dunstan replied, not taking his disdainful gaze from Amelia. "She seems not to know her place, and she compounds that error by disrupting your council."

Amelia felt all eyes on her and, looking past Lord Dunstan, could see that Sir Liam had finally noticed her. She looked him straight in the eye, and he took her signal, moving to join her. Almost immediately Brother Whilte placed his hand on Sir Liam's arm and gently held him back. Amelia was incensed by the brother's interference, daring to keep her bondsman from her.

"Have you nothing to say for yourself, woman?" Lord Dunstan demanded, though Amelia hardly heard him.

She was suddenly even more aware of the heat in the room, the sensation of it prickling at her skin. Her face was flushed, she could feel it. For a moment she thought that the ground beneath her was moving, or perhaps she was dizzy. She swallowed.

She was tired. Tired of being widowed young. Tired of being despised for her birth or for her wealth. Tired of the invaders who slaughtered her people, and tired of these arrogant men who had come to protect them but made such lazy progress toward their defense. For a moment the whole room around her swam, and she wanted to run all the way back to her bed in Dweltford and sleep until the world changed.

"I will have my man take her and teach her some manners," Lord Dunstan was saying. He reached for her wrist, and something in Amelia, something tight that she could not name, finally snapped.

She snatched her hand back, and her face contorted in a sneer. "Do not think to touch me," she all but shouted. She took a step back from him and then turned to the prince, bowing toward the dais. "Prince Mercad, I entreat you, call off this knave of yours! He presumes much upon the widow of your truest vassal."

That was her one bargaining piece, her only weapon in this tent full of arrogant men who thought her no more than a rebellious child. They would not respect her, but they would respect her husband's name. This was the Duchy of the Western Reach and here she answered only to her husband and his liege lord, the Prince of Rhales.

"Knave?" Lord Dunstan sputtered in disbelief. "I'll flog you myself, bitch! When I'm done..." His hand that had been reaching for her wrist instead snatched at her hair, and he pulled her by it.

But before he could do or say anything else, the prince spoke, his wrinkled eyes peering through the hazy room toward them. "Duchess Amelia, is that you?"

"Yes, Your Highness."

Lord Dunstan ceased pulling at Amelia but did not release his grip.

The prince looked straight at him. "Unhand her, Dunstan. She is the widow of a high peer."

Lord Dunstan withdrew his hand, and though Amelia was grateful for the prince's intervention, she did not miss the specifics of his instruction. He counted her the widow of a peer, not a peer in her own right. But she was comforted by the thought that she had anticipated the prince and this council correctly. She had rights here, even if only by dint of her husband. How far would a dead husband's authority reach?

"A woman should not be present in a Forfeits Council. A woman has no place in war!" Lord Dunstan insisted. He had a long mustache, which he groomed with flicks of his fingers, and then made a show of adjusting his cloak on his shoulder.

"In the matter of protocols, my lord," Amelia said, straightening her back and lifting her head, "I should think you would worry more about answering your violation of my honor."

"Your honor? What honor?"

"My honor, the honor of a duchess! Surely you did not think to use me so rudely, and in this august company, without my sworn men coming to my defense? Sir Liam, do you think to call this man to answer with combat?"

Duchess Amelia looked straight at Sir Liam and knew that the eyes of the crowd looked with her. Sir Liam said nothing, but his expression made it clear that he had no idea how to respond. She had pinned him in place, like a rabbit shot through with an arrow. Amelia knew how much he longed for the respect of every man around them, but now she forced him to make a choice. He could make the challenge, taking her side as a woman unwanted by virtually every man present, or he could ignore her inquiry and risk being ascribed a coward. Amelia enjoyed watching him squirm inwardly after all the trouble he had been to her since the ambush at the river. But she knew better than to alienate him.

"Of course, we are on a march to war, Lord Dunstan," she announced, turning back to the man in front of her. "It is not the time or place for petty points of honor. After the campaign I shall send my herald to you, and he will receive your apology. Or he will receive your choice of the correct time and place."

Before Lord Dunstan could say anything more, Amelia turned away, dismissing him, and quickly made her way to the front of the dais where she curtsied deeply before the prince. "Your Highness, I apologize for disrupting your council. It is most rude of Lord Dunstan and me, and far beneath the courtesy due your rank. I beg your forgiveness. I would not have come, but I felt constrained by my late husband's honor to attend and serve his memory."

She did not rise from her curtsy but looked up slightly to see how the prince responded to her words. He had an expression that reminded her of her father when he would consider a complex trade, a look of equal parts enjoyment and shrewd cunning.

"You did not feel the duchy's sworn men could serve the duke's honor?" he asked her.

In a sudden flash, Amelia had a sense of what the council was to Mercad. He was not arbitrating between competing parties, as she had thought. He saw himself as a player in the game, and he expected to win because he held all the best cards. The entire council had almost nothing to do with war and everything to do with the prince's power over his court. That was why he let them offer their forfeits and then twisted them further. He allowed them to overreach, only to spring his trap on them. With this realization, she saw the first snare in the prince's words and sidestepped it easily.

"I had thought so initially, Your Highness," she allowed, keeping her head bowed. "But so many of my men have a personal stake in crushing the Grand Kingdom's enemies. They have already shed their own blood and lost comrades to the invaders. It seemed selfish of me to not let them offer their own personal forfeits. I felt I had to represent my husband and his duchy myself."

Prince Mercad's eyes narrowed, as if he were only just noticing something about Amelia. He cocked his head quizzically. The seneschal leaned in to whisper in Mercad's ear once more, but this time the prince waved him away. He smiled at her, and it seemed to Amelia like the smile of a predator about to pounce. She kept her face as calm as she could. Her father had once told her that all merchants were liars—they had to be because every trade was about getting something for less than it was worth or selling it for more than it was worth. That was the way profit was made. So, all merchants had to learn to give nothing away, to appear like a friend but to have the heart of a bandit, ready to take everything and make off. Amelia schooled her face and readied herself to take everything she could.

"Tell us, Lady Amelia," said Mercad, lifting his eyes to the whole crowd—to remind her, she thought, that as men they would be with him, not her. "You have heard the forfeits. Do you have anything to offer? Are you, as a woman, really able to offer the duchy's forfeit? Do you even understand this council? Your loyalty to your late husband is virtuous, and doubtless God will reward you in the world to come, but is this how best to serve his memory?"

It took all of Amelia's will not to laugh out loud. The prince was so obviously trying to bait her into saying something foolish to defend her wounded pride. She was almost contemptuous, until Prentice's words sounded in her memory. *Glory and honor are the method and the measure of a knight's career.* Knights and noblemen, all the men standing around her, measured their lives in honor and glory, like her father had measured livestock in coin. But Amelia knew what the prince did not.

She was not a knight, and she valued her life in a different coin.

"You speak the truth, Highness, of course. As a woman, I do not know how to judge the value of military matters. I cannot speak to the worth of a spear over a helmet, or a slain man over a captured man." She turned to face the men behind her. In their eyes, she saw a mix of thoughts: disdain, as she expected, and some anger, but at least as many faces showed avid interest—fascination with the novelty of a woman, a duchess, in this council of men.

She smiled now, despite herself. Did the prince really hope to intimidate her with this crowd of mixed motives and crossed purposes? She had already faced her fears just to push her way through and faced them again when Dunstan had tried to dismiss her. This council no longer frightened her. She turned back to the prince and curtsied once again.

"The forfeits I have heard all seem worthy to me, Your Highness," she said. "But nonetheless, they fall short of a duke's honor. I am but a young, small thing, but I married a hero of the kingdom, and I carry his heart within me. His heart will steel me to this purpose."

She paused and drew in a breath, ostensibly to gather her courage, but also to prick up the curiosity of every ear in the room and give them all a chance to listen closer.

"I have seen the enemy firsthand," she began again, her voice louder. She lifted her head and felt like she almost had to shout to penetrate the oppressive heat in the room. She could feel her hair hanging lank on her face, but she ignored it, pouring all the strength she had into her words. "I know that if they conquer, I will be impaled on a spike and left to bleed like a tortured animal. They will care nothing for the gentleness of my birth or the softness of my womanhood. They will take everything, and so I offer everything!"

She paused one more time and then threw out her voice like a sacrist thundering a sermon. It still sounded weak and shrill to her, but everyone heard her, that she knew for a fact.

"Victory is my forfeit, Highness! We will be victorious, and the enemy driven from these lands, else the Western Reach be ceded to your throne. For if we are defeated, I assure you, Prince Mercad, it will fall to your throne to reclaim it. Our enemy is no knight or man of honor, and they will fall upon this land like a pestilence. The women will be raped and enslaved, the men and boys slaughtered. If not victory, there will be no Western Reach! Our people will be driven back across the mountains, and a new crusade will have to be called. And it will have to be done without the blood of the hero who led the last crusade to victory, for Duke Marne is dead and his heart will have died with my flesh, thrust upon a spike."

Amelia fell quiet, and for a moment there was no noise in the tent, not a sound. She did not dare look at the prince. Now that her rush of courage was fading, she fell into nervousness, fearful that the prince might simply dismiss her words, disdain her as so many of the men present wished him to, and throw her out. The silence stretched on, and her rising tension threatened to break her will.

Then she heard a low whisper. Someone behind her was speaking quietly to his neighbor. Then more whispers were heard, and in the same way that the first spatterings of rain showers grow to the hammering of true storms, so the number and volume of the voices grew, until it seemed every man in the room was speaking at once—every man but one.

Finally daring to look up at the dais, Amelia saw the prince deep in conversation with his seneschal. She wondered if they were discussing the legality of her forfeit, for the discussion seemed intense, with the seneschal explaining things at length and the prince only interrupting to ask vehement questions. At last, Mercad pushed himself to his feet, and the voices slowly lowered, though they did not fully still. The prince stood for some time on the edge of the dais, saying nothing. Then the seneschal stepped forward.

"His Highness has ridden long today, and the heat wearies him," the man said in a reedy voice. "He will retire."

Holding the prince's elbow, the seneschal began to help the prince down from the dais, but just before Mercad stepped off, he turned back to face Amelia. His skin looked gray and his expression uncertain, but he was plainly heard when he spoke.

"Your forfeit is accepted, Duchess Amelia," he said. "Either the Reach remains a victorious duchy, or else it becomes a prince's folly." Then he shuffled uncomfortably away and exited through the rear flap, into the private chambers of the pavilion.

Amelia was left facing the empty throne alone in front of the crowd of hushed knights, with Sir Carron Ironworth to one side, still standing at attention.

The knight commander nodded to her respectfully. "Your Grace."

Amelia realized that he was giving her place. She was the Duchess of the Reach, and with the prince gone, she was now the highest-ranking noble present. It was her right to leave next. She turned to look behind her and was amazed to see the armed men quickly shift to clear a path for her all the way back to the vestibule. She fitted a calm, cold expression to her face, then she faced Sir Liam, still only a few paces from her.

"Sir Liam, you will attend me," she ordered, and without waiting for him to reply or catch up, she strode regally down the aisle created in the midst of the divided crowd.

The men watched her silently as Duchess Amelia left the council.

CHAPTER 32

After the heat of the prince's pavilion, the night air outside was fresh and cool, but rather than relieving, Amelia found it like a slap to the face of a remorseful drunk. All of the doubts she had been fighting to hold back came flooding into her mind, as well as the reasonable fear that among the armed men she had just faced down, there might be one sufficiently offended to try something rash. Knights were men of honor, but as she had just shown, honor cut both ways. One rash moment by a man-at-arms who took umbrage, and she would be just a cold corpse, whether duchess, or mere merchant's daughter.

It took all of Amelia's self-control to not run to her tent. Ideally, she should wait for Sir Liam and he would be her escort, but she was not convinced he would not be one of the offended and uncontrolled. So, she moved as quickly as dignity would allow and did her best to argue with the voices of doubt in her own mind.

She had offered up the duchy entire. How could she?

No, she thought, it was good that she had. Now they were pushed to action, and she could not lose. She had been right about the invaders. If they were not driven away, she would surely be slain or enslaved, assuming they took slaves, and then honor would be meaningless to her. But if the prince won, he would be honor bound to keep the duchy in her hands, as her husband's widow. That would give her greater influence and control over attempts to marry her off. Certainly, enough to hold Sir Duggan's conspiratorial approach at arm's length, to see if she could negotiate a more favorable match for herself.

Then she remembered the seneschal at the prince's elbow and how she had not known his name. Amelia knew hardly anyone beyond the circle of ladies that Baroness Switch had kept as company and their conversation. The baroness was no longer a young woman and had not had much tolerance for court gossip. Two years ago, Amelia had been overawed just to be accepted into the circle of someone as high as the baroness.

Now, in her memory, it seemed an inadequate preparation for her present life. She had not had enough time to learn everything she needed to know or how complex and treacherous the interplays of nobility could be. No one ruled absolute, it seemed, but rather every modicum of influence and every moment of power was negotiated, even by princes. Perhaps only the king ruled above all, without uncertainty, or perhaps not even he. It could be that only the Church fathers and the Primarch answered to no one but God.

Amelia had almost reached her tent with all these thoughts roiling in her mind when a further thought suddenly burst through all others, like a flash of lightning on a black night. The pause it caused her was the delay before the hammer blow of thunder drowned out all the other fears and worries. What if the prince was defeated on the morrow but met the enemy again another day? Would he count the first defeat as meeting the terms of the forfeit? Could he even conspire to manage the battle that way?

What if he took the field against the enemy and then withdrew without engaging, calling the day a loss, and simply stole the duchy out from under her? Then she would be landless and untitled again, the widowed daughter of a penniless merchant's widow. Penniless because it had all been used to pay her dead husband's debts.

She entered her tent to find the brazier burned low and no other lights lit. It was deeply shadowed within, and while Amelia rushed in seeking refuge, she pulled up short almost immediately.

She was not alone.

There were figures waiting for her in the shadows. One person—no, two people, indistinct in the darkness.

"Who is there?" Amelia demanded.

"'Tis I, Your Grace," came her maid Teerah's tremulous voice.

"Teerah? Who is with you?"

"Prentice, Your Grace," the convict answered.

Amelia swallowed heavily and felt the heavy beat of her heart. She took a moment to calm herself. "Why are you here?"

"You did not dismiss me when you left for the council, Your Grace," he explained calmly. "I expected you would want me to await your return."

"That's what he said to me too, Your Grace," Teerah put in. "I wasn't sure what to say, so I thought I should stay here too, in case, because he's a... you know."

"Young Mistress Teerah was nervous that a convict left to himself in her lady's chamber might plot thievery or something worse."

Even in the dark, Amelia could see Teerah vigorously nodding her agreement.

"I didn't waste the time, I promise!" the girl went on. "I folded and pressed your wardrobe. You'll find everything returned to order."

Amelia smiled and took comfort in Teerah's diligent service. "You did well, Teerah," she said. "Please light some candles, and then you can withdraw to your bed."

Teerah curtsied and quickly fetched a candelabrum made from silver but without filigree or other adornment. Amelia waited patiently as she lit the candles with a taper from the low coals and then placed it on her dresser.

Prentice also said nothing, the growing candlelight showing him to be standing apart from all the other furniture, arms folded across his chest. His stance and demeanor reminded Amelia of the prince's knight commander, and she found that comforting. At last Teerah excused herself.

When she was gone, Amelia looked at Prentice. Without knowing exactly what she was doing, she rushed across to him and laid her head on his chest. Prentice pulled his arms back, clearly uncertain of the duchess's meaning or what she expected of him. For herself, Amelia felt nothing romantic, only a longing for her father or her husband, a strong presence upon whom she could rely at this time when everything was confusing and frightening. At this moment, Prentice was like an uncle to her, and she hoped he would understand it that way. She remained there for a breath, just enough time for a warning thought to come into her mind. She stepped back and straightened her spine.

"That was not appropriate," she said formally, her face schooled, but with her eyes she searched for some sign that he understood her action and its meaning. "I apologize."

Prentice' expression remained impassive, but he seemed to accept that Amelia was not offering him anything more intimate than that one moment. All young maids in the kingdom knew scandalous stories of highborn ladies who thought it a thrill to take a lowborn man, or convict even, as a lover or just for a tumble. Amelia had always been too intelligent to see such tales as anything other than folly. Such a dalliance could only ever end badly, doubly so for the man.

Amelia searched Prentice's face, hoping to see confirmation that he understood. She only realized that she was staring at him when he broke the silence with a polite cough.

"Forgive me, Your Grace," he said quietly. "but I take it the council did not go well?"

Amelia blinked and then sighed heavily. "It went..."

For a moment, she thought back over it, the tension and the uncertainty of each moment. Personally, she had reason to be pleased. She had held to her rank in the face of a whole room of men who would have gladly disregarded her. But as far as outcomes were concerned, she had no idea if she had lost or gained.

"I am not certain how..." she tried again, then stopped. She headed over to her dresser and poured herself watered wine in a silver goblet. She took a long draught. She was about to speak again when Sir Liam thrust himself into the tent. His hair was matted to his forehead with sweat, and he was red-faced from the heat of the council. There was a wildness to his appearance that was reminiscent of his rage in the church after the death of Sir Dav.

"Duchess Amelia, what have you done?" he demanded in a low, menacing voice. He stopped when he saw Prentice, his expression shifting suddenly to disbelief. "You?"

"Do you think to call your liege lady to account, sir?" Prentice asked, and he shifted a step sideways so that his body was between Amelia and Sir Liam.

Sir Liam's anger returned, but now somewhat redirected. "You should be dead in a ditch, convict. I do not know by what sorcery you have come to be here, but you do not question me!" He all but shouted the last words, and his hand rested on the hilt of his sword.

"And you do not question Her Grace, your liege," Prentice retorted, still speaking quietly but with a steely edge to his voice. He showed no sign of being threatened by Liam's lack of calm.

For what seemed an impossibly long moment, the two men stared at each other, and Amelia felt near panic rise inside her. She had been right; it was Sir Liam who was risking his honor because he could not keep his temper.

She pressed the terror down with all her will and prayed her voice wouldn't tremble as she spoke. "Sir Liam, I did not call you here to berate my convict," she said, hoping to seem as calm as Prentice did, but frightened her voice just sounded soft and weak. "Calm yourself immediately."

Sir Liam's dark glare slid coldly from Prentice to her, and Amelia wondered if he was able to get his self-control back. She swallowed but met his gaze and refused to flinch. Gradually, the tension left Sir Liam's frame, and he lowered his head for a moment.

"I take it something troubles you, Sir Liam?" she said, quickly offering him a chance to speak his mind without anger. If he felt he was about to be dismissed, she was certain his rage would surface again.

"Your Grace," Sir Liam began, and his voice sounded like he was being forced to chew broken glass. "Do you..." He paused. "I fear that you do not fully understand the implications of what you have just done. The council..." His eyes searched the ground. He was plainly struggling to order his thoughts to express them clearly.

"The Forfeits Council, Sir Liam?" she asked and moved to stand just one step behind Prentice's shoulder. She wanted his protection, at least until she was sure Sir Liam would not resort to violence, but she did not want to look like she was hiding behind a convict. Prentice, for his part, neither moved nor spoke, not taking his eyes from Sir Liam for a moment.

"Your Grace, your presence at the council offended many."

"Yourself included?"

"Your Grace, I am your man, bound to loyal service."

"I have never doubted it," Amelia lied. "But nonetheless, you have misgivings?"

Sir Liam nodded. "Yes."

"And they are?"

"You have pledged the entire of your lands and your title!" he said.

"I know that."

"If we are not victorious, that will make every one of your knights landless, cut loose in a way that declares us unfit for service. We will all be marked as failures, as stained as cowards."

"You do not think the prince will be victorious?" she asked.

"Of course I do! But the risk... to honor..." His voice was weaker now, with an undertone of pleading.

"Honor is won from risk," Amelia chided, feeling the conversation now more within her control. "Risk much to gain the full worth of the honor won! That is the point of a Forfeits Council, Sir Liam, or so I am reliably informed."

Amelia looked askance at Prentice. It was a momentary glance, hardly any gesture at all, but Sir Liam noticed it. She knew at once it was a mistake.

Her knight's expression hardened again, and his lips twisted into a sneer. "You are foolish to listen to the words of this dog!"

"You call me foolish to my face?"

"I do!" Sir Liam had mastered his rage; pride was the motivation that drove his words now. "It is my loyal duty to speak when I think my liege is acting unwisely. I did it for Sir Dav, and I would have done it for your husband, the duke!"

"Then say what you must, Sir Liam," Amelia instructed with a sigh of resignation. At every turn, courtesy and etiquette showed themselves to be two-edged weapons. No sooner did she wield them to success than they were turned back on her again.

Sir Liam turned his sneer on Prentice. "He is beneath you."

"Of course I am," Prentice said, surprising her and also Sir Liam, by his expression. "I am a convict, transported and condemned."

"You are an arrogant, uppity cur," Sir Liam spat, and he surged forward, slamming his gauntleted hand across Prentice's face. The blow dropped Prentice to one knee, and he fell forward on all fours.

"Sir Liam!" Amelia shouted, surprised by the suddenness of the strike. Her knight seemed to barely hear her.

"You see, this is his proper position, crawling before his betters." Sir Liam turned his eyes on Amelia, and there was something in his expression that frightened her even more than before. She took an involuntary step back. "This is what comes when commoners think to rise above their station. Birth tells out. Doubtless that, in time, Duke Marne would have taught you not to presume above your place—"

"Like you do?" she asked him.

"You should be thanking her!" said Prentice pushing himself up to his feet.

Sir Liam whirled on him once more, lashing out with his right hand to backfist Prentice to the ground again. This time Prentice was ready for him and stepped in, intercepting the strike. One hand on Sir Liam's elbow and the other up under his chin, Prentice pushed the knight off balance and against the tent's central pole, holding him there so he was unable to get purchase. Prentice leaned close to Sir Liam's face, a thin trickle of blood running down from his brow, where Sir Liam's gauntlet had cut him. Liam tried to push Prentice off but found himself trapped as Prentice skillfully held him out of position. The weight of Liam's armor now worked against him as well.

"You fled the field at the river bend," Prentice muttered.

"You bastard, I'll gut you!"

"But you were no coward," Prentice continued, ignoring Sir Liam's threat. "You and I both know that! The position was indefensible, and you had the duchess's life to protect. You did what you had to do."

"I do not need your affirmations, prick! Unhand me, and I'll—"

Prentice shifted his grip, and his forearm pressed hard against Sir Liam's throat. The knight made a small choking noise. It was enough to give Sir Liam pause and let Prentice finish what he had to say.

"I know you hear the whispers," Prentice said, his voice guttural and quiet. "They don't say it to your face, do they, but they say it. They wonder if you are a failure, a coward, don't they?"

Sir Liam did not speak, but the hate in his eyes still frightened Amelia. She was certain that if Prentice released him at this moment, he would likely kill them both right here.

Could Prentice hold him long enough for him to calm down? And would Sir Liam even be able to?

Her whole life now seemed balanced on the edge of a sword in Prentice's hands.

"You should thank her," Prentice said again. "She has given you the clearest chance to show your courage. She risks everything, but to them she just seems like a foolish woman, a common woman. But you? They know you know the meaning of honor, even if they doubt you have any left. They know your birth. When you ride tomorrow, they will know that you know what you risk. Let them call you coward then. Let them call a victor coward! The prince will see; every born man, blooded and sworn, will see. You will either die in glory or return in victory, but your honor will be spotless."

Prentice's words seemed to be seeping into Sir Liam's thoughts, as the knight had ceased to struggle, and his expression became more pensive. A sneer came to his lips again, but half-heartedly. "You counsel her, now you think to counsel me?"

Prentice nodded and looked to the duchess. "Her Grace orders me to speak and I tell her what I think. She has ordered you to leave me be, and you have found every chance you could to hound my steps. You call me cur, but you pay me your attentions like a lovesick page. It seems she is not going to stop talking to me, and every time you disobey her, it only threatens your honor further, so just stop. The duchess has offered me my freedom, should I survive this campaign. Halt your vendetta until then, and I swear I will meet you as a free man on the ground of your choice."

"You think I would lower myself to accept your challenge? Even were you a freed man?"

"No challenge, no duel; just two men. No whispering gossips or doubting nobles. Pick the field, and I will stand for you to vent your anger or hate until it satisfies you."

Sir Liam looked past Prentice at the duchess. "And Her Grace will allow the killing of her favorite pet?"

Duchess Amelia shrugged, realizing the part she needed to play in Prentice's argument, though she did not like it. "It seems that even the authority of a duchess is insufficient to stem the rage of two men bent on killing each other." Even as she said it, Amelia knew she was being unfair to Prentice. He had shown nothing but a seemingly endless capacity to control his own anger.

"Is that enough?" Prentice asked.

Sir Liam looked at him once more. "And in the meantime?"

"In the meantime, you swear to hold your actions against me. I lead the rogues foot under your command. I will obey without question, and all these moments between you and me are forgotten until victory or death."

Sir Liam considered the proposal for some time, and Amelia felt unsure that he would accept it.

Finally, he asked one last question. "If I refuse?"

"You can feel my hand at your throat. Your body will be dragged from here, stripped, and thrown in a ditch. You will not have a Christian burial because you will have died raising your hand to your liege lady. Your name will be cursed, and your honor gone for eternity."

Sir Liam suddenly tried to wrestle himself free, but Prentice maintained his leverage and grip.

The knight's shoulders slumped. "All right!"

"Swear it," Duchess Amelia ordered him. "On your title, before God."

Sir Liam's eyes narrowed, but he nodded. "I so swear."

"Before God?"

"Before God. I will take no action until this campaign is complete and you have freed him."

The duchess nodded. "I accept your oath, Sir Liam, and will honor it and you. Prentice?" She nodded at the convict, who bowed his head in response. He loosened his grip, but before he could release him, Liam broke his hold and pushed Prentice off.

"Remember your oath, sir," Amelia warned.

"I will never forget!" Sir Liam said through gritted teeth. He sketched a simple bow and turned without waiting to be dismissed.

"You may leave, sir," Amelia said to his back.

"You should practice wrestling in armor more," Prentice called after him, and Amelia caught her breath.

"Enough, Prentice!" she commanded, but Sir Liam left without being further provoked.

When he was gone, Amelia slumped down to sit on the edge of her bed. She sighed and looked at Prentice. "You had your victory. Why risk stirring the whole thing up again?"

"I am sorry, Your Grace," Prentice said, bowing his head again, but he had a satisfied smile on his face.

Amelia shook her head, too tired to admonish him further. "You have done me a great service."

"A reprieve, no more than that."

"It's enough for me." After a moment's silence, Amelia looked at Prentice directly. "Will you face him when I free you? He has sworn, but you have no honor to bind you to your word. Even as a freed man, no law would condemn you."

"I will stand, as I said," Prentice assured her. "Even if I did not, I think he would hunt me down. His hate is that deep now. But, of course, none of this matters very much."

"No?"

"No, Your Grace. I am a rogue, and tomorrow the best odds are I will be a corpse on a muddy field. What happens if I live long enough to be freed is too far ahead for me to worry about."

CHAPTER 33

After the duchess dismissed him, Prentice went back to the other convicts and found Turley sleeping in the grass. He picked a spot nearby and lay down, but sleep did not come. He knew it was not long until dawn and any rest would be valuable, but his mind would not settle. After staring at the stars for a short while, he rose and walked back into the main of the camp.

In spite of the hour, the entire area was a bustle of activity, with lanterns and torches burning everywhere. Pages and squires worked feverishly, polishing armor for men and horses, ensuring weapons were sharp and all the leather and tack oiled. Watching the hive of activity, Prentice could not help smiling. These were the great and the good, the best of society. On the eve of battle, they fretted and worried over every thread and tool, while not far away the dregs of the kingdom, despised dogs one and all, lay in calm and ignorant sleep because no one cared enough to tell them that there would be battle come the dawn.

Still, he thought, they would end up just as dead by sundown the next day. Prentice made his way to the stewards and told them what he would need for the rogues foot in the coming battle. He was given the obligatory sneers and cold glances, but the duchess's household had come to accept that he had some of her authority and no longer questioned his requests as long as he made them politely. When his orders were filled, he had everything loaded on the back of five hand carts and made his way back to the convicts in time for the sun to rise. He found Overseer Tuke and nudged the man awake.

"What d'you want?" Tuke demanded, rubbing his scalp as he woke up.

"I need ten men off the chain," Prentice told him.

"Oh, got a dance to go to, have you?"

"I've got five carts to fetch before the march to the siege!"

Tuke sat up, suddenly a little more awake. It seemed no one had even bothered to inform him how near the army was to Fallenhill and the siege. He rose stiffly to his feet and chased up the rest of his overseers, kicking them awake with no more respect than he would show for the convicts.

Soon Prentice had two overseers with him as he picked ten men to release from the chain. He thought about the recently captured farmers, who would all be stronger than the convicts who had come over the mountains. But they were too likely to make a run for freedom, and that would just get them killed. The army was on edge, and every man was ready for action. A fleeing convict would not last twenty paces.

One of the overseers accompanied the men as Prentice led them to the hand carts. They grumbled as they took the weight and got the creaky wooden wheels turning, but they dragged them well enough. The little column returned in time to find the convicts all awake and ready to move. One of the prince's heralds was giving orders, and Tuke was tugging his forelock respectfully. The herald had a gilded mail coat that shone like liquid gold in the dawning sunlight, and once he had delivered his orders, he rode back to the main body of the column.

"Right," shouted Tuke, cracking his whip. "Time to shift your lazy arses! Destiny awaits."

Now that the day of battle had arrived, the convicts marched first so that they were in the vanguard, first to the field and in the center. As they marched, teams of squires and lesser knights took up position around them to prevent any escape. It was onerous duty, shepherding the rogues, and Prentice imagined that none of these knights could have offered very much at the Forfeits Council.

Turley wended his way through the chained crowd and took a place next to Prentice, who marched in front of the carts. Turley looked over the five loads and their sweating bearers pulling hard. "What's this, then?" he asked Prentice.

"That's what we'll be fighting with."

"That right?" Turley assessed the loads again. "We had better options when Druce gave us the picks at the river bend."

"If we had good weapons, we'd be knights," Prentice said without looking at him.

"Aye. So we're to die today, then?"

"That's the plan they have for us."

Turley nodded thoughtfully, then he lifted his face with his customary wry smile. "In that case, let me take this moment to say that you've been a right sullen prick of a friend most of these days. Too serious, by far, but never mind that. You did fix my ankle, so thank you for that!"

Prentice returned his smile. "And you've been a pain in my arse, making trouble for us at every turn since the day I fixed your damned ankle. I should have let the thing turn septic and spared myself the trouble."

"Oh, that might have worked out for you, no mistake," Turley agreed solemnly. "But think of all the fun you'd have missed!"

It was a strange experience for the convicts to march in front of the army, especially when they crossed a rise and the road split into a dozen smaller tracks, all but disappearing into the long grass of late summer pasture. With the road gone, the convicts spread out on their long chains and moved more slowly. They looked about at the openness of the ground, eyes alert for the enemy they were supposed to fight. On the edges of the crowd, the overseers cracked their whips, and some of the riders went ahead and pointed the way forward, shouting commands that they were not to slow.

Ahead lay Fallenhill, the walled town visible just over half a league away across the gently rolling pasture. The settlement sat on a rise at the southernmost tip of a line of mountains that grew behind it to the north, like a sentry on the border between two lands—one green and pleasant, the other stony and foreboding. The nearer mountains were not so high and had some green patches of pasture on their slopes, any snow melted away by the summer sun. Further north were sterner peaks still capped in bitter white.

The ground at the foot of Fallenhill's walls was blackened and burned, and soot stains climbed the stones as well. But other than that, there was little sign of war or battle. Most especially, there was no enemy. No tents, no siege engines, and even the grass of the pasture was barely trodden. If an army had laid siege to a town the size of Fallenhill, the ground around the walls should have been churned to mud.

"Where are these bastards?" Turley muttered.

Prentice scanned the walls of the town, looking for any evidence. The gates were open, and it looked as if one hung loose off broken hinges.

Otherwise, he could see nothing untoward.

"Well, wherever they are, we need to get this organized." Prentice turned to the carts. The first had sacks of millet bread baked in small loaves and four clay pots, sealed with wax, and full of butter. He would rather have offered them roast beef, pork sausages, or lamb. Even mutton or chicken would have done, but for convicts, bread and butter to break fast was the best he could scare up. He ordered the bread to be distributed and the butter to be brought around by men, with instructions to not give up the jar. There was hardly enough for each man to get a taste; if the front ranks got greedy, the rear would revolt, regardless of the threat of their mounted escort.

"One dip of the jar each," he told Turley, setting his friend to supervise the food. He shouted his commands so that all of them heard him. "Break the hand of any man who tries to dip twice!"

Turley nodded and marched behind the butter jars with his cudgel on his shoulders. Prentice turned to the other carts. Each was loaded with staves—classic farmers poles, light but strong—and piles of rusted metal. Every sharp piece of iron Prentice had been able to find was piled in: scythe blades, kitchen knives, anything with an edge.

"Right," he shouted over them. "Every man gets a pole and a piece of metal. Tie the metal to the end of the pole, and that's your spear!"

The convict men were hardly listening, too busy enjoying the rare pleasure of their breakfast, but a couple had scarfed down their food and now looked at Prentice in a mixture of fear and disbelief.

"A pole with a sickle tied to it?" one called out. "You expect us to fight with that?"

"I do," Prentice answered flatly.

"We'll die!"

Many of the convicts grumbled their assent, and Prentice didn't know how to answer the man. He looked aside for a moment and saw Tuke and his overseers shaking their heads. They clearly did not like the idea of giving a convict even a pole and a piece of sharp metal.

Prentice felt his shoulders slump. This was the madness of the Grand Kingdom at war, and he was stuck right in the middle of it, forced to somehow make it work. He shut his eyes for a moment and then looked at them once again.

"Take the pole," he shouted. "If you don't take it, you'll still have to march to the attack. They'll make you!" He looked over the men's heads to the mounted riders stationed around the crowd of convicts. "Don't march, and they'll ride you down. Try to run, and they'll ride you down. Do anything they do not like, anything you are not ordered to, and you will be cut down here. The only chance you have to see the end of this day is to do exactly what you are told, so take the damn poles. It's the only choice you are being offered!"

"Not much of one!"

"No, it isn't."

Turley returned and supervised the distribution of the poles and the metal. No fine blades, sturdy maces, or mighty axes. Just rough bits of sharp metal, black or rusted. Just as a knight's horse stepped cleanly over puddles and mud, so the bright and pretty Grand Kingdom army rode high above a filthy collection of rogues; no more than clods of dung to be thrown insultingly at the enemy by petulant little boys.

"Discipline problems, little corporal?" called a voice.

Prentice turned to see Sir Liam seated on his warhorse and accompanied by another dozen knights. Prentice watched suspiciously for a moment, unsure if Sir Liam would keep his oath, then he remembered all the other men present and quickly ducked his head in obeisance, tugging his forelock.

"No problems, sir knight," he said. "They'll march when ordered."

"See that they do. I came today to slay the enemy, not to wet my blade on leprous scum resisting the mercy of the faith!"

Some of the knights with him chuckled or sneered, then followed as Sir Liam kicked his horse to a trot and rode to his station on the field. The last was a knight in church green with a double-crossed surcoat. The man wore a full helm with the visor pulled down, but he seemed to stare at Prentice as he rode past, as if he recognized him. Prentice bowed his head again as the man's charger kicked up the earth and trotted after the others.

"Well, that was nearly polite," Turley said, watching them go.

"The duchess got him to swear on his honor to leave off killing me until she frees me."

"That could make freedom seem less inviting, I guess."

"We've got to survive this first." Prentice gestured to the walls in front of them.

"Are they hiding inside, do you think?"

Prentice shook his head. "Not without trying to fix the gate."

"Are those trees out the front?" Turley asked, pointing to spindly black projections in the burnt region before the walls.

Prentice shook his head again. "Something more merciless, I think."

Turley nodded. "That would make sense, I suppose."

For the next half an hour, they stood watching the town and nothing moved. Behind them, the convicts wrestled with constructing their makeshift weapons, tearing rags off their clothing to bind metal to wood. Prentice knew the complainers among them were right; it was little more than a gesture toward arming them. Most would end up with an improvised tool that would break apart after the first strike. With his cudgel in his hand and the poniard on his belt, Prentice felt almost embarrassingly well-armed.

Nearing mid-morning, the prince arrived with his honor guard, with heralds riding ahead and trumpets announcing their coming. Forty strong, in royal house colors, they made an impressive company, with Prince Mercad at their head. Beside him rode Duchess Amelia. Her eye passed over the rogues as she rode by, and though she saw Prentice, she did not acknowledge him. The prince's guard stopped a little forward of the rogues, on their left. For some time, captains rode to the prince from other parts of the line and engaged him in deep conversation.

"What are they waiting for?" Turley asked Prentice, watching the nobles in conference about the royal party.

"I think they want to know where the enemy is as well. I wonder why they keep looking at us." Several of the nobles seemed to be watching the rogues, and one or two pointed toward them.

"Maybe they don't like the look of convicts with weapons," Turley mused.

Prentice shrugged as he watched the deliberations of the nobles. "They should have thought of that before they brought us out to a battle. And 'weapons' is an optimistic description."

"That's the truth!"

A herald detached from the little crowd of horsemen about the prince and trotted toward them.

"Aye up," Prentice said as the rider approached. "Looks like we're about to get our orders."

The herald rode up, and Prentice stepped forward.

"You there," said the herald. "The rogues will advance to the town."

"Yes, m'lord." Prentice nodded. "What is our goal?"

"The town," the herald answered disdainfully, then wheeled his horse and rode back to the prince's entourage.

"Well, that's our order!" said Prentice to Turley. "Let's get everyone off the chain."

They scanned the edges of the convict mass. When they spotted Tuke, Prentice jogged over to the overseer. "The order's come. Time to get them off the chain."

Tuke looked at him with incomprehension on his face, as if Prentice were speaking a foreign language.

"They can't fight on the chain, man!" Prentice urged.

Tuke looked back and forth for a moment, as if hoping a more senior man might materialize and take the responsibility out of his hands. Prentice wanted to hit him. How could Tuke have marched this far and not realized that the convicts would have to be let off the chain at some point? True, it was over ten years since the Kingdom had marched convicts to war, but it wasn't that hard to figure out. Finally, Tuke nodded and went to pass the word to his other overseers. Prentice returned to the front and jumped onto the back of one of the handcarts so that he could be seen.

"Right, you lot, listen up," he shouted. In the morning stillness, his voice carried. Knights hundreds of paces away turned to look as he bellowed. He wondered how much of his words they could make out. "We've been ordered to advance, and in a minute the overseers are going to loose the chain!"

Murmurs moved through the convicts. Prentice knew this was an important moment, the cusp of disaster. Even free men and professionals could balk at this point in a battle, maybe try to refuse, to flee. It was to his advantage that the enemy had not shown themselves, but he did not doubt some would try to hold back regardless, which would just be an excuse for the knights to do something brutal.

"Look around you!" Prentice shouted. "Look to your left and right, and behind you. See those armed men on horseback? If you try to flee, they will run you down. They are not here for the enemy, they are here for you!"

There was a further round of grumbling at this, and Prentice had a sense of how Sir Liam must have felt on the day he had him flogged. If the convicts rioted instead of marching, then the whole thing would be a disaster and he and Turley would be the first ones killed, either by the convicts or by the knights who would crush them.

"When we march," he went on, "they will make sure that no one shirks. There will be no stragglers, so keep up! Disobey and you'll be killed. Try to run and you will be killed! The only hope you and I have to see the end of this day is through the other side of this battle, so be ready. And when I call forward, you march! These bastards are waiting for any chance, any excuse to end your life. Do not give it to them!"

Prentice scanned the faces of the men in front of him. They seemed grim and resigned, but not angry at least. The rattle of the chains being drawn sounded, and the overseers stepped back swiftly, whips in hand. Some convicts shifted their feet, but no one seemed ready to run. Prentice nodded and turned to face the walls of Fallenhill. Raising his arm, he called for the advance, and the convicts behind him began to walk forward.

"Bold move, calling knights and squires bastards," Turley said, walking at his side.

"A bit of brass to inspire dogs and rogues," Prentice answered.

He felt himself smiling and for a moment he wondered how that could be. Then he realized that there was a grim pleasure in knowing that whatever brutality the Kingdom hammered down upon him, he was on the field now. In battle, all that mattered was the enemy in front of him, the man he was sent to kill or die by. It was liberating in a way, though his hands shook a little with nerves. He gripped hard on his cudgel to try to still them.

The march over the grass was eerily quiet, with just the sound of feet shuffling softened by the fronds. No trumpets sounded for the glorious charge, and no enemy shouted taunts or insults. The rogues made their way across the meadows, slowed at one point as they were forced to cross a low stone wall. They looked left and right in case an enemy might suddenly appear from their flank, but there was nothing.

It was calm. Pleasant, even.

Soon enough, Prentice and the first ranks reached the blackened area in front of the walls. At last, some sense of a war and battle entered the morning. Every fortified town in the Grand Kingdom had buildings and structures outside their walls: paupers' shanties, animal pens, and crafts too offensive to allow inside the walls, like tanners or butchers. It was these structures that had been burned at the foot of Fallenhill. The spindly projections that Prentice and Turley had seen at a distance turned out to be tree-like scaffolds, improvised but tall, and each one had a dozen bodies hanging from their branches. The feet and legs of each victim were blackened by fire.

"How's this, then?" Turley asked, pointing to another of the "trees." This one had only four victims, and they had been hanged after the fires, it seemed. The four were dressed in buckskin leathers and did not look like Kingdom folk. Turley pointed to the figures' heads, with the rictus skin pulled tight to the skulls. Each one had pointed tips to the tops of their ears.

"There's your fey folk!" Turley said.

Prentice smiled. "Well, you had to be right about something eventually."

"Don't worry, when you have your first time, I'll help you through it. So, what now?"

Prentice looked back over his shoulder. The prince's banner was clearly visible, but no signal was being given. No herald was coming with fresh orders. The whole field of knights was waiting and watching.

"If it's a trap, they want to make damn sure we spring it before they ride to the fight," Turley muttered.

Prentice agreed. He looked at the city gatehouse with its ruined gates. Most of the rogues were now well within bowshot of the walls. If it was an ambush, the enemy was clearly waiting for troops to enter the town.

"Might as well get it over with," he said and waved the convicts to follow him into the gateway.

The crowd bunched around the entry. If there was to be an attack, this was the most vulnerable moment; a densely packed group made an inviting target. Hesitantly, they crept through the gateway and into the town proper to find no ambush, but devastation far worse than they could have expected.

Instead of archers on the walls around them or soldiers hidden in the close streets and alleys, there was a scorched wasteland and a charcoal stench that stained every breath with bitterness. Everything inside the walls had been consumed, every building burned to the ground. From just inside the gates, Prentice could see all the way across the space to the walls on the other side, backed against the hills and the keep—Baron Stopher's provincial seat. No banners flew from its walls, and it looked, at this distance, that the windows had been burned out as well. It was as if the town was now just a vast cauldron full of charcoal and ashes.

The rogues advanced slowly, scanning the destruction with awe. Hands clutched staves nervously. The tension among them felt like a cloud, made real by the combinations of dust and ash kicked up by their feet. Prentice led them along a path of sorts, through the destruction that had probably once been the high street.

"Ain't nothing smoldering," Turley observed, noting no smoke rising anywhere around them. "This burned out days ago!"

"Before we marched from the crossroads, I would guess," Prentice agreed.

"I thought sieges were supposed to take weeks. Months, even."

"Normally."

Their path through the destruction took them toward the town square. Every now and then they passed collapsed mounds of brick or stoneworks, but never more than a handful still stacked on top of one another. Nothing was higher than a man's waist.

The town square was a fresh horror. The open ground contained hundreds of bodies, all burned black, most down to the bones. Lengths of chain ran throughout the crowd of corpses, wrapping around the blackened bodies and anchored to the ground by iron spikes.

"They chained 'em up and burned 'em all?" one of the convicts said, and men around him only shook their heads in disbelief.

None of them stepped into the space of the town square, for fear of stepping on one of the skeletal corpses bound to the ground. Instead, they began to shift slowly around the edges, picking a path between burned ruins and blackened corpses. As they continued forward, they were drawn to a strange mound with a figure on top of it, the highest point in the entire space.

The figure was like an iron statue, but as they neared it, they could see that it was, in fact, a suit of armor scorched black by the fire. There were chains and manacles holding the armor in place, shackled upright to a pair of crossed iron bars in an X-shaped frame. Seeing the frame and the bodies behind, Prentice knew immediately that the armor had an occupant who had died in the flames, chained in place and baked in his steel. There were little rivulets of melted metal that had flowed down the armor. It was the gold and silver that had once decorated the armor, now run down like wax on the side of a candle.

"I think we've found Baron Stopher," Prentice said, guessing the dead victim's identity. His body had been set up on a mound of what also looked like melted wax. It took a moment more for Prentice to understand what he was looking at.

"It's gold!" exclaimed one of the men next to him, and Prentice knew he was right.

The entire mound, easily many paces across, was melted gold and silver. Here and there, the glint of precious metal could be seen through the soot, and once he knew what he was looking at, Prentice's eyes found remnant shapes of jewelry and other items. The neck and handle of a silver and gold wine jug was easily picked out from the melted mass, as well as lumps of fused coins. It took only a moment's hesitation before the men nearest the mound fell on it in a lust for wealth, hammering and kicking at the soft metal, hoping to break off a piece for themselves.

"This must be almost every bit of gold the town had," Turley said, picking up an errant chunk of yellow metal and brushing off some of the soot. A passing convict eyed it greedily, but Turley pushed the man and threw the lump away. The convict watched it fall and went after it.

"I would guess that it was exactly every bit of precious metal in the town!" Prentice said.

"Why? Why burn it and melt it all?"

"It's a message." There was a cold tone to Prentice's voice.

"What message?"

"That whatever they've come for, it's not what we expect." He nodded over his shoulder to where the bodies of the townsfolk lay in chains. "They take no prisoners, so they do not want slaves. They scorch the ground, so they have not come to conquer." He looked back at the gold mound in front of him, desperate men clambering over it, hammering at it. "And they take no plunder. Whatever they want with us, it only involves destruction and death."

Prentice's face was grim as he watched the scene in front of him. Turley appeared to be lost in thought for a moment, then he opened his mouth. Before he could say something, a sound behind him caught all their attention. The men on the gold stopped, and everyone turned to look back at the gatehouse. A horn was blown, and it resounded a second time as a slow trickle of knights began to walk their horses into Fallenhill.

The riders guided their mounts single file along the path trod by the rogues, but they did not redirect around the corpses. Sounds of cracking and crunching echoed from the stone walls as the heavy warhorses ground the blackened bones under foot. The convicts were shoved aside, and all but two who had been clambering on the gold mound quickly slid off. Prentice stood aside for the knights and pushed other men to make a gap. He did not recognize the knight who came at the front, a strong-looking man with a spike on his helmet and a purple silk cape about his shoulders.

"What is this?" the knight demanded.

"Baron Stopher, I think, my lord," Prentice answered.

"Baron...?" The nobleman looked at the suit of armor in disbelief. His features distorted in revulsion, and then he stared at the mound of melted metal. "Is that gold?"

"Aye, your lordship," offered a convict eagerly, holding up a broken chunk for the knight to see.

The knight looked from the dirty lump in the convict's hand to the other convicts standing around. He erupted in rage, drawing forth his sword. "Filthy, looting dogs!" he bellowed. "All of you will die. Marrick!"

Another man behind the purple-clad knight also drew his sword, quickly followed by every man on a horse.

"No, my lord!" Prentice shouted, and the force of his shout echoed just as loudly as the knight's. He stepped directly in front of the man's mount, acutely aware of the futility of the gesture. The knight could as easily slay him as any of the others. "They act on my orders! I told them to begin breaking it down so that Baron Stopher could be laid to rest."

"Your orders?" the knight asked, his sword still raised. "What are you that you would give orders, rogue?"

"Corporal," Prentice responded swiftly and made sure to make a show of tugging his forelock respectfully. "Of the rogues foot. By order of the Duchess of the Reach, my lord."

"The Duchess of the Reach?"

The knight's man, Marrick, leaned close to his commander and spoke quietly.

The nobleman did not appear pleased with what he heard. "That shrew put a convict in charge of convicts?"

"Who else would want the duty, my liege?" Marrick said.

The commander shrugged dismissively. "Indeed. No wonder the Reach needs us to ride to its defense. The little bitch is rutting it into ruin. She needs a husband, and no mistake!" The knight turned his eyes on Prentice, lowering his sword as he did so. "All right, you little shit eater, you told them to work the baron's body free, is that right?"

"Yes, my lord," Prentice lied, and he looked around at the other convicts, who all nodded.

"So it is your fault that these untouchables are defiling the body of a ruling noble, who should be bestowed by the holy hands of the saintliest of sacrists?"

Prentice kept his head bowed and clenched his teeth to keep himself from answering back.

"Any one of these scum would slit their own grandmothers' throats for the offer of gold. Marrick, every one of them on their knees now!"

"Yes, liege." Marrick and the other knights shouted for the convicts to kneel, quickly riding to form a cordon around the massed men. Any convict too slow in getting to his knees was kicked down or given a crack across the head with a pommel. Prentice and Turley knelt where they were standing. When every convict was on the ground, the lead knight surveyed them.

"All right, Marrick, two of you dismount and check each one in turn, starting with this insolent turd." He pointed at Prentice. "Search them thoroughly, as well as the ground at their feet. If you find gold, run them through. Chasley, do you have your hunting bow with you?"

"I do, my lord," answered another man-at-arms, this one dressed in only a mail coat and chausses, wearing the same colors as the commander.

"If any one of them stands before he's searched, any one of them seems to throw something away, looks up, or even puts his head to the side, you use him for target practice. And his neighbors as well, since villains always keep company among dogs and convicts."

"I will, my lord." Chasley drew his bow from behind his saddle and nocked an arrow, scanning the kneeling men with sharp eyes.

Marrick and another knight seized Prentice and yanked him to his feet. They wrenched his tunic over his head and pulled at his waistband. He made to help them, but one punched him in the stomach, and Marrick grabbed at his hands to see if he had hidden any there. Prentice was quickly naked, the knights even stripping him of his smallclothes.

"Nothing on this one."

"And the ground at his feet?"

They kicked at the dirt. "Nothing there."

"What about that stick?"

Marrick examined the end of Prentice's cudgel. "Iron," he said.

"Very well," said the knight. "On to the next! We'll find out the thieves, won't we?"

The two men pushed Prentice back to his knees in the soot and dust. "My lord, may I cover myself?" he called to the knight through gritted teeth.

The man on the horse spared him a disdainful glance. "If you think your little dignity so important!"

Prentice pulled his tunic over his head but didn't risk standing to put his trousers back on.

When Marrick and the other man approached Turley, he was already taking off his own tunic and trousers, smart enough to be nothing but cooperative. He hesitated at his own loincloth, but Marrick cuffed him over the back of the head and soon he was naked too. When they were satisfied, they moved to the next man.

Turley landed on his knees in the dust next to Prentice. There was the sudden sound of a thrumming bow string and a short, gurgling cry. Everyone turned to see Chasley nocking a new arrow to his bowstring.

"Bugger moved." Was all he said to explain himself.

His liege looked over his shoulder to the now-slain convict. "Took him in the throat, Chasley! Good shot."

"Thank you, my lord."

From behind the crowd, nearer the gatehouse, Sir Liam's voice called to the knights. "Lord Dunstan, do you lead them at prayer?" He rode his horse forward, leading his own little squadron of knights. Unlike Lord Dunstan, Sir Liam took pains to ride around the chained bodies massed in the square.

"Bastard dogs were looting, and this bastard's bastard of yours had the audacity to deny it!"

Sir Liam looked down at Prentice kneeling in the dust and smiled. "He's not mine. It's the duchess who has a soft spot for mangy strays."

"Indeed?"

"What of the enemy, Lord Dunstan?"

"The enemy?" Lord Dunstan looked about, as if he had forgotten that there had ever been an enemy. He shrugged. "Look about you, sir. There is no enemy. They have long fled, the cowards."

"What of there?" asked Sir Liam, indicating the damaged but still upright keep.

"Burnt like the rest," Lord Dunstan said. "No doubt empty."

"You will not mind if I see for myself, I hope?"

"Be my guest."

"Got one!" Marrick shouted, like an excited boy sighting game on his first hunt. Everyone turned to see a naked, bony man being held in a vice grip while the other knight held forth a hunk of sooty gold, no larger than a peach pit.

"I told you what to do, Marrick," Lord Dunstan ordered.

Without hesitation, Marrick drew his dirk and thrust it straight into the man's belly.

"I'll leave you to your work," said Sir Liam with a nod, and he led his horsemen away toward the keep. They were mercifully out of earshot before Lord Dunstan turned back in the saddle to look down on Prentice once more.

"Well, it seems we found one already," Lord Dunstan said, his voice oily with satisfaction. "Which makes you a liar and a leader of thieves. Each one we catch will die, and then you'll be made to pay for your part in this. Put him in chains and leave him to wait for my pleasure!"

Another knight dismounted and grabbed Prentice. Near the back of the kneeling crowd, two men suddenly broke and ran for the gatehouse. One still carried his improvised spear, while the other ran empty handed. Chasley's bow sang twice, and each man fell on his face in the dirt.

"We'll get them all, every last one," Lord Dunstan said.

The knight dragged Prentice away, his new shoes—taken off when he'd removed his trousers—slipping from his grip and left behind.

CHAPTER 34

The knights left Prentice sitting in the dust in the shadow of Fallenhill's wall. They threaded a length of chain through the rings on his ankle shackles and then, for good measure, manacled his wrists with another chain. After telling him to sit, they set a man-at-arms to watch him and went back to Lord Dunstan's search for pilfered gold. The man-at-arms sneered at Prentice for a moment. Then, having satisfied himself that there was nowhere for a shackled convict to flee to in the ruin, he climbed the mound of a burned-out house and watched the movements of the other soldiers. Many more knights and their bondsmen had entered the town now, and hearing of the mound of gold, many were joining the eager search of the convicts.

Prentice sat with his head on his arms and rested as best he could. The dust and soot caked his throat and nostrils. He heard another man talking with the guard but didn't bother to look up. He was too tired and beaten to care. He did not even raise his head at the approaching footsteps, but the gentleness of the voice that spoke to him caught his attention.

"Would you like a drink?"

Prentice looked, and for a moment he couldn't see the man's face, as the sun was behind his head. It was as if his hair were a bright lantern. The man shifted, and Prentice's eyes were able to focus. The man was offering him a clay jug with a cork stopper.

"Thank you," Prentice said bitterly, turning away. "But there'll be trouble for you, speaking with a convict like me."

"Well, you're not the only one here."

Looking back at the man, Prentice noticed that he had fettered ankles; he was a convict as well, with bandages on his feet. Prentice took the jug and saw bandages on the man's hands too. He wore a simple shift of rough cotton, and there was blood on one side of that. It looked like this man had recently been through some harsh discipline.

Prentice pulled the cork, raised the jug to his lips, and took a deep swig. He nearly coughed it back up in surprise.

"Wine?" he said with a sputter, some of the red liquid running down his chin.

"I thought you could use it," said the convict as he sat on the ground next to Prentice.

"If you're caught with this, you'll really be in trouble. I can't remember when I last tasted wine." Prentice took another, longer draught, savoring the flavor. It was sweet and fine, not even watered. He swallowed and sighed. From inside his tunic, the man next to him pulled forth a small loaf of bread, tore it in two, and gave half to Prentice.

"The Church frowns on breaking bread with the condemned," Prentice said, but he took the bread willingly and bit into the soft white fiber with joy. The bread was as fine as the wine. Whoever this convict was, he had a talent for obtaining good grub.

Prentice noticed the man's bandages again; perhaps not so talented.

"The Church frowns on many things it should not," the convict said. "And smiles on things it certainly should not."

"You're happy to criticize God's holy Church?"

"I am qualified."

"Indeed?" Prentice asked, smiling through mouthfuls of bread. The man's brass made him smile. "Are you a sacrist?"

"No," the man said, smiling back. "I'm from an older priesthood."

"Well then, a handful of free advice. Criticism is heresy, and heresy is not forgiven by the holy mother church, especially not in a convict. I speak from experience."

"When truth is heresy, then the orthodox must be liars!"

Prentice slammed the jug to the ground and glared at the man. He recognized these words as a quote from Argensius, the heretical monk whose works had caused Prentice to be tried and convicted.

"Don't!" he said. "Don't waste my time. Argensius died for his beliefs, and I'm about to die for them as well. If the Church was wrong, God would not help them to slay their enemies so readily!"

"You think God is on the side of this church?" the man asked, his manner still mild in spite of Prentice's fury. "Is that what you believe?"

Of course it was what he believed, Prentice wanted to say, but even as he opened his mouth he knew it wasn't true. The fury left him, and inside himself he realized that he was sure the Church of the Grand Kingdom was wrong. Once, perhaps, God had raised it up and entrusted it with His purposes on Earth, but it had long since gone astray. It served itself, Prentice was sure of it.

"Then why doesn't He do something?" he asked the mysterious convict.

"Perhaps He does. Perhaps He's choosing to work quietly at this time. The Church has its own palaces and power, its own soldiers and princes. It doesn't really need God's help. God is in a high and holy place, but He reaches down to those truly in need: widows and orphans who starve, the desperate man and his friends who just need someone to bar the door against evil."

The image of the monstrous wolf stinging its paw on the threshold of the church at the river bend flashed into Prentice's mind. He was about to say something when the sound of shouting echoed around the walls from the direction of the keep. He looked up, then heard the clash of steel. Someone was fighting. The guard sitting on his mound stood up and ran toward the noise, perhaps seeking a closer vantage.

"They've found the scouts," the other convict said. He took a calm bite of his own hunk of bread.

"What scouts?"

"Scouts left behind by the enemy, in the keep, to observe the prince's army."

"What? Why?"

"They know as little of the Grand Kingdom as you know of them, only old rumors and bad suppositions."

"How do you know this?" Prentice asked.

The man did not answer. Together the two of them watched as plumes of dust and ash were kicked up by the fracas, twisting into the air. Knights mounted on horseback rode into and out of the oily cloud, but Prentice guessed that any men on foot would have the advantage. The ruined ground was too uneven, with plenty of obstacles to hide behind or block a horse's charge. Two of the painted men Prentice knew from the enemy's ranks broke out of the cloud through a gap in the circling knights.

"They'll be headed this way!" said the convict, rising to his feet.

Prentice stood as well. "This way? Why?"

The man nodded to the top of the nearby wall and a set of stone steps not twenty paces from them.

"They'll climb the wall?" Prentice asked. "That's no use to them. It's a thirty-foot drop to the other side!"

"If they prepared for this, say, by placing a rope up there, then they will easily be away over the walls before the knights know what is happening, since they are too busy slaying the others."

"So two will escape," Prentice said with a shrug. He sat back down.

"Unless you stop them." The convict walked away toward the gatehouse.

"Stop them? How do you propose I do that?" Prentice lifted his hands to the man's back, showing the manacles on his wrists. As he did so, the manacle on his right wrist fell loose, as if it had never been properly affixed. The chain hung from his left, still locked in place.

Astonished, Prentice stood up and the chain on his ankle irons fell away.

"It appears you have fewer excuses than you thought," said the disappearing convict, now almost lost in the ash clouds blowing across the bowl of the ruined town.

The sound of rushing footsteps and scrambling limbs drew Prentice's attention, and he spotted the two fleeing scouts through the strange gloom, tripping and clambering through the wreckage. Exactly as the convict had said, they were heading for the steps to the ramparts.

Prentice felt frozen in place.

The two men seemed not to have noticed him in their rush to escape. If he wanted, he could simply sit back down and let them go. If he confronted them, he had no doubt they would attack him, try to kill him. A part of him just wanted to hide, let the fool knights deal with the problem if they could. No matter what he did, they would take the glory and force any blame on him. Soon enough, Lord Dunstan would send for him and execute him because some convicts had dared to be as greedy for gold as Lord Dunstan himself. Prentice despised them all: the greedy convicts, the cruel nobility, the brutal invaders. He wanted to sit down in the dust and let the whole lot of them figure it out for themselves.

Let someone else take the scars for once.

The bitterness in his thoughts rushed like a torrent until it struck an unexpected bulwark, a counter thought that resisted the flow of hate catching him by surprise. In his mind he could see the slain villagers of the river bend village, their bodies ripped open, faces twisted in pain and misery. Prentice wanted to think he was on their side—on the side of the truly innocent victims, the side of widows and orphans, as the convict had said God was. But looking into himself, he saw it was a lie. Because faced with a chance to stop two of these invaders, off the chain and with only him and God to answer to in this moment, he wanted to do nothing. Prentice knew that of all the people he hated, he would despise himself the most if he did not do something.

He dropped into a crouch, trying to hide behind rubble as the two scouts drew close. None of the knights had noticed their escape, and they themselves looked to the wall or back over their shoulders. They weren't ready for Prentice. He picked his moment and sprinted around a collapsed house with half a brick chimney still standing. With a roar, he leaped at the pair, crashing into the closest one and knocking him to the ground. Prentice rolled over the man through the soot and dust, coming quickly but awkwardly to his feet. His only weapon was the chain hanging from his wrist and a brick he had managed to snag. He blinked against the stinging dust and ash.

The leading scout stopped his run and glanced back at his companion on the ground, dazed from Prentice's attack. Prentice looked back and forth between them, and they looked at each other as well. For a moment it seemed like they recognized him. Had they been at the river bend village? If so, then these men were among those who murdered the villagers. A rage rose within him, as choking as the dust.

The two scouts looked at each other, and the standing one said, "Ashen."

Prentice had no idea what that meant. The man on the ground said something to his companion in a foreign tongue. His companion nodded, then turned on his heel and ran for the stairs to the ramparts. Prentice threw the brick at his retreating back, grunting with the effort, and caused the man to stumble, but he did not fall or stop running for the steps. Before Prentice could do any more, the other scout launched himself up from the ground, lunging with a dagger.

Prentice stumbled backward on the broken ground, and the scout pressed forward, not trying to flee but committed to covering his comrade's escape. Prentice took hold of the loose manacle in his right hand and pulled the chain taut. He was not trained to fight with a short chain, but he had heard of some slave rebels from the frozen south who made manacles into weapons. He tried to mimic what he had been told of their fighting style.

The scout thrust with his dagger, and Prentice used the taut chain to deflect it as best he could. The conflict was swift, the dagger thrusts driving forward and Prentice blocking desperately. One thrust beat past the chain and cut him on the shoulder, but not deeply. The scout tried to capitalize on the strike, quickly reversing the dagger and bringing it back in a savage slash. But the move unbalanced the man, and he overcommitted. Prentice was able to block the attacking arm then whipped the chain over like a flail, smashing the heavy iron manacle into the scout's face. The man's feet almost slipped out from under him and before he could recover his footing, Prentice grabbed him behind the head and pulled him down into a brutal series of knee strikes, hammering his face and chest. The painted man went limp in his grip and slid unconscious to the ground.

Prentice tried to let him fall but lost his balance as the man's weight shifted downward. He went down on one knee and twisted around, half collapsing across his unconscious enemy. Looking up from where he was sprawled, he saw the other scout throw the coil of rope over the side of the curtain wall from the top of the ramparts. The invader looked back, and his tattooed face contorted into a hateful snarl as their eyes met. The man spat, and Prentice answered him with a one-fingered salute. Then the enemy was gone, and Prentice pushed himself off his captive. He lay back in the dirt, aching and tired, ready for this damned day to be over.

CHAPTER 35

The combat with the scouts hidden in the keep ended with victory, announced by war horns trumpeting and ferocious cheering. Prentice listened to the sounds of triumph as the slain were paraded about by the knights and their men-at-arms. Likely a page had been sent back to the prince and his entourage, and soon their magnificently caparisoned mounts pranced through the broken gates. After using his loosed ankle chain to bind his prisoner, Prentice sat on the brick pile of the broken chimney and watched the impromptu parade like a peasant on a holy day. All he needed was a sugar cake to snack on.

The sun was well past noon when a smaller group of horsemen detached from the celebration and headed toward Prentice's corner of the ruin. Seeing them come, he guessed their purpose and jumped off his mound. His prisoner was still unconscious, but Prentice maneuvered the man's body so that he was on his knees. Then he knelt next to the slumped man, propping him up.

The horses approaching were led by Lord Dunstan, and at his side rode Duchess Amelia. As she neared, Prentice thought she looked pale and miserable. He wondered if it was the smoke and ruined humanity that troubled her. At her side, Lord Dunstan had a look of gleeful triumph. Prentice bowed his head and tugged his forelock in exaggerated courtesy as they reached him. The rest of the horsemen, six in all, were men-at-arms, and they fanned out around him with lances held high, colorful pennants hanging from the ends. Eight pairs of eyes looked down on Prentice, and he felt an almost childlike glee at the confusion growing among them.

"Here is your useless dog, Duchess!" Lord Dunstan announced.

Recalling Duchess Amelia's story of the events in the Forfeits Council, Prentice guessed that Dunstan was enjoying a chance to humiliate her by placing the blame for the looting at the feet of her chosen convict. Lord Dunstan was as proud and petty as Sir Liam, it seemed, but lacked the careful cunning. It looked like he wanted to press ahead with embarrassing the duchess, but he could not ignore the extra prisoner.

"What is that?" Lord Dunstan demanded.

"A prisoner, my lord." Prentice had to force himself not to smile as he answered, keeping his head down.

"I wasn't told a prisoner was taken." Lord Dunstan's confusion was unmistakable as Prentice only shrugged. He continued with an angry bite in his voice. "What fool left a prisoner in your charge? I'll have him flogged next to you!"

"No one left him," Prentice said quietly, and now he looked up. "The man has been in my charge since I captured him trying to escape over the wall. There is a rope atop the rampart there."

Surprise caused Dunstan's anger to erupt. "You lying turd! Stand up and tell me who left this man in your charge, or I'll run you through where you kneel."

He wrenched his sword from its scabbard as Prentice rose to his feet. Although he was looking at Lord Dunstan, he watched Duchess Amelia from the corner of his eye. It seemed to him that she was thinking, her expression brightening even as she did so.

"You there," she said suddenly to one of the riders standing by. "Send to the prince's factor and see if any knights have reported taking a prisoner from the battle."

Lord Dunstan's ire was diverted toward the duchess momentarily. "You dare to command my man?"

She met his question with a stern gaze. "In my husband's duchy, I will command your man!" she said icily. "As I will command you and any man or woman, short of Prince Mercad himself, it is my right." She turned back to Dunstan's man. "You, go! And return presently. We will see the truth of this claim."

The man rode off, and Lord Dunstan chewed his lip for a moment. Prentice and Amelia shared a cunning look.

"Perhaps I should send my man Chasley here as well," Lord Dunstan said, his tone pregnant with meaning. "He'll be able to find the knight who captured this prisoner."

The duchess smiled sweetly. "I'm sure your first man will be competent to the task and return presently. No need to send others running hither and yon. Besides, in their zealousness, they might pick the wrong man for you." She had seen straight through Lord Dunstan's attempted ploy.

The group waited in silence for the four or five minutes it took for the rider sent to return, this time accompanied by the prince's seneschal. The man rode a slight roan mare, similar to the duchess's mount. It made him seem short and feminine next to the heavily armored men and their war chargers.

"A prisoner indeed?" the seneschal said, expressing his surprise. "You are to be congratulated, Lord Dunstan, Duchess Amelia. This is quite the prize. To whom does the credit for the capture belong?"

Lord Dunstan opened his mouth, but the duchess was quicker. "It was the corporal of my rogues who made the capture. Right here, as the enemy made for the wall."

"Truly?" The seneschal's nostrils flared as if the mere mention of convicts put a foul smell in the air. "Well then, this is a full day of victory for your duchy, Your Grace. Lord Dunstan, have your men bring the prisoner. The prince will want him questioned at length."

The factor wheeled his horse about and left.

"Thank you, Lord Dunstan," Amelia said as she turned her own horse as well. "I will take my man now. Prentice, you will follow!"

"Yes, Your Grace." Prentice tugged his forelock again, following the duchess at a quick step as she rode away.

He thought about giving Lord Dunstan one of Turley's infamous cheeky grins but, knowing the lord already had his longsword in hand, did not trust the nobleman to keep his temper. He could feel the lord's icy gaze on his back as he followed the duchess's horse. The whole distance to the town gatehouse, his hearing was stretched taut, listening for the sound of a horse behind him, a man coming to cut him down for his impertinence. Even once they were in the meadow beyond, his tension did not ease, not until they reached the camp a league away and the relative safety of the duchess's own men-at-arms.

CHAPTER 36

"I thought for sure that Lord Dunstan was about to succeed where Liam had failed," Amelia said to Prentice as she sat in her tent eating her midday meal late. She appeared to be in thought, as though she might offer him some food as well. But they both knew that her servants would speak of it, and rumors would result— rumors she would not want to have to deal with.

"He was so smug!" she continued. "Do you think Liam put him up to it?"

Prentice stood facing her, in the position that was now customary for him. "I doubt it, Your Grace. Sir Liam wants my head for himself. If he had conspired with Lord Dunstan, I think he would have remained to watch the execution. Can I ask how many men Lord Dunstan executed in the end?"

"Seventeen in all," Amelia said. A frown twisted her lips, and she put down the piece of cheese she had been about to eat. Thoughts of the executions didn't sit well with her appetite, it seemed. "A vile business, truly! What did that fool think, that those men were going to smuggle out the whole mound of metal and somehow escape with it?"

"Many of them would have had some thought like that."

"Did you?"

Prentice shook his head. "Escape and go where?"

"Exactly. The whole point of transporting convicts across the mountains is to make escape pointless. The mountains to the east and the empty plains to the west. Where would they go?"

"South to the Vec. Most convict escape fantasies lead there."

"I hadn't thought of that," Amelia admitted.

"A straight run down the Dwelt to the Mur, and then on into Vec lands," Prentice explained. "Assuming you can avoid all contact with people until you reach the south. I know of a few who have tried in my time across the mountains, but none who succeeded."

"And all the challenges that plan possesses are magnified for these men," Amelia said. "Aiming south through our army and past the invaders. Surely even the most desperate convict could see that was suicide?"

"As opposed to kneeling in the dust and waiting to be executed by an arrogant knight?"

Amelia narrowed her eyes and looked at him. "You think to chastise me? You think I do not fully understand the convict plight?"

"I think only someone who has been there, kneeling in the dust, can fully appreciate how wild the thoughts of a convict can get," Prentice said, shrugging. "How golden any hope can seem, no matter how thin or flimsy." He finished by bowing his head, to show he meant no disrespect.

Amelia smiled. "I suppose you are right. I would never have imagined myself taunting an assembly of knights and peers in the presence of the Prince of Rhales, yet I did. And in spite of the foolishness of it, I have profited."

"Your forfeit?"

"Sir Liam has presented the assault on the enemy left behind in the keep to the prince's court as a victory to fulfill the forfeit."

"It was no more than a skirmish," said Prentice.

Amelia nodded. "Barely twenty men. A scout force, no more."

"Your forfeit was for total victory."

"True, but today has been worthless for that." Amelia's smile took on a satisfied twist. "There was no true battle. Almost all the offered forfeits are worthless now. How can an earl who offered to kill fifty enemy soldiers deliver that forfeit when there were only twenty enemy men in total? And with no army to defeat, there is no enemy camp to sack and no loot to take!"

It was now Prentice's turn to smile. The duchess's grasp on the politics of the day was excellent. His smile became wry as he realized that the duchess would soon have little need of his advice. His privileged status could shortly be over. He hoped Duchess Amelia would honor her promises, but he'd seen nobles break their word to their lessers when it suited them. He had no way to hold her to her word if she did choose to break it.

"The prince will announce tonight that all the forfeits are void," Duchess Amelia continued. "His seneschal has confirmed this with me."

"That will cost him," said Prentice. "It's a humiliation."

"He can't claim the forfeits," the duchess countered. "The army would revolt. Every man of them stands to lose."

"It seems as though you're enjoying this."

"No, though I could do," she admitted. "They were all looking forward to their glorious battle as in the days of old but see what they found instead. They all looked like fools today. But the price for their lesson has been too high. We assumed we were marching to liberate Fallenhill, and now we find that it is a charnel pit for the slain. Did anyone escape, do you think?"

Prentice could only shrug.

"I feel like I should weep for them," she said. "But so many have died now. So many. How does one mourn for this?"

She fell silent. The sounds of the camp around them were oddly mixed as well, as if reflecting the duchess's own mind. There were occasional shouts and laughs, as of men trying to celebrate, to find humor or joy, but they always faded quickly, and muted conversations became the norm. The whole camp knew of the brutal fate of Fallenhill and the day's unsatisfactory engagement.

Prentice stood quietly waiting until a herald announced himself and entered the tent. He was carrying a summons from the prince. He presented it with a curt bow and withdrew, but Prentice noticed the herald give him a sideways glance as he left. His time in the army as an anonymous convict was also at an end.

"Prince Mercad summons me to discuss the interrogation of your prisoner," the duchess said, interrupting his thoughts. "Though this letter calls him the prisoner of the crown."

"A convict can own nothing and claim no glory."

Duchess Amelia folded the note in one hand and pinched the bridge of her nose with the other. "Today was a personal victory for me, but the Reach and its people are still in mortal danger."

"It may feel like that every day, for one of your position," Prentice ventured.

"An unappealing thought." Amelia sighed. "Why does God allow it?"

"Your Grace?"

"All this violence and evil, why does He allow it? Why does He allow innocent people to suffer so?"

"Did you ask that question when your husband was alive and you were in the flush of your marriage, Your Grace?" Prentice asked.

"What?"

"Convicts suffered at the hands of the Sir Liams and Lord Dunstans of the world when your future looked secure and your happiness assured. Were you so upset with God then?"

Amelia shook her head wearily. "I know I invite it, but your impertinence still shocks me every time."

"If it helps, sometimes it shocks me too," said Prentice.

Amelia laughed and dismissed him so that she could prepare to attend the prince's audience concerning the prisoner. She told him that she would have preferred to bring him with her to the audience to advise her, but both of them knew such a thing would be impossible.

Prentice left her tent and went looking for Turley and the rest of the convicts. He found them sitting near a stream in the meadow in front of Fallenhill, only a short distance east of the town entrance. The overseers were back in place, and the improvised weapons had been confiscated.

Overseer Tuke nodded as Prentice approached. "I heard you were to be executed."

Prentice tilted his head. "Not today."

Tuke gave Prentice a look of sly contempt. "So much for your big speech this morning, geeing them up to march to their deaths. Not much of a battle after all."

"Made your job easier by seventeen all the same, though," Prentice retorted.

"Twenty-two!" Tuke countered.

"What?"

"Five of 'em didn't want to hand back their big, sharp sticks. Thought they was going to lead a convict rebellion! Knights rode 'em down like grass."

Prentice wanted to punch the man's smug smile into his face. Five more dead? It must have happened after the duchess had escorted him away. Lord Dunstan's men might have been involved, itching to avenge their lord's embarrassment over the captured scout.

If he'd been there, maybe he might have headed off the conflict.

His pleasure at surviving the morning faded and he scowled as Tuke walked away chuckling. With leaden steps, Prentice walked around slowly, looking for Turley. Eventually he spotted his friend sitting on a tree root and chewing a long strand of grass. Around him was a group of ten or so convicts, all on one chain but clearly sitting close, as though Turley were holding court. He waved Prentice over.

"Aye up, what did I tell you all?" said Turley to his little gathering. "Too clever by half to be executed by a horse's arse like Dunstan!"

The convicts smiled and welcomed Prentice, giving him space to join Turley on the root.

Prentice sat and looked about, puzzled. "Making friends?"

"What, these gentlemen? We are all sitting together and enjoying the sun and shade and the late summer grass under us. It's entirely civilized." Smiles and chuckles circulated. Turley was entertaining to almost any audience.

"Not all of us," Prentice said grimly, cutting across the light mood.

Some of the convicts scowled, but Turley was not perturbed. "A bitter business, sure enough," he said. "But we have survived and now enjoy the rest afforded to victors."

"Victors?" Prentice hung his head. He understood Turley's happiness. No matter how bitter life was, surviving the brutality of a day like this made a man happy. Made them feel like they had won something, become victors, even though nothing significant had changed except that some had died. "What happened after Dunstan marched me off?" he asked, not lifting his head.

"They kept searching us for gold for a bit. Gutted more than a few of us."

"Seventeen!"

"That's about the number," Turley said with a nod. "Truth to say, I wasn't too frightened. After all, I didn't have any gold. I mean, what did those fools think was going to happen? That they would be allowed to just pick up some leftover gold? Loot is for knights and nobles—maybe a yeoman if he's lucky. That's why they send us in the first place! We don't get no shares."

Other convicts made noises of agreement, and Prentice looked up to see them all nodding. "What about the other ones?" he asked.

"Other ones? Oh, you mean them fools who thought they were going to fight their way to freedom? They were worse fools than the ones who wanted the gold!"

"And that's all right?"

"Sometimes death is the only cure for stupidity."

"Can't save those who won't learn?" asked Prentice.

Turley nodded, and many of the convicts with him, but Prentice already didn't care about the answer. This was convict wisdom, and it had kept them alive for many years. It was the thinking that Prentice himself had held to since his transportation, but suddenly he found he could not stomach it anymore. Cursed, condemned, and rejected already, convicts should not embrace the loathing. They should not despise each other's lives. Something had changed inside him.

"There must be something better," he muttered, and as he did, he realized that this idea was not as new to him as he thought.

It was what had motivated him since the duchess had spoken to him behind the castle in Dweltford: the hope of something better. Thinking about it, he realized it went back further. It had pushed him to carry Bellam with his wounded ankle, to risk his life to stop the spearman on the road. Prentice wanted better, for himself and others. And better *from* himself. His conviction and exile were like a stone that had been laid on him, as on a patch of grass. It seemed to kill everything under it so that nothing green would grow but shift the stone even a little and the roots underneath were revealed. Leave a light on it, let it see even a moment's water, and suddenly the dead patch would spring to greenness. And Prentice's life *was* springing to greenness; the invasion had shifted the stone, and try as they might, the Kingdom's great men were failing to roll the weight back onto him.

"Blessing conquers burdens," he said to himself, recalling again the words of Argensius, the ancient heretic.

"D'you say something?" Turley asked.

"Just something I read once. Tell me, why are we all here resting? Is there no hurry to get us back to the camp?"

Turley and the convicts shared another chuckle. "They're busy!"

"Busy?"

"The prince's man interrupted Lord Dunstan's little butcher's party, and when he heard about the gold, he laid claim of it for the prince, the throne, and everyone high and mighty under the sun! Dunstan and his men nearly had kittens, swearing about being first through the gates and having the right to the pick of the loot. 'Rightful claim' were the words that got thrown about a lot!"

"Then he wanted to know why there were convicts near so much gold," added one of the men seated on the grass with them.

Turley pointed at the man and nodded agreement. "Right! They were talking about getting us to carry off the bodies as we go, and get them buried, when one of that lord's men pipes up that maybe there was still some gold or silver—or gems, even—among them burned bodies! Well, that was the end of that. We were marched out quick smart, and they were left to sort through the bodies and that sodding lump of metal!"

More laughter passed around, and even Prentice had to smile. The thought of the proud men-at-arms having to dig through the soot and ash to the ruin of their fine surcoats was amusing.

"I suppose we better get ourselves marched back to camp," Prentice said, standing up and brushing bits of bark off his breeches.

"What for?" asked Turley. "It's pleasant enough here, ain't it? A jug of wine and some cheese, and this'd be the perfect afternoon's picnic."

"Maybe, but when those well-born men get done, they're going to be tired, dirty, and cranky. I don't want us to be anywhere near them, doing anything out of the ordinary. Best to be obedient and out of their way; they've already killed over twenty of us today. No need to give them another go around."

"Aye, that's wise thinking," Turley agreed, and he stood as well. "Pass the word, lads. The corporal's going to have us moving off."

Prentice was surprised to hear himself called by title, though of course he was in command of the rogues and had now led them on the field. He shook his head and walked over to Tuke.

"Time to take us back to camp, Overseer," he said.

Tuke looked like he was about to take offense at Prentice giving him orders, then simply shrugged and uncoiled his whip. Either he thought there was no point arguing over sensible orders that made his life easier, or else he was still uncertain about the limits of where Prentice's authority over the rogues started or finished. With a few shouts and half-hearted whip cracks, the convicts were brought to their feet and set to the march. The comfortable men grumbled a little, but mostly they were compliant. With a slow shuffle and the clank of chains, they made their way back to the army's camp and their meager evening meal.

CHAPTER 37

"The prince now knows where the invaders are," Amelia announced to the men gathered before her. She sat on a campaign chair beside a fire in front of her tent. The map of the Western Reach was spread upon the ground between them, lit by the firelight and candles placed on stands at the corners. The group of men was made up of knights under Amelia's banner, with Sir Liam in front as their captain. To one side, Prentice knelt alone on one knee, present but apart. His position as corporal of the rogues made his presence legitimate, but only just.

"The prisoner has revealed much about his army, and the prince's interrogator assures us that the enemy has encamped here," the duchess explained.

She used a long rod to point to a tributary stream of the Dwelt and a valley two days' march from Fallenhill. The fact that she was giving them the information revealed by the prisoner Prentice had captured leaned further strength to his presence in the meeting, but he found himself wondering how the prisoner could have divulged so much so quickly. Had the man not even tried to resist interrogation?

"The enemy is supposedly encamped on a hill there," she continued, "and already the prince has sent outriders to confirm this fact. He instructs the entire army to be ready to march before dawn."

"It is already past the midnight hour," one of the knights observed.

"Indeed, sir," said the duchess. "You will go straight from here and break your camp. No sleep for any of us this night!"

Some of the knights murmured at this announcement, but Prentice had to hide a smile. After the embarrassment of the day's non-battle, the prince would be in a hurry to engage the enemy, to avenge his humiliation. Prentice wondered if that was part of the enemy's plan, and it would explain their extreme violence. Humiliate the Grand Kingdom and lure them into rash action.

"We must steal the march upon them," Sir Liam said, supporting the duchess and the prince's plan. "They have shown that they are brutal cowards, slippery like eels and likely to evade us once more if we give them the chance! Prince Mercad is wise in his plan."

The other knights nodded sagely. It was obvious that a call to action suited them for the most part. For a moment, Prentice thought that Duchess Amelia cast a look at him, perhaps to see if he shared the knights' eagerness or else to see if his face revealed some opinion on their reaction. In their presence, though, he kept his eyes downcast in studied humility and focused on the map. He did look up at one point and saw that one of the knights in the group present was not a bannerman of the duchess—the man in the green surcoat who had ridden with Sir Liam that morning. Now his helmet was removed, and Prentice could see the man's face. Although he had only a single glance and the firelight was dim, Prentice was sure the man was staring at him. It was a long moment more before he realized who this knight was: Brother Whilte.

As soon as he made the connection in his mind, Prentice knew he was right. He was older by ten years, of course, but the fair hair and the narrow face were Whilte's. With so many things to worry about on the march and the coming battle, Prentice had hardly spared a thought for Brother Whilte, even though he had been so enraged by hearing of him in the army the night of his vision. In truth, Prentice had scarcely thought of Whilte at all for the past decade, except to curse him on sleepless nights. The man seemed to enter his thoughts only to bring a storm of anger and bitter memories, then fade away, as if blown by a morning breeze.

Now he was here, a fully-fledged Church knight and a part of Sir Liam's entourage. Sir Liam was the Knight Captain of the Reach, but that was hardly an impressive rank in this army. Whilte would likely only have attached himself to Sir Liam for one reason: revenge. As if Prentice being stripped of rank, convicted, and transported were not revenge enough.

Prentice kept his eyes down, but his thoughts were busy. He barely heard the duchess as she finished giving her instructions. Some part of him noted that she was obviously growing in confidence in dealing with armed men, and they were growing in acceptance of her role. Assuming the Kingdom won the upcoming battle and drove the invaders from their land, this campaign looked to be cementing Amelia's place as the Duchess of the Western Reach.

"Did you not hear me, Prentice?" the duchess asked, piercing the cloud of his thoughts. She had dismissed her knights, and she and Prentice were alone beside the red coals of the fire as it burned down. Her face was shadowed from Prentice, and he could not see her eyes.

"I'm sorry, Your Grace?"

"I said that it seems you were mistaken."

Prentice had no idea what she was talking about. "Please forgive me, Your Grace, but...?"

"You claimed the prince had no idea what he was doing on the march, sending out heralds, but now it seems that he had more wisdom than you thought."

Prentice said nothing.

"The prisoner tells us that the enemy commander is doing exactly what the prince expected him to do. He has taken up a position and is waiting for our army with his. The only difference was that he had no heralds to send out to meet ours. He left his soldiers behind to tell us instead."

"Is that Prince Mercad's understanding?"

"It is," Amelia said. There was nothing in her manner or tone that told him what she might have been truly thinking. "What do you think? Should you apologize?"

"I was not privy to the interrogation, Your Grace. The prince should know better than I."

"Should know? But you do not think he does?"

Prentice thought about his answer. Earlier in the day he had been flushed with confidence, hopeful that his capture of the prisoner had restored any flagging strength in his standing with the duchess. Now, after having Brother Whilte stare hate at him for half an hour and the duchess herself showing cool reserve, he wondered what else the prince's interrogation had turned up and how it might have been twisted against him. Every time he saw light over his head, the waters of convict paranoia closed over him again.

Or perhaps the duchess was feeling the growing confidence that Prentice could see in her. He didn't doubt that others would have seen it too. Her gambit in the Forfeits Council had paid off. Her knight captain had led the only true combat on the day of battle and won the only victory. And she had presented a prisoner to the prince, who now told them the path to the site of the true battle. If she thought to protect herself politically with the nobles in the army and the Rhales court in general, now would be a good time to begin to distance herself from him—to send him back to the convicts and forget him.

"I have another question for you, Prentice," she said quietly. "It is imperative you answer honestly."

"I will not lie," he said, though it unnerved him to say so.

"What did you talk about with the prisoner?"

"Talk about, Your Grace?" The question so caught Prentice off guard that he looked straight at her, staring in incomprehension. "We never talked of anything. I kicked him unconscious, and that's how he lay until you arrived with Dunstan's men."

"Lord Dunstan," she corrected.

Prentice cursed himself inwardly. Now was not the time to let go of his self-control and forget his place. She was no longer a frightened widow riding a riverman's barge in a desperate race for home, even though that was not even two weeks ago; he had come too far to ruin his hope of freedom with loose words.

"So, he said nothing at all in the entire time?" she asked.

"Nothing, Your Grace," Prentice began, and then shook his head, remembering. "He cursed the ashes when he saw me."

"Cursed the ashes? What does that mean?"

"When I confronted the two of them as they fled, Your Grace, they didn't see me until I was upon them. The prisoner said the word 'ash' or 'ashes' or some such. His accent was thick. I assumed he was cursing the dust and soot that kept me camouflaged as I snuck up on them."

The duchess nodded and turned, staring at the red coals for a moment. Even though they were out in the open, somehow the rest of the camp felt far away to Prentice; the sounds of stewards and squires breaking camp were muted to his ears. His whole attention was on Duchess Amelia.

"The prisoner said that he knew you," she explained quietly.

Prentice blinked. How could the man know him? It was an unbelievable claim. He half rose in his eagerness to deny it. "We had no conversation, I swear, Your Grace! He was unconscious the entire time. I do not know the man and don't even know how he could have known me. When would we have ever met? Who is he?"

The duchess sighed. "He did not name you, Prentice. He called you Ash, or the Ashen Man. He said that his captains had told them all to watch out for the man from the ashes, for he was the sign of their defeat! You, apparently."

Prentice was still confused by the duchess's previous question, but he picked the thread of her words apart enough to realize that the prisoner hadn't accused him of being their ally. The invaders counted him as an enemy. He settled back onto his knees again. "This must be a ruse of some sort," he offered. "An attempt to confuse his captors."

"That is the prince's thought," the duchess said with a nod, and Prentice breathed a little easier still.

With the knights frustrated by their abortive battle and the argument over the pile of melted loot, it was another moment when a hothead could have easily sought him out and killed him with the prisoner's words as a pretext—a chance to make someone pay for the sense of frustration.

"Is that what you thought?" he asked.

"I do not know what to think. The man was insistent that it was you they feared, even when Sir Liam pressed him."

"Sir Liam was there?"

"Yes." The duchess stood and straightened her skirts, the blue-dyed linen looking black in the bare firelight. "He pressed the prisoner to reinterpret the facts and name him the harbinger of their doom."

"Him?"

"Why not him?" she asked. "He led the assault on the enemies hiding in the keep, a clear victory—and he did it riding in the soot and ashes. It sounds similar to the story the prisoner told."

Prentice nodded. It made as much sense as naming him.

"Except the prisoner would not have it, not even when threatened with the pincers or a blade."

"The man was tortured?" Prentice knew it was probable, but the duchess shook her head.

"Sir Liam threatened to take his eye," she said, "but still he would not change his tale. Other than that, the prince had no need to even threaten the tools of the torturer. The man gave up everything willingly. The prince's commander said it showed that, under the fierce tattoos, they're simply petty bandits and cowards. No more than murderous thugs."

Prentice disagreed, but he did not say anything. He was still uncertain how his thoughts would be received.

"Today did not go well, but the Reach has emerged stronger," she continued. "Prince Mercad assures me that we march now to the swift resolution of the campaign. Victory before the end of summer. We will march south for the next day, back along the road, before turning west and fording the Dwelt. This will give us a chance to meet up with Sir Duggan, who is still delayed bringing the militia. The prisoner says that the enemy has six hundred men in their force. When Sir Duggan joins us, that will mean we are just over twice their number. Our victory is assured, God willing!"

Prentice nodded, again remaining silent. Inwardly, though, he wondered how Sir Duggan had still not caught up with the army.

The noises of the camp grew louder as servants and stewards were stirred from rest and given their orders for the march. The night's peace was overturned. For a long time, the duchess stared into the flames, and Prentice watched her.

Eventually, he dared to clear his throat. "Shall I see that the rogues are ready to march, Your Grace?"

Duchess Amelia looked straight at him, but her eyes were only dark shadows. "In spite of the difficulties it has caused me, I have favored you, Prentice. It has cost me, but I needed a voice I could trust, and I chose yours. You seemed wise and alert to the cunning of my..."

Prentice wondered if she was reaching for the right word, as if she did not want to say "enemies."

"You seemed to understand the threats I face," she continued. "When I heard the prisoner name you as the one he feared, I did not know what to think. No one present imagined the man was actually afraid of you, faced with the threat of armed knights. The only thought that has made sense to me is that you might have fixed upon some strange, desperate ruse with the man, promising him something in exchange for making you seem important in the eyes of your betters."

"Why would I do that?" Prentice asked.

"It does seem a ridiculous folly, except that the prisoner is all that kept you from death today." The duchess leaned forward, peering at his face. What was she trying to divine from his expression? "Lord Dunstan was escorting me to your execution. Evidently, he has heard rumors of our relationship; he knows I favor you, and to avenge the slight I gave him at the Forfeits Council, he was going to present me with your head. If you had not offered me that prisoner, you would have been dead. So I ask myself, What would you do, faced with that inevitability? Would you devise an impossible plan to save your life?"

Prentice wanted to curse, to rant, to swear. He had done the right thing, honoring his liege and risking his life to capture a prisoner using nothing more than a manacle as a weapon, and all she wanted to do was accuse him of the most convoluted conspiracy imaginable. Instead of venting his fury, he bowed his head and blew out a terse breath before speaking with as much composure as he could muster.

"You give me far too much credit, Your Grace," he muttered through gritted teeth, trying to seem calm and knowing he was failing. "What would I offer him? He was sat in the ashes with another man, lower and meaner even than he. What could I have done to persuade him?"

"You were his captor."

"In chains myself."

"Except that you were not!" the duchess said, and the suspicion in her face was unmistakable. "You were supposed to be chained hand and foot to await execution, yet your manacles hung loose from one wrist and your fetter chain was binding the prisoner's wrists. You were virtually free. I saw you! In the surprise of the prisoner, Lord Dunstan's men missed this fact, but I saw it."

Prentice remembered the convict who had shared his food with him and how the manacles had fallen away. How could he explain that to her when he hardly understood it himself? It was as if an angel had taken a humble form and sat with him a spell; or perhaps it was a saint, returned to earth. That was how the story looked to his eyes when he let himself think about it. It would be unbelievable to anyone he tried to tell, always assuming they weren't simply offended by the suggestion that a saint might spend time with a mere convict, filthy and condemned. No matter what humble stories the scripture might tell about God and His mercy, no one in the Grand Kingdom expected God's kindness to rest on the vileness of a convict.

"My chains were loosed," he said. The words sounded weak to him, but he could not think how else to say it.

"You were escaping! That's why the chains were loose."

"Why would I take a prisoner if I wanted to escape?" Prentice shot back too quickly, unable to keep all the anger from his voice.

"Perhaps you saw an opportunity and traded one desperate plan for another!" the duchess accused.

"Now you think I'm a complete fool? You should make up your mind, Your Grace. If I were intent on escape, it would have been smarter by far to throw my lot in with the enemy. They wanted to escape just as much! Or if not, to simply follow them at a distance, see if they were successful, and use their method after them. Why would I risk myself against two armed men with only a length of chain?"

"You did not want to escape?"

"And go where?" Prentice knew he sounded exasperated, but he could barely keep his feelings hidden. "A fleeing convict is less than a dog to every soul of the Grand Kingdom. My life would be shorter and even more bitter than it is now! Hunted and hungry is not how I want to die, nor torn apart by some man's hounds."

"You would not go to the enemy?" The duchess's suspicion seemed to have waned now, and there was another tone in her voice—something almost like relief.

Prentice wondered if she might have been more concerned about the personal betrayal that an escape attempt would have represented than about his violation of Kingdom law. Was she angrier that he might have abandoned her? It was not something he had expected.

"I could not go to the enemy," he said, more gently now. "You and I have both seen how they treat our people, Your Grace. I would not expect them to welcome me, not in any way. More than ever, the empty west holds no escape for a convict!"

Not empty any more, he thought.

Amelia nodded slowly. She picked up a fallen stick from the edge of the fire and tossed it back on the coals, where it flared again with small yellow flames. The shadows fled from her face for a moment.

"Lord Dunstan was so smug," she said. "So gleeful. I swear I think he wanted to swing the executioner's sword himself. All I could think was how I'd put you into this danger. I had visions of him tossing your head to me like a trophy, making me carry it back to my tent. I could see it in his eyes."

Prentice didn't disagree. It was the kind of thing a man like Lord Dunstan might do.

"And then, when I saw you without your manacles, I thought you had been about to flee. I was paranoid. I thought I had lost you, and then it looked like I would lose you again—and by your choice! I have risked so much for you, been humiliated in my use for you, and it looked like you were going to flee and abandon me to the likes of Lord Dunstan! Even through the interrogation in the prince's pavilion, I could barely think of anything else but betrayal."

"I wouldn't have fled," he said. "There is nowhere to go."

"You are like a brother to me," she said suddenly. Prentice did not know what to think. "My father was an only son, and when he died, I wished he would have had brothers so that I would have had an uncle to advise me. Then my husband had seemed to meet that need, but just as I became comfortable, he, too, was gone. Now God has sent you to me. I mean that—I truly believe God has sent you to me, with your straight advice and your formal loyalty. You are the brother I've prayed for."

"I don't know what to say."

"Swear yourself to me."

Prentice looked straight at Amelia in sheer disbelief. He was a convict. He could no more swear fealty than a rat could. If he even tried, it would seem ridiculous and offensive. Any knight in the camp would take a blade to him for the presumption; he'd be lucky to lose only an eye or a hand. But the duchess was serious. She wanted his pledge.

"I am a convict, Your Grace. I cannot—"

"I know that!" she interrupted with a wave of her hand. "I will make you free as soon as I can, but I cannot discard you or give you away. Swear yourself to me, now and in your freedom. When I free you after the battle, promise me now that you will stay my man, stay in my service."

"Assuming I survive the battle."

"Do not evade, not in this. Swear to me now, and I will make it known if you are slain. You will be buried a yeoman, with the debt of your conviction cleared. Swear to me now!"

"Very well."

Prentice shuffled forward and went on both knees, bowing his head before her.

She placed her hand on his head. "Swear your life in fealty to me. Name yourself as my man."

"Duchess, I am your man," Prentice said, lifting his head. He quoted the words of a knight's oath of fealty. "'My life in fealty to you and your line. My strength to build your fief. My honor bound to yours until my last breath and last drop of blood.'" He looked down at the state of his ash-smeared clothing, filthy and stained despite their newness, and then looked back up with a smile. "'My honor, such as it is.'"

"I will restore it to you, I swear!" she said, taking his hands. "I accept your fealty and will not betray you. I will be your liege and your family's, your line tied to mine."

She released his hands, and Prentice shuffled back quickly in case someone looking on saw them and asked inappropriate questions.

"Well," he said, "that was unexpected."

She laughed her gentle laugh, the one she often used with him, and he saw suddenly how much she valued him. He lifted her gloom, and it made him glad. He bowed as she sent him off to prepare the rogues foot.

CHAPTER 38

Prentice had to chase through the dark fringe of the camp to find Tuke and his men, who were sleeping a little distance from the convict chains. As he expected, they had not been informed of the army's early departure. What surprised him was the way in which Tuke and his small group accepted his word. They only grumbled quietly about their loss of sleep; not one of them dismissed him as a mere convict. He had anticipated another round of contempt and condescension, but they simply found some lanterns and set about waking the convicts to ready for the march.

With the noise and the limited light, it took him a while to find Turley, who was sleeping on some hay a short distance from the rest. A pack mule was quietly cropping the edge of the mound of hay, but it seemed not to have disturbed Turley, who Prentice had to wake himself.

"It's too early," Turley complained as he stretched.

"Dawn in less than two hours," Prentice argued.

"Oh, hell's bells, that's the middle of the night! If you hadn't come to find me, no one might have known. I could have been left behind."

"Thinking of escape, are you?" Prentice asked.

"Wouldn't you?"

"Second time tonight someone's asked me that."

"Oh, sounds like a story," Turley said, pulling his shoes on. He'd been using them as a pillow.

Prentice sat next to him and told him everything that had happened in the evening. Turley nodded along to the tale but made no comments. Even when the story was finished, he still said nothing.

"No pithy observations?" Prentice asked. He had left out the part of the night where he had sworn himself to the duchess, but he still expected his friend to say something about the rest.

Turley frowned and nodded to himself one more time. "So, do we call you Ashes now or what?" he asked in mock seriousness.

"What?"

"Maybe I should fetch some water and a sacrist, baptize you and make it official-like."

Prentice turned his head away and spat on the ground. "That's what you take from my tale? A nickname?"

"What else did you want me to say?" Turley grinned. "I'm a humble convict, and I used to be a farmhand. I ain't got no way with these highborn things, like questioning prisoners or making strategy. The only time I've ever seen questioning done, it was when the bailiffs had me tied to a post. But a battle name, that's something I understand."

"This isn't a battle name," Prentice said. "He was trying to sow dissension, create problems for the Kingdom army."

"Nope, I don't see it like that." Turley shook his head and stood up at last. He headed toward the rest of the convicts, talking over his shoulder to Prentice, who followed him as quickly as he could. "See, it looks to my simple mind like the enemy's got themselves someone they fear. They're afraid of you, and you're one of us!"

"You're being ridiculous."

"Oh no, indeed! You remember what you've been saying you wanted every step on this blasted march? That you needed to find a way to keep these poor sods strong and alive in a campaign where they're worth less than dog crap? This is it!"

Prentice stopped dead. He had no idea what Turley was talking about. His burly friend grabbed a small barrel and, carrying it under his arm, marched into the midst of the crowd of manacled convicts, stepping over chains until he was in the center. Then he put the barrel on the ground and stood on it. Prentice pushed through the crowd to stand near him as he spoke.

"Listen up, you crotch fleas!" Turley's voice carried in the torch lit dark. "I got someone I need to introduce to you all."

Prentice wanted to punch his friend, but he knew better than to make the scene worse by objecting. Even if he knocked Turley off the barrel now, others would only ask him later what it was all about. Bored men gossiped, and when they weren't terrified for their lives, convicts were very bored men.

"You see, while we were getting shanked for gold theft in Fallenhill and the high knights were off playing war with a bunch of enemy scouts, our corporal here"—Turley paused and then corrected himself—"our *captain* was busy being a damned hero!"

There was a curious murmuring among the men, though many looked snide and cynical to Prentice's eye. *Why go calling me a captain*, he thought to himself.

"Oh, I know he ain't much to look at, all dirt and scars," Turley continued, "but after Lord Dunstan had chained his feet and his wrists, they left him by himself, and he captured an enemy prisoner!" He paused for dramatic effect. "That's right. Unarmed, manacled, and chained, this stallion took an escaping enemy officer prisoner. Beat the bastard senseless into the bargain."

This notion drew appreciative chuckles from many, but Prentice was annoyed by Turley's embellishment of the story. The prisoner wasn't any kind of officer.

"The prince and the duchess themselves have just finished the questioning, and I'll bet ain't one of you dogs had a bailiff so pretty ask you for your testimony!"

More chuckles.

"So now we are marching, and I need to tell you what our prisoner said. He told us where the rest of these scum bastard cutthroats are making their camp. So that's where we're marching, even before dawn! And he told us one other thing. Turns out they've got a name for our mighty captain, a man who can take a beating and then take prisoners. They call him Ash! Do you know why?"

The men shook their heads, and Prentice wondered nervously where Turley was going with his little speech. He was a charming rogue, charismatic whether he was seducing a scullery maid or addressing a crowd of convicts, but Prentice didn't trust him not to make problems worse.

"Why?" called a voice from the crowd.

"Because after the fire, no matter how long it burns, there's always ash left, isn't there? Just like in Fallenhill! That's why they call him that, 'cause they know they can't kill him. No matter how long the fires of war burn, no matter how hot, Ash will always be left at the end. The Grand Kingdom sent him out here over ten years ago, and ain't no other convict lasted that long on a chain. They can beat him with whips, and he won't break! Put manacles on him, and he'll still beat his foe to a bloody pulp. No wonder the enemy's pissing their kilts—and we march with him! He's our damned captain. If they're afraid of him, then they're afraid of us. Stuff the pretty knights and their damn horses. This is our captain. Captain Ash!"

The convicts did not shout or cheer. They were the wrong men for that. But they nodded, and many smiled. They liked the idea of a hero leading them, a convict like themselves, chained but unbreakable. Turley hopped off the barrel and motioned for Prentice to step up.

"What are you doing?" Prentice asked.

"Time to address your men," Turley said with a grin. "You're leading them to war now, Captain Ash!" He leaned in to whisper in Prentice's ear. "Pricks like Sir Liam aren't wrong. Men need inspiration in war, but a potter needs good clay to work with. This is the best clay you're ever going to get. What can you make of it?"

Prentice shook his head but couldn't help smiling. He had spent the last ten years hiding, tugging his forelock and using a shield of calculated obedience to keep himself alive. No ambition, no hope, no pride. That was how he had survived. But there was no freedom in that life either. He needed to hope, if he was to be free, and he needed ambition to pursue it.

He put his foot on the barrel and stepped up. The flickering firelight played over faces that were unmistakably attentive. They wanted to hear what he had to say. Even in that poor light, he could see it, and he could also feel it in himself—an eagerness for more than just groveling on a chain, beaten and half-starved.

"The duchess has spoken to me," Prentice started, forcing himself to speak with a strong voice, to give no sign of the hesitancy he felt. "We're to march a day back down the road, and then we strike west. We'll ford the Dwelt and meet the enemy in a valley a day beyond that. In two days, we will face them, and the duchess has promised me that every man who lives through that day will be cut from the chain, pardoned, and freed. That means that some of us are only two days from freedom."

That caught all their imaginations, and eyes glittered in the filthy faces. He could see them better now and realized that the sun would soon broach the horizon. He could not have timed his speech better if he had tried.

"That doesn't mean it's an easy road, the road to freedom. No, it is not!" he said. Prentice felt he had to add that. Hope was well and good, but the chances were that most would die, perhaps even all of them. He could not lie to them that much. "Two days from now, when we face our master's enemies, you'll have weapons in your hands, and I want you to remember this one thing: the road to your freedom is a path you must cut for yourself through that enemy, because your freedom is on the other side of that battle. So be prepared to cut your way through!"

Prentice took a page out of Turley's book and paused for dramatic effect. He looked as if he was going to step down, then added with a smile, "And be prepared to keep up because I'm going to be right out front cutting my own path! Freedom is my harvest, and any weed that gets in my way's going to be mown down. Now, get ready to march!"

He hopped down.

Turley shook his hand. "That's how you do it!"

Prentice nodded.

A convict drew close to them, apparently prodded by his fellows standing nearby. "Is it true? You captured a prisoner?"

"It's true, but I was lucky. I had to use the manacle chain."

"But you were unarmed?" the man pressed. "And he had a blade?"

"Yes."

"Bugger!" The convict returned to his mates to confirm the details.

Prentice left them. "We best find them some food for the march," he said to Turley. The two of them went looking for food, while behind them the overseers had the easiest job they'd ever had arranging the gangs and getting them set for the march.

CHAPTER 39

The return journey south on the road passed quickly, even for the convicts on the chain. News that the enemy army had been found lifted spirits, and the bitter confusion of Fallenhill was left behind. The melted lump of precious metal had been claimed by the prince, though he ceremoniously presented Lord Dunstan with a chunk cut away by two men with hacksaws. The ugly lump looked like a sooty log of wood, a broken stump with a shiny end of silver and gold that was two feet long and too heavy for one man to carry. Prentice, of course, was not at the presentation, but the object made such a ridiculous trophy that the story of the audience had spread quickly through the army.

By the time the army began crossing the river Dwelt, Sir Duggan still had not arrived from the south, and the duchess sent two more riders to find out what delayed him.

"Can he have turned craven with age?" she asked her advisors.

Sir Liam would not hear a word of it, refusing to believe that a hero of the last crusade could have lost his nerve or heart. When she pressed him for a possible explanation, however, her knight captain could offer none. Prentice was just as confused and could not think of a plausible explanation either.

"Surely this is a betrayal," Amelia wondered aloud.

"At the least, he is failing in his duty," Prentice agreed. "He is disobeying you, mitigated only by the fact that, strictly speaking, he is not yet your sworn man."

"A fine legal point that will not save him when we return!"

Prentice cocked his head thoughtfully. "Perhaps he does not expect you to return. He might think he is fulfilling the greater duty by keeping Dweltford garrisoned."

"Then he truly is a rebel and a coward, and I have even less care for his fate. To think he wanted my hand!"

It was clear to Prentice that the duchess was not comforted by their conversation, but he was more aware of the way in which she was embracing the army's new mood. Her usual uncertainty was diminished. Instead, she was happy and confident, giving orders and making her presence felt in the camp in a new, stronger way.

At sundown on the day of the river crossing, a number of hedge knights gathered at her tent and begged to pledge themselves to her service. She and Sir Liam spent the evening conducting the swearing ceremonies. Unlike the pledge she extracted from Prentice the day before, this was a truly formal ceremony, overseen by a sacrist ridden from Dweltford with the same knights. Though the sacrist was late to the campaign, he was glad to be in time for the key battle. When the last knight had been anointed and the final prayer recited, the whole group stood and raised a cheer.

"They seem happy," Turley said, watching from a servant's fire some distance away. He tried to steal some meat from a pot on the coals, but the maid who was stirring slapped his hand with her spoon. He made a show of wincing, then licked the juices from his fingers.

"I guess." Prentice sighed and rubbed at his beard.

"Glum, are we?"

"We're convicts. What else would we be but glum?"

"That's not so true as it used to be, not these last few days."

Prentice looked at Turley, but he knew exactly what his friend meant. The rise in spirits that had spread throughout the army seemed to have infected the convict foot as well. Despite the demands of the fast march and the rushed fording of the river, there was a sense of determination among the convicts. No one straggled, and the chains kept good order so that Tuke and his men had barely raised their whips all day.

"Maybe they still should be glum," Prentice said.

Turley nodded thoughtfully. "You feel bad about what you said? Worried that you tricked them with your little exaggeration? Got them going happy, like little lambs to the butcher's knife?"

"It wasn't an exaggeration. It was an outright lie, and you know it!"

"It's not like that," Turley countered. "Sure, the duchess never gave you her exact word for every man, but you know that convicts can purge their souls with service. Hells, that's even in the words they use to convict you when they send you over the mountains. 'Go and purge your guilt with service.' Remember that!"

"I said they were promised their freedom. *I* promised them freedom!"

For a while they sat quiet. The maid with them tasted the stew in her pot, then nodded and held out her hand for Turley's plate. He gave her the wooden dish, and she filled it. She was not so young as Prentice had first thought, seeing her now as she leaned around the fire to give him his meal as well. Her eyes were bright, but there were lines on her face, and her hands had the typical burn scars of one who'd served a long time at a kitchen hearth. After Turley and

Prentice had their plates, she lifted the iron pot with a carry stick and went to feed the other servants.

"She's not as young as your usual," Prentice said.

"No, but sweet and fine no less," Turley agreed. "Widowed young. Pox took her first man."

They ate for a moment, chewing the soft meat with relish. Prentice looked at the fire as he did. "I don't think you should be with the rogues when we take the field next time."

Turley spat the bone in his mouth back onto his plate with a splash. "What?" he demanded. "Why not?"

"You don't need it," explained Prentice. He picked a piece of gristle from his teeth and flicked it at the flames. "The duchess has already promised you your freedom at the end of the campaign. You've nothing to win on the field. Stay with her servants, get your pardon, and make an honest woman of that widow. Make a life."

"And what about you? She promised you freedom too, you know."

"I'm the corporal of the rogues—or captain, apparently. I have to be there! Besides, I'm their lucky charm now, thanks to you."

"Don't blame me," Turley protested. "I didn't name you. And you're the one who ran around being all heroic."

"Oh, shut up! And stay off the field."

Turley swallowed another mouthful. He gave Prentice one of his wry smiles. "I don't think you'd have made a good knight, even if they hadn't convicted you."

"Is that so? And why not?"

"You've got too much conscience to make a good knight!" Turley scoffed. "Caring what convicts think of you? Worrying for their lives? What kind of knight does that?"

Prentice knew Turley was trying to cheer him up, but it did little good. The reality of battle had not changed for the convicts, no matter what new intelligence the prince and his commanders had. They were just as condemned as they had been on the meadow in front of Fallenhill. Except now they had hope, and that was his fault.

Hope had been his enemy for over ten years, ever since he had been accused of heresy and locked in the Ashfield college cellars. Hope had disappointed him time and again. Prayer had gone unanswered as well, so he had turned his back on them both. Injustice ruled his life instead. He knew he wanted to hope for a better future, and Duchess Amelia offered him a better chance than any other in his decade of exile. It felt so wrong to use hope now to motivate the other convicts, like he was telling them a lie and trusting in hope that it would turn out to be true.

Turley did not care, that was obvious. He seemed happy to get his satisfaction from the little pleasures he could eke from life and let his conscience tend to itself. Prentice could not do it. He did not want happiness without righteousness. Perhaps it was his time in Church schooling, the training to be a holy knight that had shaped him this way.

He shook his head. Men were going to die, and he would be leading them. Didn't he owe them the truth, at least?

"The truth is all I have," he muttered to himself.

"You say something?" Turley asked.

"Nothing. Self-pity, I suppose."

"Self-pity? Now you really sound like a convict, but a new one—not one with ten years over the mountains."

Prentice nodded. "I've been having some old thoughts over again lately, remembering some things the Reach tends to make a convict forget."

"Ah, we all have nights like that."

"So what do you do with them?"

"Me?" said Turley. "I try to find a sweet and willing maid to curl up with. Or at least willing—sweet's not always on offer. Or some hooch, if I can charm it or swipe it."

"I'm not that kind of man," Prentice said.

"And thank God too! If you were, then I'd have been dead long ago."

Prentice looked at him in surprise.

Turley drained his plate and smacked his lips. "You don't think I hooked onto you for your winning personality, do you? You've been helping keep me alive and out of too much mischief for years now. I know a good thing!"

"Even if I get you flogged?"

"Oh, well, lately you've not been doing so well, but even a thoroughbred gets tired some days."

The maid returned with the empty pot and a handful of straw, saying that she needed to clean it up at a nearby creek and asking if Turley would like to come and keep her safe. Turley told her there was an army all about and that she could not be safer. She objected, saying that after washing the pot, she was thinking to bathe herself and would need a man to defend her honor. She winked as she walked off toward the creek.

"Defend her honor?" Prentice asked with a mock stern gaze.

"And you expect a rogue like me to make an honest woman out of *her*?" Turley responded, standing and heading after her. "The Israelites had an easier time crossing the desert!"

Prentice could not help but smile as he watched his friend go. He did not want to lead that man to his death.

CHAPTER 40

The army marched before dawn the day after fording the Dwelt. The land on the western side of the river was covered in low rolling hills, finally falling away from mountains to the endless westward plains. By late morning, outriders were reporting signs of the enemy force, exactly where the prisoner had said they would be. The prisoner himself had not been seen since the army had marched from Fallenhill. Prentice assumed the man was still alive and being questioned, but if the prince was sharing anything else he had learned, the duchess was not forthcoming.

"I have heard a rumor of a new name for you, Prentice," she said to him as he marched barefoot beside her horse. "I am told that the convicts have taken to calling you Ash. I'm assured even the overseers and others are using this new name."

"Yes, Your Grace."

"I have heard that they are calling it a battle name. Is that right?"

Prentice nodded.

"You do not think it provocative to take a name given by our enemy? One that Sir Liam tried to claim a right to?"

She looked at him pointedly.

"I hadn't really thought of that."

"Convicts are not typically given honors like this, are they?"

"Not typically," he said, "but I do not think that should matter to Your Grace."

"And why is that?"

"Because of the coming battle and your promise, Your Grace. Either I will survive the battle, in which case you will free me, and my name will be my own problem as a free man..."

"Or?"

"Or I will be dead, and the problem will have gone away by itself."

"Very well." The duchess nodded and spurred her horse ahead, leaving Prentice to return to the convicts.

Nearing noon, the army marched into the shallow bowl of a meadow valley with a stream running from the north to the southeast. At the valley's western corner was a hill with a broad grassy slope leading up to a blunt crown. On this slope the enemy army waited. Their position was defensive and strong. To the north, the hill's slope merged into other rolling hills, with unseen gullies and other features. On their south was a ridge of black rock that formed a natural wall, preventing any possibility of outflanking them on their right. The slope in front of the invaders was not steep, but it was long, so that the Kingdom army would be charging uphill for three or four hundred paces. The stream across the valley floor at the foot of the hill meant that forces coming from the east would not be able to build momentum either, since any speed they gathered coming down into the valley would be lost crossing the stream, and the tightness of their lines would be broken up. Prentice appreciated the enemy's position; it was well chosen. The odds were good that the little stream would be crimson by the end of the day.

As Prentice did a rough count of the enemy in his head, a herald in Reach livery rode up and summoned him to the duchess. He rushed to keep up as the man led the way, bare feet slipping in the grass. His shoes were lost somewhere in Fallenhill, from when Lord Dunstan's men had dragged him off. He was still some distance from the duchess when the ring of a bell pealed around the valley. It was so clear and pure that, for a moment, the whole army looked around, trying to find the source. Soon enough, some pointed.

Following their indications, Prentice could make out a single enemy soldier standing out in front of their lines, twenty or so paces forward. He was tall and powerfully built, bare chested and wearing only dark breeches. He stood strong with two items in his hands. In his right was a sword, long bladed with a heavy gilt pommel and cross guard. In his left was a bronze bell. Holding it by the iron ring on top, the man struck the pommel on the bell with rhythmic strikes. Prentice counted the strikes, then looked at the sky to judge the sun and realized what the man was doing. He was keeping time, ringing the hours of the day.

Prentice contemplated this as he approached the duchess on her horse. "Your Grace?"

"Attend me, Prentice," the duchess instructed. "Watch and listen carefully, but keep your tongue. I will want to consult you before the battle begins."

Prentice tugged his forelock and fell in discreetly beside the duchess's saddle, like any dutiful servant. The duchess rode forward until her horse was amid the prince's entourage, though slightly back from the front. The knights and lords were discussing the ground and the enemy, and tactics for the coming battle. Their tone was light, even happy, as they all seemed relieved to be finally able to come to grips with the foe.

"There will be no Forfeits Council this time," Amelia said quietly to Prentice. "The prince has declared that there will be no time, with the enemy so close and ready, but I think he mostly wants to avoid another debacle of unfulfilled claims."

Prentice nodded but did not speak in reply. Many of the prince's entourage were pointing forward of the army, to a spot just this side of the stream. It looked as if something or someone was crouched to the ground there in the rushes. Two knights spurred their mounts and swiftly crossed the intervening distance, circling the creature. They splashed in the shallows and waved their swords until the figure of a woman arose. She lifted her hands to one of them and then cringed away as the knight hefted an axe and struck downward. The woman had been chained to a stake, and the knight's axe struck the links from the wood, freeing her. She was naked, it seemed, with her dark hair loose down her back and full of grass and nettles. Even at a distance, she was clearly dirty and bruised. The two knights pointed to the prince's place in the army's line and escorted the woman to him.

She struggled forward, dragging the heavy chain and trying to cover her nakedness as she came. She seemed to plead with the knights as she walked, but they ignored her, only pointing again at the prince and using their horses to keep her walking. When she was ten or so paces from the royal company, she stopped, hiding her head in shame in the sight of so many men.

As they watched, many made cold comments, some even crude. Prentice heard one low voice claim that she was doubtless a witch, left by the enemy to put a curse on the Kingdom army.

It was the duchess who spoke out loudly, surprising all present. "Oh, dear God!" she cried. "Baroness Stopher?" She spurred her mare forward, leaving Prentice standing alone as she quickly rode to the woman on the grass. Amelia dismounted and took the woman in her arms, searching the bruised face closely for a moment. "It *is* you!"

Duchess Amelia immediately slid her cream-colored cloak from her shoulders and wrapped it about the woman, covering her. "This is the baroness!" she declared.

The muttering changed tone, and many men shifted uncomfortably in their saddles.

"Well, will no one offer her aid?" Amelia demanded. "Is the sight of an abused woman on a battlefield all it takes to rob you of your wits?"

The knights and lords looked at each other for a moment before several finally moved. In a hesitant confusion, they started and stopped until, at last, one knight was most forward and dismounted to offer his horse to the baroness.

"We must remove those chains!" announced Sir Carron Ironworth's strong voice. "Send for a blacksmith."

"I will take her to my tent," said Amelia. "Have the blacksmith attend us there!"

Sir Carron nodded, and Amelia pressed the baroness to mount the horse. The woman put her hand on the saddle, but before she could mount up, she turned to the prince and looked at him with a strange clarity in her eyes, as if she only just recognized him. She rushed forward and fell on her knees before his horse, Amelia's cloak slumping over her.

"Your Highness," she said.

"Baroness, your homage is welcomed, of course," said the prince, his voice dripping with distaste. "But it can wait until later. The business of the Kingdom's wars must come first, and you are hardly fit to be received."

"I... I know, Your Highness, but I must beg leave to speak. I beg of you! Those..." The baroness fumbled for a moment as she obviously struggled to find the right words. "Those men, they told me to give you a message. They made me swear! Swear to our god."

The prince held his chin high, disdainful of the baroness's groveling before him. It made Prentice want to curse. *For God's sake*, he thought. *Let the bloody woman speak.*

The prince looked to his closest advisors, Sir Carron and a richly dressed sacrist who Prentice guessed was the prince's chaplain. "Very well. Speak!"

"Your Highness, the leader of the men who sacked our town and burned..." the baroness began, but she fell to sobs as she no doubt recalled the burning of the townsfolk and her own husband, cooked alive in his armor. Several of the men listening tutted or sighed loudly. At their impatience, the abused woman lifted her head in wild-eyed defiance. "Their leader's man gave me a message for you, Highness. He made me swear to God to give it to you. He dragged me out and had me stripped in the dark, in front of his men all lined up there!"

She turned and pointed wildly at the waiting enemy ranks. "They took me down to the water and chained me there like an animal in the muck with insects! I shivered until the sun rose, and now I have burned."

"You have a message for me, Baroness Stopher?" the prince coldly interrupted.

"Yes! Yes, a message from our enemy." The baroness nodded, her ruined hair bouncing in a cloud about her head. "He says he has come here to wait and can wait all day. He knows how hard it is for old people to march, and he understands if you wish to rest. He will gladly crush you at sunset or wait another day and do so at dawn. His army will fight in the day or night, whenever you are ready. They fight and fight and kill and burn..." Her words faded as the peal of the bell strokes rang across the field again.

The baroness turned at the sound, treading on the hem of Amelia's cloak, so that it half fell from her shoulders. She was exposed but ignored her nakedness as she looked back at the army and their bell-ringing herald.

"That's him!" she screamed. "He stands there and rings that bell. Kill him! Kill him, or they will kill us all. Kill us all!"

"Her mind is broken," intoned the sacrist beside the prince, his voice deep and melodious, as though he were pronouncing a sermon in a church rather than sitting his horse in an army. "A battlefield is no godly place for a woman."

"I will take her now, if you will, Your Highness," Amelia offered, sparing a cold glance for the sacrist.

"Sacrist Porlain is correct," said the prince. "Take the baroness to your tent and await the outcome of the battle. With rest and a return to a lady's duties, doubtless she will remember herself."

"I will see her safely," the duchess replied, covering the baroness once more and then curtsying in the grass. "But I fear I must return. As my husband's wife, I cannot rest or return to a lady's duties until this foe is driven from our land!"

"Do as you will," the prince said wearily. "You have done so thus far on this campaign."

Prentice did not doubt everyone present heard the tired rebuke carried in the prince's words. He was certain the duchess had heard it. Amelia pointedly led the baroness to her own horse, ignoring the previously offered mount. Once the brutalized woman was in the saddle, the duchess handed the reins to Prentice, who bowed his head as he received them. Amelia then led them from the field, looking for stewards to order the setting of her tent and to fetch a blacksmith for the chains.

CHAPTER 41

As she waited for the tent to be set, Amelia sent for Sir Liam. The baroness slid from the saddle of her horse and sat on the ground in the grass. Every attempt to talk with her was met with only silence. Her mind truly did seem broken.

"That could have been me," Amelia muttered to herself as she paced back and forth. Her head was crowded by memories of the ambush at the river. Until now, being slaughtered so brutally, as her maid Dianda had been, was the worst she had imagined for herself. But as she looked at the baroness, other fates became apparent. Stripped, beaten, and thoroughly humiliated, then sent back to face the contempt of the Grand Kingdom. Amelia found herself hard pressed to tell which fate she would more fear.

"Your Grace?" Prentice asked quietly. He stood by as the stewards began to set the tent, holding the horse's reins as she had ordered and not speaking until now.

"I was musing," Amelia told him.

He nodded. "Your Grace, the battle will commence soon. After the insults the enemy offered in his message, I doubt anyone will urge the prince to wait."

Amelia agreed. "You think the insults were deliberate? So do I. The message was given to goad the prince into quick action."

"It will be a mistake. You should not return to the field!"

Amelia turned to him; her eyes narrowed in disbelief. "You think so? You heard the prince. Already he is seeking revenge, as well as any opportunity to put me back in my solar, darning and embroidering until a new husband is found for me!"

She would have continued, but at that moment Sir Liam arrived, accompanied by Brother Whilte. Prentice's hand went reflexively to the handle of his cudgel, where it hung from a rope around his waist.

"Your Grace, this is no good time to summon me from the field," said Sir Liam, not bothering to dismount.

Amelia marveled at how fickle his manners were. If her fortunes were strong, he followed her loyally enough, but let the prince even sneer in her direction and instantly he was too good to serve her.

"A moment, Sir Liam," she said, holding up her hand. "Prentice, why would you tell me not to go?"

Brother Whilte turned to Sir Liam and made a show of being offended by the duchess's offhanded manner. "She summons you from battle, to waste your time waiting while she confers with a convict! The foolishness of women was never more obvious." His voice was not quiet.

Sir Liam scowled but did not correct his companion.

Amelia kept her eyes on Prentice. No matter what Whilte or any other nobleman thought of her, she was yet the Duchess of the Western Reach, and they would wait upon her.

"You should not go because it is a trap, Your Grace," Prentice said, his voice level.

"How can you know?"

"Yes, convict," Brother Whilte said with an arch tone, "share with us your heretical wisdom."

Prentice whirled to face the two knights, and for a moment Amelia thought he might launch himself at them, so furious was his expression. She had never seen him so close to losing control. His breathing was heavy, and his eyes narrowed like a raging beast. When the moment passed and Prentice reasserted his self-control, Amelia felt herself breathe a sigh of relief. She almost didn't hear Prentice's words as he presented his reasoning to the two disdainful knights.

"Why have they waited for us? Have you asked yourself that?" he said.

Sir Liam did not respond, seeming too impatient to return to the battlefield and his chance of glory. Whilte shrugged dismissively and waved away Prentice's question.

"They could have led us a merry dance for months, perhaps the whole rest of summer and autumn," Prentice persisted. "They want no plunder or slaves, so what are they doing?"

"They have chosen their field for battle, fool," Whilte answered.

"Why?"

"Because that is what armies do! Truly, Duchess, every time you indulge this miscreant and allow him to speak to his betters like this, you only reinforce the court's disdain for you. Clearly, allowing you to marry above your station has made you forget the true order of things. You will doubtless soon have to be taken in hand, or you will just run wild and let your late husband's demesne be overrun by mongrels and bastards!"

Amelia was stunned by Brother Whilte's directness. He was surely only saying what many in the Rhales court thought, but to be so blunt was beyond rude—it was an insult. And was the comment about bastards insinuating that she was licentious? Was he implying that she and Prentice were lying together?

"Enough of this!" Sir Liam said curtly, cutting her off before she could rebuke Brother Whilte. "The prince has made the call to battle, and his authority supersedes even yours, Duchess Amelia."

With that, Sir Liam wheeled his horse with an angry pull of the reins. The beast whickered and snorted and then broke into a canter.

Brother Whilte leaned forward and fixed cold eyes on Prentice. "She won't be off the leash forever, you little dog's prick. Once she's brought to heel, there'll be no one to protect you anymore—and I'll be there!"

"Your brother was the one who needed protection," Amelia heard Prentice say under his breath as the two knights rode away. Then he said to her, "You should have dismissed Liam!"

"You told me not to!"

"I know. I was wrong. You can't have him treat you like that in public or let his companions do it either. If he covers himself in glory on the field today, it will only be worse."

"I thought you said this battle was a trap."

"I am certain."

"Why? Just because they waited for us?"

Prentice nodded.

On the ground nearby, Baroness Stopher moaned softly, then her chains clanked as she pulled the cloak further about herself and lay outstretched on the grass. She looked to be asleep. Amelia both pitied and envied her.

She motioned for Prentice to continue.

"They've waited days for us here," he explained. "Since before we reached Fallenhill. So, this is the ground they want. Why?"

Amelia looked west to where the battlefield lay just beyond a low ridge. She thought about what she had seen and compared it to the works she had been reading. There were factors she recognized, but there were so many new pieces of information that she was not sure.

"The field they stand on means our knights cannot sweep around their sides, the flanks," she began, thinking out loud. "But surely we can just ride straight at them."

"Except for the stream."

Amelia nodded thoughtfully, then suddenly shook her head, realizing the enemy's mistake. "They're too far up the hill!" she declared. "Even if charging knights are disorganized by the stream, the enemy is too far away to use the confusion. The knights will have time to re-form their lines."

Prentice smiled. "You've been reading, I see."

Amelia returned his smile, pleased with herself. The political part of her mind registered that the approval of a convict was not something that a duchess should concern herself with, but she was too buoyed by the thought that the enemy had made a strategic blunder.

"So, we will win?" she said. "They've made a key error, and we will win!"

"I don't think so."

"Why on earth not?"

From the field came the ringing notes of the bell again. The baroness whimpered in her sleep, her soft mewling muffled further by the cloak pulled about her face.

"Because that army stands ready and marks time," said Prentice, looking in the direction of the ringing. "They have had days to prepare the ground. They are skilled and experienced and have never once lost any encounter with a Kingdom force. They are too good to make so simple a mistake. They are not resting; they are watchful and ready."

The stewards erecting Amelia's tent stood a short distance away and bowed, telling her they were done. Her furniture was being taken down from its carts.

"Leave those," she told her stewards. "Only bring my cot for the baroness and a chair for myself."

The servants obeyed.

The duchess thought for a moment about Prentice's words. "Go to the rogues," she told him. "Whatever happens now is beyond me. I only pray it is not beyond the prince and our army."

Amelia knelt and shook the baroness on the shoulder, to move her to the cot in her tent.

"Just one thing more, Your Grace," Prentice said. "You should know that I have promised your full emancipation for every convict who survives this campaign. It was all I could think of to motivate them to fight."

Amelia sighed inwardly. It was too much to think about. Prentice had overreached himself, but she could not bring herself to care. Her position as duchess still felt precarious in spite of all her gains so far, and soon men of the Grand Kingdom would be dying in her name.

"Go, Prentice," she said. "And help us win, or else I won't be able to emancipate anyone."

Prentice smiled and bowed before jogging off toward the field. A blacksmith arrived carrying a hammer, chisel, and some other tools. Amelia took the baroness by the arm and led her to the tent, helping her onto the cot. She woke when the blacksmith began his work but was soon after sleeping again, and Amelia sat in the chair next to her.

CHAPTER 42

The rogues were still on the eastern side of the stream and well back from it when Prentice returned to them. The weapon carts were nearby but still loaded. The overseers had not even pulled the chains from the shackles. The whole mass of men was standing, watching as the knights and their squires were fording the stream and lining up on the other side to begin their attack on the invaders.

"What's happening?" Prentice asked Turley, who was standing near Tuke.

"You ain't in this one!" the overseer answered before Turley could. "They don't want ya!"

"What?"

"Word came from mighty Knight Captain Liam," Turley explained. "We are to wait here. 'The army will not need convict dogs to win this glory.' His words."

Prentice shook his head. "Fine. Overseer Tuke, I need five men off the chain to distribute the metal and poles."

Tuke looked unimpressed. "What for?" asked the greasy overseer, chewing what smelled like rancid tobacco, black spittle on his lips.

"To arm the men."

"Don't you hear good? You ain't in this one!"

"What I heard was an order to stand this ground," Prentice said. "A quarter hour from now, I could hear an order to attack, or advance, or to hold ground to cover a withdrawal. Whatever orders come to the rogues, I'll have them bloody armed for the task. Now get five men off those damn chains for me!"

Tuke grunted and spat some stinking muck into the grass, but he turned and ordered his men to the task. Soon, five convicts were handing out the poles and metal. Many of the inferior weapons needed remaking with their makeshift fixtures, but some were still useful as they were.

"You're taking to command quite natural," Turley said quietly, careful to not be heard by the overseers. "Don't think I've ever seen you lose your temper with a free man like that before. You always said it was the surest way to judgment day."

Prentice said nothing.

"Thing is," Turley went on, "we all kind of trust you, even knowing the limits of a convict. These men are waiting to follow the hero Ash—Prentice Ash. That's you. If you're planning on some glory charge to end it all, well, that doesn't seem a fair use of their loyalty, leading 'em to your early grave."

Prentice turned on him. "Is that what you think I'd do?"

Turley shrugged. "I dunno, maybe. Like I said, I never seen you this wild, ever. You were always the smart, calm one. Kept my mischievous hide out of trouble all these years now. You know that's why I'm friends with you?"

Prentice wanted to smile, to reassure his friend, but he could not shake the grim certainty that there was a trap set for the Grand Kingdom army on this field and they were falling right into it. He turned back and scanned the field, watching the two armies. The knights had forded the little stream *en masse*, their warhorses crushing the sedge grasses flat in a hundred-pace-wide path and churning the crystal waters to murk. On the other side, they formed up in perfect ranks, little or no jockeying for position. Behind them, squads of squires and pages set themselves ready with supplies, replacement lances and shields, and tools to make running repairs for any knight whose equipment was damaged before he was ready to quit the fight.

Last of all, the prince and his honor guard waited on the east side of the stream, a small pageant of the finest colors and armor, watching the attack from the closest vantage point.

Prentice turned from watching the Grand Kingdom army, which was almost ready for the charge but still somewhat disorganized, to the enemy, still in ranks and waiting patiently. Their leader remained standing out in front, sword and bell in his hands. This would have been the perfect time for them to charge, to engage the knights while they were fording the stream. A downhill charge by disciplined spearmen could have delivered a stinging first blow, a serious advantage in morale, even if it didn't do much actual damage—which it could.

What are they doing? he wondered.

It was possible to disrupt a charge of knights. A pit or trench only needed to be a handspan deep to disrupt a warhorse's charge, even possibly injure the animal, weighed down by rider and armor as it was. But Prentice could see no sign of any digging, just the rising grass slope with the enemy at the top. It was almost as if they wanted the knights to charge successfully, but Prentice could not imagine why. Could the enemy be as proud and foolish as the leaders of his own side?

There was a drumbeat from the prince's entourage and the waving of colors. All along the lines of knights, shouts went up. There was a pause, and then the trumpet sounded.

And with one great roar, the charge began.

The tightly restrained destriers were given their heads, and with snorts the powerful beasts leaped forward. In seconds, the hoofbeats of hundreds thundered over the valley.

"Damn, you can feel it in your bones," Turley observed. "Those bastards'll go down like windblown grass! That much steel running at you? I'd be pissing me-self."

Prentice watched the charge. The herald, with his bell, retreated to the safety of his own lines. Even with the heavy objects in his hands, he sprinted that short distance to avoid being overtaken. Faced with that earthshaking wall of steel-clad muscle, the average man would bolt in terror, self-preservation telling him there was no other choice. But disciplined men knew better.

This enemy, with painted face and unfamiliar equipment, was clearly very disciplined. Rank after rank of them stood fast, their long spears held forward to receive the charge. Prentice could not see it, but he was sure that the front ranks had rammed their spear butts into the earth to reinforce them against the enemy mass. From the first time he had seen their work, defeating the angry Sir Dav at the ambush at the river bend, it was clear that these men knew how to fight against horsemen.

The moment of impact was a cascade of clashing steel metal along the two lines, like the roll of a steel wave on an iron beach. A knight's warhorse was trained to run down men on foot, crashing bodily into a man and then trampling him where he fell. But even the best-trained mount would shy from sharp steel, however, especially thrust at its face on the end of a spear. Some of the horses had closed blinders, and their riders were able to force them into the lines, thrashing and kicking as the knight's lance punched through boiled leather armor. Others could not help but shy, or else their riders did not wish to risk them too much, and so many of them balked at the end of the charge, wheeling in place.

The front two ranks of knights and spearmen dissolved into a cruel melee. The few mounts that plunged deep into the enemy were soon slowed by the press of bodies and their riders were dismounted too easily. Most of the knights, seeing the enemy's discipline began to withdraw. No orders were given, since these men of war knew their business. They pulled back about one hundred paces and began to re-form. Squires rushed forward with fresh lances to replace broken shafts and to check the horses' tack. As they did so, the enemy spearmen also re-formed their ranks. The ones at the back stepped forward, filling the gaps in the line, their slain and wounded passed quickly back.

"This is going to be a brutal business," Prentice said to himself.

"They took that!" Turley marveled. "They took that bloody well. Too bloody well!"

"Kingdom knights." Prentice spat on the ground as he said it. "Normally, they'd have us convicts up the middle and let us bog the enemy down. Then they sweep to a flank and attack from the side. That's how you rout an army."

"But there's no space to sweep around here, so they've just jumped to the charge and hoped for the best?" said Turley, following Prentice's train of thought. "Well, more fool them; least we're not getting thrown into the fire!"

Prentice understood Turley's attitude, but he was still worried, even as the knights charged again. This time the crash of steel was just as loud, echoing discordantly down the slope, but no knights sought to smash through. Now they fought with more discipline, knee to knee and protecting each other's flanks. The enemy spearmen had a more desperate time, their painted faces contorted in snarls as they screamed and bellowed battle cries. Again, though more slowly, the two fronts broke into the confusion of melee, and slowly the knights began to disengage once more, riding away to re-form yet again.

"How many times are they going to charge?" Turley asked.

"As many as it takes."

Prentice knew the conflict was devolving into a battle of wills, both sides seeking to grind the other down; the first side to break would lose. The knights charged again, but their mounts were already tired from rushing uphill twice, and they struggled to keep up more than a canter. This time their line was uneven before it struck, and the melee even more confused. Horses shied without even reaching the line, and wounded knights staggered out of the confusion and dust, seeking refuge on the fringes of the conflict—a moment to take a breath or assess an injury. Prentice couldn't see them, but he knew the enemy spearmen had to be suffering similar losses.

"So why hold the line?" he said to himself.

"What?" asked Turley.

"When the knights withdraw to re-form, they should just start marching down the hill."

"Who?"

"The invaders. They've got themselves covered on the flanks and backs to the peak. Why let the horses back into line? Push them while they're re-forming."

"Maybe they're tired too."

"Tired?" Prentice repeated. The notion caught in his mind.

"Just look at them horses," Turley kept on. "They're going to have to rest them soon or else give them to the knackers. They'll be too broken for anything else."

Prentice had stopped listening to his comrade. Another question came to him, the most important one. "Where are their wolves?"

"What? Oh yeah, where are the wolves? Or the other beasts those farmers said."

Prentice looked over Turley's head to the north. The hills and gullies looked narrow and twisting. They would be awkward for a force of any size to move through. He looked south. On one side the rocky ridge stretched all the way down to the stream, but on the eastern bank was a broad, flat meadow. What was on the other side of the ridge? Prentice peered back and forth, judging the distance between the ridge, the stream, and the two clashing forces.

Suddenly, he knew the enemy's plan.

"Tuke!" he shouted. "Get them off the chains now!"

"Say what?" asked Turley, distractedly watching the knights' fourth charge.

Prentice was already rushing toward the little clutch of overseers calmly spectating, and he ran right up to Tuke. "Keys, man! We need them off the chains now!"

Tuke sneered. It appeared he was willing to have Prentice wield his strange convict's authority in some contexts, but not to be ordered about in front of his own men. He was doubtless still smarting from Prentice's earlier rebuke, so this new set of orders seemed too much for his pride. He drew himself up, puffing out his flabby chest. "Now you look here, boy—"

"I don't have time for this, Tuke!"

"Is that right?" Tuke asked, looking over his shoulder at his fellows.

Prentice knew the name of this game: laugh at the uppity convict and then teach him the painful lesson that can only be learned at the tip of a lash. He wasn't interested. As Tuke turned his face back, Prentice thrust the end of his cudgel into the man's gut. The overseer bent at the waist, huffing in pain. Prentice followed up with a heavy punch that smashed across the side of Tuke's head, dropping him unconscious to the ground. The other overseers stood by stunned a moment, then reached for their whips.

Their eyes grew wide with utter shock as the five men they had unchained to distribute the convicts' weapons abruptly stepped up, shoving their makeshift spears and bills forward, protecting Prentice. For a moment, he, too, was surprised by this unexpected support.

"We need to get these men off the chains and marching now!" he ordered the overseers, who still had their hands on their whips.

"You'll hang for that, convict!" one of them said, looking at Tuke's fallen form.

"Maybe," Prentice retorted. "But looks like you won't live to see it if you don't give up the keys."

The nearest overseer reluctantly handed over the key on his belt, and soon the others followed suit. One of the unchained convicts took them and passed them to Prentice, who gave them to Turley.

"Go pull those chains, and be quick!" Prentice said to his friend, then turned to the overseers. "You lot, go back to camp. Your work is done. If I live through this, feel free to tell how I led a convict revolt. One way or another, it won't matter by then."

"What's going on?" Turley asked as the overseers fled, none of them thinking to take Tuke with them.

"Just unlock them!" was all Prentice said, looking past his friend to the ridge. He wasn't certain, but it seemed as though there was dust rising from the land beyond the rocks. He heard the chains sliding back and squinted as the early afternoon sun flashed off the armor and weapons of the prince's retinue. The royal crowd still sat their horses on this side of the stream, eyes fixed on the battle up the slope. The next nearest soldiers were the pages and squires, almost two hundred paces or more up the hill, still re-arming the knights. The prince was dangerously exposed.

"Is there somethin' down there?" someone called from among the convicts.

From the south, a column of dust, plainly separate from the dust of the conflict up the hill, was wafting on the light breeze. Whatever waited beyond the ridge was on its way. The chains rattled loose, and Prentice turned back to the convicts to see that they were all looking to him. They were as ready and eager as he had ever seen any convicts, and he had a sudden, bitter thought. This was as close to freedom as many of these men would ever come. He briefly imagined telling them to run, giving them a chance of freedom by fleeing what was almost certainly about to become a Kingdom defeat.

At that moment he remembered the raging conflict he had witnessed between the white lion and the many-headed serpent, and the voice that had chased him out of the vision.

"Three times you will challenge me," it had said. "Three times, and then I will defeat you and give you victory." It was God who had spoken, he knew it. The Lion of Judah.

Was this his third time? The vision by the pool had been the first, when he prayed in bitterness. The second had been in Fallenhill, when he had thought to let the enemy scouts flee, even knowing their evil, surrounded by so many innocent victims slain. If he told these men to flee, would he be defeated? And if he was, what would be the victory after? It seemed as if time had stopped around him for a moment, and the whole rush of thoughts had whirled through his mind and moved on. He reached a decision almost before he realized. He nearly smiled to himself as he turned to face the men.

"We're going to run down to that stream and stay there," he shouted at them. "When we get there, bunch up behind me, facing south." He looked toward the ridge, and the dust was thickening; they didn't have long. "Fast as you can, but stay together!"

He turned on his heel and ran toward the stream, picking a spot halfway between the prince's entourage and the ridge. It was possible that the enemy would sweep wide, but he gambled that the more likely plan was that they would try to charge straight at their target, the prince. He deliberately did not run too fast, concerned that he would leave the half-starved men behind, but he was astonished when he saw many of them quickly catch up to him.

"My father commands many hosts. Will you let him command you too?" a voice beside him asked, and Prentice turned. The convict who had offered him food and wine at

Fallenhill ran next to him in the midst of the others, hands and feet no longer bandaged, but apparently already healed with ugly scars.

"I know who you are," Prentice said.

"I am pleased."

"But I don't know why."

"This day is the first of a number that must come. Today's battle is but a shower. The next season will bring floods that will rise to test the foundations of nations."

"So why me?"

"For He says unto Moses, 'I will have mercy on whom I will have mercy, and I will have compassion on whom I will have compassion.'"

Prentice chuckled and shook his head. "You're saying I'm not chosen or special, aren't you?" The men around him kept up, but somehow felt distant. "I could still die at any time in this battle, couldn't I?"

"You are chosen, and you are special," the convict replied. "And you could still die at any time in this battle, or after. Do your duty, seek what is righteous, and trust the Lord of Hosts for the outcome."

Prentice looked at the men around him, recognizing in them his task, his duty. He turned back, but the convict was gone again.

From somewhere behind him a voice cried out, "Oh God! What is that?"

To the south, a company of enemy soldiers burst from behind the ridge, riding in two-wheeled chariots. Each vehicle was drawn by a pair of powerful horses, like knights' destriers, and had two or three men riding in them. The chariots and horses came up from what must have been a ford in the stream, hidden beyond the ridge, and they were already at a trot. The men were all painted like the spearmen on the hill, but they were larger and heavily built, like the herald who had kept time with the bell. They were the enemy's heroes, there could be no doubt, the equivalent of the Grand Kingdom's knights. Their weapons were heavy, and they each wore bronze mail or even some plated armor.

There were over twenty chariots, and in the middle was their leader. He rode taller than the rest, and Prentice knew immediately that he was the one the farmers had seen. He had no helmet, but long hair that streamed about his face and two enormous antlers, like those of a great stag, that sprouted straight from his head. The brute wielded a polearm as long as a knight's lance, with a heavy head of black iron. He thrust the blade into the sky and made an inarticulate cry, like the rage of a monstrous animal. From all the other chariots came answering cries, and a man threw himself from each one, even as they were picking up speed. Every one of the men was naked, and before any of them struck the ground, their shapes shifted, like a shimmering of shadow in deep water. Suddenly, they were wolves and beasts of many kinds, running beside the accelerating chariots.

"Oh, well now we're bloody stuffed," said Turley.

Prentice came to a halt beside the stream and let the others gather around him. "Form up here, tight as you can!" he shouted. So many of the convicts were already panicking. Some had broken off from the rest and were trying to flee, exactly as he had thought of telling them to. As he watched, though, Prentice saw two of the beast-men break away from the chariots to pursue them. The creatures' shapes were like those the farmers had described—hounds with birdlike, beaked heads. Those fleeing were doomed, but the main mass had little better chance. He turned his back on the onrushing enemy and did his best to organize his men.

CHAPTER 43

Sir Liam walked his mount as quickly as he dared over the churned ground to find his squire. Broken bodies and fallen weapons littered the trampled grass and ruined earth. He had extracted himself from the melee for the fourth time, finding his way out of the dust more by instinct than sight. His horse was all but exhausted, and he had shattered three lances and lost a mace in the charges and combats. He could barely believe that the enemy line yet held, but behind him the sounds of combat still rang out.

Sir Liam's squire, a new boy he hardly knew named Croftlin, rushed forward, carrying his sword belt and second shield. Before the last charge, he had told Croftlin to have the shield ready in case his first broke, but the one on his arm still felt sound. Its colors were half lost, scratched away by spear strikes and sprayed with blood, but otherwise it was good. He took the sword by the hilt and pulled it forth, leaving scabbard and belt in the squire's hands. He waved the boy away and then looked back to the battle. More knights were emerging from the chaos, and the breeze was blowing back the dust for a moment.

Why don't they charge us? he wondered.

Liam had expected the first charge to scatter the lighter-armored footmen easily. When they had held for the first, he had thought the second charge would do the job. Now they had held for four charges and the subsequent melee, and Sir Liam had to respect their nerve. No Grand Kingdom footmen were so disciplined. Even the militia and mercenaries of the Vec realms to the south would not be so brave, not in his opinion.

The invaders had suffered what looked like heavy losses, maybe one in five or even one in four of their number, but still they held and fought off the Kingdom army. From where he sat his horse, he thought their own losses were not quite as high, but each melee left more knights unable to fight. There was no doubt this was a difficult conflict, but it only inspired him to thoughts of greater heroism. The harder the fray, the higher the glory. Certainly, the dog Prentice and his convicts would have been hacked to pieces in seconds by this foe.

Sneering, he looked back down the slope to see Prentice leading the rogues to the stream at a run. He watched for a moment, wondering what the fool convict thought he was doing.

"Wine, Sir Liam?" asked Brother Whilte, approaching on his own mount and offering a skin for his thirst.

Sir Liam accepted a swig with a nod of thanks. He eyed Whilte's condition. The brother's surcoat was torn, and there was a filthy mud of blood and dust down the front of his breastplate.

"Got my horse cut out from under me," Whilte explained. "Had to hack my way out on foot to get my second mount. Thing's as old as my grandmother, but level-headed and stout enough for the rest of this fray, I think."

Sir Liam nodded at his words, but he was not really listening. The convicts were coming down the hill, and his eyes were drawn to a small cloud of dust at the southern end of the valley.

"What's the heretic doing now?" Brother Whilte asked, eyes following where Sir Liam was looking.

Chariots burst into view, and beast-men fell to the ground amidst their wheels, sprinting forward with inhuman speed.

"It's a trick!" Sir Liam said. "It's a damned trick!" He looked back to the melee where the two lines were now more disengaged than not. Weary knights were returning to re-form again, and the enemy was letting them go once more.

"Where the rutting hell did they come from?" Whilte said, plainly horrified by the sight of an attacking force bearing down on the prince's company with only the rabble of convicts for protection.

Sir Liam had already turned his horse and was waving his sword about his head, trying to draw the attention of every Kingdom knight he could.

"The prince!" he bellowed, his voice hoarse and cracked from the shouts and war cries of battle. "To the prince! We must defend the prince!"

Other weary knights looked up and saw the dire situation in the bottom of the valley. Dirty and hammered, many of them seemed too tired to even comprehend what they were looking at, but Liam continued to shout, trying to rally them to ride to the Prince Mercad's defense. He could not ride away by himself, a lone hero. One man would add nothing to the royal protection against that enemy force, and to the other knights he might well only look like a deserter fleeing the field.

"Mercad! The prince!" he shouted. Slowly—too slowly, it seemed—the other Kingdom warrior nobles realized the situation and moved to respond. Sir Liam wanted them all, but when he had gathered thirty or so around him, he lowered his sword, and they rushed down the slope. He trusted that the other knights would understand soon enough and either fight a rear guard or else join him in fighting off the ambushing chariots.

As they thudded over the ruined ground, Sir Liam knew that their charge was the slowest of the day, their near-exhausted mounts barely lifting above the rate of a trot, even with the help of the downhill slope. The invaders had set their trap well, holding the knights in the battle far from the prince and the army's other leaders, tired by over an hour of charges and fighting. At least the duchess was safer in the camp, though if the enemy succeeded, then she and all the other camp followers would certainly be taken prisoner.

Liam knew the fate of prisoners. For the first time, he accepted in his mind the thought that the Grand Kingdom might not carry the day. He had never faced defeat like this, and the thought of it made him desperate.

———————◆○◆———————

Prince Mercad had watched intently from the moment the knights of the army had crossed the stream and prepared their first charge. He had willingly accepted the suggestion that the Grand Kingdom's finest take the battle to the enemy by themselves, especially in the light of the debacle at Fallenhill. It was usual for the rogues to be sent forward first—it had been so as far back as the prince could remember—but never had the enemy simply not been there to engage with their own rogues or other footmen. The tiny skirmish fought at the town's burned keep had done nothing to redeem the day's honor and finding Baron Stopher's roasted body and his slaughtered townsfolk had only infuriated the prince further.

Even the duchess, intent on playing the loyal widow, seemed sent to plague him with her repeated involvement. Of course, if the rumors of her dalliance with a convict rogue proved true, it would be a further embarrassment to the court. Mercad had to return from this campaign with some kind of victory.

So, he watched the battle intently. When the dust had started to rise, he had even wanted to suggest that the whole party move up to stand with the pages and squires, to see better the progress of the clash, but looking quickly about him, he dismissed the idea unspoken. He was sure these popinjay courtiers, with lace and silk under their spotless armor, would find the stream's edge quite close enough. They would doubtless protest any suggestion of getting closer, and he could not bear to hear them whining again. Their bloodless countenances only reminded the prince of his own age and frailty. He wanted his youth back. Then he would not be forced to watch; he would lead the charge.

"What is that?" Ironworth asked from beside him.

The prince paid little heed. He was saddle sore after only a couple of hours and had long since grown to ignore the foolish prattle of the sycophants around him. As if they would know the first thing about battle. Except for Ironworth, of course. He was an experienced and skilled knight, as his father had been before him. The Ironworth line had served the Grand Kingdom as knights, champions, and captains for nearly six generations.

"Did someone order the convicts up after all?" asked Sacrist Porlain. The prince had asked his chaplain to bless the troops and pray for victory, and the man had taken it as a general invitation to ride with them. He had hardly shut up the whole day, offering his ill-informed opinion on every turn of the deployment.

"Your Highness?" Ironworth pressed, and Mercad was finally persuaded to drag his attention from the hill slope.

His knight commander was pointing south, and the prince saw the convict foot running to the stream's edge. He was about to curse when he noticed figures and carts running on behind them. Blinking in the bright sunlight, he realized these were not carts but chariots, the sunlight flashing from their tack. Armored warriors rode proudly while painted drivers whipped the horses to frenzy. For a strange moment, Mercad sat high in his saddle and stared at them in disbelief.

"Who fights with chariots anymore?" he muttered. "Are we being attacked by ancient Egyptians?"

Then there was the scrape of swords being drawn forth, and Ironworth ordered the honor guard to form up.

"We should flee!" someone shouted.

"It's too late!" squeaked Porlain, snatching at his embroidered reins in panic and causing his horse to wheel about, knocking into others.

The prince could see he was right. War beasts were barreling across the higher ground behind them, cutting off retreat.

"God in heaven, save me!" Porlain cried.

Trust a sacrist to pray for himself first, the prince thought.

Then there was no time for bitterness. The enemy seemed to gather itself to pounce among the panicked convicts, but even as they did, something flashed from the stream—a blinding white light with a shape inside it. The figure seemed to leap up from the water toward the charging enemy, not quite touching the ground.

"An angel," the sacrist exclaimed. "God hears my prayer. We are saved!"

"Angel or no," the prince muttered, "we're a long way from saved."

He tried to give orders to the others, but his words were swallowed up in a thunderous explosion as noise and flame erupted where the flash of light fell in the midst of the charging enemy. Mercad was thrown from the saddle, and his vision swam as he lost consciousness.

CHAPTER 44

The white lion flashed into Prentice's view just as the chariots drew near, leaping up from the water of the stream as if it had stalked there among the reeds and rushes. The creature was easily as large as the chariot horses, and its mane streamed behind it as it bolted out. It was every bit as majestic as he remembered, glowing in the high sunlight. This time, however, Prentice was not the only one who saw it.

"What's that?" screamed a man to his right.

A crackling filled the air, like the sound of a roaring fire, and the lion's approach came with a rushing wind. Many of the convicts recoiled, momentarily distracted even from the charging enemy. Then the lion leaped in front of them, and the ground exploded in fire. The chariots' charge was smashed apart, and the convicts were thrown to the ground. The grass was scorched by flame, and many of the dark beast-men were scattered, incinerated. The lion fell upon the others, tearing and ripping with fang and claw.

Prentice got back to his feet as quickly as he could, his vision swimming and his head throbbing as he did so. He staggered a few steps before he got his balance back. His ears were ringing. All around him the ground was scorched with fire, the golden grass burned black. He rubbed at his face, and his hands came away sooty. Just like at Fallenhill, he was ashen again. He wanted to laugh. He looked about him and tried to get any of the convicts he could find to join him.

"For the Kingdom! The Grand Kingdom!" he shouted, but his voice sounded quiet and distant in his ringing ears. "God has made a way!"

He found his iron-ended cudgel in the scorched grass and retrieved it. The ground smoldered and smoked so that Prentice's eyes stung as he tried to see around him. Through the chaos he saw an enemy spearman with a face colored half red and half vibrant green, like spring growth. His spear had a strangely fluted blade with numerous spines and flares, obviously designed to tear flesh with any jab or cut. The edges dripped blood already, and the man thrust again, disdainfully slaughtering a dazed convict.

Prentice snarled in rage and threw himself at the enemy. He struck furiously, the cudgel hammering so hard against the shield that the enemy staggered backward. Before he could bring his spear to bear, a convict seized the enemy from behind and threw him down. The convict had a scythe blade in his hand, broken away from its haft, and he thrust it downward like a dagger into his enemy's throat and chest. When he was done, he stood and smiled at Prentice. He waved the makeshift dagger near his face in a vague approximation of a military salute. Prentice returned the gesture and pointed at the fallen spear.

"Take that and follow me!" he ordered and led off through the smoke.

The thunderous snarls of the lion and the fighting war beasts flew through the air like hateful curses. All the chariots were overturned or smashed as they burned, but many of their crews had survived and were on foot, armed and hounding clusters of frightened convicts. The convicts had numbers, but the enemy soldiers were well trained. They were champions, men of rank, like knights, and

Prentice could see that they had won the right to be driven into battle in their chariots. He charged without hesitation as he encountered one or two, using the confusion to his best ability and leading a growing band of rogues behind him.

He laughed out loud when he found Turley, standing in another small crowd of ten or so men. They all kept their poles forward, making a defensive hedge, while three chariot warriors stalked about them, darting in and out, looking for weaknesses. Even as Prentice watched, one of them surged again as another used the distraction to slide his shield under another convict's spear, pushing it out of the way, and thrusting him through the belly. Turley did his best to drive them back, swinging his cudgel wildly, like a crazed axeman who couldn't decide which tree he wanted to chop down. The enemy warriors simply stepped back with wolfish smiles, protecting themselves with their shields. They were not afraid.

Prentice felt the rage rise within him again, and he burst into a sprint, straight at the nearest enemy. The painted man yelled in surprise as Prentice vaulted from the smoke, kicking forward so that he landed bodily on the man's shoulder, knocking him aside. The invader fell toward the convict spears while Prentice barreled on to the next attacker. This one had his shield up in time, but he was unable to deflect the weight of the charge as it crashed into him. He staggered with a cry, and Prentice brought his heavy cudgel down on his skull.

The convicts who had been following their leader had already dispatched the first enemy as Prentice came up from his crouch to face the third. This man had the time to reset his guard and was ready for the attack. His face showed no fear, only battle lust—a wild, eager grin. Prentice found that eagerness inside himself as well and he gladly charged again.

The man aimed his spear to let Prentice impale himself with his own force, but Prentice saw it coming and knocked the spearhead away with his cudgel while pressing forward for the man himself. The enemy tried to withdraw and awkwardly swung with his shield, but the rage inside Prentice seemed to lend him strength; he simply took the hit as he pressed in close and drove his cudgel up under the man's chin. The blow crushed his windpipe, and the man collapsed in agony, gasping for breath.

Turley stepped in swiftly and finished him off. Then he looked at Prentice with a broad smile. "I always knew you were good in a fight, but hell's bells, I ain't never seen you like this!"

Prentice nodded and looked about for more of the enemy. He wanted to slay them all. The desire coursed through him like the heat of strong drink, making him drunk on battle. As he cast his eyes about, he saw the lion once more, distant now through the rising smoke and dust. It had a beast in its jaws, a scaled thing with a flicking, serpentine tail, which it tossed about until the thing's back broke and then cast it away with a toss of its head. Then the lion looked straight at Prentice, and there was a seriousness in its expression, a calm sternness that seemed to wash all the rage out of him like a rush of icy water.

"It is my rage that you feel, rage at the unrighteousness of sin," said the voice in his mind that had spoken to him that night in the willow grove. "But never does it rule me. Though I know it, I never forget myself. Do not forget me either, or my rage will consume and destroy you as well." The lion bounded away, and the sounds of its conflict faded from the battlefield.

Prentice turned back to the convicts—his men—for he realized now that that was who they were. They were all looking to him.

"Right. Keep together!" he shouted at them, calm and commanding once again. "We're not out of this yet."

Several convicts were scavenging the enemy polearms from the ground, or the fallen themselves, and they all eagerly pressed together to make a close knot of spears.

Even as they did so, the smoke began to clear. Through it came the leader of the charioteers, the enemy's great champion, the Horned Man. He was over seven feet in height, with broad shoulders and mightily thewed limbs. The antlers that sprouted from his head branched to over a dozen tips, and each point was chased in silver or gold, ornamented like arrow tips. He carried his thick-hafted pole weapon, as long as he was tall. It was a glaive, with a heavy, single edged blade and a barbed spike on its back side.

"The Ashen One?" said the Horned Man, his voice deep but grating, like the grinding of rocks. His dark eyes flashed with fury. With one hand still holding his weapon, he slapped his armored chest with the other, a challenge beat upon a drum. "The day has come!"

"If you know me, then know this," Prentice said, a commanding tone in his voice. "I will not quit this field until you and your people are slain or driven from it!"

Many of the men around him nodded and muttered their agreement, drawing confidence from Prentice's bold words. They shook their weapons at the monstrous enemy commander. In return, the Horned Man only sneered and cast an eye up the hill. Prentice followed his gaze and saw that the remaining invaders on the slope were at last advancing toward the stream. As they came, they quickly overran many of the squires, as well as wounded knights or those too confused to have joined Sir Liam's defense of the prince. The spearmen moved in open formation, and they unleashed their whooping battle cries, charging to catch as many knights as they could in the fording of the stream. The second half of the trap was closing on the Grand Kingdom forces.

"The seers can say what they like," the Horned Man said, smiling as his plan succeeded around him. "I did not become Vindicator by being afraid of old coward's visions!"

"Leave now or die. Your choice!" Prentice shouted, hoping it sounded like a final warning.

The Horned Man only continued to smile.

One of the convicts burst from the group, charging with his improvised pike. "Die, bastard!"

The Horned Man let the convict come on, barely even shifting his weight. He flicked the heavy blade of his glaive with almost casual strength, knocking the charging weapon aside and then slicing forward at the man. The black blade struck at the left collarbone, and even as it checked the charging man's momentum, the Horned Man slashed it downward across his chest. The man died with his head and one shoulder sliced away from his body.

The Horned Man gave them all a contemptuous look before pulling back his weapon and standing relaxed once again. "Next?" he mocked.

"How in all of heaven and hell's crap are we going to fight him?" Turley muttered as murmurs of panic sounded among the convicts.

"He'll kill us all, Ash or no!" someone else said.

"We're not going to fight him," Prentice said quietly.

"We're not?"

"When I give the order, everyone is to run for the prince's company!"

"Truly?"

"Truly! We'll need knights with heavy armor to beat this bastard. Pass the word quietly."

Prentice never let his eyes leave the Horned Man. He had no doubt that the enemy champion could easily slaughter a dozen poorly armed convicts, Turley and himself included. He was thankful for the warning to not embrace the rage; if his blood had been up, he would likely have led the little squad in a suicidal charge.

He waited as long as he dared for the convicts to be ready, then gave his order. "Run, now!" he shouted, and the men bolted as one.

Prentice stood his ground as they fled, in case the Horned Man tried to pursue. It seemed little more than a futile gesture. The Horned Man only watched the convicts go, as if amused by their retreat. Prentice backed away slowly, keeping watch for a long moment. When he had a good gap, he turned and sprinted after his men. His legs ached, and the dust and soot around him tasted acrid in his mouth. He was bone weary, and the battle was only half over.

CHAPTER 45

The convicts rushed toward the prince's colors, the elaborate banners still held aloft, though Mercad himself was nowhere to be seen. They gathered other men as they ran so that there were nearly sixty in number following Prentice and Turley. As they approached, three knights were killing one of the beaked war beasts, running it through with lance strikes. Corpses of other beasts lay around.

At first the knights seemed unnerved by the approaching rogues, but Prentice pushed quickly to the front and tugged his forelock. "The rogues foot attends the prince's orders, my lord!" he called. The knight in the center of the three lifted his helmet's visor to reveal a gray-bearded face. Prentice took a moment to recognize Sir Carron Ironworth, the prince's knight commander.

"You're that Reach convict they say is rutting with the little duchess?" the knight said.

Prentice could not tell from the man's tone if he disapproved or was merely putting a face to the only information he knew. "Yes, my lord." There was no point arguing.

"Was it you that gave the order to advance the rogues foot?"

"Aye, my lord!" Turley chimed in. "It was him!"

Ironworth's eyes switched disdainfully onto Turley for a moment and then back to Prentice. He chewed his mustached upper lip a moment, thinking. "Yes, well, bloody good man," he said suddenly. "We'd be up to our necks in this puddle of shit if it weren't for you receiving that charge for us! As it is, we're still up to our waists, so it's not over yet. We're going to get the prince off the field." He nodded to the two knights flanking him.

"My lord, the enemies on the hill are charging." Prentice pointed in their direction.

"And their bloody leader's still out there somewhere!" Turley added.

"We'll hold them at the stream," said the knight captain.

One of Ironworth's men pointed to something Prentice could not see. "They're already trying to encircle us. Our men die at the water's edge!"

Ironworth looked over the battlefield, and Prentice could see him making a swift calculation. "Right. You two, take the prince now!" he said to the knights. "Carry him on your bloody saddles, royal dignity be damned. Break through as best you can, and don't stop until you are safe." He looked down at Prentice and the other convicts. "All right, you damned rats. Today you become war dogs, and we're going to rally this shambles to make a stand. Time to shed some blood for your prince, and may God bless every man who fights!"

With that, Sir Carron spurred his mount toward the river, while his companions rode the short distance to another rider less horse standing by a man lying in the grass —the unconscious prince.

"Now that's how you give a speech!" Turley said.

Prentice gathered the convicts to follow the knight commander. "Stay together," he told them. "Any man off by himself is a lamb to be taken."

The once-clear stream was awash of crimson and brown. The knights riding to defend the prince were now pressed down to its banks so that it hemmed them in as effectively as a moat. Some crossed, their horses clambering out the other side to face what remained of the charioteer force. Others reached the stream only to become mired, their tired mounts slipping in the mud. Many were slain this way as the spearmen reached the western bank of the stream; the height advantage of the knights' horses was canceled by the height of the western bank, little though it was.

Prentice arrayed the convicts on the eastern bank, ordering them to strike down on any enemy in the stream. Horses whinnied in panic and men shouted incoherently—rage, fear, and confusion mixing in equal measure.

"We need to get our men out on this side," Prentice shouted over the din.

"We will shield you!" Sir Carron declared, and he began to order the knights around him, commanding them from the saddles of their exhausted mounts.

The convicts formed small teams, each one focused on pulling an armored man or horse out of the mire. Ironworth then sent the rescued men back to the stream to protect the convicts as they did their rescue work. Every now and then an enemy spearman leaped into the water for an easy kill, or else a spear was thrown like a javelin. Many of the convicts fell wounded or slain, their unarmored flesh too vulnerable. The knights fared better against enemy weapons, but the press of bodies and the water were their own hazard. Several sank in the muddy water and drowned, their heavy armor too great a weight for their tired limbs.

Soon enough, every knight or squire who could be saved from the stream had been, and the two forces, now heavily depleted, faced each other over the short gap, only ten paces between them. The Kingdom men stood close, shoulder to shoulder, rank and privilege forgotten, knight beside squire beside convict. Behind them, Sir Carron had a tiny force of ten or so knights still mounted. These he held ready to respond if the enemy should try to flank.

The invaders pressed themselves as tightly together as the Kingdom army, and for the first time, Prentice could see the weariness of the day in their wild, painted faces. Since that first skirmish at the river bend, the invaders had seemed implacable, utterly tireless in their bloodlust. Now they were looking almost close to defeat. Prentice would have been happy if he did not know that the Kingdom men almost certainly looked just as weary and weak. For a long moment, the two forces watched each other silently.

"What we need now is some of them crossbows you mentioned from the last war," Turley said.

Prentice nodded. If either side had invested in even a token force of archers or the like, they would take this battle right now. He knew why the knights of the Grand Kingdom had no use for bows, but he wondered why the invaders didn't bring them.

There was a series of shouts from among the invaders, orders being given in their foreign tongue. Then two things happened. From the ranks behind, shields were passed over the heads of the men to the front so that the first line soon had built an effective shield wall without any gaps. The front was only twenty men wide, but the whole body of them formed a tight unit, with shields across the front and down the flanks.

The second thing that happened was that the Horned Man pressed his way to the center of the front, his massive glaive held high like a battle standard. The iron and bronze no longer glinted in the sunlight, too filthy with blood and gore. Next to him stood the bell carrier, who had commanded the spearmen and kept time on the hill, his longsword ready. Neither champion had any shield of his own, but they were the only gap in the wall.

The Horned Man gave a bellowed order, a savage animalistic shout, and all the invaders began to thump out a cadence, men at the front beating on their shields and others stamping their feet. Then they began to advance slowly, one step at a time. As the front rank reached the edge of the stream, the men behind grabbed belts or armor tack, holding them steady so that they didn't slip or fall but were able to keep their cohesion. As the ranks in front reached the stream, they acted as a brace for the ranks coming behind, also keeping them upright. Like a vast armored insect, slow but inexorable, the invaders edged forward in this impressive and frightening display of discipline.

A shiver of fresh uncertainty passed through the Kingdom men. They shifted their feet, and a soft hum of muttered fear washed through the little crowd.

"Steel yourself," Sir Carron commanded from the rear.

"We must retreat!" called an unseen voice.

"No!" Prentice and Sir Carron shouted at the same time.

Several heads about him turned to look at Prentice, surprised in spite of their fear. Prentice did not care about what they thought. "Either we hold them here or they run us down."

"You heard the man," Sir Carron added. "This day ends with victory or death!"

The invaders' front rank reached the other side of the stream, and they held their shields high as the Kingdom hammered down with whatever weapons they had. Spears thrust upward and the front rank tried to climb, but the Kingdom pushed back. Every now and then, a Kingdom man was speared in the leg, lost his footing, or slid into the enemy mass to be ripped apart. It was a near stalemate, but the Kingdom lost a few more than the invaders and, at every moment, drew closer to their breaking point, like a taut rope stretched and stretched.

"We can't beat their bloody shields!" Turley shouted, thrusting down with a captured spear.

"We need a gap," Prentice declared. "And that's it!" He pointed down the line to where the Horned Man and his captain were hammering on the shields of a small knot of knights.

"You're mad!"

"If we can't beat their shields, then we go where they have no shields."

Prentice pushed his way left along the edge of the stream bank. As he did so, the man beside him fell into the water, one leg hacked apart by the Horned Man's polearm. The next fell as well. Prentice stepped straight into the sudden gap and locked eyes with the Horned Man. The twisted champion sneered, but there was a flash of recognition in his eyes, and Prentice knew that uncertainty was undermining his inhuman calm. Prentice did not wait, did not hesitate. He threw his heavy cudgel head-first at the Horned Man's face and then leaped into the air, poniard in his other hand.

The Horned Man flinched from the unexpected throw. The cudgel's iron head struck his antlers, cracking one but doing little real damage. It was the flinch was his downfall, though. Prentice fell on him, using his free hand to grasp the enormous man by one of those antlers, while he stabbed again and again at the monster's neck with his long dagger. The massive glaive was nothing but an overlong weight in the Horned Man's hands now, and Prentice added his own mass, driving the vile commander down into the mud.

It seemed for a moment that there was no one else on the field, only the two of them locked in their struggle. Blood sprayed over Prentice while his opponent wrestled to get free. In spite of his wounds, the monstrous warrior was still strong, and he dropped his weapon, trying to grapple Prentice and tear him off. Prentice gasped as the thickly muscled arms wrapped around him, threatening to crush his spine. He cried out but kept hacking and thrusting at his foe's neck and face. Then there was a snap, like the crack of an axe on a tree trunk, and the brute fell limp; his neck had broken.

Horned Man and convict tumbled in the mud of the stream, and for a moment Prentice was rolled under the water. He thought he would drown, held down by the weight and the suction of the mud. He fought his way free and came up gasping—but without his dagger. He refused to let go of the Horned Man's antlers, however, and he pounded the enemy's skull with his bare fist until he realized that, finally, the man was dead. Blinking through the mud and blood, Prentice struggled to his feet. As he did so, the last of his opponent's flesh tore around his neck, and the mighty antlered head came free.

Struggling to keep himself upright, Prentice looked around him. A kind of calm had fallen. In the stream about him, the enemy had pulled back a handful of paces, as if fearfully giving him room. Only the other champion, bare chested with his longsword in his hands, seemed ready to take up the fight. Prentice fixed wild eyes on him and then raised the decapitated head of his enemy. He bellowed a feral shout, as furious as the Horned Man's own battle cry, and wanted to laugh when the shout was echoed by the Grand Kingdom soldiers. Even as he looked at the second champion—expecting to be cut down by the longsword at any moment, but not afraid—the Kingdom men surged into the stream, and the rout began. Prentice let the fighting move past him quickly and sank, exhausted, to his knees in the water, his hand still gripping the Horned Man's antlers.

CHAPTER 46

Prentice sat in Duchess Amelia's chair, at her insistence, while a chirurgeon bound a wound on his arm. The black-clad man was old and bald, and he peered at his work down a long, hawk like nose in the dim lamplight. Nevertheless, his hands moved with gentle competence, and soon enough the long gash was washed and bandaged.

The chirurgeon had been on hand in the duchess's tent, attending to the Baroness Stopher. He had given her a warm draft of white laud, which had taken the distressed woman into a deep sleep. She lay on the duchess's cot, breathing softly.

"Her mind is wounded and may even be broken," the chirurgeon told the duchess. "There is no physic for this that is as good as sleep."

Duchess Amelia had been quietly observing the sleeping baroness when the soldiers had begun to return. She watched them enter the camp slowly, in small numbers at first. So many were filthy and bloodied that she was sure they must have been defeated. Even in the gathering darkness of evening, they looked ruined. But soon a crowd of men returned, and they came carrying loot in bundles and slung over shoulders. They wore enemy armor, ill-fitting and damaged, and carried their weapons, as well as the natural plunder of any camp: pots, pans, blankets, and clothing. The army had routed the enemy and looted their camp afterward. A page, surely no more than twelve, trotted past the front of her tent. He was so filthy that she could not tell what the colors were on his torn surcoat. He limped slightly on one foot and had a bruise on the left side of his face so swollen he could not open that eye. Yet he was smiling ferociously.

"Boy?" she called.

Before she could say more, he turned to her. With a voice like a herald, he shouted, "Rejoice! We are victorious. The enemy is put to rout!"

He marched off into the camp hollering these words and trying to rouse any servant he found.

Behind him, a further crowd walked closer, and the duchess was surprised to see them turn aside toward her tent. As they approached, she began to make out faces and identities among them. Some were men-at-arms and even knights, she was sure, though they were all on foot. Most, though, were convicts—her rogues. Soon the crowd formed around the opening of her tent, leaving a small space. From their midst emerged a single filthy man carrying a grotesque trophy. It took Amelia a long moment to recognize Prentice and to realize that the trophy was the head of the enemy commander that rumors had spoken of—the Horned Man.

Prentice moved to stand right in front of her and then sank to his knees like a man who had no more energy left to keep his feet. He bowed his head and presented the Horned Man's severed head to her, placing it on the ground before her. The battered thing repulsed her, but she forced herself to look down into the dead eyes of the monster who had led the invasion of her lands and commanded the slaughter of her people.

The crowd seemed to hold their breath, a distinct hush falling over them as they watched her. What were they expecting?

She looked at Prentice, and he smiled at her and nodded. It helped her to understand somehow, and confidence built within her. Surely no man could now doubt her competence or her right to her husband's lands. To her lands. She had chosen her own captain, and here he was, laying the enemy's head at her feet. Duchess Amelia looked over Prentice's head and scanned the faces of the expectant crowd. Squaring her shoulders, she drew her skirt back and lifted her slippered foot. She raised it and placed it firmly down on the Horned Man's head. The crowd erupted in cheers, and she accepted their adulation.

This was the army's victory, the Grand Kingdom's victory, the prince's victory. But she would never let them forget that it was her victory too.

From the crowd, Sir Liam emerged. Had he come to still the cheering, to try to rob her of this moment?

Instead, he went to one knee before her. "Victorious lady," he shouted to be heard. "You must present your trophy to the prince! I crave your indulgence. Allow me to escort you."

She had never seen Sir Liam seem so sincere in his courtesy. Not a handful of hours before, he had been happy to disdain her to her face. She did not trust him and looked quickly at Prentice, cautious that there was some treachery she might be missing. Prentice nodded, as if to say that she should do as Sir Liam suggested, making the gesture look like a respectful bow of the head.

The duchess straightened up again. "Sir Liam, I will require your escort," she announced. "I will attend the prince with news of victory. Commission a man to bring this with us." She pointed to the head still beneath her foot.

"I should be honored if the duty fell to me," Sir Liam replied, rising once again.

Amelia withdrew her foot so that he could take the head. She looked over the crowd and was able to just make out

Turley's face through the darkness and dirt. "You there," she ordered him, then glanced down to Prentice on the ground in front of her. "Send to the chirurgeon in my tent and have him attend this man. His service to me has been..."

She paused, wondering what the appropriate word would be to use. She felt like she owed him her station and all her lands. Without him, she was sure she would already be in a nunnery, the army of the Grand Kingdom routed, the Reach in flames. But too much flattery or praise would count against her. The rumors about the pair of them were already unspeakable.

"...worthy," she said at last. "His service to me has been worthy."

The crowd cheered again, and she led them away, a filthy procession through the dark. Sir Liam walked at her heels, the Horned Man's head grasped in both his hands by the antlers, like the handles of a perverse chalice.

Prentice remained behind, taken into the duchess's tent by the chirurgeon. The doctor gave him a physic mixed in wine to ease his aches and ordered him to strip his shirt. The thing was little more than bloody tatters at any rate, and Prentice had half winced, half laughed as he pulled it over his head. Many of the wounds from his lashing, which had begun to heal, were now torn again from the exertions of the battle. They had been joined by an array of new injuries, mostly the kind of small cuts that were inevitable when one was unarmored in the press of battle. The chirurgeon systematically bathed each wound he found and mixed compresses and poultices to bind them with.

Prentice was still seated and having his arm sewn when the tent flap opened and Duchess Amelia returned. Beyond her in the lamplight, Prentice could make out Sir Liam and Sir Carron. The prince's knight commander stopped the younger knight on the threshold and said something to him that Prentice could not hear. Sir Liam nodded and then remained outside, while Sir Carron entered and closed the flap behind him.

Prentice stood awkwardly, feeling the combination of his injuries and the sleepiness of the chirurgeon's painkilling draft. He bowed and had to catch himself against the tent's center pole before he fell over.

The chirurgeon tutted and turned to the duchess. "If you wish this convict treated, then I need him to sit." He nodded his head in a bare gesture of respect.

"Of course," she allowed, and Prentice felt himself pushed gratefully back onto the chair. He blinked as Sir Carron stepped up beside the duchess.

"We come from the prince's bedside," the knight commander began.

Prentice nodded and realized that Duchess Amelia was not smiling. He thought to brace himself, expecting bad news, but found he could not help smiling. With the white laud and the fact that he had lived through the battle, he was more relaxed than he had been in years. If they dragged him now behind a horse through filth and thorn bushes, it would take him a moment even to think to object. Nonetheless, he did his best to school his face and to seem sober.

"The prince is gratified to be given news of his victory and now rests," Sir Carron continued. "Sacrist Porlain regales all with the tale of the angel that turned the battle in answer to his prayers. He's calling it a miracle. I swear the man thinks he'll be canonized a saint within the hour."

"The angel, my lord?" Prentice asked.

"The great flash of light and thunder," the knight captain explained. "Everyone saw it. It fell upon the enemy quite near where you were."

"The thunderclap? The great lion men saw, wreathed in light? An angel?"

"I've not heard about any lion, though the stories peasants tell grow quicker than bamboo grass, so I suppose someone might have seen a lion or a horse or a dragon in the glare. For me, I saw no more than the flash of light, like lightning that did not come from the sky. As well as the flames on the grass, of course."

"Of course, my lord."

"The prince rests now. The day was exhausting for him; he carries the weight of his years more heavily than many know. It has fallen to me to see to the remainder of the day's business."

That would mean the dispensing of honors and the shares of loot and booty, as well as further duties. Many of the knights and noblemen, having served and gained their honors, would be eager to return to the comfort and duties of their own lands. The prince's authority would be needed to press some to pursue any fleeing enemy and ensure they did not return.

"Prince Mercad has thanked me personally and ordered the preparation of an edict honoring the contribution of the duchy and the men of the Reach," Duchess Amelia explained. "The prince did not say, but Sir Carron assures me that the edict will be to the duke and duchess's praise, both by name."

"It is right," said Sir Carron. "The duke chose his young bride well! Her steel will not be forgotten."

"It is well deserved, Your Grace," Prentice said, bowing a little as he sat and eliciting another angry tut from the chirurgeon, who was not finished tying off the stitches.

Sir Carron and Duchess Amelia exchanged a look, and the knight commander continued. "The contribution of the duchess's men on the field will also receive special mention. The men of the Western Reach rallied to the prince's defense and turned a cunning trap back against the enemy. For this reason, there will be an elevation."

Sir Carron let the last word hang in the air a moment, and Prentice tried to penetrate his meaning.

What was he trying to say?

"The knight captain of the Reach," he explained, and suddenly Prentice could see what was coming. "Sir Liam rallied the other knights and led them to the prince's defense. For this he has been awarded hereditary title of baronet and named Defender of Halling Pass. He will have the right to raise taxes and men from the valleys of the pass and will remain in service to the Western Reach Duchy as a fiefed bannerman."

Prentice nodded and closed his eyes.

"Sir Liam will be invested with his own heraldry," Sir Carron continued, "and the prince has awarded him the right to wear antlers on his helmet, as a trophy of the victory he led over the enemy captain. The prince has given Sir Liam the head so that he may wear the very same ones, with their gold and silver."

In spite of himself, Prentice laughed at the irony, especially at this final insult. "Of course he has," he said, which was all he could think to say. He had swallowed his pride for too many years to waste his breath now.

"I understand there has been some bad blood between you and the new baronet. Is that so?"

"I am but a convict, lord knight," Prentice said, and he could not keep the bitterness from his voice. "I have no blood but to shed for the Kingdom's sake."

"Very good," said Sir Carron. "Nevertheless, I have explained to the young baronet how far beneath him a conflict with a convict would now stand and how it would diminish him in the eyes of the Rhales court—and in my eyes as well. I expect he will now consider any matter between you settled."

With that, Sir Carron bowed to the duchess and turned to leave. He walked a few paces, then turned back and looked Prentice in the eyes.

"One more thing," he said, and his tone was suddenly less formal. "I have stood on many battlefields, and I know the character of war. Men are born to their rank, but courage and skill are forged in actions. The Kingdom must regard rank, for birth is from God, but rank can receive rewards that are forgotten to courage, even when action is more deserving. In my life I have learned that a good soldier remembers, even if the Grand Kingdom forgets sometimes. So I give you this as a small remembrance, as one soldier to another. You stood as well as any could this day, no matter your station."

Sir Carron plucked a purse from his belt and tossed it into Prentice's lap. It jingled heavily as it fell. Then the knight commander left, and Prentice held the purse in his free hand. The chirurgeon finished his work and then he, too, withdrew.

"Have my lady-in-waiting sent to me," Duchess Amelia instructed him as he left.

Then they were alone. Prentice tried to stand again, but she gestured that he should keep his seat. He turned as she moved to her cot and sat on its edge. Baroness Stopher stirred in her sleep but did not wake. The duchess sat quietly for a long moment, eyes on the ground.

"Do you hate me?" she asked at last. "For what has happened with Sir Liam?"

"Hate you, Your Grace?"

"You brought me that hideous head. That means you took it yourself. I know that because there was no way Sir Liam or any of the other knights would have left it in your hands if you had not killed him yourself!" She looked straight at him with a plaintive expression, like a child begging forgiveness.

"No, Your Grace, I do not hate you," he told her.

"Even if I tell you that I did not protest or even make a sound as the prince heaped honors on Sir Liam? Baronet Liam now."

Prentice sighed. His bandages itched, and his eyes felt heavy. He wanted to lie down. Whatever fresh indignity the

Grand Kingdom wanted to visit on him, he wished it would just wait until morning.

"What else could you do, Your Grace? Correct the prince? For a convict? I think not."

"I owe you, Prentice, as much as I owe any man. I cannot give you the battle honors you deserve, but I will reward you. In a moment I will have you taken straight to a smith, and those shackles will be struck from your ankles. I pronounce you freed!"

"Thank you, Your Grace."

"Do not thank me yet. I will see you rewarded. I commission you now as my scholar advisor and name you to the rank of patrician among the freemen of my lands. It is hardly a battle honor, but it is the best I can do without recourse to politics and the prince's court. I will have a household provided to you in Dwêltford, and a stipend."

"I have the purse to put it in now," he said with his wry smile, waving the little leather bag so that it jingled.

Amelia smiled back. "I will never forget what you have done for me, Prentice," she insisted. "I want you to tutor me and, whenever they are born to me, my children. I will make my husband's fief strong, regardless of the man I eventually marry. Pity the fool who thinks me to be the ticket to an easy title now! I am the victorious Amelia, Duchess of the Western Reach, widow to Duke Marne and bearer of his legacy."

"You have done well, Duchess."

"You will call me Amelia, Prentice. You are my friend."

"Amelia."

"I have one last word, and then to the smith."

The duchess stood and moved until she was in front of him, looking down on him regally. She rested one hand on his shoulder. "Given the station of patrician, Prentice, you have the right to a name—a family name that will be inherited by your sons, and their sons in perpetuity. It will be written in the annals of the Reach and known to the Church and God."

Prentice blinked in surprise as he realized just how far Amelia was going for him. With an inherited name and the rank of patrician, she was raising him as far as a man could be raised short of admission to the nobility. He was as high now as he would have been had he never been expelled from the Ashfield academy.

Amelia continued. "I cannot give you the honors of the field, for rank has stolen those from you, but I will give you the honor that our enemy gave you—the name they feared you by! I call you Ash and give the name to your descendants in perpetuity. Rise, Prentice Ash."

Prentice stood and almost immediately fell forward. Amelia caught him and held him in an embrace. He felt so little emotion, but blinked in surprise as he realized he was crying tears of relief. He tried to straighten himself to relieve her of his weight, but they only slipped about, and he fell back into the chair. He felt himself drifting into sleep, and the last thing he heard was the duchess say, "Perhaps I'll have the smith come here!"

It did not matter to Prentice. He fell into sleep knowing that when he awoke, he would be free. He hoped the smith would not steal his purse while he slept.

EPILOGUE

Newly titled Baronet Liam made sure the oilskin bag containing the Horned Man's head was tightly bound to his saddle tack. The task rightly belonged to Croftlin, but the youth had lost two fingers on his right hand during the fighting and could not possibly tie the knot. Liam felt some sympathy for the boy. With the fingers missing from his sword hand, there was virtually no chance he'd ever be knighted. He could never acquire the necessary skills and would be a squire for the rest of his life. Ultimately, though, that was the way of battle, and Liam felt little enough pity. They all took the risks on the field, and God rewarded the righteous and punished the rest.

That thought gave Liam an extra smile as he looked at the bag and thought of the trophy inside. The duchess may have been seduced by her bastard-heretic-convict, but God had spoken in Liam's favor and the prince had named the victory to him. Liam had no doubt that it was a sign of divine approval, and he longed to share a drink to his success with Brother Whilte. A drink with an ordained man would seal the holiness of his success in his own eyes. What did he care if Ironworth forbade him from finishing off the duchess's little dog? Liam was the hero of the Reach and a baronet now. Let Prentice lick her toes all she liked. Liam would be magnanimous and let the dog live. Everyone knew now who the better man was, and the prince's edict would confirm it.

Liam looked about for Croftlin. He had sent his squire to find Brother Whilte some time ago and still the boy wasn't back. He was tired and needed to rest. This wait was too long. He took up one of the pewter cups he had laid to warm by the fire. He thought of uncorking the brandy now and giving himself a dram, but that would seem rude, to invite a man to drink and then start before him. Instead, he put the bottle back next to the second cup and filled his with some wine from a skin on his saddle horn, watered piss though it was.

At last, Croftlin emerged from the dark, but alone.

"Where the bloody hell have you been?" Liam demanded. "And where's Whilte?"

"I could not find Brother Whilte," Croftlin explained, wincing in pain and cradling his bandaged hand. "Some knights from Calmain said they think they saw him leave the melee with a wounded leg, and one of Sir Quarn's bondsmen said he saw a knight with the brother's livery dragged from the field by his horse with one foot twisted in the stirrup!"

"Damn!"

Whilte was no great loss to the world or to Liam—not now with his new title. There'd be companions enough in the days to come. But Whilte's place in the Church had offered extra benefits. With a sigh, Liam threw the wine from his cup and picked up the brandy. He pulled the waxed cork with his teeth and poured himself a generous portion. He downed it and was pouring a second when he saw Croftlin looking at him. "What? You don't expect a cup for yourself, do you?"

"No, sir. I mean, my lord! It's just that there is other news."

"What other news?"

Liam was not interested in camp gossip. Any other battle, there'd be singing and feasting all night, with maidens to deflower and legends to establish in tales and song, but this paltry campaign was too bitter and too poor for any of that. Liam had deliberately set his camp away from the rest a space because he didn't want to be reminded of the victory's half-heartedness. If he had to be disappointed at his elevation, he didn't want the rest of the court, his new peers, to see it in his face. Better to drink alone with a clergyman and claim one dedicated the victory to God. After all, wasn't the prince's chaplain prattling on about miracles?

"Well, boy?" he insisted. "What bloody news?"

"The prince, my lord," Croftlin began tremulously. "Prince Mercad... he has passed."

"Passed?"

"Dead, my lord, only just now."

The prince was dead? Liam's mind did not know which way to go first. The old fool had been frail, everyone knew that, but Liam hadn't thought him in danger, not once his guards had removed him from the field. And the death of a prince was no small matter. It had repercussions throughout the Kingdom. He had no way of knowing what this would mean for the Grand Kingdom, the court in Rhales, or the campaign, but he did have one desperate thought.

"The edict? Has the prince's edict been issued?"

He threw the brandy and his cup down and seized Croftlin by his arms. The boy flinched and cried in pain. If the edict was not yet published, then it was possible the prince had not sealed it. It might not even have been drafted yet.

"The edict?" he asked once more. "Has it been published? Has the edict been published?"

Croftlin shook his head. "I don't know!"

Would he retain his new title without the edict? Liam didn't know the law well enough to say.

With the prince dead, he might have just lost everything.

GLOSSARY

The Grand Kingdom's social structure is broken into three basic levels which are then subdivided into separate ranks: the nobility, the free folk, and the low born.

The Nobility

King/Queen – There is one King, and one Queen, his wife. The king is always the head of the royal family and rules from the Denay Court, in the capital city of Denay.

Prince/Princess – Any direct children of the king and queen.

Prince of Rhales – This title signifies the prince who is next in line of succession. This prince maintains a separate, secondary court of lesser nobles in the western capital or Rhales.

Duke/Duchess – Hereditary nobles with close ties by blood or marriage to the royal family, either Denay or Rhales.

Earl; Count/Countess; Viscount; Baron/Baroness – These are the other hereditary ranks of the two courts, in order of rank. One is born into this rank, as son or daughter of an existing noble of the same rank, or else created a noble by the king.

Baronet – This is the lowest of the hereditary ranks and does not require a landed domain to be attached.

Knight/Lady – The lowest rank of the nobility and almost always attached to military service to the Grand Kingdom as a man-at-arms. Ladies obtain their title through marriage. Knights are signified by their right to carry the longsword, as a signature weapon.

Squire – This is, for all intents and purposes, an apprentice knight. He must be the son of another knight (or higher noble) who is currently training, or a student of the academy.

The Free Folk

Patrician – A man or woman who has a family name and owns property inside a major town or city. Patricians always fill the ranks of any administration of the town in which they live, such as aldermen, guild conclave members, militia captains etc.

Guildsmen/townsfolk – Those who dwell in large towns as free craftsmen and women tend to be members of guilds who act to protect their members' livelihoods and also to run much of the city, day to day.

Yeoman – The yeomanry are free farmers that possess their own farms.

The Low Born

Peasants – These are serfs who owe feudal duty to their liege lord. They do not own the land they farm and must obtain permission to move home or leave their land.

Convicts – Criminals who are found guilty of crimes not deserving of the death penalty.

Military Order

Knight Captain, Knight Commander & Knight Marshall – Every peer (King, Prince or Duke) has a right to raise an army and command his lesser nobles to provide men-at-arms. They then appoint a second-in-command, often the most experienced or skilled soldier under them. A duke his Knight Captain; a prince his Knight Commander; and the King his Knight Marshal.

Knights – These are the professional soldiers of the Grand Kingdom. All nobles are expected to join these ranks when their lands are at war, and they universally fight from horseback.

Men-at-Arms –A catch all term for any man with professional training who has some right or reason to be in this group, including squires and second and third sons of nobles.

Bannermen – This is a special form of man-at-arms. These are soldiers who are sworn directly to a ranking noble.

Free Militia – The free towns of the Grand Kingdom have an obligation to raise free militias in defence of the realm.

Rogues Foot – A rogue is a low born or criminal man and so when convicts are pressed into military service, they are the rogues afoot (or "on foot") which is shortened to rogues foot.

Other Titles and Terms

Apothecary – A trader and manufacturer of herbs, medical treatments and potions of various sorts.

Chirurgeon – A medical practitioner, akin to a doctor or surgeon, especially related to injuries (as opposed to sickness, which is handled by an apothecary).

Estate – A person's estate can be their actual lands, but can also include their social position, their current condition (physical, social or financial), or any combination of these things.

Fiefed – A noble who is fiefed possesses a parcel of land over which they have total legal authority, the right to levy taxes and draft rogues or militia.

King's Law – This is the overarching, national law, set for the Grand Kingdom by the king, but does not always apply in the Western Reach.

Magistrate – Civil legal matters of the Free Folk and Peasantry are typically handled by magistrates, who render judgements according to the local laws.

Marshals/Wardens – Appointed men who manage the movement of large groups, especially of nobles and noble courts when in motion. They appoint the order of the march and resolve disputes.

Physick – A term for a person trained in the treatment of medical conditions, but without strict definition.

Proselytize– Attempt to convert someone from one religion, belief, or opinion to another.

Republicanists – Rare political radicals, outlawed in the Grand Kingdom and the Vec who seek to create elected forms of government, curtailing or overturning monarchical rule.

Seneschal – The administrative head of any large household or organisation, especially a noble house of a baron or higher.

Surcoat – The outer garment worn by a man-at-arms over their armor. Typically dyed in the knight's colours (or their liege lord's colours in the case of a bannerman) and embroidered with their heraldry.

Te tree – A tree, known for its medicinal properties.

The Rampart – A celestial phenomenon that glows in the night across the sky from east to west in the northern half of the sky.

ACKNOWLEDGMENTS

To faithfully list all who have inspired me in my writing
would be a book unto itself, and I would doubtless do some
the disservice of forgetting them.
Suffice to say, the Lord knows how great is the debt I owe
and so, to paraphrase an expression used by the US military,
I shall thank them all and let God sort them out.

MORE FROM PUBLISHER

Be sure to check out our other great science fiction and fantasy stories at:
bladeoftruthpublishing.com/books

ABOUT AUTHOR

Matt Barron grew up loving to read and to watch movies. He always knew he enjoyed science fiction and fantasy, but in 1979 his uncle took him to see a new movie called Star Wars and he was hooked for life. Then Dungeons and Dragons came along and there was no looking back. He went to university hoping to find a girlfriend. Instead, the Lord found him, and he spent most of his time from then on in the coffee shop, witnessing and serving his God. Along the way, he managed to acquire a Doctorate in History and met the love of his life, Rachel. Now married to Rachel for more than twenty years, Matt has two adult children and a burning desire to combine the genre he loves with the faith that saved him.

Learn more at:
https://www.bladeoftruthpublishing.com/mattbarron

ALSO BY MATT BARRON

Rage of Lions

Prentice Ash

Rats of Dweltford

Lions of the Reach

Book 4 TBA

Made in the USA
Monee, IL
17 February 2022

91344841R00225